GHOST OF A CHANCE

Mike Brodie is tired of people thinking she's a man, and right now, she is tired of everything. As well as keeping an eye on Raffi, her undergraduate goddaughter, she's been running her music shop, doing voice work and playing the saxophone. Her pushy manager, Paul, is filling her diary to bursting point. When Mike decides to take a well-earned break, she heads for Berwick Grange, but being ambushed by armed men on her arrival is just the start of her troubles. When she discovers a body floating in an ornamental pool, mishap turns to murder.

GHOST OF A CHANCE

GHOST OF A CHANCE

by

Susan Hepburn

Magna Large Print Books
Long Preston, North Yorkshire,
BD23 4ND, England.

British Library Cataloguing in Publication Data.

Hepburn, Susan
    Ghost of a chance.

    A catalogue record of this book is
    available from the British Library

    ISBN   0-7505-2452-9

First published in Great Britain in 2005 by Allison & Busby Ltd.

Published in Large Print 2005 by arrangement with
Allison & Busby Ltd.

Magna Large Print is an imprint of Library Magna Books Ltd.

Printed and bound in Great Britain by
T.J. (International) Ltd., Cornwall, PL28 8RW

For Dom, Mary and Joseph,
most treasured of friends,
with love always.

Chapter One

I thought they were going to kill me. They melted out of the dusk-cloaked trees, silent and almost invisible. How many were they? Four? Six? My mind was as frozen as my limbs, and I seemed to have lost my ability to count.

My chest constricted with fear as I hit the brakes and skewed to a halt, seemingly no more than a couple of feet away from one of the men. He stood in the middle of the track, pointing some sort of weapon right at the middle of the windscreen. More accurately, right at the middle of my head.

I sat transfixed, like a rabbit caught in car headlights. Ironic, given that he was standing in the glare of my own. Dark clothing, face only semi-visible, obscured by something I couldn't quite make out, maybe a scarf. God, I couldn't even see straight! Nothing was making sense. I felt like I was suffocating, that somehow, everything was happening in slow motion. Most of all, I felt that none of this could be real. It simply couldn't be happening to me.

A tap on my driver's side window shocked me out of denial and into taking a huge gulp of air. I must have been holding my breath. Reluctantly, I moved my gaze to the source of the sound to be confronted by a figure identical to the first. He motioned at me to lower the window, the gesture illuminated by the flashlight he was holding. *Not bloody likely!*, I thought.

There was a sudden blinding flash of headlights racing up behind me, accompanied by the blaring of a car horn. I don't know who was more startled, me or the heavy mob, but I had no intention of hanging around to find out. Shocked into action by the intervention, I swung the wheel savagely, hitting the accelerator as hard as I could to get the car off the track and into the woods. Not a good idea, as it happened, because I smacked heavily into a tree before I got very far. The impact winded me but I had enough adrenaline racing round my system to ensure that it didn't slow me down. I was out of the car and running blind, without even having to think about it.

Behind me, I could hear sounds of confusion, voices raised and undergrowth being trampled. Not that there was much to trample on. The late February ground was iron hard, icy and unforgiving, as I found to my cost when I caught my ankle in an unseen root and sprawled headlong. Cursing and frantic, I thrashed around, freed myself and stumbled on.

The track had been bad enough with the gloom of dusk upon it but here amongst the trees it was a nightmare world of shadow upon deeper shadow. I had shied away from the beam of my one remaining headlight, instinctively wanting to keep myself from being seen, being an easy target. What I could do nothing about, however, was enabling myself to see where I was going, and I stumbled on blindly, chest heaving, breath coming in great gulping rasps, from terror as much as from physical exertion.

The voices were still behind me, although I now began to hear the pounding of feet getting closer. That may have been my imagination but I had no desire to turn round and check it out. I heard someone yell, 'He went that way! Leave this one to me!' That's when, half-turning at last, I ran into a tree, cannoned off it and fell into the lacerating embrace of a thorn bush, screaming as its naked arms whipped across my face.

I could definitely hear the pounding of feet now and thought, too, that I could sense bobbing light. I wrenched myself upright, tearing my clothes as well as more skin, and sought desperately for a way to go. My sense of direction was now zero, my brain a whirling mass of wordless prayer and non-thought.

'Will you stop running, goddamit! We don't mean to hurt you!'

Dear God, the feet were thundering now, and somehow, my upper body was trying to drag the rest of me forward as I hit the ground again.

This time, I didn't hit it alone. I was face down, the air crushed out of me by the weight of the body on top of mine. My hands clawed the earth and I squirmed for room to turn myself over. I lashed backwards with my right elbow, making a contact that elicited strong verbal objection from my assailant. The weight eased fractionally and I heaved myself half over before it crushed me back into the earth. I tried to bring up my right knee and failed. Thrown flat on my back, I was pinned to the ground, my opponent's breath hot on my face.

'Will you lie still, dammit! I don't want to hurt you. Whatever you may think, I am not your enemy!'

It's funny the way your mind works in a situation like that. The only conscious thought that registered in my head at that moment was that this man's accent told me that he came from Texas. I lay perfectly still, the only sounds those of two sets of laboured breathing.

'I'm gonna let you up, now. No running for it, OK? We have to get this sorted out.' I grunted my agreement. I was barely in any state to stand, let alone run off anywhere. He backed off and pulled me to my feet.

'Jesus, you're a mess!' I was blinded by the beam of light aimed at my face. He immediately turned it back to illuminate his own. All that registered because of the mud was a long, straight nose, startling blue eyes and dark hair.

'My name is Jake Tyler and I run the conference centre at Bewick Grange. Now who the hell are you?'

An American running a conference centre at an English stately home? 'Mike Brodie,' I told him. 'I've come to stay in the holiday cottages as a guest of Maggie Mallory.' My teeth were chattering so much that the words jerked themselves out of my mouth.

'*You're* Mike Brodie?'

The tone of voice he used as he said it pushes my button every time. Energy came from somewhere. I took a deep breath. I usually manage the litany in one.

'Don't tell me. You were expecting a man. So

was my mother, and she never forgave me for it. I got lumbered with a minor variation of the name she'd already chosen for a boy. Michal. That's M-I-C-H-A-L. Like King David's wife, in the Bible.'

He looked at me for a second. At least, I assume he was looking, because he said nothing. Then, 'Well, *Michal*, can you walk?'

I nodded. Right then, between the cold and the shock, I was feeling an urgent desire to move.

I started off unsteadily but at least now, thanks to his flashlight, I could see where I was going. I heard a crackle, not of twigs, but the kind of static you get from a walkie-talkie, and heard, 'Jake, this is Martin – what's going on?'

'One of our intruders appears not to be an intruder at all. Can you get Maggie for me? Over.'

'Sure. What about the second intruder? Over.'

'Wait one.' He touched my elbow, signalling a halt. 'A car came screaming in behind you. You know anything about that? Someone with you?'

I shook my head. 'No, but I did have trouble on the way here. Some maniac kept flashing his lights and trying to tailgate me. That's why I missed the turning and got lost.' Maggie had given me a clear set of instructions on how to get to the village and which way to access the estate. I really had got lost, trying to get away from Mr Road Rage, and had wound up taking the first turning I thought might lead me back in the right direction. I realised that the old Chris Rea number, 'The Road to Hell', was going through my mind. Trust me to have found it.

Jake spoke into his radio. 'OK, Martin, the

13

second intruder is nothing to do with the first. Carl and Terry went after him. You get hold of Maggie yet?'

'Maggie here, Jake. What on earth is going on?'

I could have cried with relief at the sound of her voice.

'Your guess is as good as mine. But first, give me a description of your friend, Mike Brodie.'

'Mike? But ... oh my God! Is she hurt?'

'Walking wounded. Please confirm you just said "she"?'

'Oh no! I mean yes, she's a she! Five foot four. Slim. Green eyes. Red hair. Always wears trousers. Oh – and she drives a Volvo estate and she'll have at least one saxophone in the car.'

'OK, Maggie, I'm bringing her in. She's gonna need a lot of hot soapy water and about half a box of Band-Aid...'

We walked on. I was glad someone knew where they were going because, even with the benefit of the flashlight, it all looked the same to me.

'Saxophone, huh?' He swung the torch at me. 'Which one do you play?'

'Tenor, mainly, though I have another three – alto, soprano and baritone.'

'Now that's what I call greedy!' He chuckled as the beam of light went back to the path.

'Not really. I play in three bands, stand in for assorted other people when I'm needed, and I do session work.' *So stick that in your pipe and smoke it...*

'Talented lady.'

I grunted again, too tired to take the compliment. Night had fallen and the silence was

14

eerie now, broken only by the crackling of twigs under our feet and the sounds of our breathing. I shivered.

'I can't hear your friends.'

I sensed, rather than saw the shrug. 'The other guy took off like a guided missile, and in the opposite direction to you. They'll find him. They can always call for the dogs if they have to.' My blood froze at the thought.

There was light ahead now, the single, lop-sided beam that was left on my car. It loomed baleful rather than welcoming, as if in reproach for what I'd done.

'Well, let's take a look at the damage.' The flashlight swung along the car's length. Maybe seeing it like that, stark against the blackness, was what kicked in the anger for me.

'Oh my God...!' The front was crunched, near side lights shattered. I didn't wait to see more. Just rounded on Mr Jake Bloody Tyler, the full realisation of what I'd just experienced flooding through me in a swell of indignation.

'Just what the bloody hell did you think you were doing? Holding me up like that, pointing weapons? Dressed like Rambo on a bad day? Jesus, I could have been killed!'

'Look, I'm really sorry. There was obviously a big misunderstanding and...'

'Misunderstanding?' I kicked the car viciously. Totally illogical, of course. I really wanted to kick him. Problem was, he was a lot bigger than me.

'You just assaulted me!'

'I thought you were an intruder. A trespasser. And I didn't mean to assault you – just stop you

15

getting away. I'm truly sorry. You can kick the shit out of me once I get you to the Grange, if that will make you feel any better. I'll explain things properly to you then, but not out here, and not while you're upset.'

'Upset? Upset? I am NOT upset, I am bloody well angry, and with good reason!'

'I couldn't agree more. Let's take that as read, but let's also get you inside, in the warm, and into the bathtub, OK? I'm doing my best here to give you an abject apology. Short of grovelling at your feet, I figure the best way is to get you to Maggie asap. Now where are your saxophones?'

His spiel had temporarily deflated my anger and filled me with longing for those things he'd spoken of. Maggie. A hot bath. Oh let me just lay down my head and sleep... I rubbed my eyes, concentrating on his question. My saxophones.

'Just brought the one. In the back of the car, with my suitcase.'

'Keys?'

I patted my pockets, distracted, then realised. 'Still in the ignition.'

'OK. Look, I want you to come over here.' He led me back to the track, now pitch black under the moonless sky. I didn't like this at all.

'My vehicle is just a little way down there.' The flashlight cut an arc in the direction in which I'd originally been heading. 'I'll bring it down here when I've salvaged your stuff. There's nothing we can do about the car tonight – I'll have it brought in first thing tomorrow, OK?'

'OK.' My tone was churlish, but what choice did I have? The light hung on me for a moment.

'Did you have a purse? When you ran off in the woods?'

It took me a second to understand what he was asking. 'You mean a handbag? No. Stupid things. I don't even own one.' He went back to the car and the blackness enveloped me completely.

Moments later we were bumping down the track towards Bewick Grange and what I trusted would be warmth, safety, a hot bath and a good night's sleep. On the way, Jake had pulled up alongside the car abandoned by the evening's other interloper, asking me if I recognised it. It was a dark coloured Rover, and I didn't.

Tiredness had overcome me, making it difficult to concentrate when Jake explained that this track led, not directly to Bewick Grange, but to the conference centre, from where we would have to loop round to get to the holiday cottages. I grunted in acknowledgement. Grunting seemed to be turning into a habit. I simply wished I were back home and in bed, that I could turn back the clock and relive the day minus the histrionics. On second thoughts, that wouldn't make a lot of difference, given the way it had started out. It was all the fault of that Greek and my bloody brother...

Chapter Two

The insistent ringing of the phone had penetrated my sleep, dragging me up into a confused state of semi-consciousness. I have an ancient answering machine, but had obviously forgotten to reset it after checking my messages when I got home in the early hours of the morning. I also have a bed and a bedroom but was aware of a cricked neck and dead leg which appeared to be the result of having slept on the sofa in the living room all night, something I hadn't exactly planned on doing.

Groggily, I managed to haul myself upright, becoming aware of my dishevelled state with irritation. My tie was loosened, my waistcoat unbuttoned and, apart from my shoes, which I stumbled over in my haste to answer the phone, I was fully dressed. I didn't think I'd been *that* tired when I got in from the gig in Birmingham.

Lurching through the kitchen door – my dead leg had pins and needles by now – I grabbed the handset and mumbled, 'Mike Brodie,' stepping into the cat's water bowl as I did so. Cursing silently, I shook my wet foot and resisted the impulse to stand stork-like on the other one as I watched the water spread magically across the floor in an ever-expanding puddle.

It took me a moment to realise that I wasn't understanding the sounds coming through the ear piece. This was largely due to a heavily laboured foreign accent on the part of the speaker. Rubbing my hand across my face, I made an effort to concentrate. Finally, I tuned in.

'Raffi – I wish to speak to Miss Rafaella Orsini, please.'

Raffi is my goddaughter. She doesn't surface until at least midday on a Sunday and is like a bear with a sore head if you wake her other than for a life and death situation. Rather like me, in fact, but I managed now to keep the bear in check as I responded.

'May I ask who's calling?'

'My name is Adonis Clerides. I have the right number for Raffi, yes?'

'Yes,' I confirmed, 'but I'm afraid she's not available at the moment. Can I take a message for you?'

'Sure. Please. That is very good of you. I want to offer her a job.'

'A job?'

'Yes. I spoke to her several times last year. She said she would come and work for me. I have a holiday place near Athens – chalets, bar, that kind of thing. Last year, she couldn't come. This year, she said she would, that she would come after she finished her finals at University. Did she speak to you of this?'

Of course she had. I remembered it now. Her friend's brother had worked for this man as a chef and had said that everything was legitimate and above board.

'Yes,' I told him. 'She'll be pleased you've come back to her on it.'

19

'Well,' he continued, 'You will perhaps tell her that I need someone else as well – one of her friends, perhaps? Do you think she will know someone willing, yes?'

I smiled to myself. 'Oh, I should think so! Can I take your number and I'll get her to give you a call as soon as possible.'

'Sure,' he agreed, and gave it to me slowly. I read it back to him from the planner board on the wall where I'd scribbled it, before hanging up.

I leaned against the door frame for a moment before forcing myself upright and crossing to the sink, where I filled the kettle. I mopped the floor whilst the water was boiling watched by Stix, the cat, who perched on one of the working surfaces doing her vulture impression and eyeing me with her usual disdain. She was Raffi's cat and put up with me only on sufferance. I chucked a couple of slices of bread in the toaster, made the tea and fed her while I was waiting for it to brew. It was only then that I noticed the time on the microwave clock. 8.15 a.m. What a great start to a Sunday morning...

I cleared away my breakfast dishes and went upstairs for a good hot shower, stuffing my dirty clothes in the washing machine on the way. Despite having had only five hours' sleep, I didn't think of going back to bed. I'd only feel worse if I did. Just take things nice and steady. I had only just reached the bottom of the stairs when the phone rang again. Bloody hell! What was this? A 'Let's disturb Mike Brodie Day'? Who the hell was up at this time of morning on a Sunday besides Greeks with job offers?

'Mike Brodie.' I said it in the tone of voice that dared anyone to do anything other than hang up on the spot.

'Mike – I know it's far too early, but I have an emergency situation. Please don't rip my head off...'

'Mitch!' The middle one of my three brothers.

'Sorry about this – look, you know I'm supplying waiting staff for a big opening? Three weeks' time? Well, the arrangements have gone a bit tits-up and...'

'Mitch...' I interrupted. 'Why are you bothering me, on a Sunday morning, about something that's taking place in three weeks' time and has nothing to do with me?'

'Ah. Well. The thing is, I thought you could give Raffi a shout. She has lots of student friends, and students are always desperate for cash. And secondly, well, it does concern you, in a way.'

'I don't do waitressing,' I reminded him. 'Why don't you cut the crap and tell me what it is you want?'

'That's precisely why I had to phone you today. Because you'd need as much notice as possible.'

'Mitch...' I warned him, 'You're sounding horribly like Paul.' Paul is a wheeler-dealer music-business friend of mine who, much as I love him, irritates the shit out of me with his convoluted approach – wheedle, wheedle, all around the bushes before he gets to the nitty-gritty. 'I'm going to count to three,' I continued, 'and if you haven't spilled the beans – *con*cisely – *pre*cisely – I'm going to hang up on you. One...'

'The band's dropped out and I need you to

rescue the occasion.'

'What?' My brother owns a recruitment company which supplies catering and administrative staff – since when had he taken to producing the entertainment? 'Well, speak to Paul. Go to an agency,' I told him, irritation clear in my voice.

'I thought you'd like first crack at it.' He sounded affronted.

'You're really cruising, Mitch! *Why* would I want first crack at it? I'm booked up to my eyeholes as it is.'

'How's this for succinct, then? Just two words for you – Stevie Carlisle.'

'What?!' I almost rocked on my heels.

'Thought that would get you hooked! Wait till you hear this...' Stevie Carlisle and his band were huge in the charts about fifteen years ago and since then he'd carved out an even more successful solo career as well as going into record production. Seemed the big opening was another diversification on his part – he was opening an exclusive and very expensive health club.

'So why isn't he playing himself? That would be a mega-draw,' I asked.

'Oh, he'll jam at the end of the night. But he's there as owner. Businessman hat on. Also, he wants jazz, to start with. "Cool", if that makes any sense. Get people nice and relaxed. Seems the band he originally asked bottled out. Can you believe it?'

I could, actually. He was a formidable talent with an equally formidable reputation. Some people might thrive with a challenge like that. Others would find it too intimidating. I told Mitch I'd talk

22

to the guys and get back to him.

When I re-entered the kitchen a couple of hours later I was in a much better mood, having made my phone calls before locking myself in the basement and playing the sax. Raffi was emerging from the pantry with a cereal box in one hand and a banana in the other. Her long black hair snaked down the back of her dressing gown as if possessed of a life of its own and her brown eyes flickered to the clock in surprise when she saw me.

'Didn't think you'd be up yet!' she smiled. 'Weren't you playing last night?'

She always reminds me of one of those great Renaissance paintings. Vibrant. Voluptuous. Must have been her genes coming out. I said that she's my goddaughter, but there's rather more to it than that. Her mother, Nicola – English, and a childhood friend of mine – had eloped with a titled Italian at an indecently early age and Raffi was the result of this union. It hadn't lasted, however, and, Nikki, now used to a very luxurious lifestyle, had jetted off in pursuit of the same, figuring that having a five-year-old-daughter in tow was not the best way to do it. Not that she'd been that blatant, of course. At least, not to begin with. So I was 'just looking after Raffi for a while...' Oh, she came back now and again, from increasingly exotic places, and always with a new man on her arm and in her bed. Couple of marriages later, and the arrangement had become more formal after she'd suddenly plucked Raffi out of my hands and sent her to a boarding school, where she'd rebelled big-style, saying she

23

wanted to stay at home with me. So I had become her legal guardian and she'd been with me ever since. She was coming up to twenty-one now, and in the final year of her undergraduate course at the local university. I smiled and brought myself back to her question.

'Yes, I was playing last night. In Birmingham. I'm only up because I got woken by the phone.'

She shook her head. 'You forgot to reset the answering machine.' It wasn't a question. She knew me too well. I gave an embarrassed shrug.

'Mike, you should get a new one. One that resets itself.'

'You're not implying that I'm deficient in my ability to use modern technology, are you?' It was a running joke between us. She calls me the Last of the Luddites, not that it's true of course.

'Me? No.'

'I drive a car, don't I?'

'An automatic!'

'That's not Luddism!' I laughed. 'It's convenience.'

She looked at me sceptically. I wondered if she remembered some of the taunts I'd had in the days when I drove a manual. One of my brothers' favourite expressions had been, 'If you can't find it, grind it!' Better change the subject... 'You're right about the answerphone, though – I'll get a new one.'

'I'll believe it when I see it!' She peered dubiously at the scrawl on the planner board, gave up trying to decipher my handwriting and sat down at the kitchen table. I use that planner primarily as a reminder to myself and more often than not it's written on whilst I'm juggling a cup in one hand and the telephone in the other. I do try to makes notes as legibly as possible. Not always successully, if comments like, 'This looks like it was written by a spider on acid!' are anything to go by.

'So which band were you playing with? Last night?' She sat at the table.

'Rude Rhythm.' I replied, passing her the milk. I play regularly with four bands, this being the Latin outfit.

'Not the Green Glittery Jacket mob, then?' she teased as she began to eat. I groaned. As I said, I regularly play with four bands. I just wish to God it were only three. The Green Glittery Jacket mob, otherwise known as the Frederick Penfold Quartet, is not my favourite. Why men in their seventies should wish to dress in black dinner suit trousers, green glittery jackets and spotted bow-ties to play Tea Dance music late at night is a mystery to me. Why I, more than thirty years their junior, should do likewise, is an even bigger mystery, especially as we invariably end up sounding like a cross between the Death March and Mickey Mouse on helium. George, the drummer, operates like a wind-up soldier with a damaged spring, alternating between Speed Metal tempo and that of a tortoise in hibernation. Sometimes, all in the space of a single number.

I had been trying unsuccessfully for three months to get out of the band, quite reasonably pointing out that I'd been hired only as a temporary replacement for Sid, who'd died. By now, I wasn't convinced that they were looking for a permanent replacement at all. That's to say,

I rather thought *they* thought that I was it, which was not our original agreement.

'But good tenor players are hard to find!' Frederick had objected.

No they're not. What he meant was, good tenor players who are alive and fully functioning in their seventies are hard to find. Most of them are dead from the effects of booze or illegal substances before then...

'But your youth brings new life and vigour to the band!'

This from Albert, the only upright bass player I know who performs in his sleep. Honest. I swear to God, he just nods off and it holds him up while his arms go onto automatic pilot. Not ruthless enough, that's my trouble.

Frederick had presented me with my Green Glittery outfit at the first gig I'd played with them. Like, about ten minutes before we were due to go on. They'd played in plain clothes when they'd auditioned me, I'd remembered, with more than a touch of sour grapes.

'I think you'll find everything is the right size,' he'd said with a knowing look. He used to be a tailor. Be grateful for small mercies, I reminded myself. At least he didn't need to take my inside leg measurement...

'So who are you playing with tonight?' Raffi's voice broke into my churlish thoughts. I would, I decided, get a new answering machine and I would get out of that band.

'Howlin' Blue Horns,' I grinned. They were the antithesis of the Green Glittery Jacket mob. Playing mostly R&B and Soul covers, which

26

somehow never seem to go out of fashion, they were hugely popular and very, very good. 'Well, actually, I'm not,' I corrected myself. 'I've got Patsy to stand in for me.' Patsy Snell also played in several bands and we had an arrangement whereby one of us would stand in for the other if we were ever ill or got double booked. It had worked very well. So far.

'What? Are you sick?' Raffi looked at me anxiously.

'No. You missed some developments, being away on your field trip. I'm going off for a long overdue break.'

She broke into a torrent of her father's native tongue. I think it was the equivalent of 'Jesus, Mary and Joseph,' only a lot longer.

'It's not that miraculous!' I laughed.

'Oh yes it is! You work far too hard and never take proper time off! So where are you going? When?'

'Well, today, as I've bummed out of tonight's gig. I'll leave late afternoon or early evening, I think. And I'm going to Bewick Grange to spend a few days with Maggie.'

Maggie Mallory and I went way back. We'd met on a British Theatre Association course, more years ago than I care to remember, and had instantly clicked. Back then, she was working in her home town of Liverpool as a Senior Fraud Officer with the DSS. We'd written and phoned regularly and she would usually come down to visit two or three times a year. She was single and, given my erratic lifestyle and Raffi's schooling, it was easier for her to come to us than the other way around. Some years after we met, she'd done an MBA and God knows what else, and moved into Hotel Management, thereafter moving about quite a lot herself. Just a few months ago, she'd landed the post of General Manager at Bewick Grange, a minor Stately Home which had never been opened to the public before. As it was located in Oxfordshire and I live in Cheltenham, it means that at last, we're in easy striking distance. The only reason I hadn't visited earlier was that she was flinging herself into the job in order to get ready for the Grand Opening, now only weeks away at an early Easter. That hadn't stopped her nagging me about it, though, so I'd finally taken the bait, spurred on by increasing tiredness which, as this morning's interruptions had shown all too clearly, had turned me into a female version of Mr Grumpy.

'That's brilliant, Mike! A rest will do you good.'

'Yes – I can even take the saxophone.' That's another reason I don't like going away. I play every day and hate being unable to do so. 'I suppose I ought to think about packing,' I continued. 'Tell you what – how's about we go out to lunch before I get ready?' She may only just have finished breakfast but I knew she'd find room. Raffi has nothing if not a thoroughly healthy appetite.

'Great!' she beamed. 'Anything I can do to help?'

'I don't think so.' I was about to leave the kitchen when I caught sight of the wall planner. 'Ah! On second thoughts, there is. Find me some cash-starved students for Mitch for a big black-tie do in three weeks' time. Oh – and find me someone – besides yourself, of course – who wants to work in Greece for the summer...'

I would gladly have gone myself, I thought, as images of sun, sea and sand clashed rudely with the reality of bumping down a track to Bewick Grange. Not that I would have known we were approaching it had Jake not said so. The headlights picked out the sweep of a drive and the sound of gravel crunched beneath the tyres now, in contrast to the hard-packed soil we'd bounced over earlier. I expressed surprise at the lack of lights.

'The private apartments can't be seen from this side and that's the only place you'd see lights at this time of the evening.' He swung onto what appeared to be another earthen track. 'It's Rosemary Cottage you've been allocated, right?'

'I think so.' All I could remember was that it was something vaguely edible.

'Ah yes – Maggie beat us to it, see?'

I could see. A blaze of light, an open door and Maggie, standing in the doorway. I almost fell out of the jeep in my haste to get to her. I'd never seen her dressed so casually before. She was wearing what looked like old jeans and a sweater and had splotches of something that looked suspiciously like paint on her face. Her raven hair, shoulder length when I'd last seen her, was now cut into a geometric bob which hung beautifully along her cheekbones.

'Mike! Oh, look at you!' Her voice almost disappeared into a squeak. She hugged me fiercely and pulled me inside where, ever practical, she'd had the forethought to put down newspaper to protect the carpet from whatever bits of woodland I might be trailing in. Jake brought in my suitcase and saxophone and put them on the floor. I could see him better now. Tall, lean and filthy about summed him up. I wondered if I looked as bad.

'I'd better go see how the other guys are doing. Catch you later.' He nodded at me and left. As he turned, I was surprised to see that his hair, dark and sleeked back from his head, was long and plaited into a thick, single braid.

'Come on, you!' Maggie laughed. 'Let's get your clothes off and get you into the shower! You'll need that before you can even *think* of sitting in a bath!'

I allowed myself to be pushed, pulled and prodded towards the bathroom, only too eager to get to soap and water. Before I could set foot inside, however, the front door burst open and several figures seemed to be battling to get through it at once.

'Mike! Oh my God! Thank God I found you!'

'Do you know this man?' The question came from Jake, who stood to one side as two other men prevented a third from approaching me. Not that he looked like a man. He was covered in more leaves and mud than most trees possessed at this time of year. The voice was a different matter, though. I would recognise it anywhere. I shut my eyes in disbelief.

'Paul Barnett. A Musical Mr Fixit of my acquaintance. Not that I was expecting him, and I have no idea how he knew I was here.' A horrible suspicion skittered across my mind...

'But that's just it, see? I dashed around to your place because of the emergency and young whatsherface told me you were coming here so I went like a bat out of hell until I caught up with you and Jesus, Mike, I hooted and flashed – God, I was nearly up your arse at one point – didn't you know it was me?'

Mr Road Rage... 'You? That was YOU?'

'Of course it was me. I just said so. I was trying to get your attention.'

'Oh, you got my attention all right!'

'I thought you knew where you were going and you go and get lost and look what happened!'

'I DID know where I was going until you scared the pants off me, you pillock!'

'I just don't understand how you didn't know it was me! God, I must have got close enough for you to see my face!'

'Oh you did!' I spat back. 'But excuse me for not paying enough attention and not having an illuminated magnifying rear view mirror just so I could read your number plate – backwards – and while your headlights were blinding me while I was breaking the speed limit trying to get away from what I thought was a homicidal maniac! Which reminds me – last time I saw you, you owned a white BMW! And whatsherface, for your information, has a name, and it's Rafaella.'

'Whatever. I knew it was something I couldn't pronounce.'

'So you guys are friends, right?' The Texas drawl was thicker than molasses. 'We can all go home now you're happily reunited?'

31

If looks could kill, I'd have dropped Jake Tyler at fifty yards.

'But, ohmygod, Mike, you're a mess!' Paul was off again.

'I look a mess? Have you looked in a mirror lately?'

'That's not the point – what I mean is, you can't go on television looking like that!'

I stood with my mouth open, wondering why everyone was suddenly eyeing me with such interest.

'Run that by me again?'

'Television. You're filthy. Look like you've been in a fight or something.' His gaze swivelled and fixed on Maggie. 'Can't we get her cleaned up – asap?'

'We were actually just about to do that...' She was about to giggle. I could hear it in her voice.

'What television, Paul?' I had a bad feeling about this...

'Life and Death Job, Mike; Life and Death. You'll love it. It's perfect. No problem for someone of your calibre.'

'Paul...'

'Just two numbers, Mike. That's all I'm asking. Just two numbers. Originals.' He mumbled the last word, smothering it under a half-cough, hoping I wouldn't hear. 'I know it's short notice and I know it's live television and you've never done live before, just pre-recorded...'

'Live? Did you say LIVE? With ORIGINALS? You're off your head!'

'Now, now, Mike – we've got plenty of time...' He rubbed at the mud-spattered face of his watch. 'Actually, scratch that. We haven't got much time. It's in Bristol. Well, don't just stand there – get in the shower, woman!'

Maggie shoved me through the bathroom door before I could hit him. 'I'll get some clean clothes for you.' She patted my shoulder. I threw her off.

'Just hold on a minute!' I shoved my way back into the hall. 'I never said I'd do it. I AM *NOT* GOING TO DO IT!'

'Just two numbers, Mike, I told you. I don't know what all the fuss is about. I have a tape in my car and I even have the dots if you want them.' 'The dots' is Paul's way of referring to written music.

'My car is wrecked, I'm wrecked…' I protested.

'Mine's not. And you're not wrecked. Just not fit to drive. I'll take you.'

'Oh no you won't! I've had enough frights for one day and I do not – repeat – DO NOT want any more!'

He actually looked hurt. 'There is nothing wrong with my driving. I have never yet had an accident.'

Right. Quite apart from there being a first time for everything, and whilst he may never have *had* an accident, the number he'd caused was a different matter entirely.

He pushed me into the bathroom, coming in behind me. Maggie, her arms full of clean clothes, stalled him with a raised eyebrow.

'You – out!' she ordered.

'Mike…' He threw a last desperate glance at me as she manhandled him through the doorway.

'No way, Paul. That's my final word. No way!'

Chapter Three

Hurtling along the motorway at ninety miles an hour is not my idea of fun at the best of times. When Paul is driving and I'm strapped in the back with my eyes closed and a pair of headphones clamped around my ears, it's a different ballgame again, and one I like even less.

I had my eyes closed on two counts. One, I had no desire to see for myself just how closely I was being diced with death and two, having my eyes closed enabled me to concentrate more intently on the music. I was listening to it on Paul's very expensive personal stereo. He had offered to play it on the in-car system but I'd blathered about needing to concentrate and rewind. It was bad enough that I was getting in a car with him at all, but some part of me reasoned that maybe it would be safer in the back if we crashed.

He was so thrilled, delighted and grateful that I'd changed my mind. Not that I had – I'd just got myself coerced by Jake and Maggie, who seemed to find the whole thing hilarious. I don't think I was born without a sense of humour, but right then, it was singularly lacking. According to Paul, I was a star, a life-saver, a trooper, a real pro. No I wasn't. Just not ruthless enough...

His transformation was spectacular when I'd emerged from the shower. Jake had apparently hauled him off for a similar clean-up operation

34

and had lent him some clothes. Personally, I would have hosed him down with cold water and told him to run round naked in the cold to dry. Still, you can't have everything.

'This is a great favour you're doing, Mike, and the boys will be SO grateful. I'M grateful. Thank you. Thank you, God. There IS a God!'

I was getting thoroughly confused by this stage as to whether he was thanking me or God at any particular time, and didn't like to ask. The mere thought of a theological discussion with Paul would have been enough to have the Spanish Inquisition running for their lives. Not to mention their sanity.

Whenever Paul comes up with an emergency – and his life seems to be in a constant state of crisis – I'm always stupid enough to start out by asking, 'What's the problem?' It's a sort of Pavlov's dog thing on my part only worse, because I know it's a stupid thing to ask, and still do it. I'm led to believe that other, more sensible musicians, at least brace themselves with a good slug of something alcoholic before opening their mouths when Paul is on the other end of the line.

'Problem? There isn't one now, not now you're available. Thank you, God. Thank you, Mike.' He definitely sounded like he was getting religion. I decided to interrupt the flow before he dragged me off on a pilgrimage of thanksgiving.

'So what's the craic?' I'd asked after my clean-up. After being press-ganged by Jake and Maggie on Paul's behalf...

'It's a doddle, Mike. An absolute doddle for someone of your calibre.' I sometimes wonder if he's got a needle stuck. Now there's a thought – a voodoo doll...

So here I was, concentrating for all I was worth on two numbers – originals – which I'd never heard before and would have to play live on television in about an hour's time – whilst trying my best not to think about the speed we were doing or the likelihood of Paul having a heart attack at the wheel.

I didn't fancy having a heart attack myself which, come to think of it, made reason number three for keeping my eyes shut. Not that it really worked. The way I was being thrown about, even with the benefit of a seat belt, indicated not only horribly high speed but a hellish bent for lane-changing more suited to a race track.

Look on the bright side, I told myself. At least wearing the headphones insulated me from Paul's verbal diarrhoea. I'd been bundled into that car with a speed and efficiency of which the SAS would have been proud. One of my other sources of income is down to my skills as a voice-over artist, so I turned green with envy at the speed and clarity with which Paul had delivered his synopsis of the situation.

'New Band. Red Hot. Your sort of music. Sax player slipped getting out of the bath and broke his arm. Bastard. So you're it.'

I did think the 'bastard' was a bit unkind. I would have been demented if I'd broken my arm and it's not exactly something you'd want to do, even if you weren't a musician.

Even before we'd got to the motorway, Paul's driving was living up to my expectations.

'What keys am I in?' I'd asked, unable to find the sheet music. He'd roared into the village, startling a passing fire crew with a rude gesture that took both his hands off the wheel. I just knew I was going to feel sick. Starting right now...

'Oh – er...' He fumbled for the pieces of paper that showed the dots, his head disappearing below windscreen level. I closed my eyes and held my breath, squinting through one eye as if death wouldn't be quite so terrible if I didn't see it coming with binocular vision.

His head reappeared and he swerved deftly, narrowly missing a motorcyclist who'd had the temerity to turn into the road when Paul wasn't looking.

'B flat and E flat, I think.'

'Concert?'

'No – just the two numbers – I told you.'

'The keys,' I persisted. 'Are they concert keys or my keys?'

'There's a difference?' He turned to look at me as he asked, still fumbling for the music, and a cat used up one of its nine lives, missing the transition to squashed cat by the merest tip of a whisker.

'Paul...'

'What?' He peered through the windscreen again. 'God, Mike, you're a bloody awful passenger! You really make me nervous.'

'I make YOU nervous?' He turned to look at me again, apparently surprised by my reaction. I hastily told him that the tenor sax is a B flat instrument for which music is transposed, in the hope that he'd be so uninterested that he'd turn

37

back and look where we were going.

'Really? Well, you learn something new every day!'

For a Mister Fixit who moved almost entirely in music circles, he displayed an almost total lack of knowledge which never ceased to amaze me. He was also tone deaf, which I'd learned to my cost a couple of years ago, but that's a different story. He finally passed me the sheet music. I was in C sharp and F sharp. My favourite keys. I buried myself in the headphones and didn't emerge until we screeched into the car park of the television studios.

To say I was jet-propelled into the Green Room would be something of an understatement. At least we'd arrived in one piece and at least now, I could have a run through with the band. All hell was let loose the minute we walked through the door.

'Jesus Christ, Paul! I've heard of cutting it fine, but this is ridiculous! And where the bloody hell is the sax player you promised us?'

The rising, panic-induced pitch took the speaker beyond soprano and into castrati range in my estimation. Shame I'm a vegetarian. I could have had Paul's balls for breakfast.

'What do you think this is?' Paul snapped, pointing at my sax case. 'A handbag?'

'But you promised us Mike Brodie!'

'I am Mike Brodie,' I assured him.

'Who played on the Sting album? And...'

'Yes. I know.' I took the requisite breath. 'You were expecting a man. So was my mother, and she never got over it. Lumbered me with a slightly edited version of the name she'd chosen for a boy. Michal. That's M-I-C-H-A-L. Like King David's wife, in the Bible.'

'Shit!' The speaker – Mr 'I'm in a panic' – was tall, blonde and what Raffi would have called Drop Dead Gorgeous.

'Shit happens.' I shrugged.

'Like to your face, you mean?'

I was somewhat taken aback. I hadn't actually seen my face since my foray into the woods, and come to think of it, Maggie had placed herself rather strategically between me and the bathroom mirror.

'Ah, yes – I'd better have a word with someone about that...' Paul did a disappearing act and left me to be stared at by Drop Dead Gorgeous and his Three Unhappy Men who were, by the look of it, stuck somewhere between a rock and a hard place.

I put the sax case on the floor. 'I may not be male and I may not be pretty, but I didn't know either condition was a prerequisite for playing the saxophone. Do you want me to play or not?'

'Do we have a choice?'

'Not unless you want to cancel.' This little gem came from the Floor Manager, a good-looking guy in his thirties. He nodded towards the clock. 'You've got twelve minutes.'

'Until the run-through?' I asked. Paul had cut it fine.

'Until you're on. Capital O, capital N.'

Paul returned even as he spoke, six pairs of eyes swinging towards him like a compass to North.

'Bloody hell, Paul!' I exploded.

'Now, now, Mike! It's not a problem. You'll be fine. You'll all be fine.'

'Eleven minutes. If you're lucky.' It was the Floor Manager again. 'Yes or no?' The question was addressed to Drop Dead Gorgeous. This time, he didn't hesitate.

'Yes. Let's do it.'

I quickly unpacked the sax and started to put it together. As I did so, the front left-hand keys fell off. There was a collective intake of breath. One of the Unhappy Men sank in to the nearest chair like he'd been pole-axed. I reached for the screwdrivers in the case and set to work.

'Some people call me the Last of the Luddites,' I began, my casual tone belying the speed of my fingers. 'That's because I'm computer illiterate. When, however, it comes to things like this....' I twiddled away deftly. '...it's really quite simple. If you put it in your mouth to play it, I can fix it. Let's go.'

We sprinted across to the studio, taking our places with barely enough time for me to sign the release form for the appearance. Paul had disappeared again, no doubt talking his way into the Gallery from where he would get to see the camera's eye view of things and have sixteen kinds of fit, having to keep quiet for the duration.

I had just enough time in hand to get an acute attack of nerves. I switched automatically into deep breathing exercises. Quite apart from anything else, I would need all the breath I could muster. The band looked to be, on average, about half my age and their now broken-armed sax player had immaculate breath control and phrasing if the tape was to be believed.

Just as the presenter introduced the band, I realised that I didn't know which number we were to play first. The drummer started an intricate pattern of delicate cymbal work. *Right*, I thought – *the slower one*. I breathed through a fixed smile as a camera operator moved in on him. Dry mouth and sweaty fingers were threatening, the precise opposite of what I needed. The bass came in, swiftly followed by guitar, with swelling keyboards not far behind. This was it. Two-two-three-four. We were in. That is, me and Drop Dead Gorgeous, who was the trumpet player.

Thank God I have perfect pitch and the auditory equivalent of a photographic memory. We played tighter than a duck's arse, then he was away into a solo. I knew I'd be next and kept my breathing deep and slow until I recognised my cue. I just glimpsed the camera moving in as I shut my eyes and went for it.

Nice one, Mike, I thought, as I came through the other side without a bum note. *One down, one to go*. As the cameras left the band and an interview with a controversial historian was cued, I ventured a glance at the others. They seemed a lot happier than they'd been earlier and gestured their satisfaction.

It seemed like only seconds before we were cued in again, this time to scream into the other number, the tempo of which had frightened the pants off me back in the car. I slipped into Liquid Fingers mode as the tempo wound up and up, leading into one hell of a sax solo. I seemed to be accelerating towards a cliff edge, soaring, swooping, screaming and honking in a flurry of notes so fast I no longer knew what I was doing. My whole body was vibrating, from the top of my head to the soles of my feet, then I was over the cliff edge, hurtling down to hand over to the trumpet.

Then it was over. I was in a daze, on a high from the exhilaration, and it was only when the back-slapping started as we headed back to the Green Room that I realised what I needed. I headed off for the toilet, crashed into a cubicle and was promptly sick.

My reflection stared at me from the mirror as I washed my face. It took me a moment to register that it was actually myself I was looking at. True, the light was unflattering but even so, I gave myself a fright. I should have been an actress, I thought. Looking like this, I'd have been a natural for the latest remake of 'Bride of Frankenstein'. I was coming up with at least one black eye and my face was criss-crossed with lacerations. I'd sailed close to the wind in more than one respect tonight.

I joined the others at the bar, where there was a drink waiting for me at the band table.

'Well played, Mike! I knew you'd be fine!' Paul beamed at me. 'Just had to warn the cameras to stay off your face and concentrate on your fingers.'

'You were great, and we owe you one.' This was from Drop Dead Gorgeous. 'I also owe you an apology for the reaction when you arrived.'

'Forget it,' I shrugged. 'Paul had everyone walking a tightrope. I would have killed him if I'd

42

known there wouldn't be time for a run-through.'

Paul chuckled and raised his glass of mineral water. 'If you'd known in advance, you wouldn't have come, which is why I didn't tell you. They ran through without you. Only possible way.'

'Paul, you are irascible!'

He beamed at me again. 'As I don't know what that means, I'll take it as a compliment. Do feel free to have another drink. That's a little bonus for you this evening – you don't have to worry about drinking, with me driving you home.'

Oh bugger. I'd forgotten about that...

Chapter Four

Peace. Perfect peace. I opened my eyes, relishing the silence, warm beneath the duvet, not wanting to move. I hadn't set the alarm the previous night, not having got back to the Grange until one a.m. But I had got back alive and in one piece, despite what passed for driving on Paul's part.

Curiosity finally got the better of me. I don't sleep with my watch on, so I leaned across to the bedside table to see what time it was. Leaning, of course, meant moving. And moving hurt.

I couldn't believe how stiff I was. Every muscle hurt. I ached in places I didn't even know I had places, let alone muscles. That's a lot of pain, just to find out it's 9.30 in the morning. To say that I crawled to the bathroom would be an exaggeration, but it would probably have been easier than walking. A shower wouldn't get rid of this, I thought. This called for a long, hot soak in the bath.

I emerged some time later, now able to add 'scalded lobster' to my 'Bride of Frankenstein' look, which had not improved with the benefit of a good night's sleep. Quite the reverse, in fact. I now had two definite black eyes and bringing a face cloth near my battered visage felt rather like an encounter with industrial grade sandpaper. Maggie had provided me with antiseptic cream the previous evening and I applied it liberally. Bugger the anti-wrinkle stuff. Wrinkles I could live with. They didn't hurt.

As I sat with my first cup of tea, I reread the note I'd found on my return from Bristol. Maggie had propped it against the bottle of wine she'd also left for me.

'Sorry about the apparently hostile welcome! Will let you sleep. Meet you in my office for lunch, 1 o'clock. If you see Jake, don't go ballistic – it wasn't his fault and he's probably already sorting out those responsible! Lots of love, Maggie.'

I made an indeterminate noise and smiled – which hurt – more at Maggie, than through any sense of forgiveness over the events of the previous evening. Right then. What was I going to do until one o'clock?

It was half past ten by now and my first thought was to play the sax. Breakfast, however, had reminded me that my jaw hurt. Not a lot, but enough for me to think twice about it. I marvelled that I'd played as well as I had for television, but that had been with adrenaline to override the pain. I decided to leave it until later. I looked at the plan of the estate and the village which Maggie had left with her 'Welcome Pack' and looked out of the window. The sky was that particular shade of blue that says 'cold', but lifts the spirits. There was snow on the ground, but it looked powdery crisp rather than icy and lethal. I decided to risk it. A good walk after my bath might ease the aches still further.

Taking the plan with me, I set off down the track with Bewick Grange peering through the trees some distance to my right. It was a beautiful day, the low yellow sun reflecting from the snow which covered everything in sight like sugar frosting. I was feeling better already. I had put on coat, scarf and gloves, my Doc Martens boots making easy work of conditions underfoot. I felt like a child again, with that wonderful sense of newness as you plant your feet in pristine, virgin snow. I even turned to look at the trail I'd left behind, remembering childhood snowball fights and the making of snowmen with Alan, the boy who'd lived next door. Pieces of coal for the eyes, a carrot for the nose... Laughing at the memory, I strode determinedly to where the track met the road to the village.

Checking the plan, I turned left, crossing the road in order to walk facing oncoming traffic. There was no pavement here, the snow folding its thin coat over rough grass verge and hedges, now bare, beyond which stretched open fields for as far as the eye could see. Occasionally, they held a cottage or small house and as I continued my walk, I met no one and was passed only by a single car, an old blue Vauxhall Astra, coming towards me.

It wasn't long, however, before I began to hear the sound of occasional traffic and as I rounded a bend, the road rose steeply, its end flanked by buildings, and I found myself meeting Ruttersford High Street. It seemed rather a grand name for a thoroughfare barely wide enough for two single lanes of traffic to pass without hindrance. I turned left into it, with the aim of taking a leisurely walk to see what was on offer. A surprising number of people were about, mostly mothers with pushchairs or small children, and elderly people making a rather more cautious foray along the street. It didn't take a genius to work out why. Constant trekking had turned the snow to ice, and the pavements were far from innocent.

My boots gave me confidence, and I marvelled at the unsuitability of some of the footwear on display as one or two foolhardy souls tottered along, slipping and struggling for balance or, in one case, losing it completely and sitting down with a thump. This was a young woman wearing stiletto heels. I rolled my eyes at the sight, as did the elderly man who helped her to her feet. He, I noticed, was wearing thick woollen socks over his shoes.

The shops, mostly bow-fronted, provided a rich assortment of outlets. Apart from the usual grocer, chemist and newsagent, there was also a tearoom, which I earmarked for later use, and a variety of shops aimed at the tourist trade in the summer months, selling arts and crafts, pottery, perfume and the like. On the right-hand side of the road, the shops gave way to a high stone wall behind which a church declared itself on a raised bank of ground overlooking the village. From this vantage point, one could gaze even further and see the Grange. A woman in sensible shoes and a beautiful overcoat emerged from the church porch.

'Beautiful, isn't it?' She smiled her welcome at me.

'Must be stunning in the summer.'

'An unsurpassed view, in my opinion. And the weddings we have here – brides brought to church in horse drawn carriages, the trees and fields ablaze with colour. It's breathtaking.'

I smiled, which hurt a little but didn't matter. I love enthusiasm.

'Have you always lived here?' I asked. She had barely any accent to betray her origins.

'Lord, no! Moved here five years ago. I'm the vicar, Alison Clarke.'

She was taller than me and had a lovely open face with wide blue eyes and wisps of blonde hair peeping out from beneath a stylish hat. How I envy people who can wear a hat! I resisted the temptation to try and flatten my unruly curls into some semblance of order, and took the proffered hand.

'Mike Brodie. I'm staying with Maggie Mallory at Bewick Grange.'

'Oh, I know Maggie! Comes here most Sundays with Steve and Katie Anderson. Lovely woman. Incredible laugh. Friend of yours, I take it?'

'Yes. We go back a long way.'

'Here for a break, then?' I realised that Alison

was scrutinising my face with a concerned look. I grimaced.

'I'm not a refugee from domestic violence – honestly!' I explained what had happened, briefly and as best as I could, given that I still didn't really know yet. Nor had I forgotten that Jake had promised me an explanation.

'Oh Lord! Sounds to me like you may have had an unscheduled meeting with the Companions of the Crooked Staff!'

'The Who?'

'Battle re-creation lot. They can get a bit over-enthusiastic, I'm afraid. Maggie is having them do a big re-enactment for the Grand Opening, I believe. Warren Myatt is very keen to put the Grange on the map, so to speak.' Warren Myatt, I remembered, was the new owner of The Grange and Maggie had said that he'd asked to meet me.

'Oh, sorry – must dash!' A horn had sounded and I walked down with Alison to the car waiting for her on the road in front of the church.

'Nice to have met you, Mike, and I hope the rest of your stay is rather less eventful than your arrival! Any chance I'll see you on Sunday?'

'In church? No. Not my thing, I'm afraid. Come to that, I'm not sure how long I'm staying, anyway.'

'Left it open, eh? Well, feel free to drop in if you want to.'

She waved as the car pulled away and I looked at my watch, deciding I had time to scout round the shops before taking advantage of the tearoom. Sore jaw or not, I was feeling decidedly hungry even though I'd eaten breakfast not too

48

long ago.

I soon spent some money. One of the shops had just the sort of pottery I'd been on the lookout for and I bought several pieces in taupe and cream with delicate leaf-shaped filigree work around the rims. I also bought handmade cards and hair ornaments for Raffi. I had called in at the newsagent-cum-post-office, buying newspapers and a pile of magazines, and was walking past the chemist shop, now toting two carrier bags, when disaster struck. A man leaving the shop cannoned straight into me and both of us went flying. I managed to stay on my feet but dropped my bags, whilst he sprawled headlong with his shopping.

'Are you all right?' I asked, as I helped him to his feet. It always seems such a stupid question, but what else can you say?

'Dear me. Yes. My fault entirely. Mind on other things, you know. But how about you?' He blinked at me from behind wire-rimmed spectacles which were thankfully intact, combining an owlish look with the ramrod straight carriage often seen in ex-Service personnel.

'I'm fine,' I assured him. 'Really. No harm done.'

'Oh good. Oh dear.' He'd looked down at our shopping. It was strewn across the pavement. I didn't like to think about the pottery. The two of us crouched down to pick it all up, nearly banging our heads together in the process.

'Ah. That's not mine.'

'This is, I think.' We scrambled around until we'd finally managed to get everything back into our bags. One of mine now made dubious noises. Rattling noises.

'Are you sure nothing is broken?' His face was anxious.

'No. No, really. Everything is fine,' I lied.

'Ah. Well. Thank you very much for your help and I'm most awfully sorry to have been such a bother.'

'Not at all. Mind how you go.'

'I certainly shall. Leather soles, you know. Must change them when I get in. For when I come out again.'

'Yes. It's a bit treacherous.'

A Land Rover hooted and the man waved to its occupants. He hovered for a moment, opened his mouth, changed his mind and backed off, raising his hat as he did so. Someone else who could wear a hat, I realised. As he walked away, I shook my head and looked ruefully at the bags. Oh well. No use worrying now. I'd look at the damage when I got back.

I had just crossed the road to take a closer look at the tearoom when a voice called, 'Can I give you a lift?' Jake was sitting in a Land Rover in a tiny side road as the twin of his vehicle, the one that had just hooted, pulled away.

'Aren't you blocking the traffic?' I asked.

'No. Your face looks like shit.'

'Thanks a lot. Yours doesn't look too brilliant, either.' He had a large bruise along his right cheekbone.

'Comes from a strange, red-headed woman socking me with her elbow.'

'I did that?'

'You sure did.'

'God, I'm sorry!'

50

'Don't be. I could have been Jack the Ripper for all you knew. You'd have been well within your rights to have inflicted a damned sight more than this.'

I didn't like to admit that I'd tried but failed. An impatient hooting emanated from behind him.

'Now I am blocking the traffic!' he grinned. He pulled round into the main road. 'So – can I give you a lift or are you going to keep me on double yellows all day?'

'I'd love a lift. But I was hoping to get a cup of tea first.'

'No problem. There's parking round the back. I'll meet you in there. Mine's coffee, black, no sugar, with a raspberry Danish – my shout.'

'You're on!'

The interior of the tearoom was every inch Ye Olde Englishe Tea Shoppe with gleaming copper, whitewashed walls and black beams. The raspberry Danish wasn't bad, either. I had one with my tea.

'So – how was your life and death business with Paul last night?'

I grimaced. 'Fine, so long as they kept the camera off my face.'

'You play for a living?'

'It's one of three ways I make a living, actually.'

'Multi-tasking, huh?'

I laughed at the way he said it. 'Well ... I started out with my music shop. I sell and repair new and second-hand instruments. The sort you blow.'

'Locally?'

'Cheltenham.'

'So who's looking after it now?'

'Alex, my partner. Actually, we're closed on Mondays, anyway.' I stretched carefully and contentedly, glad to be warm again.

'And you play saxophones. Even on TV at short notice.' He smiled. 'Even after being frightened out of your wits and knocked about in the dark.'

'You noticed! Well, it wasn't that bad. Could have been worse.'

He raised his eyebrows. His eyes, I noticed, were a very deep shade of blue. I felt instantly embarrassed for noticing.

'I understand I may have had a run-in with the Companions of the Crooked Something?' I asked, burying my face in my teacup.

'Crooked Staff. Yes, you did. Now where did you hear that? I asked Maggie to let me deal with it and give you the low-down.'

'Maggie never said anything. I met the vicar. She told me.'

'Not much goes on around here that Alison doesn't know about. Or get to hear about. Yes. Maggie's organising a big reenactment for the official opening of the Grange. They'd been practising and some of the younger ones, on the way home, got a little carried away, spotting a potential trespasser on the Estate. Just so happened I was near them at the time. On my way to the pub.' He shook his head. 'Needless to say, I have had more than a few words in certain ears, and those words have been noted. Your car repair bill will be met in full and they also owe you a new jacket, I believe.'

'Thanks very much.' He'd certainly dealt with

everything promptly.

'So what's number three?'

'Pardon?'

'Your multi-tasking?'

'Oh. I do voice-overs. TV and radio commercials. Narrating documentaries and training videos. That sort of thing.'

'My, my! A woman of many talents. And how does the estimable Alex cope with all this?'

'I'm not away that much,' I shrugged. 'I mean, the gigs are invariably evenings and we juggle around the voice work. Anyway, I haven't had a holiday in ages, so he doesn't mind. He had extra time off when his mother-in-law was ill and took an extended break when she died. Lynda – that's his wife – took it very hard.'

'Hold on a minute – I thought Alex was your partner?'

'He is.' I suddenly realised his mistake. 'My business partner.'

'Ah. So how does your other partner cope? I'm sorry – I'm making assumptions. When you said ... I thought you meant your husband or boyfriend.' He raised his eyebrows. 'Girlfriend, even.'

I laughed. 'Wrong on all counts! I was married, briefly, and I have a kind of surrogate daughter, but no – my husband died fourteen years ago.'

'I'm sorry.'

'His name was Duncan, and he was my original partner. In the business, I mean. We bought it together after we'd trained. That was how we met. On the training course.'

'So he was musical, too?'

'Oh yes.'

'And you played together?' I nodded. 'So how long have you been playing the saxophone?'

'Over twenty years.'

'That's a long time.'

'Don't remind me!' I noticed he was looking at my hands.

'And you never remarried?'

'Never met anyone mad enough to want to live with me.' I omitted to say that there had been two men I'd been mad enough to want to live with, neither of whom had wanted the package responsibility of Raffi as well. Time to turn the tables. 'So what about you?' I asked. 'What's an American doing working at an English Grange?'

'Point one, I work at the conference centre, not the Grange. And point two, despite my accent, I'm not American.'

'You're not?'

'Comes of my Mom being American and my Dad being British.'

'But you've lived there. That accent is unmistakable.'

'Till I was seventeen,' he acknowledged. 'Then we came to England. Then my parents split, and I spent a lot of time going backwards and forwards. Eventually, I settled here properly but I visit often and still have that damned drawl. Well...' He looked at his watch. 'I'd better get you back for your lunch with Maggie. She'll have my hide if you're late.'

'It's that time already? Hell, where did the morning go!' I scrambled for my things and shivered as we walked across the car park. The wind was up, raw and biting.

'You ought to get a hat,' Jake commented. 'Seventy per cent of your body heat is lost through the top of your head.'

I gave him a withering look. 'Find me one that will stay on and not make me look a complete prat, and I'll be glad to!'

He laughed. 'You do have rather a lot of hair!'

'Right.' It's not so much the length as the thickness and curliness that's the problem.

The drive back to the Grange was short, and as I got out of the car, Jake suddenly said, 'You did everything wrong, you know. Back there in the woods last night. If that had been for real, you'd be dead meat.'

'What?'

'Just a thought. Maybe I could show you what you should have done.'

Right. Fancied a wrestling match, did he? An image sprang to mind and I blotted it out before it showed on my face. 'I really don't think that's necessary,' I smiled. 'Um – how do I get to the Tower from here?' He'd dropped me at the cottage so I could dump my shopping. What was left of it...

'Follow that path and you can't miss it. They used to throw people off the top, you know. Years ago.'

'Alive?!'

'Only till they hit the ground...'

Chapter Five

'By God, Maggie!' I spluttered as she enveloped me in a hug. 'Those stairs must keep you fit!'

'Don't they just! I'm up and down more often than a whore's drawers! Have to eat a chocolate bar after every ascent just to keep me from wasting away! It's easier going down, though.' She held me at arms' length and scrutinised my face. 'Ouch!'

'That just about sums it up!' I agreed, looking around me. 'So this is your office?'

'Yes – welcome to my domain!' She gave a sweep of her arm which encompassed the whole room.

'Wow!' I said, and meant it. A mullioned window overlooked a breathtaking view of gardens below, beyond which sloping fields led to the woods. The interior had been thoughtfully designed to accommodate modern technology and practicality whilst maintaining the beauty and dignity of the ancient building. Her desk was large and of solid oak, well capable of supporting the computer, telephone and other things necessary to her job, whilst a smaller version, against the back wall, was home to a fax machine and other accoutrements. The walls were hung with tapestries and other hangings rather than paintings. The effect was quite stunning.

'I thought we'd have lunch in the village – give

ourselves time for catching up.'

I groaned. 'I had to climb all those stairs, just to go straight back down again?'

'I wanted to show off my office! Besides, it will do you good – keep you fit!'

'Give me a heart attack, more like! I don't know how you do it!'

'You can laugh, Mike Brodie! One poor soul did have a heart attack up here and it was no joke for the paramedics, getting him down!'

'Jake said there was a short cut – something about people being thrown off the top, alive? I take it he was joking?'

'Afraid not. At one period, this was used as a sort of jail. All a bit gruesome, I'm afraid.'

'Not a tradition you're planning to revive, I hope?'

'Oh, I don't know...!' She laughed. 'It might go down quite well. Providing you're not the victim, of course.'

'Remind me not to piss you off...' I trailed behind her as we made our own conventional descent.

A short time later we were seated at a table in the Three Tuns, making ready with a bottle of wine whilst waiting for our lunch to arrive.

'To present and absent friends – you and Raffi!' She gave me a long look. 'So how are you, Mike? And I don't just mean after last night's little excitement, either.'

'Little!'

'Well, if I know you, that's how you'll have shrugged it off to Jake this morning.'

'Oh? And what's that supposed to mean?'

'Nothing...' She was giving me her 'I'm-all-innocent' look.

'That's all right then,' I grinned, 'because there's nothing to talk about on that score!'

'Michal! Don't tell me you don't fancy him! Tall, dark hair – *long* hair, which you're a sucker for – baby blues that look like ocean depths and that voice–' she lowered her own – 'like deep brown, melting molasses...'

I sat with my glass half way to my mouth and spluttered. 'If you find him that attractive, how come you're not after him yourself?'

'Not my type. Doesn't do a thing for me.'

'So who does?'

We were used to sparring and had left subtlety behind years ago. She'd been trying to fix me up with a second husband as long as I'd known her, as well as trying to find a first for herself.

'Who says anyone does?'

'Your face. Your letters – between the lines. And possibly the vicar.' I was remembering my conversation with Alison, the way she'd looked when she'd said what she had.

'Alison? And what's she been saying?'

'Oh, this and that ... Steve and Katie, was it? So who are they?' I cast about, thinking of things she'd written. 'Wasn't there a Steve who makes hand-crafted furniture from reclaimed timber? Is that the same one?'

She was quiet for a long moment. So long, I wished I hadn't asked. She sighed.

'It's serious, Mike. I didn't want to say anything until I was sure. Sure of his feelings as well as mine. And ... it's just – well – a bit complicated.'

I couldn't believe she'd get involved with a married man. 'Oh, Maggie...'

'What?' She burst out laughing at the look on my face. 'Not that kind of complicated! Katie's Steve's daughter, not his wife!'

Our meals arrived and we waited until we were alone before resuming our conversation.

'But Katie has a mother, I presume?'

'Yes. She did a bunk with some American when Katie was ten months old. Steve's brought her up single-handed since.'

'And how old is she now?'

'Six. So how did you pick up on Steve, you mindreader?'

'We're too alike, Maggie. Remember how you rumbled me at that party a couple of years ago?'

'Oh ... HIM! What was his name ... Chris!'

'Chris.' I shook my head at the memory.

'I remember...' She twirled a forkful of pasta and grinned. 'We were packed like sardines, people sitting all over the floor because there were no chairs left, and you needed to leave the room...'

I nodded. 'And at the end of the evening, after we left, you said, "You fancy Chris, don't you?", and I couldn't work out how the hell you knew, because I'd been so careful to hide it.'

'Which was precisely how I did know! When you were trying to get to the door, he caught your leg with his arm – completely accidental – and had any other man in the room done it you'd have quipped, "You can touch my leg anytime!" It was because you didn't say that, that I knew!'

59

'Like the dog that didn't bark in the night.'

'What?'

'Sherlock Holmes.'

'Right, Dr Watson! So what does all this have to do with Steve?'

'It's exactly the same thing. You described lots of people you'd met – what they did, what they looked like, their idiosyncrasies, whether you liked them or not. But Steve was completely matter-of-fact. The alarm bells were ringing in the background, but it took Alison to bring it up again. I remember you liked her.'

'Yes, I do. But how come you've seen her? I didn't know she'd been to the Grange.'

'That's because I met her in the village. And Jake, come to that. Not that I got as far as this pub, though.'

'Good, isn't it?'

I had to agree. The food was outstanding and I was feeling wonderfully replete.

'Jake will probably be taking you to the other pub, though.'

I put my knife and fork down none too gently. 'Maggie!'

'Don't look at me like that – it has nothing whatsoever to do with me. No matchmaking or romantic interest, I promise. I just happen to know that he has a pretty good reason for wanting to take you there.'

'Like what?'

'That's for me to know and you to find out...' She tapped the side of her nose.

'Maggie...'

'What's the big deal?' The Innocent look again.

'You did say you don't fancy him? Or did I misunderstand you?'

Given that we're both pushing forty, I sometimes think we're really going on fifteen…

'You did not misunderstand me. I do not fancy him.' I avoided her eye by resuming the shovelling of food into my mouth.

'Even if you did, you wouldn't do anything about it. That's your problem, Mike. You were just the same with Chris. He was available. As was whatshisname, a couple of years earlier.'

'What's availability got to do with anything?' My fork was poised in mid-air. 'Just because something is available, doesn't make it an obligatory try-out.'

'You're being obtuse.'

'I am?'

'You are.'

I pushed my plate aside. 'Maggie, if there's something on your mind, just come out with it, will you?'

'OK. It's just that – it's such a bloody waste! You being single. I know this is getting a bit personal, but it upsets me, seeing you like this.'

'Like what?'

'You know perfectly well what I mean. When was the last time you went out on a date?'

'I have loads of male friends,' I began, evading a direct answer. 'Work with men ninety-nine percent of the time…'

'That's not what I mean, and you know it! A date, Mike – see – you can't even remember!'

I started pulling apart an uneaten bread roll. 'Maggie – I don't need a man to be a complete person. You've known me long enough: There is nothing missing in my life. I am not walking around with a gaping hole. I'm working well – rather too hard, perhaps – which is one of the reasons I took this opportunity to come and see you at last – but honestly – I'm OK. Really.'

We looked at each other. She reached across the table and squeezed my hand. 'I'm sorry, Mike. I don't mean to try and organise you. It's just that – well, I know it sounds corny, but I'm so happy with Steve and I want you to be happy, too.'

I smiled and squeezed her hand in return. A young man at the bar, behind Maggie's back, mouthed something to his friend about 'lesbians'. I ignored him.

'I'm really happy for you, Maggie. And I do know how you feel. I had that with Duncan. I was lucky. But maybe hoping for another stab at it is just being greedy.'

'We'll have to disagree on that! And how come you can have four saxophones but not more than one husband? That's really logical, Mike!'

'That never was my strong point! Oh my God...!' The dessert trolley had arrived. 'Is that real old-fashioned treacle tart?'

'Absolutely the best! I can personally recommend it.'

'I'd better have some, then!' We ate in silence for a moment. 'So when am I going to meet this lucky man? And his daughter.'

'How about teatime tomorrow afternoon?'

'Sounds good to me. And what time is teatime?'

'Oh ... five-ish. If you meet me at the bottom of

the Tower, we can walk over together.'

'As long as I don't have to throw myself off the top, first!'

'It's not compulsory!'

'Then I'll pass.' I had never seen Maggie looking so well. She was somehow both animated and peaceful, as if, for the first time since I'd known her, her life was in perfect balance. I envied her that.

'So tell me about your job. What exactly do you do?' She'd told me bits and pieces in her letters, but I wanted to be able to put the whole picture together.

'Oh–' She swallowed a mouthful of lemon meringue pie, waving her fork in the air. 'As General Manager, I'm responsible for business – visitor business, corporate events, special dinners, that kind of thing. My primary task is to attract visitors. What we want apart from the locals – and not-so-locals, come to that – is organised tour groups and foreign tourists through tour operators and agents.'

'That's a hell of a responsibility. And you're doing all this from scratch?'

'Yes and no. I mean, the commercial side has been going for some time – the conference centre, holiday cottages, the fitness centre and gardens. It's just the Grange itself that hasn't been open to the public before, but it's fascinating, Mike. There are Tudor connections, Civil War connections – I've arranged for educational packs for schools to slot into the National Curriculum.'

'You must have worked your socks off!'

'You're not wrong! It's been a tight run thing,

with my predecessor doing a bunk and all.'

'Your predecessor? But I thought this was a new post?' We shared the bill and set off back to the Grange, walking at a leisurely pace.

'Well, again, yes and no. This kind of thing has to work on forward planning. Jake is responsible for the day to day running of the conference centre and the Myatts already had someone in my job, supposedly getting ready for the opening. Anthony Byers. But as I said, he did a bunk.'

'With the family silver, you mean?'

'No.' She looked surprised at the question and pulled a face, trying to find the right words. 'To tell the truth, I think it was a bit much for him. Sort of like a breakdown, I think. Anyway, he left a note saying he was very sorry but he had to go to Italy and wouldn't be back.'

Mention of Italy reminded me of Raffi and I made a mental note to phone her. 'So you just had to pick up the pieces?'

'I'll say. And there were a lot of them. Which reminds me – you have a free pass to all the facilities.'

'Thanks!'

'It was Elynore's idea. I'll fill you in on that later.'

We huffed and puffed our way back up the Tower stairs to Maggie's office. She put the kettle on. 'Pot of tea?'

'Lovely!' I was ready for one after the walk back.

'You and your tea!' She shook her head. 'The day you turn one down, I'll know you're ill!' She tossed me a brochure, rapidly followed by a

64

second one.

'First's the standard one, second's for corporate hospitality.' A third quickly followed. 'And that's the run down on the conference and fitness centres.'

'You have been busy!'

'Told you so! I'm a superstar, that's all!'

I leafed through the brochures while Maggie took messages off her answer phone and made a couple of calls. She had no problem with technology.

'These brochures are really good,' I enthused. 'The photography alone must have cost a packet.' It was first rate and captured stunning views throughout the seasons. I stopped at a picture of the Myatts. Elynore and Warren. Warren seemed an incongruous name for the owner of the Grange.

'What are they like?' I asked, indicating the page.

'Super. Never known people with so much energy. Actually, you're invited to lunch with them tomorrow, in the private apartments.'

'Thanks.' I raised my eyebrows.

'You're not offended?'

'No. Just wasn't expecting it, that's all.' A meeting was one thing, but lunch? I hoped I would know which cutlery to use.

'You'll like them. They want to meet you because you're a friend of mine. Also ... they may have a little business to put your way.'

'Oh?'

'I'll leave it to them to tell you. God, Mike, I'm sorry! Here I am saying I don't mean to organise you and I've already set you up for tea with Steve and Katie and lunch with the Myatts!'

'That's all right. Those sorts of things, I don't mind – just don't try organising my love life, OK?'

'I'll try... I'm just sorry we're not going to see that much of each other while you're here. With the opening only three weeks away, I'm up to my ears.'

'Maggie, stop apologising. I'm just glad to be here at all and I'm quite capable of looking after myself. I'm sure I'll find plenty to do.'

'Oh – that reminds me – there is one other thing I've sort of arranged.'

I watched the grin fighting for room on her face. 'What are you up to, Maggie?'

'It's not your love life, honestly! It's just that … tomorrow morning … I've got a little job for you…'

Chapter Six

'What DO you think you're doing?' The voice was female, Scottish and highly confrontational. My eyes flickered upward, the barest of glances, and not far enough to see the speaker's face.

'What's it look like? Changin' the baby, ain't I? Couldn't see no signs nowhere and 'e needs changin', 'e does. Done a pooh.' I was aware of a stifled giggle to my right.

'He's WHAT?!'

66

'Shit 'imself, ain't 'e? They do it all the time, you know. Babies.'

'Madam – this is neither a public lavatory nor a baby changing facility. I shall have to ask you to come with me.'

I stood up slowly, patting my imaginary baby's back. ''Ere – what's your problem, then?' I glowered at Mary, one of the recently appointed Guides, who was going positively red in the face with simulated anger.

'What's my problem? What's my problem? YOU'RE my problem! This is the AUTO-GRAPH ROOM! You can't change a baby in here!'

'Well, I just 'ave, 'aven't I? And I didn't put 'im on the cabinets or nothin'. See – I changed 'im on the floor.'

'Yes, I can see! Have you any idea what this carpet cost?'

Diffidently, I allowed my gaze to follow her accusatory finger.

''S'only a little bit of a stain,' I shrugged. 'Soon come out, that will, with a splash of disinfectant.'

'Disinfectant?' She sounded as though she were ready to blow a gasket.

'Yeah.' I pushed past her, imaginary baby clutched to my bosom. ''S'on offer at the local supermarket. Dunno what you're gettin' your knickers in a twist for.'

I marched out of the room, followed by a scampering Mary calling, 'But ... but ... but...' like a record with its needle stuck.

'Lovely, ladies! Well done!' Philippa, the Head Guide, called us back into the room, where we were met with a scatter of applause.

'More butts than a billy goat!' she smiled at Mary. Turning to the small group of trainees, she said, 'Now that was a wonderful example of how NOT to deal with a difficult situation. And in case you're thinking it was a ludicrous or exaggerated one, let me assure you that it happened more than once in my previous place of employment. That's why I particularly asked Michal to act it out and Mary to handle it badly.'

She glanced at me and nodded. I resumed my baby-changing position on the floor, absorbing myself completely in the task, talking to the baby, tickling its tummy, wrinkling my nose in distaste as I removed the offending nappy.

'Now then – Carol – perhaps you'd like to give this situation a try?'

I heard approaching footsteps and a startled 'Oh!', followed swiftly by, 'Can I help you, Madam? You look like you need six pairs of hands there! Actually, we have a baby changing room just along the corridor – shall I give you a hand? I'm sure you'd be more comfortable, and so would he. Isn't he lovely? What's his name?'

'Albert.' This time, there were several splutters to my right.

'Hello, Albert!' Carol was obviously game for the exercise. *She* was tickling the imaginary Albert's tummy now. I picked him up.

'Shall I help you with your bag? Marvellous, all the stuff they make for babies nowadays, isn't it?'

'Yeah.' I replied absently, suddenly noticing the stain on the carpet again. 'Oh dear. He's made a bit of a mess on your carpet. I'm ever so sorry.' I bent down and scrubbed at it with a tissue, nearly knocking the imaginary Albert's imaginary head into one of the glass cabinets as I did so.

Quick as a flash, Carol moved to intercept me. 'Don't you worry about that! That'll come out, no trouble at all. You leave it to me.' Chucking the imaginary Albert's imaginary chin, she led us out into the corridor carrying our imaginary baby bag and chattering away about how much he looked like me, asking how old he was and generally being as nice as pie. She was brilliant and Philippa told her so.

'Right, ladies! I think you've earned yourself a tea break. Let's adjourn to the guides' staff room.'

Once inside, Maggie ambled over, mug in hand, smiling broadly. She had stayed at the back of the group, watching the whole performance with pen and notebook at the ready.

'I love watching you work!'

'Hardly work! But I thoroughly enjoyed it.' I nodded to where Carol was standing, listening intently to Philippa. 'She's good.'

'Yes, I'm pleased with her. No-nonsense approach but with a generous helping of both tact and charm. Couldn't ask for more, really. Philippa said she'd be good. Has a nose for these things.'

'But where did you get them all? Never having had Guides here before?'

'Advertised in the local rags. We were very lucky with Philippa. She'd just moved down here from Derbyshire when her husband retired. She was Head Guide at a Stately there. Much bigger than this, of course. Very experienced and highly recommended. I hope you were all right last night.'

Her sudden change of tack threw me for a moment. She'd been worried about leaving me to my own devices, having had a prior engagement.

'I was fine. I told you, I don't need baby-sitting and I don't expect to be constantly entertained. I know you're up to your neck at the moment and I'm just glad to be here, OK?'

'So what did you do with yourself? This place is hardly a hive of activity.'

I used my fingers to tick off points. 'Phoned Raffi. No one else for Zorba the Greek yet, but three volunteers already for Mitch's black-tie bash. Played the saxophone, full blast. Watched TV. Had another good long soak in the bath.'

'Your face doesn't look quite so raw.'

'No. I'm not quite so stiff, either.'

The guides were disappearing now, off for another session where my services were not required. Carol flashed me a smile as she left the room and I winked at her.

'You haven't forgotten lunch with the Myatts?'

'No, Mother.'

'Sorry! I'll meet you by the Tower at twelve-fifteen. It's half past twelve for one o'clock.'

'I'll be there.'

The morning was again bright and clear but the wind had dropped, making it feel marginally warmer. The snow was melting and patches of grass now showed through its thawing blanket. I had read the brochures last night – a point I had forgotten to tick off – so now took the time to

70

walk around and take in the sights with better orientation. I left the building via the great oak door through which visitors would pass to commence their guided tours, and paused beneath a giant Lebanon Cedar which stood proud and magnificent against the blue sky and dappled earth. Crocuses were pushing their way up in scattered clumps around its trunk, their yellow and purple heads like multicoloured exclamation marks.

I breathed deeply and clapped my gloved hands together simply because I felt like it. To my left was the main drive by which visitors would approach, and beyond that, a play area for children. The roof of its wooden fort, protected by trees, had not yet lost its covering of snow and looked for all the world like an illustration from a fairy tale. Hansel and Gretel, perhaps, with the snow as the icing on the gingerbread house. To my right was the road to the chapel, with another fork snaking off towards the back road to the village. I did a double take. I hadn't expected the large white tent, which certainly hadn't been there the previous day.

I walked towards it, doubting the trustworthiness of my eyes as through its plastic window, I thought I saw a zebra. Not a live one, you understand. Had that been the case, I'd have been legging it in the opposite direction as fast as I could go. Vicious creatures, so I'm told. Unpredictable. I crossed onto the grass and peered inside. This one was definitely motionless. Looked like it hadn't moved for a very long time. I wasn't going mad. It was a zebra. Of the stuffed variety.

Gruesome, I thought, averting my eyes to take in the other scattered contents of the interior. A couple of potted palms. A large, Grecian-looking urn. An intricately carved trunk, inexplicably making me think of sandalwood. Curious.

I stood, undecided for a moment, then elected to walk along the chapel road. This placed me with the back of the Grange to my right and the chapel to my left, with small gardens laid out on either side of the path. It must be beautiful in the summer, I thought.

The chapel, to my surprise, was unlocked. I entered cautiously, peering around the door before actually stepping forward. It was noticeably colder inside, weak sunlight playing with the stained glass windows above the altar. I quietly closed the door behind me and made my way down the single, central aisle. Plain dark wooden benches sat solidly on either side, looking as if between them, they'd be hard pushed to accommodate more than fifty backsides. It was totally silent. No, that's not right. Silence implies an absence and there was presence here. I had a sense that somehow, the very stones were breathing. Evenly and anciently drawing breath to a primordial rhythm different to that of the world outside.

To my left, before the altar, was a tomb, set back against the wall. On top of it lay the effigy of a man, his hands in an attitude of prayer. He was dressed as a knight, though without a helmet, and a sword was hanging along his left leg. On his right was a long dagger and his feet were clad in what I supposed to be a representation of metal shoes, broad at the toes and with small spurs at the heel. Absently, I ran my hand along the ancient stone

'Who were you?' I wondered, making myself jump as I realised I'd spoken aloud.

'Sir John Howard,' came the reply. I nearly fell over with shock. 'Sorry to startle you.'

I took a deep breath to steady myself and turned to see a dark-haired, good-looking man of about my own age approaching, dressed in outdoor working clothes, a rough jacket and trousers with string tied around the bottom of the legs. I looked at his boots, even bigger and dumpier than my own, and shook my head.

'I can't believe I didn't hear you come in.'

'No, I've never understood that myself – it's as if footsteps disappear into the stone. I'm Edward Fairfield, by the way. Head Gardener.'

'Good name for a gardener!'

'I can't deny it. You must be Maggie's friend.'

'Mike Brodie.'

We shook hands, mine disappearing inside his, which seemed the size of a ham. His grip, though firm, fell short of crushing, which was a relief. I need my fingers.

'Yes,' he said, indicating the recumbent knight. 'Sir John Howard. Died in the Year of Our Lord 1500 and owned the original Grange which was built on the site of an earlier building. Only bits of that left now, of course. There's a nice inscription – see?'

I squinted at the carved words, struggling to make sense of the ornate lettering. 'Pray that my sowle at rest may be...?' I hazarded.

'...I can no longer pray, pray thee.' Edward completed it for me, obviously knowing it by heart, and we stood in silence for a moment.

'So – just having a look round then, were you?'

'Yes. Ambling till lunchtime.'

'Seen the gardens yet?'

'Not properly, no.'

'Would you like to?'

'I'd love to.'

We left the chapel, the unexpected brightness outside making me realise just how dim the interior had been. No wonder I couldn't read the inscription.

'Have you worked here long?' I asked as he led me to the Italian Garden – another reminder of Raffi. He was wearing a cap now, having retrieved it from a pocket where I assumed it must have been stuffed before he entered the chapel. Another one with a hat, I thought. Wouldn't have stayed on my head for two minutes.

'Since just before Sir Ranulph died.' He pointed to a figure working a little way ahead of us. 'Jim there, though, worked here all through Sir Ranulph's ownership. He just does a bit part-time, now. Knocking on, you know.'

Jim looked positively ancient, with skin beaten to leather by long exposure to the seasons. There was nothing wrong with his hearing, though.

'Oh aye,' he said, straightening up. 'I came here when Sir Ranulph took over. Kept these gardens ever since, though this young whippersnapper reckons he knows more about 'em than I do.' Both he and Edward smiled, but I was aware of an undercurrent of genuine resentment not too far beneath the surface. 'The gardens has changed a lot since them Myatts took over,' he continued. 'For the better, I has to say. Shame about him, though. Sir Ranulph. A recluse, that's what he was, and no relatives, see? Let this place go to rack and ruin, he did.'

'So you were pleased when the Myatts bought the place, then?'

'Aye.' Did I imagine it, or had there been a slight hesitation? 'I was. They'm done wonders, of course. Spent a fortune, fixing everything up. I'm glad people will get to see the Grange now.'

'But?' I prompted. He shot me a sidelong glance and chuckled, saying to Edward, 'She don't miss a trick, do she?' Edward said nothing, and the old man looked back at me.

'Well, call me old-fashioned, if you like. Which you can, because I am old. As old as my tongue and a bit older than my teeth. Not that I've any left, nowadays. Anyway, what I don't hold with is conferences and saunas and all that fancy stuff and suchlike. Things has to be run as businesses these days, I'm aware of that. Money's one thing as don't grow on trees. But commercialisation ... well, it's not the same. Not so homely.' He turned away abruptly and went back to his work.

'Thank you,' I said. He nodded and Edward and I walked on. 'Must have been difficult for him – you taking over his gardens, sort of thing.'

'Oh, it wasn't too bad. He's no fool, and like he said, it's a completely different ballgame now. Takes far more than one man to look after this lot. There was a hell of a lot of work to be done, just to clear it after Sir Ranulph died. The Myatts, though, gave me pretty much a free hand on the redesign. Wanted to take it back to how it was in earlier periods, make the best of it.'

'It must be very satisfying for you.'

'It is. I'll see you later, I hope. You won't have time to look at the gardens now.'

'I won't?'

'If I remember right, you have a luncheon appointment with the Myatts?'

'What is it round here?' I laughed. 'Telepathy? Everyone seems to know what I'm doing.'

'Sheer nosiness on our part. Do you have friends in the village?'

'What?' The question threw me. 'No. I just came to see Maggie, have a break.'

'Well, enjoy your lunch.'

'Thanks.' I realised I would have to hurry to meet her. I flew off as fast as I could.

'Time flies when you're having fun...'

The slow drawl startled me and I turned to see Jake leaning in an alcove on the side of the house. I couldn't think of anything to say to that.

'It's OK.' He stepped forward, smiling. 'I was looking for you, is all, and heard you were on Nature Watch.'

'Oh. Is anything wrong?'

'No. Just wanted to let you know that your car will be ready tomorrow afternoon.'

'That's quick.'

'Not as bad as it looked and the guy at the garage is a friend of mine. Hope you haven't been too inconvenienced.'

'Not at all. Besides, the walking is doing me good.'

He fell into an easy step beside me as I increased my pace, glancing at my watch.

'You doing a White Rabbit?'

'I will be, if I don't get a move on.' I spotted Maggie at the foot of the Tower, still some distance away. She waved, and we raised our hands in reply.

'Thanks about the car. That's handy, actually. I have a voice-job in Birmingham on Thursday morning.'

'Now that was the other thing.'

'Sorry?'

'The other thing I wanted to see you about. Thursday. Are you free in the evening? There's someplace I'd like to take you. You'll need the saxophone.'

'Oh. Right. Yes. Thank you.' I felt incredibly stupid. The man had reduced me to monosyllables. He smiled and I cursed inwardly as I felt myself blushing.

'So you'll be in Birmingham on Thursday?'

'Yes. I should be back by mid-afternoon.' I'd arranged to stop off and meet Raffi for lunch on the return journey.

'Well, if you'd care to come on down to the conference centre – with the saxophone – I'll show you around before we head on out.'

'Great. Thanks. I will.' Still bloody monosyllables.

'I think you're late, Rabbit. Maggie's looking agitated.' He nodded towards the Tower.

I ran the rest of the way.

Chapter Seven

Galloping down the corridor to the private apartments, I was panicking about whether I should have changed for lunch. Maggie had divested me of coat, scarf and gloves and left them somewhere along the way. I was wearing teal green woollen trousers, cream shirt and a Liberty fabric waistcoat bearing an abstract Celtic design in soft shades of brown, green and blue.

'You look fine – you're not meeting God!'

'My hair's a mess, though, right? It's always a mess!'

'Will you stop worrying!'

I pushed my hair back, fighting a losing battle with what felt like an explosion in a mattress factory.

'Here we are.' Maggie had come to a halt in front of an imposing pair of gilded double-doors. She knocked briskly.

'Welcome!' The doors were flung open by an enormous man with a mane of blonde hair, blue eyes and a perfect set of teeth.

'You must be Mike! I'm Warren and this is my wife, Elynore.'

Good Lord, I thought, faintly, *another American*. Not what I was expecting at all. Maggie was watching me, the 'Innocent' expression back on her face. She's loving this, I thought. I smiled sweetly and decided to get my revenge later.

Elynore Myatt had come forward, unfolding herself in one easy, liquid movement from a cross-legged position on an enormous green sofa in the middle of the room.

'So nice to meet you! We've heard such a lot about you from Maggie.' She was tiny, though wiry rather than delicate, with dark brown eyes and hair to match. Although not big myself, I felt like a galumphing blob in comparison. Unlike her husband, she was English, and the clothes she was wearing would easily have cost a couple of months of Edward's salary.

'Sherry? Such a quaint English tradition, I always think.' Warren was poised, ready to pour.

Maggie and I accepted. Elynore said nothing and was furnished with a glass of mineral water. 'Teetotal,' she explained, raising her glass. 'Comes of having had an alcoholic father.' There's not a lot you can say to that.

'What part of the States are you from?' I asked Warren. I was having trouble placing his accent. Both Myatts laughed.

'Oh no – you're not getting away that easily! Maggie tells us you have an uncanny ear. You tell me.' His voice may have laughed but his eyes held a challenge and something else, something I couldn't read. I hate being put on the spot. I looked at him evenly, wondering just how good he thought I was. I smiled and tilted my head.

'Mmm. I'm not that good, you know. Just know the main ones needed for commercial work. But I'd guess ... New England. Not Boston, but I couldn't pin it finer than that.' It was half the truth, anyway. He may have lived there, may have cultivated the accent, but unless my ears were deceiving me, it certainly wasn't where he'd been born. I kept my face bland as I searched my memory for where I'd heard that undercurrent before. No luck. It would come to me later, no doubt.

'Madam, you are a witch! Portsmouth, as a matter of fact.'

'All your life?'

His eyes narrowed. 'Generations.' He smiled when he lied. I do, too, but I know my reasons. I didn't know his. He turned and looked at his wife.

'She's perfect, Elynore, don't you think?'

'Absolutely, darling. I'm going to enjoy this lunch.' It sounded horribly like I was on the menu.

'We saw the documentary you did.'

'Which one?' I asked. Maggie certainly had been talking.

'About two weeks ago?' Warren looked at Elynore, who nodded in reply. 'About the mummification cult in Utah.'

'Interesting. And expensive.' Elynore added.

'But I cannot believe it's you in the luxury car commercial!' Warren accused.

That was my latest and was getting a lot of air time. I smiled, dropped into slinky, sexy motor car mode and whispered the ad, word for word. Elynore shrieked and Maggie bowed.

'I told you she was good...'

What is this? I thought, beginning to feel like a performing seal.

'So where are you from, Mike? I'm hopeless with accents.' Warren turned the tables on me rather neatly.

I kept the smile in place. 'I was born in Derby-shire but that's not what you're hearing. Probably down to having been an Army brat and moving around a lot. You learn to speak like everyone else in order to fit in.'

'Survival tactics, you mean?'

You don't know the half of it, I thought, but nodded easily.

'Shall we go through?' Warren linked his arm through mine, towering more than a foot above me, while Elynore and Maggie followed on behind. I couldn't have a relationship with a man that tall, I thought suddenly. His size was intimidating. Just too damned big.

'I hope you're ready for this, Mike, and by the way, we do know you're vegetarian.'

'Oh I'm ready! Worked up quite an appetite this morning, one way and another. Must be the fresh air.'

'But that's not all, is it?' Warren gave me what I presumed was meant to be a playful dig, nearly knocking me sideways. 'Did you really say "shit" in the autograph room?'

I rolled my eyes at Maggie, whose face was suffused with laughter.

'You can't get away with anything here, I'm afraid,' Elynore informed me as I slid into my seat. 'And by the way, did Maggie warn you? We're going to ply you with drink and make you a little business proposition...'

'Christ, Mike – you're pissed!'

'No I'm not. Just ... pleasantly plonkered.' I

stared at my accuser intently for a moment. 'Paul. What are you doing here? Again?'

'Da-da!' He whipped his right arm from behind his back, producing a bouquet of flowers. I looked at them, looked at him, and hiccuped.

'You ARE pissed!' he repeated.

'No I'm not. Have you ever seen me in a state of inebriation?'

'Not until now. But...'

'Well, there you are then. I just had a glass or three of lunch at wine time, that's all.' I seemed to have a hazy recollection of sherries and liqueurs, too, but couldn't add them up. 'I'll be fine.' I told him. 'Just need a little walk to clear my head.'

I set off at the best clip I could muster. Paul hesitated, then caught up with me, still clutching the bouquet.

'Where are we going?'

I stopped, trying to get my bearings, then cut across a lawn, neatly tripping over a 'Keep Off The Grass' sign.

'Mike...!' I was yanked back on to the path, where he pointed out the sign to me. After he'd put it back.

'Oh.' I said.

'You'll get us into trouble!'

'That's good, coming from you!' I giggled and looked at him again. 'You haven't got the squits!'

'What?'

'The squits. Diarrhoea.'

He looked suitably mystified. 'Why should I have diarrhoea?'

'Verbal diarrhoea. You've always got it.' I sat

down heavily on the nearest available wooden bench. I had the stirring of a memory of Maggie's mobile ringing when we were eating dessert. That had rum in it, I remembered. I concentrated, trying to think what she'd said.

'Mike – Paul is apparently at the conference centre, looking for you. Can you see him later? Jake will send him over here.' I assumed I must have said yes. I poked him in the ribs. Being bigger than me, he didn't fall over sideways.

'So what's the craic, Batman? Need my red-hot saxophone?'

I was developing a headache. I knew this because of the dull throb forming right in the middle of my forehead. I had the sudden, horrible knowing that if he DID need my red-hot saxophone, he'd have to wait. I *was* pissed. Two glasses of wine or three halves of beer is my limit, so it didn't take Einstein to work out the formula. I thought of Shanna, an alto player I used to gig with. At twenty years old, she could drink any man I knew under the table. At one dreadful, never-to-be-forgotten gig in Wales – The Gig From Hell, as far as our drummer was concerned – she'd drunk enough to sink a battleship and we were worried she wouldn't be fit to play. 'I'm in control,' she'd assured us. 'Just point me at the microphone and I'll play.' So we'd pointed her at the microphone, she'd played a stonking solo and promptly keeled over sideways into the trumpet player. Odd that, I thought. She never drank as much afterwards.

'Mike...' Paul rudely interrupted my reminiscences by pulling me to my feet. 'I think you need some coffee. Where's your cottage from here?'

I had to think about that, but we got there eventually. I never knew Paul could make coffee. It tasted like shit, being at least four times as strong as I make it myself.

'What are you doing?' I asked. He was poking about in cupboards and waving his arms.

'Looking for a vase. They need water.' This time, he waved the flowers.

'Oh.' I hadn't noticed a vase. Then again, I hadn't been looking for one.

'I know!' Inspiration hit me. I lurched to my feet and bumped my way into the bedroom where I picked up the carrier bags from my previous day's shopping expedition and shook them. One rattled. That was it, I thought with satisfaction.

'I think I bought one yesterday.'

Paul took the bag from me, looking dubious, and thrust more disgusting coffee at me.

'Some of this stuff is broken.'

'I know. I just haven't looked at it yet. How about the vase?'

He rummaged further. 'It's fine. What shall I do with the stuff that isn't?'

'Bin it.' He did so, and a couple of minutes later the flowers were passably arranged and standing on the kitchen table.

'You're a man of hidden talents,' I remarked as he sat down opposite me. 'So to what do I owe the honour?' He looked puzzled. 'The flowers, Paul. I've known you a long time and you've never bought me flowers. Got me into plenty of scrapes. Nearly got me killed on a couple of occasions. So why flowers? Why now?'

He scratched his left eyebrow carefully. I'd

never seen him do that before, either. Then again, he'd never seen me drunk before. Maybe it just itched.

'Mike, you misjudge me. Even I have the good grace to admit that Sunday was a little OTT, even by our usual standards. The flowers, therefore, are just a way of saying thank you. You did a sterling job. The boys were delighted and I was – ah – proud of you.'

'Thank you. That's it?'

'Well...' His right hand fluttered negligently. 'They – the boys, that is – would like you to do a couple of gigs with them if you're free. I'm not sure you're sober enough to check your diary, however.'

'I'm not drunk!'

'Of course not, darling. Just a little bit puddled. So why don't you drink some more coffee and tell me all about it? And where is your diary?'

'In my saxophone case.' I gestured vaguely towards the living room, where the sax stood on its stand, strap hanging from its neck.

'That's the sax. Where's the case, Mike?'

'Oh. The case. In the bedroom. Wardrobe, I think.'

The latest cup of coffee was just too much. I poured it down the sink while he was out of the room and drank a glass of water instead.

'Now then...' He came back, glanced at me, poured a jug full of water and set it on the table. Doesn't miss a trick, I thought.

'I've got a headache.' I announced.

'I know you have, darling. You drank too much at lunchtime.'

'You never drink, do you?' I'd never once seen him with alcohol. Something stirred at the back of my mind. 'Is it because you had an alcofrolic father?'

He nearly choked on a mouthful of his own coffee. Must have a cast iron stomach, I decided irrationally.

'No. I don't have an alcoholic father. I'm allergic to it.'

'Allergic to alcohol?'

'Yes.'

'But you can't be allergic to alcohol!'

'You can be allergic to anything. Now, why don't you tell me about lunch and drink some more water?'

He topped up my glass and I dutifully downed it. I thought about things for a minute.

'Well, you see, it was with the Myatts. They own the place. He's huge and American and Maggie didn't warn me and I'm going to get her for that. And she's English and very posh – all "terribly, terribly" – and she's teetotal and – ah – SHE has an alcoholic father! Or did. I think he's dead. Probably from drinking too much, you see, though I suppose he could have just died anyway. Or not.' It was coming back to me now. After a fashion. I drank more water and concentrated. 'They made me do my voices, you know, and he lied, because he's not from New England at all, though he says he is, though I lie about my background, too, but you didn't hear me say that, did you, and anyway, he said his family were there for ever, see? Generations, and all that. Generations, my arse! He's from...' I frowned, trying to hear again the vowels and diphthongs he'd worked so hard to eradicate. I would get it eventually.

Paul had a sort of polite expression on his face which was partially obscured because he had his fingertips steepled together just above his nose, elbows on the table. *That's bad manners, that is*, I thought.

'Anyway,' I continued, 'I don't know why he lied, but he did, and that's his business, but then, you see, they said they were going to ply me with drink and give me this business thingy ... whatsit ... proposition. And they did, because they want me to do these promotional videos, one for the home market and one for abroad, primarily the States and Japan and – oh, wherever, I suppose. They want to pull the tourists in, you see. Cut glass job. Terribly, terribly. Posh, you see.'

'And Lady Posh doesn't want to do this herself? Didn't you say she was "terribly terribly"?'

'Yes. But no. And she's Mrs Posh, not Lady Posh. Mrs Myatt, actually, and she said she wouldn't be comfortable. Anyway, she snorts, you know, and that's not good on a promotional video.'

'Cocaine?'

'What?'

'She snorts cocaine?'

I put the glass down and stared at him pityingly. 'No, you pillock. She SNORTS snorts.' I demonstrated and wished I hadn't.

'Mike – where's the lavatory?'

'First on the left, through the living room. Do you need to pee?'

'No Mike. You're going to be sick...'

I was very sick and Paul never turned a hair,

which is more than can be said for me. I cried and wailed and panicked and made a complete idiot of myself. Never in my life had I been sick through drink. Until now. I kept trying to apologise, which only made me feel worse.

'Mike, it's not the end of the world. I deal with vomit a lot. Some of my hard rock/heavy metal bands, you just wouldn't believe. This is nothing I haven't dealt with before and I shall doubtless be dealing with it again. Comes with the job. Talking of which...' He slapped the diary in front of me, along with a list of dates. 'Let's have a look, shall we?'

I was pencilling in gig number five when I stopped. 'Paul — I thought you said it was a couple of dates?'

'That's right. Nine.'

'Paul!'

'Ten's a few and more than that is several, OK?'

'You're taking advantage of me!'

'No I'm not. You'll love it. The next one's at Ronnie Scott's, God rest him.'

'All right, you bastard. Now I know why you brought the flowers.'

He cleared his throat. 'Erm ... actually, no you don't. Yet.'

'What? You mean there's more?' I was stone sober now. Fragile, but sober.

'Well ... it's just a teensy-weensy favour. You'll love it, Mike; right up your street. You remember the Floor Manager on Sunday?'

I nodded. Slowly. I was worried my head might fall off otherwise.

'Well, we got talking you see, and he told me

about this place – not too far from here – so it's not as if it's out of the way, you see – and it's a sort of audio-visual training centre, for established people as well as trainees, so the ones who work in the studios learn Outside Broadcasting, and the ones who are normally on radio learn video and vice versa and well, the long and the short of it is, they need bands, you see, especially ones with brass, because brass is difficult to engineer because of dripping or dribbling or some such – I can't remember – but the thing is, they have this slot on Friday and...'

'Friday? This Friday?' I moved too quickly and squealed.

'I know it's short notice, Mike, but I thought if 7th Avenue South or the Howlin' Blue Horns could do it, it would be a feather in everyone's cap, a really worthwhile experience, free DVDs and so on...'

'Do you know how many band members there are in the Howlin' Blue Horns?'

'Nine. Almost all self-employed. Including you. You can do it, Mike. I know you can. Where's the telephone?'

'Just like that?!'

'Just like that. No problem at all. And this will be daylight hours, so you'll get to keep your evening free. Speaking of which – no time like the present! Strike while the iron is hot, and all that. Come on, Mike – pretty please...?'

Not ruthless enough. That's my problem.

Chapter Eight

I didn't see the body to begin with. I was simply looking at the huge ornamental pool, admiring the clean lines of the fountain and imagining how, in the summer, droplets of water would soar and fall like a shower of diamonds in the morning sunlight.

Only as I dropped my gaze to the water's surface did my mind register something not quite right. Only as my eyes focused on the uninterpreted strangeness was the shape able to register in my consciousness.

A human hand.

Disbelieving, I allowed my eyes to follow it, making out an arm, a shoulder, a head. An incoherent cry rent the silence, confirming that what I was seeing was, in fact, a body. I saw a woman, closer to the pool than I, break into a run. She reached the edge of the pool before I did, had the body half out of the water before my stricken legs had covered half the distance. By the time I reached her, she was giving mouth to mouth. My mind revolted. It was surely too late. The woman shot me a look of mute desperation. It was Alison, the vicar.

'Phone – in the vicarage. Door's unlocked.'

I stood stupidly for a moment, averting my eyes, not wanting to see the body. Alison raised her head abruptly and pointed.

'That way – go!'

I ran like a mad thing, praying that the vicarage wasn't too far away. I felt as though my lungs would burst as I crashed through the back door and spent what seemed like an eternity in a frantic search for the phone. Why had I come out without the mobile? Because on a pre-breakfast walk, you're not expecting anyone to call, let alone to need the bloody thing for something like this, I told myself savagely.

I found a phone in the study and dialled 999, trying to clear my head sufficiently to make sense to the Emergency Operator. Describing where the incident had occurred was the biggest difficulty for me, but thinking of it in terms of being some distance behind the vicarage helped. At any rate, they were on their way. I put the phone down, trying hard to stay calm. *Oh God*, I thought. *I don't want to do this*, but knew I couldn't leave Alison on her own. I ran back to the pool as fast as I could.

Even from a distance I could see she was still giving mouth to mouth, now with chest compressions, and I could hear her shouting, wincing as I heard her pleas to the man to 'Breathe, dammit, breathe!' For one awful moment, I thought I was going to faint, as long-buried memories threatened to overwhelm me. As I got closer, I could hear her sobbing.

'Arthur, you old fool! Why couldn't you just leave it alone!'

I approached her from behind, touched her shoulder, still unwilling to look at the dead man, forcing myself to say, 'I know how to do this. Let

91

me take over.' Furiously, she pushed me away and carried on. I felt useless. There was a crashing in the undergrowth to my right and a uniformed police officer appeared, taking in the situation at a glance and running towards us. He spoke briefly into his radio – giving our precise location, I think – then literally pulled Alison away, taking over the resuscitation without a break in rhythm. She rolled over onto the grass, exhausted, and I sat down beside her, cradling her head in my arms. I heard a siren approaching and soon a second man appeared, this time in civvies. He swore profusely as Alison pulled herself into a sitting position and hung her head between her knees.

'Can you get her home?' I realised he was talking to me. 'Ambulance is on its way. No good just sitting here. I'll wait with Tom. Spell him, if necessary.' He used his thumb to indicate the labouring policeman. I nodded and helped Alison to her feet. She took a long deep breath, letting it out slowly.

'I'm all right.' We hugged each other silently and made our way back to the vicarage.

She went up to the bathroom whilst I made tea in her kitchen. I leaned against the sink, hanging my head in shame. Fat bloody help I'd been. I heard footsteps on the stairs followed by the sound of a door closing. 'Alison?' There was no reply. I went through to the hall and called again. The house was silent apart from the sonorous ticking of the long-case clock beside which I was standing. I opened the front door and looked outside. There was a path leading to the church. I'd suspected as much and sighed heavily as I went to find her.

She was sitting at the front of the church, eyes fixed straight ahead, face expressionless. I hesitated before sliding into the pew beside her. I felt awkward and out of place. This was her patch. She probably wanted to be left alone and I could understand that, wanted to respect it, but knew the police would be coming before too long. She didn't turn her head when she spoke.

'I hate it. Death.'

'Doesn't it come with the job?' I asked. 'As well as being part of the human condition?'

'Yes. And I still hate it.'

We sat in silence until she spoke again, this time turning to look at me. 'You're not a Christian, are you? Maggie said ... she wasn't gossiping, you understand. I was just telling her I'd met you yesterday. You know how it is.'

'Yes, I know. And no, I'm not.'

'So. You think death should be easier for me because I am?'

'No.'

'Why not?'

I shuffled uncomfortably. Why did I so often get embroiled in theological discussions? Still, at least this one was understandable. There's nothing like finding a dead or dying person to focus your mind on questions like these.

'Believing something is one thing. In your head, mainly, though I know faith is supposed to be deeper than that. Being human, however ... well, that's sometimes another thing.' I thought for a moment. 'Descartes was a fool. If he'd said, "I feel, therefore I am" or "I am related, therefore I am", he might have been nearer the mark. You're human, like anyone else. Why shouldn't you hate death? That's what comes of dualistic thinking, sticking everything in an either/or box. We're so out of touch now with natural cycles. It's not life and death. It's a life/death/life cycle. At least, that's what I believe. And even if you believe in an afterlife, it doesn't stop the pain, the sense of loss for people left behind.'

She looked at me as if seeing me for the first time. 'A musician who knows Descartes?'

'Musicians look for answers, too.'

She smiled wryly. 'Of course they do.'

'We ought to get back,' I said gently.

'Yes. The police.' She stood up and threw her head back. 'God, I could murder a cup of tea.'

I told her I had one waiting.

Steve and Maggie waited until Katie had gone to bed before asking me about the morning's events. I'd phoned Maggie from the vicarage after the police had gone, leaving a message on her machine to say that I was taking the bus to Oxford but would meet her as arranged to go to tea with Steve and Katie. The news about the body had reached her long before then, of course.

'I can't believe you didn't tell me, Mike! Why didn't you come straight back to the Grange?'

The question had irritated me. *I don't always need tea and sympathy*, I thought. Sometimes, I just like to be by myself, and that was how I'd felt after leaving Alison. I was shaken by the memories evoked by the morning's occurrence. Years had passed since Duncan's death, since my own abort-

94

ive attempts at resuscitation, yet it had jumped up and hit me in the face as if I were reliving the experience all over again. I also didn't want to go over and over things, answering the same questions from different people. The police had been quite enough for one morning and although I knew Maggie would want to know, I'd decided it would be on my terms, when I was ready.

My irritation had soon evaporated on meeting Steve and Katie. He was a solid looking man, strong and stocky, though considerably taller than Edward, who was of similar build. He had green eyes and brown hair, the merest hint of grey showing at the temples and flecking his beard.

'Come on in, Mike! It's lovely to meet you at last! This is my daughter, Katie. Katie, this is Maggie's friend, Mike.'

'Hello,' she beamed up at me. 'You're Mike, but not a man, and you play the saxophone. I've got a picture of a saxophone in my bedroom. Would you like to see?'

'Yes please!' She led the way, an unselfconscious child, with her father's colouring but slight build. She was dressed in shirt and dungarees in a startling combination of primary colours. Her bedroom was a jumble of games and books, topped off with a menagerie of soft toys, all of whom I had to be introduced to by name.

'My goodness, you'll never be lonely with all these friends!'

'Maggie bought me these,' she said, indicating Lucy the Lemur and Henry the Horse, 'I love Maggie. She's going to be my Mummy.'

'You're very lucky to have found each other,' I

told her. When Maggie had said it was serious, I hadn't realised she'd meant quite this serious. Perhaps it was wishful thinking on Katie's part. I thought about Maggie's face, the way she'd talked about Steve and his daughter. I shook my head. No, I didn't think it was wishful thinking at all.

Katie's picture of a saxophone was part of a poster showing a variety of musical instruments.

'Is yours like that?' she asked, pointing.

'I have one at home exactly the same. It's an alto sax. The one I've brought with me is bigger and is called a tenor saxophone.'

'Does it have a name? Daddy says instruments often have names, just like my toys.'

'Er ... Dexter.' I made it up on the spot.

'Why is it called Dexter?'

'Because there was a famous saxophone player called Dexter Gordon. He was very, very tall and wore a special kind of hat and I have a tie with a picture of him on it.'

'Can I see?'

'Perhaps another day. I'll bring it and show you.'

'Will you bring Dexter, too? I play the piano and we could play something together. That's called a duet.'

'So it is!' I laughed. 'I think that's a very good idea. I'll see what we can arrange.'

After Katie was settled, Maggie and Steve curled up together on the sofa with a glass of wine. Following yesterday's performance, it should have been my turn to be on mineral water, but Steve didn't have any so I settled for fruit juice instead. I hadn't seen Maggie since lunch with the hosts from hell, and wondered if she'd comment. She did.

'You usually like a glass of wine, Mike.'

'Yes, well, after the Myatts... I'm sorry. I know I drank far too much.'

'Sorry? For what? You were brilliant, had them completely entranced. I must admit, I did wonder if you'd fall over or start burbling or something because you've always said you have a low tolerance for alcohol and I've never seen you drink that much. You're a real dark horse, Mike. You were as right as rain.'

'I was? I didn't make a fool of myself?'

'Don't tell me you can't remember? You were fine when you left to go and meet Paul. What did he want, by the way?'

I gave her a highly edited version of his visit, relieved by her assurances. I decided I must have come over peculiar – in other words, got really pissed – when I went outside into the cold air. I censored the end of the story by saying that I had, in fact, had rather a headache.

'You're full of surprises!' she laughed, then shook her head, suddenly serious, 'Not the sort of surprise you wanted, though, finding Arthur this morning.'

'You can say that again. It wasn't just me, though – more Alison, in fact.' I told them what had happened. 'Alison was apparently saying her morning prayers. Does a walking meditation, or something. As for me – one of the leaflets you gave me had details of walks around the village, and I decided to take one.'

The wrong one, I thought. Well, it was almost the

whole truth, What had really happened was that I'd woken early, while it was still dark. The reason for that was that I'd fallen asleep after Paul had left, doubtless due to the excess alcohol and having been sick, and had slept like a log. Paul had been delirious with triumph after bagging the Howlin' Blue Horns for Friday. Well, almost all of them. Our guitarist was away felling trees in Staffordshire – or was it planting them? Anyway, his opposite number in Rude Rhythm was going to stand in for him. So. I'd woken up early, pottered about for a bit and gone out when it was light.

'What happened after you and Alison got back to the vicarage?' Steve prompted.

'The police came,' I shrugged. 'They have to, in cases of sudden death.' There hadn't been much we could tell them, of course. Neither of us had seen the victim fall into the pool, so had no idea how long he'd been there. Too long to have been revived, that's for sure, but I couldn't blame Alison for trying. She'd been working on gut instinct, especially as the dead man was someone she knew. Tom, the young policeman, had known him, too.

'Everyone knew him,' Alison had explained, after my admission to Tom that I hadn't been able to bring myself to look at the body. 'He was a real local character, though not a villager born and bred. He came here when he retired – he was a University Professor.' She'd frowned and looked at Tom. 'How long had he lived here?'

'I'm not rightly sure. I remember him when I was at secondary school, but not before.' They had debated his age, eventually agreeing that he must be around eighty now, or, as they corrected themselves, must have been around eighty when he died.

'When he first came, he was always pestering Sir Ranulph for access to the Grange – he had a bee in his bonnet about its history, some obscure happening that was supposed to have taken place during the Civil War – or was it the Reformation? Anyway, Sir Ranulph wouldn't allow it.'

'Always was a cantankerous old sod,' Tom had chipped in. 'Sorry, vicar.'

'Well, it was his house and he could do as he liked. When the Myatts bought the place though, it was a different story. They gave him a free hand, were very keen to have it researched, though I think they got a bit fed up with him recently. He was writing a book, you know. And it was he who helped Maggie find one of the two priests' holes that are supposed to be there.'

I must have looked puzzled, because Alison had smiled and said, 'Sir Ranulph didn't give a damn about the place. Even when he inherited it – I believe from his uncle – the Grange had gone downhill and was in quite a shoddy state. I think he felt it was a millstone round his neck. What was it Arthur told me...? Yes – some of the rooms had been locked for so long that the keys couldn't be found and no one had a clue as to the whereabouts of the priests' holes.'

'If Sir Ranulph didn't allow him access, how did Arthur know all this?'

'He talked a lot to Jim, the old gardener, got what information he could through him, before the Myatts came. Then, of course, they had the same trouble and he could see for himself.'

'So there's no one else from Sir Ranulph's time around?'

'No one who had access to the Grange. Except Jim, of course. And Edward, I suppose – he's Head Gardener now, though he came not long before Sir Ranulph died. I think there was a housekeeper, but that was very brief and donkey's years ago.'

'So where's she?'

'Oh, she wasn't local. Haven't a clue.'

I'd waited until Tom had left before asking Alison what she'd meant when she'd shouted at Arthur about 'leaving it alone'. I wondered if he'd heard her. Hearing is supposedly the last sense to go. With that in mind, I'd thought it best not to remind her that she'd called him an old fool. She had shaken her head sadly.

'He was getting exhausted, Mike. Had worked himself into a frenzy, especially over the last few weeks. On about tobacco smuggling, asking to see basements in houses in the village, the cellars in the pubs. When I saw him on Sunday afternoon, he was ecstatic, almost feverish. He said he'd finally cracked it, had just one last thing to do to verify his theory.' She had shifted in her seat, rubbing her neck wearily. 'He said it was all in the latest part of his manuscript. I told him he was overdoing it, but he wouldn't listen. He said, "You don't need much rest or sleep at my age, my dear, Time enough for that when I'm dead."'

Her eyes had filled with tears. 'He was probably roaming about out there half the night, and fell in. He did that, you know – walked during the night, all over the place. "Looking for clues", he called it.'

Maggie was in tears herself by the time I'd finished telling the tale. Steve put his arm around her and hugged her gently.

'Poor old devil. All that work and now nobody will ever know what it was he thought he'd found,'

'You'll have to come and see the priests' hole, Mike.' Maggie blew her nose noisily.

'Sure,' I agreed. 'In fact, if I'm going to do these promotional videos, I really ought to do the whole guided tour.'

'Oh, more than that. I'll speak to the Myatts. I'm sure they'll give you the run of the place. Apart from the private apartments, of course.'

'Thanks.' I wriggled out of my chair and went to fetch my coat, 'I really ought to be getting back. I need to make an early start in the morning for the voice-work in Birmingham.'

'Are you sure? I can come back with you.' Maggie started to get up.

'Oh no you don't!' I shoved her back onto Steve. They needed some time alone. I suspected they didn't get much of that, with a six-year-old around.

'Are you sure you'll be all right in the dark?' Steve asked.

'Absolutely. It's not far, and I have my trusty torch.' I produced my mini-Maglite from my coat pocket. 'Handy for when I stagger home from gigs at three in the morning. Besides, I'm a lot safer here than in Cheltenham. A country village like this is hardly a hub of criminal activity, is it?'

How wrong can you be?

Chapter Nine

It's not easy, being a chicken. Especially when you're face to face with a couple of strapping men who are not only making hen and cockerel noises, but are also standing on one leg and flapping their arms like wings.

I studiously avoided eye contact as I read the script. For the 7th time.

'When it comes to eggs, consult the eggsperts – the hens of Meadowsweet Farm...'

Squawkings and cluckings, along with what were meant to be brooding noises, punctuated my homely, farmyard tones. Three times, we'd only got this far.

'Our hens are fed only the finest ingredients with no antibiotics so...' We'd fallen here twice.

'...when it comes to the best, freshest eggs around, think free-range...' This was as far as we'd got last time.

'...think freshness, and insist on the best. Meadowsweet eggs.'

Silence. Three lots of bated breath. Three frozen bodies. The tape was still running. Then yes – oh yes – Will's voice came through my headphones saying, 'That's a wrap – it's in the can.'

The two men sagged with relief, I shrieked with long-suppressed laughter and, shaking their heads, they beat a hasty retreat. I fumbled for a tissue as Will's voice came through the cans again. 'That was great, Mike – come on up!'

Voice sessions are not usually as demented as this, though small jobs, like Will's, are often funny. Normally, please God, there are sound effect CDs to take care of things like revving engines and broody hens. Not today, however, though it was the first time I'd known them fall down in that department.

'We did our best to isolate a cock crowing. Just didn't sound right,' Will had apologised. Hence the two men doing impressions of the feathered variety. Hence the seven takes because they'd kept cracking up in splutters of laughter, which was why I'd avoided eye contact as much as possible. One of them was a musician I was on nodding terms with; the other could have been dragged in off the streets, for all I knew.

We had been in the smaller of the two studios today and I made my way upstairs to the control room or 'Flight Deck' as Will always called it. The downstairs studio where I'd just done my bit for free-range farming was soundproof and bare except for the microphones we'd been using and several sets of headphones. Up here was major high-tech with a brand new mixing desk and enough paraphernalia to make a Trekkie drool.

Mick, the sound engineer, was leaning back in his chair with his hands clasped behind his head and a beatific smile on his face.

'You look like the cat that got the cream!' I observed.

'And you're the cat that got it for me!' he grinned.

'What are you on about?' I asked, as he played

back the recording we'd just made. We listened in silence. It was good.

'That's what I'm talking about. All down to your reputation as a one-take wonder. I took a bet with the lads. They reckoned they could crack you up. I said they couldn't. You're a beaut, Mike!'

I grinned happily, though I certainly felt far from beautiful, I'd had to explain my face when I arrived. Will had said, 'I'm sorry, lady – we don't have any call for Mrs Quasimodo or Bride of Frankenstein scripts at the moment. Don't call us – we'll call you!'

Mick slapped half his winnings into my hand as Will said, 'Right! Couple of sax tracks and you can get back to your holiday!'

Not until I'd seen Raffi, though. I left the motorway and drove into Cheltenham along the Tewkesbury Road. The car was running perfectly and it was good to have it back. I'd found it parked outside Rosemary Cottage when I'd returned from Oxford the previous afternoon. The keys had been put through the letterbox along with a note which read, 'Returned as good as new. See you tomorrow. Jake.'

I wanted to call in on Alex at the shop on my way to meet Raffi. Traffic was bad on the London Road due to repair work, so I cut through side streets to avoid the queues and finally pulled in to the car park on the opposite side of the road. 'Horn Blowers' was sandwiched between a chemist's and an antiques store, and I noticed with pleasure that Alex had changed the window display. A fine family of saxophones was spread across the big window with trumpets and trombones suspended above them.

Alex was sitting behind the counter, head bent over something he was working on and didn't see me crossing the road. He looked up, smiling, as the doorbell tinkled when I entered, blue eyes crinkling and blonde hair flopping across his face. He did a double take when he saw me.

''Strewth, Mike! You look like you've gone ten rounds with Mike Tyson!'

'Don't be silly – my ear's still intact!' My eyes fastened on the dull gleam beneath his fingers.

'Thought you might like it,' he said, setting it upright. 'Couldn't believe it when it came in. Bloke's uncle died and they found it when they were clearing the house.'

'Oh yes...' I breathed, running my fingers down the body. 'Complete?' I glanced behind the counter as Alex nodded and saw the crook and mouthpiece on the bench.

'Original case, too.' He could have won a Cheshire cat competition as he said it. My body hair was standing on end. This was a Conn Lady-face, so named because the bell was engraved with the face of a woman.

'Please tell me we bought it?'

'We bought it.'

'Yes!' I did an impromptu twirl.

'Want a blow?'

'Is the Pope a Catholic?'

I took off my coat and, kneeling on the floor behind the counter, put the sax together. Alex asked what reed I wanted. I looked at the mouthpiece.

'V16. 2.' He obligingly stuck one in my mouth.

'It's not perfect yet,' he warned me. 'Still some work to do on the tuning. I did think of leaving it for you to do, then I thought it might be a nice surprise to have it ready for when you came back. Only you surprised me first.'

I fixed the reed in place and stood up. 'Well – here goes.' My fingertips were tingling as they hung over the keys. I ran through a few scales and arpeggios to get the feel of the thing.

'G sharp's a bit ropey and not all the B flats are sorted yet,' Alex apologised.

'I know. But the tone is just wonderful. What a voice!'

The sound was big and fat and voluptuous. I played 'Stardust' slowly and extravagantly, then slipped into 'Moonglow' and 'Don't Get Around Much Anymore'. My eyes were still closed when I finished.

'We can't sell this!' I told him. 'What did you pay for it?'

Alex laughed and told me. I raised my eyebrows. He hadn't swindled anyone but it would be fair to say we'd got a real bargain.

'How did you manage that?'

'Told the truth. Said it needed a lot of work. I've done a complete re-pad and recork, just for starters. And they really weren't interested. Just wanted to get rid of it.'

I put her down carefully. She was definitely a she, the first one I'd ever come across. I pulled my cheque book from an inside jacket pocket and wrote out a figure for its retail value after repair. It was Alex's turn to raise his eyebrows. 'That's more than generous, given that you own the place!'

I shrugged. 'I can think of people who'd pay three times as much for her.'

'Her?'

'Oh yes.' I ran my hands along her flanks, smiling as I thought of Katie, with a name for everything. 'She's Lady Day...'

Raffi was already waiting for me when I reached the restaurant. I'd told her about my face on the phone, so at least I didn't have to go over all that again.

'I've got an interview!' she announced, nearly squeezing the breath out of me.

'That's great!' She was due to complete her degree in Environmental Policy and Management in a few months' time and was already applying for jobs.

'I have to go to London for it,' she told me as we ordered food.

'When?'

'Well, the interview's tomorrow but I think I'll go this evening, stay overnight with Corinne.' Corinne was a friend of hers, doing a degree at Goldsmiths. 'Which reminds me–' she went on. 'Are you free tomorrow evening?'

'Tomorrow?' Friday, I realised. 'Depends on what time you're thinking of. Why?'

'Beanie's Band is playing at the Paradox Centre – thought you might like to come.'

Beanie's Band – band name 'Beanie & The Boys' – comprised several friends of Raffi's and they were very good. I pulled a face and told her

107

about the audio-visual training centre. 'I'm not sure what time we'll finish,' I explained. 'We're scheduled for the morning and part of the afternoon – we get a break for lunch – then there's another break and we do the video late afternoon into the evening.' Paul, needless to say, hadn't been entirely honest with me.

'A video? There's going to be a video?'

'Yes. Well, DVD, by the time it's done. What's the big deal?'

'I must tell Beanie and the Boys. I'll be seeing Greg and Tim this afternoon.' The corners of her mouth were twitching.

'What's so funny? You've seen me on TV before.'

'Oh ... it's just that I might get to prove a point, that's all.' Despite further coaxing, she refused to elaborate. 'I'm asking round for the Greek job, by the way. No firm takers yet, though one or two people might be interested.'

'Great.'

I told her about Lady Day over lunch, but didn't tell her about Arthur, not wishing to spoil her mood over the interview and also, for purely selfish reasons, not wanting to have to go over it all again.

'Sounds wonderful!' she enthused. 'Will you be using her at this training place tomorrow?'

'No. She needs a lot more work yet. Besides, she's special. I wouldn't use her for the Howlin' Blue Horns or Rude Rhythm. She's not their style.'

'7th Avenue South, maybe?'

'Maybe...' And then, of course, it dawned on

108

me. The band she'd be really perfect for was the Frederick Bloody Penfold Green Glittery Jacket Mob Quartet.

There's always a price to pay...

Chapter Ten

I made sure I used the correct entrance for the conference centre on my return to the Grange later that afternoon. Jake was standing in the car park talking to Elynore Myatt, who had a leash-less cocker spaniel at her heel. I switched off the engine and sat in the car. Jake waved and Elynore turned to flash a smile at me. When I still didn't get out, they came over, dog included. I could feel myself sweating. I lowered the window carefully, trying not to look at it.

'Car's perfect. Thanks.' I nodded at Jake.

'My pleasure.'

'Aren't you getting out?' Elynore asked.

'Oh, not for a minute. Sometimes it's nice just to sit.'

The dog barked and I sweated some more.

'Quiet, Oscar!' Elynore commanded. It did as it was told but quivered with excitement, looking at me. Elynore looked, too, with renewed interest. There was nothing wrong with her arithmetic.

'I say ... you're not afraid of dogs, surely?'

'No – just terrified.' I admitted. She tossed her head in a half-laugh, half-snort.

'But my dear girl – Oscar wouldn't hurt a fly!'

That's good, I thought. I'm her 'dear girl' when I've got a good ten years on her and whilst I was prepared to believe that darling Oscar wouldn't hurt a fly – no doubt because he couldn't catch one – I was willing to bet he wouldn't be averse to a nice piece of my ankle.

'I know it seems stupid, but I ... um... had a bit of a bad experience with a dog a few years ago.' I didn't add that I still had the scars to prove it.

'Well, not to worry. I must be off, anyway.' She really did pronounce it 'orf' and I had to smile. 'Terrible business about old Arthur. I don't know what I shall do about Warren's birthday, now.'

She turned on her heel and walked away. I was relieved to see Oscar follow her. Jake waited until they'd covered some distance before opening my car door.

'I think you're safe now.' I looked at him sharply but his face, like his voice, held no hint of mockery. I got out, keeping a close eye on the disappearing dog.

'Sax is in the back,' I told him, moving to get it.

'You remembered!'

'Yes.'

'Bring it inside.'

Our footsteps crunched together over the gravel path leading to the entrance of the conference centre.

'What has Arthur's death to do with Warren's birthday?' I asked.

'It's spoiled her surprise. She was planning to present him with the History of Bewick Grange. And as Arthur was writing it...' He shrugged, leading me into a small but airy office. 'You can leave the sax here. It'll be safe.'

We stepped back into the hall and he locked the door.

'Must've been tough on you and Alison, finding Arthur like that.'

'Yes.'

'You OK?'

'Yes.'

He searched my face and nodded. 'How about a coffee before I give you the tour and the spiel?'

'Why not?'

'Do I take that as a yes then?'

'Yes.'

The conference centre was an old building, restored in keeping with its original layout and features. A sweeping central staircase led up to a galleried second level. The effect was breath-taking. Jake followed my gaze with a smile.

'We have conference suites on both floors, plus a lift, ensuring access for wheelchair users.'

'Good thinking.'

'Oh, they haven't missed a trick.' He strode across the floor, throwing open a pair of elabor-ately carved wooden doors. 'This room is kinda special.'

'Wow!' It was plush with fabrics and lush with the greenery of exotic plants. I shook my head and laughed. The opulence was overpowering. 'How on earth can anyone concentrate on business in here?'

'They don't. It's the Banqueting Suite. Usually Corporate Hospitality, the emphasis being very much on hospitality. We also have Murder Mys-tery Weekends. They can be...' He weighed his

111

words carefully. '...interesting.'

'Interesting?'

'Uh-huh.'

'You're having me on, right?'

'Wrong. We've had more bodies and budding detectives in here than you'd believe.'

'But where does everyone stay?' I asked, my mind going back to conferences. 'You only have a few holiday cottages.'

'They're a separate item. Not used for conferences. Most meetings are no more than a couple of days, though, having said that, we have a few that run to five, and last year, we had a couple of arty-crafty workshops that ran for seven. Anyway, for them, and when we're playing host to Murderers and Detectives, we have something else.' He led me to the rear of the building and out into a courtyard.

'Clever, don't you think?'

'Like a hotel annexe!'

'A high-class hotel annexe,' he corrected me.

The low, grey stone single storey buildings were complete with the seemingly obligatory mullioned windows and oak doors.

'Converted stables – like to see one?'

I nodded. He produced a giant key ring and ushered me into one of the guest suites.

'My God!' I breathed. It was immaculate, but then, how could I have expected anything else? Even the ends of the toilet rolls were neatly folded.

'Talk about "no expense spared"!' I shook my head in admiration. 'This place must have cost a fortune! Where does all the money come from?'

'Elynore's money is inherited. From Daddy and Husband Number One. Warren earned all his – he's one hell of a good businessman. So money married money.'

'Warren's something to do with shipping?' I was trying to remember The Lunch from Hell again.

'A shipping line, a Container Logistics Company and fingers in several other pies.'

'Even so, they must have spent a small fortune.'

'A couple of large ones would be nearer the mark. Mind you, they've also received a lot of money in grants – regenerating the countryside and stuff.'

'And there's a Health and Fitness centre, too?'

'Right this way.'

We cut across the courtyard and down some stone steps, turning a corner which revealed the complex.

'I'm impressed.'

'Thought you might be. Come on in.'

Like the courtyard accommodation annexe, this was also a single storey building but with a lot of length.

'Don't tell me – there's an indoor heated swimming pool.'

'There sure is. We got everything here except a climbing wall.'

I followed Jake to the reception area where a smiling young woman, whose name badge told me she was called Claire, gave me a selection of leaflets. Two rather large middle-aged women, wrapped only in bath towels, trooped out of a door, giggling like schoolgirls.

'Now, now, ladies! Dress code, please! I can't have you frightening our young gentlemen!' They scuttled off, laughing.

'Mixed saunas today,' Claire informed me.

I scanned the leaflets. Apart from the gym facilities, sauna and swimming pool, a wide variety of things was on offer including aromatherapy, body wraps of various descriptions, reflexology and the usual beauty treatments.

'Anything take your fancy?' Jake asked.

'Lots of it!'

'Good. I understand you now have a free pass to the facilities. You should make use of them.'

'Bribery as well as corruption!'

'Corruption?' For a moment, I thought he thought I was serious. Embarrassed, I told him about the lunch date. And the state I'd been in afterwards. He laughed.

'So – you can let your hair down after all!'

'Being drunk is hardly my idea of a good time. It was awful!' I booked a couple of aromatherapy massages, including one for the following Monday morning.

'You're staying then? Or coming back after the weekend?'

'I haven't thought about it, to be honest. Now I'm temporarily on the payroll, so to speak, I just think I ought to get to work on learning about the place.'

'It's all work with you, isn't it?'

I shifted my weight uncomfortably. 'No. Music is my way of letting my hair down. I don't look on playing as work.'

'Mmm-hmm.' He gave me a long look that

brought heat to my face and had me cursing my hormones again. 'In that case, I'd better get you ready for letting your hair down again this evening. Let's go get the sax.'

We went back to the conference centre and collected it. I stood awkwardly in the hallway.

'Where are we going?'

'My place. Don't look so worried – I don't bite.' He took the case from me and headed behind the stairwell. 'I have an apartment on the premises.'

The sitting room was a riot of vibrant colour. Marsha Hammell musician prints scattered the walls along with Native American art. I stepped closer to look at a shield.

'That's beautiful.'

'I made it a long time ago.'

'You made it?' I examined it more closely. 'Does it have meaning? I mean, are the things you've used symbolic?'

He didn't answer immediately and I glanced back at him. 'I'm sorry. I shouldn't have asked. If it's personal...'

'You can always ask.' He looked at me and for once, I didn't blush. His eyes went back to the shield and he indicated a patch of white fur. 'Rabbit. One of the issues I was dealing with at that time was fear.'

I looked at him curiously, finding it hard to imagine him being afraid of anything. He tapped my sax case with his foot.

'So – what do you like to play?'

'Just about anything. Jazz. R&B. Old standards. Oddly enough, I was classically trained.'

'Classical sax?'

'There are over two thousand pieces written for it.'

I was glad he'd changed the subject. I was on firmer ground here. Business, not personal. He left the room and came back with a trumpet. I looked at him, astonished. Excited.

'Well, I'm not classically trained. But I hear from Maggie that you have a liking, amongst other things, for the Brecker Brothers.'

'Oh man! You're talking the god of the tenor saxophone in my book!'

'You have impeccable taste.' He watched as I put the sax together. 'OK then!' he said as I stood up. 'Let's make some music, lady!'

Chapter Eleven

The grin was still on my face as I drove to the audio-visual job the following morning. After our little run-through, Jake had taken me to the Green Man pub, as Maggie had predicted he would. Whatever subconscious illusions I may have been harbouring about the quiet country life and local yokels had been thoroughly shattered there. Thursday night was jam night and the place was packed.

'Where do they all come from?' I asked as we squeezed and shoved our way through punters packed tighter than a rugby scrum.

'From miles around.' Jake had had to shout

above the noise, which at that point owed nothing to music and everything to a babbling cacophony of conversation. The bar staff, when it was possible to glimpse them through the crush, looked as though they were sorely in need of several extra pairs of arms. We finally made our way through to a less densely packed area.

'This is where we play,' Jake announced. I knew from our earlier conversation that he was a regular here. A tall, gawky man with receding hair and heavily framed spectacles struggled to join us.

'You got her, then?'

'I sure did. Mike, this is Dave Williams. We play here as a duo every Wednesday and usually chip in on jam night.'

We shook hands. He had incredibly long fingers. 'Guitar and keyboards,' he volunteered, noticing my attention.

'Whatcha drinking, Mike?' Jake asked,

I looked around, already uncomfortably hot. 'Iced water, I think.'

'One pint coming up. Dave, why don't you take her through the back and introduce her to the boys?'

I lugged my sax case behind Dave and followed him out the back door and across a flagstoned area towards a long, low building, brightly lit and marked 'Function Room'. I had assumed that 'the boys' I was about to meet would be musicians, but I was wrong.

They were the Companions of the Crooked Staff.

'They wanted to meet you. To apologise. I understand there was a bit of a contretemps when you arrived.' Dave spoke awkwardly, confessing to a set-up.

'Well, I don't usually look like this!' I indicated my face.

'They did that?'

'They did.'

They – now far greater in number than had greeted my arrival at the Grange on Sunday – had pushed together several long tables and were seated along the sides, banqueting fashion, I noticed Steve and Maggie, trying and failing to look innocent. They rose as I approached. All of them. I felt acutely embarrassed. I don't like being singled out for special treatment, or, for that matter, being the centre of attention. Which may sound odd, coming from someone who spends a lot of time on stage, but up there, I'm part of a band, a whole, a collective. Strangely enough, it makes me feel safe, gives me a sense of security. It took me years to be comfortable playing solos. I didn't like the exposure, feeling I was up on my own, under scrutiny.

It seemed that Edward Fairfield, the Head Gardener, was to be spokesperson for the group.

'Mistress Brodie!' He bowed. They all followed suit. I put the sax case on the floor, unable to decide whether to bow back, attempt a curtsey – silly in trousers – or simply turn tail and leg it.

'These, thy humble servants, Companions of the Crooked Staff, are gathered together to crave pardon for their excessive zeal in protecting yonder Grange these five nights past.'

'Their eyesight left much to be desired through seasonal lack of carrots!' a young upstart on his

118

left chipped in. Edward silenced him with a glance.

'We trust thy carriage hath been most heartily restored and herewith present thee with replacement for thy torn apparel.'

A parcel was hastily passed down the table. I took it, wondering what presents had been wrapped in, back in the relevant time. This one was wrapped in brightly coloured paper scattered with saxophones, musical notes and ribbons. I suppressed a smile.

'Prithee check 'tis to thy liking.'

Jake's voice came in a whisper behind me. 'Maggie gave us your old one when Paul whisked you away for the TV gig. So we'd know the right size.' He moved to one side and set our drinks on the table.

The jacket was beautiful. Raw silk, the colour of evergreen. I cleared my throat. 'I give thee thanks, good Companions, for such fine replacement.' I bowed awkwardly.

They roared their approval, hammering on the tables with their fists. It was a bloodcurdling sound. Edward silenced them with an upraised hand.

'Furthermore, my lady, in honour of thy great daring in seeking to escape such a dangerous foe, we hereby create thee an Honorary Companion of the Crooked Staff, and, moreover, no mere dainty damsel but a fighting Companion...' The room erupted again. Once more, they were silenced. '...A fighting Companion, for thy good friend, Mistress Mallory, doth tell us that despite thy fair sex and littleness of stature, thou art a worthy and brave-hearted foe, being known in one of thy minstrel bands as...' He paused for effect. '...Scrappy!'

A great roar of approval and more hammering upon the tables entailed, Maggie had dissolved into laughter, her face scarlet as she pointed at me helplessly. I was presented with a scroll and managed a suitably flowery speech thanking ye gathered assembly for ye honour bestowed. My good health was toasted and I gave the scroll to Maggie for safe-keeping.

'Scrappy, eh?' I muttered. 'I'll see you later...'

'So how does it feel, Mistress Scrappy?' Jake asked as we made our way back to the bar with Dave, ready to jam. I glanced behind me.

'They're not all coming as well?!'

'Oh yes. Now you're an Honorary Companion, you'll be their Musical Champion.'

'They take it awfully seriously, don't they?'

'Indeed they do. And old Arthur was a mine of information for them. He'll be sorely missed.'

I assembled the saxophone and slung it round my neck, tapping the bell.

'I feel like a misfit, As if I'm in a time warp or something. This wasn't invented until the nineteenth century. Still, at least this one is called Dexter.' I was remembering 'Dexter' and 'Sinister' from childhood history lessons.

'Not good enough!' Jake laughed. 'You'll have to bring something more in period when you take part in anything.'

If the bar had been noisy before, it was sheer bedlam now. Microphones and PA were in place as was, unknown to me, the pub's secret weapon.

First up in the jam was a solo artist, a refugee, by the look of him, from the Sixties, who sang and played blues harmonica. He seemed, however, to have percussion accompaniment when no drummer was evident. Hippy Blues was followed by an outfit comprising singer/guitarist, bass player and a teenage boy on trumpet. They were not bad, and seemed, like their predecessor, to have a phantom drummer. Next up was a really funky fusion-style set up. They had their own drummer but there was no way he was playing everything I was hearing. Even Dennis Chambers couldn't have pulled that off without extra limbs.

As they wound up the tempo, not only did the phantom drumming become more frenetic, but the crowd of people around the bar lurched pack-like, in a wave, away from it. Stepping neatly backwards to avoid being trampled on, I heard both laughter and swearing.

'Tony's on good form tonight!'

'Yeah, but God help us by the end of the evening!'

Puzzled, I turned to find Jake struggling to my side with fresh drinks.

'Who's Tony?' I shouted above the din.

'The landlord.'

'I don't suppose he's also the Phantom Drummer?'

'Got it in one. But you ain't seen nothing yet. I suggest you use the mike furthest from the bar and keep your eyes open.'

I've played some places in my time. Pubs, clubs and all manner of hotels. Marquees of all shapes and sizes. I've played places you most certainly would not take your Granny, even if she were dead, because the punters look like Necrophiliacs Anonymous. Places where I've nearly had my head torn off because the moron who gave us the booking thought we played an entirely different kind of music or booked us in – unknown to us, lambs to the slaughter – on Death Metal night. Nothing, though, had prepared me for Tony the Phantom Drummer in full flight. The pub became hell on wheels.

Before Jake and I started playing, he'd limited his phantom drumming to hands on the bar or a couple of upturned ice buckets. By the time we were in full flow, he'd progressed to stealing drumsticks and adding bottles and glasses to his repertoire. Sometimes they broke and sometimes they didn't. When they did, showers of glass went everywhere. It soon became apparent which people were regulars and which were visitors. Regulars took it in their stride and, in any case, had the forethought to keep out of range. Visitors swung between amusement, disbelief and out-rage. I don't know what's worse – having to duck deliberately aimed missiles or trying to avoid randomly flying slivers of wood and shards of glass. At any rate, it kept us on our toes.

Later, as Jake turned into the conference centre car park, switching off the lights and the engine, the night, devoid of the street lighting I was so used to, was brilliant with stars.

'I've had a wonderful evening! Thank you!' Impulsively, I turned and kissed him on the cheek. He caught my face with his fingers, held it fast.

'You missed,' he said softly.

'I what?' My heart was hammering at his touch, his nearness, and I was glad of the dark to hide my burning cheeks, wondering if he could feel the heat that betrayed me.

'It was supposed to go here.'

Slowly, his lips covered my own. I froze for an instant, then melted as passion lit up, rocking my control, shocking me with its intensity. Warmth exploded across my belly, making me ache with wanting. We broke apart and he stroked my neck. It was all I could do to stop myself from groaning.

'How would you like it...' he asked slowly, 'if we went inside, sat by the fire, shared a bottle of wine and swapped life stories?'

Oh shit! I thought. *I'm not ready for this.*

'I ... um ... I'd like that very much but ... ah ... maybe some other time?'

I could feel him looking at me but didn't want to meet his eye.

'I just might hold you to that.'

He smiled slowly and let me go. My breathing was back under control now.

'The audio visual thing tomorrow, you know. I need an early night.' God, couldn't I come up with something less stupid than that?

'I think you already missed it. It's way past turning-into-a-pumpkin time.'

I opened the door and got out of the car, Jake turning on his headlights to illuminate my own vehicle, opposite.

'Thanks again,' I babbled.

'Mike?'

'Yes?'

'The saxophone would help. For the audio visual.'

'Oh. Right. Yes. Sorry. Thanks.' I wanted the ground to open up and swallow me.

'Trunk's unlocked.'

I removed the sax case and took it over to my own vehicle. He kept his lights on until I got inside and had the engine running. He switched them off, got out and stood watching as I drove away.

The dull ache in my belly was still there, accompanied by a long unaccustomed dampness between my thighs.

Mistress Scrappy of the Crooked Staff, nothing, I reproached myself.

I was just such a bloody coward...

Chapter Twelve

'Not another Honkin' Blue Horn!' The security guard, an older man with iron grey hair and crinkly blue eyes, smiled as I filled out my details on arrival at the gatehouse to the studio complex. '*How* many of you are there?'

'Nine,' I grinned, knowing full well that he knew as well as I did.

'And I could have sworn I'd been booked in at least fifteen of you this morning!' He watched as I stuck one of two necessary passes onto my jacket.

'That's it – and leave the other one clearly

visible in your vehicle.' He gave me instructions on how to get to the studio and where to park.

Paul had supplied the powers that be with a list of personnel, using our full names, and I was pleasantly surprised not to have had a grilling about mine for a change.

'Nice name, that,' the guard nodded as I left. 'Wasn't that King David's wife, in the Bible?'

I had come from virtually one end of Oxfordshire to the far end of Worcestershire, the studio complex lying in the Vale of Evesham and not too far from my home in Cheltenham. I'd brought Raffi near here for picnics in the spring and summer months when she was little, following the Blossom Trail.

Parking the car, I waved to Richard and Chris, who were sitting on a low stone wall, rolling cigarettes. They played, respectively, trombone and trumpet.

'Hiya, Scrappy!' they chorused. There was no sign of their instrument cases.

'What's this?' I laughed, gesturing at empty space. 'Only doing backing vocals today?'

'Inside.' Richard cocked a thumb. 'First left, then right until you get to the end of the corridor.'

'Just follow the noise,' Chris pulled a face. I nodded and went inside.

I could hear Paul a mile off, garrulous as ever. I closed my eyes for a second, wondering how I was going to face him after my little drunk and disorderly the other day. I needn't have worried.

'Mike! Darling!' He emerged from the control room and grabbed me as I tried to slink past. He also grabbed my sax case, thrusting it at John, our singer, who was standing in the doorway of the studio.

'Take this in for her, will you?'

John rolled his eyes at me, tugging an imaginary forelock behind Paul's back.

'No good going in there at the moment,' Paul confided. 'Utter chaos, but I expect you're used to that.'

I heard a steady thump-thump as Brian, the drummer, commenced his sound check. John reappeared, told Paul he was needed and ushered me back outside, laughing once we were out of earshot.

'He's a nutter, that guy! Absolute bloody fruitcake!'

We joined Chris and Richard, who were still perched on the wall. They looked at John expectantly.

'They'll call us when they're ready,' he said. 'They want the horns one at a time to sound check to start with, then all of you together. Something to do with dripping or dribbling... I dunno.' He shrugged, then pointed to a building further down the road. 'You can get tea, coffee and food down there, but don't go any further, OK? Sorry guys – we're going to have to do a lot of hanging around today.'

I'd anticipated that and as an afterthought, just as I was leaving the Grange, had chucked the carrier bag containing my still unread magazines in the back of the car. I thought about going to get them but Richard slid off the wall, pulling me with him.

'Come on' he said. 'Might as well case the joint.'

126

We certainly had plenty of time for it. We played pinball, ate too much, had our back teeth floating with tea and coffee and played a rather rude, outdoor version of 'I-Spy' before sound-checking. Once that was over, we had a crack at the business in hand, namely laying down three tracks. We'd had a debate over what we should play and settled on 'Almost', 'Sweet Soul Music' and 'Take Me To The River'. Richard, who did a trombone intro on 'Almost', suddenly found he couldn't play it. He had, of course, played it faultlessly on at least three hundred occasions, but would it come out right now? Would it hell. He got more and more embarrassed, we all fell about laughing and taking the mickey, and were eventually evicted from the premises to give him time to get it sorted.

It was my turn to cock-up on 'Take Me To The River'. One of the engineers, a middle-aged man wearing corduroy trousers, tweed jacket with leather elbow patches and half-moon glasses, *asked* me to cock-up.

'On purpose?'

'Yes, if you wouldn't mind.'

'Ooh – I don't know about that! She makes mistakes all the time, but doing them to order...' Nick, our keyboard player, grinned. If I play anything wrong or that he doesn't like, he tends to join the others in asking me 'Was that the jazz version..?' The engineer looked a bit nonplussed and said he needed a mistake so I could be edited back in – 'dropped back in' – at the correct spot.

'OK,' I said. 'No problem.'

Oh yes it was. I began to appreciate the talents of men like Victor Borge and Les Dawson. It was my turn to be laughed at now. Finally, I got it right. That is, I got it wrong. On purpose. A spectacularly horrible couple of notes.

'Wonderful! Now, just start again from the middle eight and do it right this time.'

Right. Wrong! Having done it wrong the once, could I now play it right again? No. We all fell about laughing. Once more, everyone was evicted, except me, left behind to get it right.

All in all, it was a good morning's work and we were allowed to adjourn to the bar at lunchtime with strict instructions not to drink too much. Paul didn't join us, being left deep in conversation with a couple of men also wearing tweed jackets with leather elbow patches.

'Maybe it's a secret uniform,' John suggested.

'No – that's the sweaters – have you seen the sweaters? All Nordic bum-warming jobs – they probably work for radio stations in the Arctic Circle.' Richard disagreed.

'Bullshit!'

'You look – count the sweaters – I'm telling you...'

We counted a lot of sweaters, talked nineteen to the dozen and ate huge ploughman's lunches in the bar. Time ticked by. We interrogated Chris – day job, farmer in the northernmost village in the Cotswolds – about how the lambing was going, got Richard – day job, graphic designer – to design a new business card for the band, and teased Brian mercilessly about the hats he'd taken to wearing to cover his receding hairline.

'Right – you all got your diaries?' John interrupted as he returned from the bar with a tray of drinks. We all mumbled and rummaged and eventually produced an assortment ranging from filofaxes to scraps of paper.

'Gold Cup Week!' John announced. A collective groan rippled round the table.

'I know we weren't going to play this year BUT...' He fended off the protests by raising his voice.

'...BUT I think I made an offer we'd be mad to refuse.' He sat with an ear-to-ear beam across his face. That expression is just one of the reasons he's such a good front man. Short and wiry, he's a bundle of energy with the wackiest face imaginable. He was probably a court jester in a previous life.

'Wait till you hear this,' he told us. 'There's a new pub opened in Cheltenham, right? And the landlord is worried about getting the punters in there when there are so many established places, most of them with bands already booked. Didn't think he'd be able to get anyone at such short notice.'

He beamed happily round the circle of sceptical faces. It's not that we've anything against Gold Cup week, *per se*. We'd just rather be out and about enjoying it, rather than entertaining the drunken hordes.

'Well, I said, you just might be in luck there. Gave him some garbage about a cancellation, bunged him a tape and the publicity material and *voilà!* Three consecutive nights.' He looked at me and said, 'I told him one of your other bands would play the rest of the week.'

I choked on my pint. No one spoke for a

second. Chris pushed a loose piece of tobacco off his lower lip with his tongue.

'So what's so great? He's paying us a fortune, is he?'

'Too right, he is, though he doesn't realise that yet! The thing is, he was dubious about paying our going rate, see? Worried there wouldn't be enough punters. So I told him, I can understand that, new pub and all, big competition in Race Week. Tell you what, I says to him, how about we make a deal where you can't lose out?' He paused for effect. We stared at him. The smile never wavered.

'So...?' urged Richard, unwilling to drag it out any longer.

'So...' beamed John, raising his glass, '...I told him we'd play for ten percent of his takings.'

Several mouths began to twitch. I was having a hard time not to laugh out loud. Ian, who had only been with us for a couple of months, didn't get it.

'But what if he winds up with hardly any customers? He's got a point there, you know.'

Brian rattled his drumsticks against the edge of the table.

'No, my son – the Commander's right.' He always calls John 'The Commander'. Sort of a Dad's Army joke gone wrong. He winked at the rest of us. 'It's like this, see. We all press-gang all our family and friends...' Hoots of derision all round. Ian looked startled.

'Even you've got friends, matey – am I right or am I right?' Another wink.

'But...'

'Oh, put him out of his misery!' Richard laughed.

'All right, all right!' This time, the wink was for me.

'Now, Mike here, she's got a couple of friends, see.' A gasp of mock astonishment greeted this news. Ian was trying his best to make sense of things. I sat po-faced.

'You will be seeing them, of course?' John checked.

'Of course.'

'But...' What Ian didn't know and the rest of us did, is that I have a couple of friends, Joan and Deborah, who run hotels in Cheltenham. They are, like everyone else, bursting at the seams during Race Week. And if I ask nicely, they get their regulars to support anything we have going. I made a note in my Filofax to phone them. Little did I know I'd need Joan for rather more urgent reasons before long...

'What do you think this is – a bloody holiday camp?' Paul stuck his head round the door. 'Come on – you've got a video to make!'

I wondered how Raffi had got on with her interview and wondered how much longer we'd be here. Video. The word conjures up such glamorous connotations for a lot of people. It did for me until the first time I shot one. Forget glamour. Think 'repetition' and 'automatic pilot' and you've just about got the reality. This time, we were in something resembling a giant hangar which, at this time of the year, meant it was freezing. Brian grumbled about brass monkeys. John said he should be used to it, being a builder.

Chris came to Brian's defence, saying he was a farmer and out in all weathers but it didn't mean he had cast iron bollocks, either. Richard leaned against a wall, wearing a woolly hat and a long scarf as well as his overcoat. We all breathed on our hands, rubbed them together, stuck them in our groins or armpits to stop our fingers seizing up or dropping off. Eventually, the building was transformed from drab, cold and grey into a blaze of multicoloured lights, the cameras were ready to roll and we got started.

We had chosen to do the old Blues Brothers' number, 'Everybody Needs Somebody', so we played it. And again. And again. And again. The cameras shot from this angle, then from that. They shot close-ups of all of us. They particularly wanted the horn section to do a little dance. Great. We didn't have too much room on the plinth we were standing on and Chris and Richard are both over six feet tall, with shoe sizes to match. I had a bad feeling about this...

Tom, on guitar, who was always breaking strings, broke a string and had to change guitars. Dave, on bass, who never broke a string, broke a string and had to change basses. We kept dancing. The movement, along with the lights, was keeping us warm.

After what seemed like an eternity, they'd had enough. We'd had more than enough. I wondered if we'd ever be able to play that damned number again without thinking about this crazy evening. Still, they were pleased and we were pleased. We'd had a good time, their people had gained experience and we'd get some free publicity material into the bargain.

As we packed away, I looked at my watch and shook my head when asked if I wanted to go for a drink in Evesham.

'I'd love to, but I promised I'd be elsewhere if we finished at a reasonable time.'

The session had taken a long while, but not nearly so long as I'd anticipated. Paul waved at me from the other side of the hangar. I wish I'd noticed what he was waving. I wish I'd known why he was waving at me. It might – just might – have saved at least one life if I'd gone over to see what he wanted. As it was, I thought it was just a wave, and waved back and walked out. I was too busy looking forward to the rest of the evening now I knew that I had plenty of time to get over to Cheltenham, meet Raffi at the Paradox Centre and catch the gig with Beanie and the Boys.

Chapter Thirteen

'Mike – can I have a word?' Gaffer, one of the chefs at the Centre, placed a bear-like hand on my arm. I had just arrived and was standing at the bar, scanning the crowd for any sign of Raffi and wondering if she had already gone through to the cavernous extension at the rear of the building where the band was playing. They didn't sound like Beanie and the Boys to me, but maybe it was a double bill.

'Sure. Nice to see you, Gaffer. How's it going?'

Gaffer was a very good guitarist, currently in search of a new band. I had first come to know him through his Aunt Joan, my friend with the hotel. Over six feet tall, his shaven head glinted in the light, his face holding a sombre expression at odds with his usual cheerfulness. We moved over to one of the rough wooden tables, his jeans straining to contain his thighs. Gaffer was built, as the saying goes, like the proverbial brick shithouse.

'Oh – I'm OK, but – I assume you haven't heard?'

'About what?'

'You haven't heard.' His face became even more sombre. He took a deep breath. 'Right. Well, Raffi's in the office with Sandy. Pretty upset. We're all pretty upset.'

'Gaffer – what?' My mind was doing overtime. Had she had an accident? Been attacked? He must have read my thoughts.

'Sorry, Mike – I'm not explaining this very well, Raffi's fine. It's Tim. From Beanie and the Boys. He's dead.'

'Dead? You're kidding!'

'Afraid not. It's bloody horrible, to be honest, mate.' He took a pull on his pint. 'There was a fire. At his house. Last night.'

'Oh my God!'

'Yeah. You wonder if there is one, don't you, at times like this? Someone like Tim dies, and yet you get out-and-out bastards living to a ripe old age and fucking up people's lives something chronic.'

'I know.' I shrugged helplessly. 'How did it happen?'

Gaffer gave me an old-fashioned look. 'That's

134

what the fire brigade's trying to find out. I mean, we assumed it was an accident, right? The whisper on the street says it was arson.'

'Arson!' I looked at him, unable to take it in. 'You don't think...'

'It had crossed my mind.'

Tim was white. His girlfriend, Sherrill, was black. They'd had their hassles over it, but arson..? This was a different league altogether.

'What about Sherrill?'

Gaffer shook his head. 'Don't know. Only one body, as far as I know. Definitely a bloke. She could be away, of course – does field trips and stuff, doing research or something. Anyway, somebody's got to find her and tell her. Wouldn't fancy that job.' Both Tim and Sherrill were PhD students at the University of Gloucestershire. He sighed heavily. 'What a bleedin' mess. First I knew anything was wrong was this morning. Beanie phoned. In a terrible state, he was. He'd gone round to Tim's, wanting to make sure he was up. They had some sort of meeting at Uni, I think. Anyway, when he got there, the house was gutted.'

'Bloody hell!'

'Well – look, do you want to come and have a word with Raffi? She was pretty upset. I already told you that, didn't I? Sorry, mate. Anyway, the point is, Sandy took her to her office because she was crying. Gave her a stiff drink. Raffi said something about you might be coming and you might not, so I kept an eye out for you. She wasn't making a lot of sense, to be honest.'

Sandy was the manager of the Centre. We made our way to her office, where Raffi was sitting quiet and very straight in a hard-backed chair. She jumped up as soon as she saw me.

'Mike – Tim's dead!'

'I know, sweetheart – Gaffer just told me.' I enveloped her in a hug and she cried quietly.

I glanced across the top of her head. 'Thanks for looking after her, Sandy.'

'No problem, Mike.'

I walked Raffi through the bar and out into the cold night air. Gaffer followed.

'Where's your car?' I asked Raffi.

'At home. I came straight from the station.' I cursed myself for forgetting. She hadn't felt confident enough to drive to London, so had taken the train instead.

'Never mind. I'll take you home.'

'No! I want to see it!' She pulled away from me.

'What?'

'Tim's house. I want to see. For myself.'

Gaffer raised his eyebrows. I looked at Raffi. Her face was flushed and she was clenching and unclenching her fists.

'I don't think she'll settle till she does,' I told him.

He nodded. 'OK. But I'm coming with you.'

I was glad of his company. Tim hadn't lived in the most salubrious part of town, so Gaffer's presence, as we walked to what remained of his house, gave reassurance. I also thought the walk might do Raffi some good, help get rid of the excess adrenaline.

The streets were dark and damp, the fine rain which fell causing the orange street lamps to diffuse their glow into a Lucozade-like fizz of

136

colour. We were in the backstreets now, and the only signs of life we passed were a drunk, a cat and two foxes. Apart from our own footfalls it was eerily quiet, though I knew that not far away, the Promenade and High Street would be alive with activity as people made their way between pubs and clubs in varying degrees of sobriety.

We came to the house at last, black on black, broken windows gaping like missing teeth, the roof collapsed as if overtaken unawares by a terminal tiredness. We stood on the opposite side of the road, still and silent as the reality hit us.

After that, Raffi didn't want to go home to be by herself, so I took her back to the Grange with me. She fell asleep in the car and I had difficulty getting her into the cottage. I left her fully clothed on the sofa, simply covering her with a duvet.

My own sleep that night was disturbed, haunted by strange images. I dreamed of a faceless man, dripping pond weed, and watched Tim's house ablaze, flames shooting skyward, smoke, thick, black and choking, billowing after them. An unknown, translucent figure, shimmering in and out of vision, was pointing at me, voice deep and distorted as it ordered me to 'Get him out!' I wanted to. I tried to move but couldn't. I could feel the heat now, closer and more intense. There was the smell of singeing, like hair, my hair... I screamed, trying to run away, but my body simply would not respond. 'Help me! Help me!' I screamed again, but there was no one there. The figure had gone. The pond-weed man had gone. All I could see was Duncan, my husband, and he couldn't help, either. His head was slumped over the steering wheel of the car, his sightless eyes staring through me as his life-blood seeped away and the icy water rose over my head...

Chapter Fourteen

'I hope you're ready for this!' Maggie smiled.

'No, I'm not.' I scowled at her over my cup of tea.

'Ready for what?' Raffi asked.

'I'm sorry. I'd forgotten all about it when I brought you here with me last night,' I apologised. 'There's a trip to the stables.'

'It's a sort of Saturday morning ritual,' Maggie explained, helping herself to one of my slices of toast. 'We all troop off and have a ride, then come back here for lunch with the Myatts.'

'Sounds like fun,' Raffi said. I scowled at her, too.

'It is,' Maggie enthused. 'Katie's having lessons and loves it. Then again, most kids love animals of any kind. Must be the soft and furry connection.'

'Yeah, right,' I grumbled. 'Horses have teeth and hooves and just one of their back legs weighs between eleven and twelve stone.'

'How do you know that? I thought you'd never been near a horse?'

'I haven't,' I confirmed. 'But I have a friend who does a cross between shiatsu and osteopathy on horses. He told me. That's why he gets lower back pain when he's been treating them and has to have regular massages and stuff. Are you sure it's safe?'

'Of course it's safe! What is the matter with you, Mike?'

'The slight matter is, I heard this morning that someone from here was killed by a horse just the other day.' I'd been for a walk to clear my head of bad dreams before Raffi woke up and had bumped into Alison. At least we hadn't found a dead body this time, but she was having to arrange a funeral, and it wasn't Arthur's.

'That wasn't at these stables!' Maggie shook her head vigorously. 'These are just ordinary horses at the stable in the village. Warren's horse is with a trainer. That's where Jack Bignall died.'

Raffi looked shocked. Maggie filled her in on the story.

'Warren Myatt has a horse that's going to be running at Cheltenham. It seems someone tried to nobble it and Jack got in the way, trying to fight the intruder off.'

'So much death!' Raffi said, biting her lip. I'd told Maggie what had happened yesterday, so she knew what Raffi was referring to. 'And what about the horse? It must have been terrified.'

'He's in a bit of a state,' Maggie conceded. 'They're not sure he'll be fit to run. Come on – we should be getting over there.'

The morning was brisk, the sky filled with scudding white cloud, fast-moving in the wind. I zipped my jacket, looking at Maggie, who was properly dressed for riding in jacket and jodhpurs, looking for all the world like she'd been born to it.

'This country living is doing you good,' I told her.

'I think you're right. I could get used to this. I am getting used to this!' She slapped her hands together, as if underlining the point.

I was wearing jeans, and Maggie had sorted out a pair for Raffi, who, due to my lack of foresight, had woken up in a strange place with no clean clothes of any description. I'd promised to run her back to Cheltenham after lunch. At least she was over the worst of the shock of Tim's death, and that's what mattered.

'It's gorgeous here, Mike!' Raffi waved her arms expansively. 'Are you sure you're coming back to Cheltenham at all? I can just see Alex running the business by himself and telling people how you gave it all up for open fields, trees, and a mysterious man.'

'What mysterious man?'

'Jake, did Maggie say his name was?'

'Oh God!' I groaned. 'Two of you on my back now!'

I spotted Katie a mile off, or rather, she spotted us. Hard-hatted and with her feet in little boots, she looked terrific.

'Mike! Mike! Are you really going to come tomorrow and bring Dexter?'

'There's TWO mysterious men?' Raffi punched me on the arm.

'My tenor sax – I'll explain later,' I hissed under my breath.

'That sounds great, Katie.' I turned to Maggie. 'What's the arrangement?'

'Brunch. We'll sort it out later.'

140

'Probably noon-ish,' Steve volunteered. 'Hope that's not too early?'

I shook my head. Steve was definitely not dressed for riding. His corduroy trousers, sweater and loafers looked distinctly out of place.

'Noon is fine. I'll be there.'

'And Dexter?' Katie tugged at my sleeve anxiously.

'Dexter wouldn't miss it for anything,' I assured her. She ran away happily.

'You don't ride?' I asked Steve as we entered the stable yard.

'Not if I can help it. Lethal both ends, as far as I'm concerned.'

I laughed in agreement. I could see Elynore, Warren and a man I didn't know, talking animatedly. Between them, they looked like a glossy advert in some exclusive huntin' shootin' and fishin' magazine.

Raffi fell into step beside me, Maggie having skittered off after Katie.

'So tell me more about the Mystery Man.'

'You're pushing it! And I haven't a clue who he is,' I told her, being deliberately obtuse and indicating the stranger.

'Howard Harrison, Warren's business partner. Mr Shipping Company.'

The Texas Treacle had come up out of nowhere on my left. Raffi did a double-take.

'Morning, Jake.' I made the introductions.

'So how'd you get on yesterday? At the studios? Hope I didn't keep you up too late.' He was laughing at me and Raffi was almost agog. He was dressed in blue jeans, a checked shirt over a

T-shirt and a navy blue zip-up jacket.

'Fine. It was fun.'

Elynore had marked our arrival now and left the men to come and greet us. I made the introductions again. I was, in fact, beginning to feel like an introduction agency, a feeling further reinforced when Edward joined us, too. Elynore must have been feeling chummy this morning because she put her arm through mine and drew me slightly away from the others before asking, *sotto voce*, if I were afraid of horses as well as dogs.

'Not as far as I know,' I told her. 'I've never met one.'

'Good Lord, girl, you haven't lived!' She didn't so much smile as bare her teeth. 'So you don't ride, then? Maggie didn't seem to think you did. Well, never mind – there's a first time for everything. I'm sure we can find you something suitable.'

They certainly did. After a word with Mary, the owner of the stable, I was taken to be introduced to my mount for the morning. His name was Jasper.

'Strewth!' I complained as we trooped into the refectory at the Grange some time later. 'I'm aching in places I didn't know I had places!'

'Sore butt, huh?' Jake grinned as I eased myself into a seat.

'And legs. Especially inside my thighs.'

'You did real good for your first time up. Edward will agree with me, right?'

'Yes, indeed.' He grinned as he looked approvingly at my legs.

'Flattery will get the pair of you everywhere! All

I did was "walk-on" or whatever they call it. It's like a whole new language.'

I was surprised I'd managed to get up at all. The horse was huge, certainly to my uneducated eye, and I had severe reservations about my ability to mount it. Jake watched as I made a couple of abortive attempts. Embarrassed, I'd shrugged at him. 'Look – I really don't think I can do this.'

Jasper stood placidly, apparently unfazed by my bumbling efforts. Jake looked at Mary, who was trying to encourage me to have another go.

'There's a simple solution,' she assured me. 'Back in a sec.'

She disappeared and left Jake holding the reins. He was stroking the horse's face. It nuzzled his hand in return. Elynore, now astride a beautiful grey, urged it towards us.

'Sorting you out, are they? Good, good!'

'How was your appointment with Arnold Niedermeyer?' Jake asked her. She looked completely blank. 'He's from my Mom's neck of the woods, back in the States.'

'I didn't know you knew him.'

'I don't. We got chatting, is all, when he first called to speak to you. Familiar accents.'

'Quite. Yes, well, he didn't turn up, I'm afraid. I was rather hoping we'd be able to do some business.'

Mary returned and sure enough, the mounting block did the trick. Elynore rode off and left me to my first riding lesson.

'Did you enjoy yourself?' Warren asked as we settled around the long table.

'Yes, I did.'

143

'You sound surprised!'

'I suppose I am, never having tried it, but yes. Lovely horse.'

'How's the Ghost?' The question came from Howard and was addressed to Warren.

'You have a ghost?' I interjected. 'Maggie never told me!'

'Ghost of a Chance. My racehorse.'

'That's the name of a Lester Young number.'

'Really? Well, the Ghost is still jittery. I am not a happy man.'

Jake sat down beside me. Raffi kicked me under the table. I ignored her.

Maggie got Warren's attention. 'Warren – Mike was telling me she has a friend who does some sort of therapy on horses. What was it, Mike?'

'Sort of a cross between shintai, shiatsu and osteopathy.'

'On horses?' Warren looked sceptical.

'I know it sounds crazy, but he apparently gets first-rate results. He specialises in racehorses.'

'Is he qualified and insured?'

'Oh yes.'

'And does he have satisfied owners and trainers – veterinarians, even, to back up these claims?'

'Absolutely. I'll give you his name and number.'

'You really think he could do something for Ghost, in time for the race?'

'I don't know,' I admitted. 'You need to speak to him.' Maggie supplied a notebook and pencil and I duly noted down the details.

Food started to appear. Masses of it, along with several bottles of wine. I put my hand over my glass.

'Sorry, I won't. I have to drive Raffi back to Cheltenham.'

Elynore looked at her in surprise. 'You're leaving so soon?'

'Well, I wasn't supposed to be here at all, really. Mike sort of kidnapped me because I didn't want to be on my own last night. A friend of mine died. In a house fire.'

Silence fell around the table as all attention focused on her.

'You poor girl – how awful!' Warren said.

'Yes. We were at the same Uni, you see, although Tim was a PhD student and I'm just an under-graduate. He was doing an MSc and converted, you know? He was in a band, which is how Mike knew him, and they were supposed to be playing last night and when we got there...' Her voice tailed off.

'How frightful!' Elynore turned to her hus-band. 'Warren, we ought to drink a toast to his memory, don't you think? What was his name, did you say?'

'Tim. Tim Williams.'

'Then here's to Tim. God rest him.' Warren had taken over, standing with his glass raised. We drank, though I stuck to mineral water, and the conversation turned to other things.

Elynore and Warren dragged us to their end of the table and made rather a meal of extolling my virtues to Howard, the mystery-man business partner, who, looking straight into my eyes, said he felt there was nothing sexier on God's earth than a woman playing a saxophone. I've heard it all before, of course, but it was Raffi, muttering,

'Someone should tell him that you don't suck, you blow...' that cracked me up. I choked so much that Jake had to slap my back.

My mobile rang while I was still recovering, and Raffi answered it, saying, 'Mike Brodie's mobile...' while I struggled to get my breath. She listened, then handed it to me, swearing in Italian as she did so.

'Hi, Paul!' I knew enough Italian to know what she'd said, and only one person could make her that mad. 'Yes ... we're in the refectory ... it's to the left of the Tower... OK, see you in a minute.'

'Paul again!' Maggie laughed. 'What is it this time? Playing the NEC?'

'I think romance is in the air,' Jake drawled. 'The guy can't leave you alone.'

'It's not what you think,' I laughed, although I had no idea what he wanted. Probably eighteen gigs in twelve days across five continents, if his recent form was anything to go by. I *could* learn to say no, I told myself. Well, maybe...

Paul made his entrance wearing a brown suit with loud black checks that only he could get away with. He hesitated when he saw Raffi, who tossed her head and scowled at him. I would have to stop setting her such a bad example, I thought, remembering my own scowling fit at breakfast. Paul's never one to lack brass neck, give him that. He took her hand, kissed it and said, 'Ah! It's Miss ... Unpronounceable. Italian. Definitely not Whatsherface.' She pressed her lips together. I looked from one to the other. Although they'd met numerous times, I felt obliged to reintroduce them all over again, hoping for a cessation of hostilities and a fresh start between them.

'Paul Barnett – Rafaella Orsini – Raffi, for short.'

Grudgingly, she made room for him.

'Michal Brodie,' he accused, 'Do you realise the amount of mileage you've put on my car this week?'

'Oh, no, Paul! Do tell!' I raised a hand to my face in mock horror. 'And just think – if you'd phoned me before you set out, I could have told you that I'd be back in Cheltenham this afternoon because I have to give Raffi a lift home!'

He collapsed his head into his arms on the table and sighed theatrically.

'The things I do for you...!'

'So what are you doing this time? People here are beginning to think you can't stay away from me. That you have designs on my body...' My mouth twitched.

'I don't think Pete would be too happy about that! I'm a bit old now to suddenly discover hidden heterosexual tendencies!' From the corner of my eye, I noted revulsion flickering across Warren's face, disappearing as quickly as it came. 'No, darling, it's just that you made your escape from the studio complex rather too quickly yesterday.' He regaled the table with a highly colourful account of the band's exploits. Jake sat back, grinning. 'So, there I was – I could see you were heading off, so I waved at you. Waved this at you.' He took an envelope from his pocket.

'Say, Michal – do you always run off without waiting to get paid!' Warren asked.

'Never.'

'She's either blind as a bat or was simply

ignoring me, as usual.' Paul did his affronted voice.

'Since when do I ignore you?' I protested. 'I do everything you ask! Meekly, obediently, and with my right arm twisted up to my shoulder blade!'

'Yes, and pigs might fly! Anyway, here it is.' He pushed the envelope towards me. 'It was brought in for you when you were in the studio, so, as I'd told them I was your Manager – well, the band's Manager – they gave it to me and I said I'd give it to you.' He smiled broadly.

'Paul!'

He glanced at his watch. 'Did you say you were taking Ravioli home? I'll do that. Save you a journey.'

'What did you call me?' It was Raffi's turn to choke.

'Ravioli. It's Italian, and it begins with R. That's close enough for Rock and Roll...'

How he survived the rest of the meal, I don't know. Eventually, however, he and Raffi had to make a move, and I got up with them.

'I'll be back in a minute,' I told the others, and walked with Paul and Raffi over to the cottage, remembering that I still had her presents here. I gave her the carrier bags, watching and waving as Paul's car pulled away. She was young and would probably give him such a hard time over his latest misuse of her name that she wouldn't notice his driving...

I rejoined the group in the refectory, now heavily into desserts. I picked up the envelope, still lying on the table, turned it over and opened it. Another envelope was inside. Messy. Muddy.

Trust Paul to have dropped it, I thought. I held it gingerly and read, *'Mike Brodie, Howlin' Blue Horns, The Studio Complex, nr. Evesham'* and yesterday's date. Who would be writing to me at a gig? I didn't recognise the handwriting. I opened it and frowned again. God knows what Paul had been up to, but the paper looked – I flinched – almost bloodstained. What was this? Some kind of joke? It wasn't even a proper note. There wasn't any writing – well, not that made much sense. Just the words, *'Cogito, ergo sum'*, then a picture. Of what? Vines? Poles? A vineyard?

Another picture. Three monkeys, playing musical instruments. And a further picture of monkeys, this time in the classic old pose of 'See all, hear all, say nothing'. My grandfather had had a brass set like that. Finally, in the bottom right-hand corner, a cartoon face, clearer than any written signature.

What the hell? My blood ran cold.

There could be no other explanation.

The note was from Tim...

Chapter Fifteen

'Are you all right?' The voice seemed to come from a long way off.

'What? Sorry?'

'You're white as a sheet. Not bad news, I hope?' Jake's face was creased with concern.

'No, no. It's just – it doesn't make sense.

Probably a practical joke.' My mind was whirling, putting the pictogram together. Descartes' Vineyard. It had to be. A pub at Coombe Hill, near Cheltenham. Also a warning. A warning to keep my mouth shut, my eyes and ears open. 'I need to get to the bottom of this.' I rose from the table. 'If you'll excuse me...' I left, not waiting for anyone's permission.

Back at the cottage, I phoned the studio complex. It took a while, but I finally got the information I needed. The note had been hand-delivered by a young man on Friday morning.

'There's no problem, I hope? We gave the note to your Manager, Paul Barnett.'

'No. No problem. That's fine. It's just that Paul forgot to ask where it had come from. I was just interested to know. Thanks very much. You've been really helpful.'

'You're welcome.'

I sat back, trying to take in the implications. Seven o'clock, Friday morning. At seven o'clock on Friday morning, Tim was supposed to be dead. What the hell was going on? And if Tim hadn't been killed in the fire, then who had? Nothing was making any sense.

I looked at the note again, desperate for every last piece of information. *Dammit*, I thought. *What's the point of 'Descartes' Vineyard' when there isn't even a hint of a date or time?* If Tim were really alive, really needed to contact me, why couldn't he use the bloody phone? *Not fair*, I shook my head. He doesn't have my mobile number. He knew my home number, though, through Raffi. But anyway, why me? Why send a note to me? I didn't know him that well. I looked at my watch, thinking back to when Paul and Raffi had left, trying to estimate what time she'd be home. A while yet, I thought. Almost long enough for me to get to Descartes' Vineyard...

If Descartes' Vineyard didn't exist, someone would have to invent it. Standing above a T-junction whose roads lead respectively to Cheltenham, Gloucester and Tewkesbury it looks ordinary enough from the outside, its exterior clean but unprepossessing. To the right, bounding the car park, run the rows of poles which support the vines. It was all bare now, but I tried to imagine it on a summer's day and was pleased with the image I conjured up.

Locking the car, I crossed the car park and walked down the steps and into the entrance hall. Sure enough, at the end, on my right, stood the three mechanical monkeys from Tim's drawing. Dressed in red, white and blue sweaters, they were immobile at present, their lugubrious faces staring vacantly. For some reason, they reminded me of my nightmare and I shuddered. One was holding a guitar, one a tambourine and French flag, while the third, with a cigarette and bottle, looked as if he should have had a drum, but didn't. Plaited bulbs of garlic hung on the wall behind them and they were surrounded by a sea of empty bottles.

I turned my back on them and walked towards the bar, passing a couple of fruit machines and one that looked like a refugee from a fairground. I looked again. You probably know the sort of

151

thing I mean. It comprised a closed glass cabinet containing a miniature crane which, if you have the money and the skill, you can manipulate to pick up goodies. There were lots of sweets, which was to be expected, but, unlike any machine I'd seen at the seaside as a child, nestling amongst them were miniature bottles of spirits.

I scanned the place quickly as I stepped up to the bar. What was I expecting to see? Tim, lurking beneath a table? I felt frustrated and incredibly stupid. This was probably going to be a total waste of time. I ordered a mineral water, found an unoccupied table in a corner and sat down. As far as I could tell, I should be able to see anyone entering or leaving from here.

I tried to relax, which wasn't too difficult given that a Stephane Grappelli tape was in full swing. I looked around, staggered by the visual variety of the place. Wouldn't the lads just love to play I-Spy here! The bar itself was an L-shaped top supported by casks, barrels, kegs – I don't know the difference, if any, between them, so take your pick. I imagined the boys from the band. 'I spy with my little eye... something beginning with G.S.' Green Shirt? Gin Short? No – a Grinning Skull, behind the bar. It was, moreover, wearing a gendarme's cap which had a French flag sticking out of it. Hops and continental sausages hung around it with more plaits of garlic.

To my right – oh, the boys would love this! I spy with my little eye ... something beginning with ... P.P.H.O.R.D. Pissed Punter Hollers, Overturning Richard's Dinner? Pulled Pint Heavily Overflows, Ruining Decor? How about Painted Plaster Head

152

of René Descartes! Unbelievable! I looked at it, shaking my head. The bastard was smiling. Looked far too cheerful for someone who'd wreaked such havoc on the way the Western World thought of Life, the Universe and Everything. He really should have hit his head in that bloody lime kiln. I realised, uneasily, that it was also one of those heads which, like the eyes in some portraits I've seen, seemed to follow you around.

I moved my body and settled further back into the corner, noticing now that what I'd taken for ordinary bar tables were largely old sewing machine housings. My new viewpoint also revealed dark wooden panelling decorated with *fleur de lys* and pictures of people in – I hazarded a guess – seventeenth century costume. I wondered fleetingly who they were meant to be and then noticed – oh my God – here was one for the lads with a vengeance!

I Spy with my little eye... something beginning with D.W.H.A.T.S.O.. Get that, if you can! Dirty White Hat and Tangerine Socks On? Do Whatever Horniness and Tickles Seem Okay? Very funny, but one word was almost right... Dirty Wazzock Hovers at the Sodding Office? My mental language was getting worse by the minute. Wrong! Wrong! It's – wait for it... Devil With Horns And Tongue Sticking Out!! Beat that, you bastards!

It was a remarkable looking thing, the head, bearded and red-horned, leering from a wall with long, thick tongue protruding snakelike between equally thick lips. *Up yours, too,* I thought, hoping those eyes wouldn't be following me all night.

153

Still no sign of Tim. No sign of anyone I knew.

I glanced at the ceiling, which was a series of arches crammed with wine bottles, and wondered about the logistics of actually getting them all into place. For some illogical reason, it made me feel as if I were in the bows of a galleon. *Well, this is no good*, I thought. *I can't stay here all day. Dexter has an appointment with Katie...*

I looked at my watch, working out just how much longer I could give it before going back to the Grange. What the hell. Stephane was still keeping me entertained. I went to the bar and ordered another mineral water.

'Ah – you are staying a little longer, Madame?' The barman was French, as was the woman who'd served me earlier. I wondered if they were husband and wife or father and daughter.

'Yes,' I confirmed. 'It's a fabulous place.'

'But you drink only mineral water?'

'Driving, I'm afraid.'

'Of course. Very sensible. We quite understand, do we not?' A conspiratorial glance passed between them as he tapped the side of his nose.

'Well, I shall definitely come back another day without my car,' I offered. '–maybe have a meal.'

'Oh yes. You will be most welcome.'

Friendly lot, I thought, as I re-staked my corner and practised more of my solitary version of band-style I-Spy. There were lots of amphorae. There was – I Spy with my little eye ... P.S.O.T.B.V.M. Painted Sign Over The Bar, Very Maudlin? Poster Says Oliver Tugwell Bought Variegated Monster? No. Plaster Statue Of The Blessed Virgin Mary. She was all expansive blue cloak and pious

154

expression as she knelt in prayer.

There were violins and an accordion hanging from a beam, and right by my head, a tarnished bugle. People came and went. Still, I didn't recognise a single one. A framed blackboard told me, in boldly chalked letters, that I could expect *Le Folk Music*, live, if I came on a Tuesday night, and *Le Jazz*, live, if I came on a Thursday. I thought I might come on a Thursday. I read, with gruesome fascination, a 'Pork Map' of England, showing a live boar, a gammon leg, black pudding, haslet, pork pie and – oh God – my stomach squirmed in protest – brawn. I almost cricked my neck trying to read the circumference of a huge black plaque holding the head, in relief, of Peter Paul Rubens, only to discover that all it said was *'Petrus Paulus Rubens'* or, if you want to be really pedantic, *'Petrvs Pavlvs Rvbens'*.

It was whilst I was doing this that I noticed a French road sign, blue with white lettering, which declared itself to be the *'Rue de la Piscine'*. Knowing no French, I couldn't work out whether it was the road to the toilets or the road to the swimming pool. The point was, it hung over an archway which led to another part of the pub. I felt a moment's panic. Suppose I'd been sitting here and Tim was through there? And had left? I hurried towards it. This was ridiculous. I was getting paranoid. I nearly missed the step down in my haste.

No Tim.

No one I knew.

What a surprise.

This smaller area was filled with small square tables, each covered with a red-and-white-

155

checked tablecloth. Several couples were tucking into an assortment of meals. I began to feel hungry and realised I hadn't eaten since lunch time and even then, hadn't finished my meal due to the interruption by Paul with Tim's note.

Frustrated, I turned to go back to my seat and found myself face to face with another fairground refugee. Eerily lit, it announced itself to be a *'Madame Finali'* fortune telling machine. The bottom half of it was painted red and embellished with flourishes of green and yellow, supporting the glass booth above through which a gypsy woman's head peered into a crystal ball. *'Learn Your Fate!'* I was admonished. I smiled to myself and stuck a twenty pence piece in the slot. Fortune telling technology had obviously moved on a bit since the last time I'd used one of these things. As a child, I'd had to put my hand, palm down, on the glass in order for it to be read. Madame Finali obviously did it by telepathy instead. There was a little rush of air as a printed card slipped down a slot, rather like those instant passport photos you get from a booth at the post office. I bent to pick it up, shaking it gently, as if it really might still be wet. What a wally. Slipping it into my jacket pocket, I decided I'd had enough. My date with Katie had to be kept and there seemed to have been no further clue here. I walked back through the bar.

'Madame! You are leaving?' It was the bartender.

'I'm afraid my friend didn't turn up.' I shrugged.

'Ah-ha. But you are leaving and the likeness, it is perfect.'

'It is? What likeness?' I was beginning to think

I'd found myself in the middle of a French farce. Maybe I was really back at the Grange sleeping off lunch and dreaming all this.

The young woman ducked beneath the bar and pulled out a sheet of A4 paper. She showed it to me triumphantly.

'Your friend is a very good artist, no?'

'Yes,' I agreed, looking in amazement at a picture of myself. 'Um – did he give you anything else, by any chance?'

'Oh yes! It is to help you escape, no?'

The barman leaned forward, lowering his voice. 'He told us they are remaking a TV programme from some years ago, and you are on it. The one where the bad guys, they are out to get you, and you have a secret camera and are on the run, aided only by your trusted friend, no?'

First I'd heard of it. 'No. I mean, yes. I do hope you won't give me away.' This got weirder by the moment.

'No way, Madame! Your secret is safe with us. Your friend, he said you are a very good jazz musician and that you will play for us when this is all over.'

'Um – why didn't you pass on the information when I arrived?'

He gave a decidedly Gallic shrug. 'Because your friend, he told us to tell you when you leave, but only if there is no trouble, and if we are sure you are not being followed.'

'So I take it I'm not being followed.'

'Oh no, Madame. No one has paid you the slightest attention. Except us, of course. Your friend said if there was trouble, if for any reason

157

we could not give the message to you by lunch time tomorrow, he would find another way to reach you.'

'Right. So what is this message?'

'This, Madame.' His accomplice turned and opened the till, lifted out the cash drawer and handed me an envelope. I slipped it straight into my pocket.

'By the way, Madame...' the bartender lowered his voice even further, leaning across the bar. '...where is your hidden camera?'

'Um...' I looked around carefully, as if making sure that no one was watching. *Think, Michal, think!* I turned back to him, raised my eyebrows and said nothing, fingering my silver saxophone tie-pin with exaggerated care.

'*Mais non!* That is amazing! The wonders of miniaturisation!'

Too right, I thought, as I left. *Too bloody right...*

Another note. I sat in the car with the door open, reading it with the aid of the interior light. If reading is the right word. There were no words at all, this time. Just two pictures apart from the cartoon-face signature. Well, the first wasn't even a picture. It was a set of what Paul would have called 'the dots', that is, a couple of bars of music. I hummed it under my breath. It was a traditional folk piece called 'He Moved Through The Fair'. Then came the picture. A very old-fashioned ambulance with a rail of clothing alongside it. Once again, no time and no date.

I tapped my finger absently against the paper, more confused than ever. How the hell did Henrietta Satterthwaite fit into all this..?

Chapter Sixteen

'Not much further now – ach, brace yourself!'

I gripped my seat as Henrietta's ancient converted ambulance lumbered over yet another bump. Between Jasper the horse yesterday and her vehicle today, my rear end had taken quite a hammering. I remembered, with relief, that I had an appointment for an aromatherapy massage the following morning and wondered if it would include that part of my anatomy. Not too long to go until I'd find out.

I ought to explain about Henrietta's ambulance, I suppose. It's a decommissioned one, and she uses it as a mobile shop for second-hand clothes. Not just any old clothes, either, though 'old' is appropriate. She sells collector's items from the 1920s to the 1970s. She has a shop in Cheltenham but goes out and about to fairs, car boot sales and the like.

Henrietta herself is Scottish but was briefly married to a Yorkshireman and must be in her fifties now, though she doesn't look a day over thirty. Sickening, really, She's a natural blonde, petite, and has flawless skin and a wonderful eye for colour and style. She lives in a converted railway carriage on land owned by a local farmer and her unconventional lifestyle had rubbed off on her Amazon of a daughter, Roxy, so named because she was conceived in the back row of a cinema. So Henrietta told me, anyway.

I'd phoned her on my return to the Grange the previous evening. I'd tried Raffi, too, but she was out. Probably as well. What would I have said, I wondered? 'Hi, Raffi, any messages from dead people on the answerphone?' I had spoken to her this morning, though, and she'd reported nothing untoward, so I had to assume that meant there really was nothing.

I hadn't been sure what to say to Henrietta, either, not knowing how, if at all, she fitted into things, so I'd blagged it, figuring I'd have to play it by ear.

'Hi, Henrietta – it's Mike. Mike Brodie. I'm at a bit of a loose end and was wondering if there's a fair or anything happening? I know you sometimes take the ambulance and...'

'You couldn't have timed it better!' I could hear the smile in her voice. 'I'm off to one tomorrow – it's in Oxfordshire, though.'

'Great! I'm actually staying with a friend at a place called Bewick Grange...'

'Near Ruttersford? Perfect. You're not far away at all. Why don't I just come and pick you up? You've never been in the old girl, have you?' 'The Old Girl' was her nickname for the ambulance.

'That's OK. I'm having lunch with my friend, so why don't you give me directions and I'll make my own way there?'

'Don't be daft, woman!' Her tone overruled any further objection. 'It's no trouble. I'll come and get you and drop you back afterwards. It's on my way home. It'll be nice to catch up on gossip – haven't seen you for a while.'

My lunch date, needless to say, had been with Maggie, Steve and Katie, following on from my visit the previous evening. Unbeknown to me, Jake had also been invited, so Katie was ecstatic. Not only had she met Dexter, she'd had Chet the trumpet to entertain her as well. Jake, like me, had had to make up a name on the spot. She fell in love with the instruments. Maybe it's the shininess as much as their sound. Sonny Rollins said that he'd seen a saxophone in a music shop window and it had been love at first sight.

I'd shown her which side keys to press while I blew, so she could change the notes from B to C, F to F sharp, or B to B flat. We'd had a whale of a time. Both Jake and I had played duets with her, and they were a scream. She'd sat on a high stool, concentrating for all she was worth, and had kept us hugely entertained. Jake and I had staggered about, suitably shocked by the surprise ending, loud and discordant, of a joke piece she'd played. At the end of the evening, I'd solemnly told her that I'd have to warn my keyboard players that they had stiff competition coming up. Jake said Dave Williams had better look to his laurels as far as jam nights in the village were concerned, though we weren't too sure how to smuggle her into the pub. And after the wonderful time with her, that's where Jake had taken me again.

Quieter now, I'd been pleased to see Edward, the Head Gardener, with a couple of young men from the Companions sitting at a table.

'I understand you're in charge of this lot!' I told him.

'Afraid so!' He spread his hands. 'I daren't tell

161

you when I first met you in the gardens in case you knocked my block off! Thought it might be better to get our apologies over with first.'

'Wise move!' I agreed.

Jake and I had talked, mostly about music, which got me nice and relaxed, and he had promised to come and see me play in Cheltenham the following evening. By the time we left, I was inwardly panicking about what I would do if he asked me in again. He didn't. We got back and had only started to kiss when he was beeped about a problem with an alarm in the Grange, and he had to go off and sort it out. I was still debating whether I was relieved or disappointed.

I was jolted back to the present, this time not by a physical bump but by Henrietta mentioning Tim.

'Sorry – what was that? I was miles away.'

'Looks like it! No, I was just saying, you know young Tim from Beanie and the Boys, don't you? You know about the fire?' I nodded. 'Well, they reckon now that they found another body in the basement. A woman.'

'Oh God, not Sherrill, too!'

'Terrible business, eh?' She swung a deft left onto a rutted track. 'Well, here we are. Lots of choice, by the look of it. Was there anything special you were looking for?'

How about a supposedly dead man, for starters? I kept the thought to myself and was suitably vague in reply. If Tim were here, it would be like looking for a needle in a haystack. The place was packed, and it wasn't with just your average Sunday market shoppers. There were jugglers and stilt walkers, there were stalls all over the place, there were cars, vans, a large tent, a lot of children and a lot of noise.

'Right then! I'll leave you to it!' Henrietta jumped down from her driver's seat. 'I left one of the lassies watching my rails.'

'Where exactly are we?' I asked, wondering about the legality of the site. In the middle of a field in the middle of nowhere, by the look of it. It was huge, and bounded by trees on three sides, the road being at the back of us.

'God, Mike, you're so straight!' Henrietta laughed. 'It's not illegal, OK? We know the farmer here, hold a bash a few times a year. That's his wife, see?' She pointed to a woman serving hot drinks and soup from what looked like a converted hot-dog stall. 'Why don't you have a look around? Roxy's here, doing her sword-swallowing and fire-eating business.'

She was often away with circuses and I'd never actually seen her perform. It would be nice to make up for that deficiency now. I squelched my way forward, a further rise in temperature having made a rather muddy mess of the field. Half-a-dozen youngsters instantly tagged along, a motley assortment of boys and girls difficult to tell apart in their unisex clothing, all booted and duffel-coated. I could hear the drone of at least one didgeridoo, with flutes and penny whistles competing for attention above it.

Some of the goods on sale were fantastic. Hand-crafted jewellery. Stained glass. Wood carvings. I wished I'd brought more cash with me. I lingered at each stall, wondering if another envelope would be passed over with my change. This cloak and dagger stuff was getting to me. There was no note and no sign of Tim.

I bought a steaming mug of tea from the farmer's wife. Maybe she would give me a cryptic note or invite me back to the farmhouse. She didn't. I curled my hands around the mug to warm them and wondered what to do.

There was plenty to look at and get involved in but it was quite some time later that the clanging of a hand-bell alerted me to the passing of one of the stilt-walkers, a man wearing a red top hat, red tailcoat and red and white striped trousers. He was announcing that Roxy the Magnificent and Sloppy Joe, the Clown, were in the tent, already delighting and entertaining their audience. Oh well, I thought. Might as well give it a try.

You know what thought did...

Roxy was stunning, and I don't just mean her act. I'd only ever seen her in ordinary clothes before. Close to six feet tall, like her father, and blonde, like her mother, she was built like an Amazonian goddess, and seeing her in her performance costume was something of a shock. She had the kind of body that women would die for and men have heart attacks over. She was wearing thigh-high black boots, fishnet tights and a tiny blue flared skirt – more like a pelmet, really, which clung to her hips. Above that – well, it was all one piece, the bodice and skirt, but let's just say there wasn't a lot of bodice and there was a hell of a pair of breasts trying to stay in it. I think this kind of thing is where you get the expression about trying to put a quart into a pint pot. Snaking down from her right shoulder and across her right breast was a tattoo of what looked like a dragon, its head disappearing into her cleavage. The crowd was enthralled, the men slaves at her feet. When God was giving out the various bits of female anatomy, I figured I'd been short-changed. I'd definitely got the short end of the stick.

She was just finishing her act and as Sloppy Joe the Clown took over, I pushed my way through the crowd to say hello to her. She towered above me, glistening with sweat and smiling a bigger and wider version of her mother's cheek-dimpling grin.

'Hiya, Michal! Good to see you! This must be the first time you've actually caught my act.'

I didn't like to admit I'd just missed it, so said instead, 'Impressive! Majorly impressive!' At which point my mobile rang. It seemed completely incongruous in a place like this, and I answered it furtively as Roxy laughed. What I should have been doing was keeping an eye on Sloppy Joe...

'Mike – it's Patsy – you're going to die! I may be about to ruin your holiday!' The voice was high and fast.

'What? Patsy, slow down!'

'They say there's a first time for everything and we've been lucky to get away with it for this long, right, but – Mike – I'm double booked. I can't do the gig you asked me to cover in the week.'

Is that all? As long as there are no deaths or fires involved, I really don't give a shit! 'Don't worry,' I reassured her. 'It's really not a problem. Look,

I'm in a field in the middle of nowhere and I don't have my diary with me, so I'll give you a ring later and sort it out, OK?'

'Sure.' She sighed heavily. 'I'm really sorry, Mike.'

'Don't be. Everything's fine.'

Was it, hell. No sooner had I put the mobile back in my pocket when he struck. Sloppy Joe, that is.

'...just the person we're looking for! Give her a big hand, folks!'

I was yanked into the Arena. The crowd applauded and Roxy bent double with laughter, nearly spilling out of her top in the process.

'But I...'

'And don't you think she'd look great in this?'

'Yes!' roared the crowd.

I backed away from the advancing Sloppy with my hands in front of me, shaking my head. A mixture of laughter and another 'Yes!' from the crowd greeted my action. The clown kept on advancing, beckoning to Roxy to come and help him. She bounded back into the arena, rubbing her hands with glee.

'Come on, Mike! It's just a bit of fun!' She held me fast as he came towards me, waving a one-piece clown costume that looked like an oversized babies' romper suit. It was pukey pink and bright purple.

'No! Roxy – you don't understand – I...' Anything else I wanted to say was muffled by a mouthful of material. When I emerged – after a long and useless struggle – Sloppy Joe clasped me to his chest before twirling me round for the audience.

'And she doesn't even need a wig! She's already got the hair for the part!'

What a bloody cheek! I take exception to people getting personal. I rounded on him.

'Aaarrgghhh!' he shrieked! 'She's after me!' He ran swiftly to a props table while Roxy held on to me, stuffing a variety of hats on my head and inviting the opinion of the audience. They loved it. She tried a pointy one that fell off. A bowler hat that fell off. A top hat that fell off. The crowd fell about laughing as I struggled. All I wanted to do was fell Roxy or Sloppy the bloody Clown in one swipe. Preferably both of them. She stuffed another hat on my head, shoving my hair up under it, none too gently.

'Ow!' I wailed. It didn't fall off. I was rendered speechless. There was a tap on my shoulder. I turned. Stupid, stupid woman! Splat! Pie straight in the face. I couldn't believe it. I shrieked, Roxy roared, the crowd roared and Sloppy Joe, arm around my shoulder, said straight into my ear, 'Friend to see you. In the van, when you get cleaned up.'

'What?' I turned towards him and got another face full of pie. I stood quivering, trying to wipe it out of my eyes, hearing only, 'Shall I! Shall I!' from Mr Clown Features.

Why can't a crowd yell 'NO'? just for once? This was mob rule. An affirmatory chant was ringing in my ears. I was pushed towards Roxy – I had one eye clear by now – and in my haste to get away, she clutched at me, I wriggled and she grabbed my hat. It and I parted company and I felt my hair tumble once more around my face as the crowd shrieked their encouragement. But the shriek changed timbre, which didn't make any sense. Mr Clown Features spun me round, picked me up from behind, lifting my feet clean off the ground. I could see again now, and what I could see frightened me half to death.

Trouble had broken out and Henrietta seemed to be a part of it, from what I could gauge, directing help towards three men who seemed to be at the centre of the altercation. Fists started to fly and the next thing I knew, Henrietta hurtled towards us, yelling at Roxy, 'Get Mike the hell out of here!' For a split second, all three of us looked at the fracas, then Sloppy ran one way and Roxy pulled me hard enough to almost have my arm out of its socket. It's amazing how fast you can run in an oversized baby's romper suit...

Chapter Seventeen

I don't know if you've ever tried explaining to a couple of police officers what you're doing in a music shop at twenty past eight on a Sunday evening, apparently stealing saxophones whilst dressed as a clown and with Roxy, the Pneumatic Tattooed Amazon as your accomplice.

Believe me, it's not easy.

They wouldn't take me seriously, for a start. Looking like an oversized baby in a romper suit didn't help, I suppose, but then it didn't help, either, that they were so overcome by the sight of a Pneumatic Tattooed Amazon with both breasts not only intact but positively overflowing, that they couldn't see straight for trying to work out exactly where the Dragon's head tattoo went.

I was nearly demented. The gig was due to start at nine and it should have been a simple matter to stop off at the shop, pick up the saxes and get to the pub on time. But I hadn't reckoned on my friendly, highly zealous Neighbourhood Watch, had I? Yes, I told the police, of course I owned the shop. No, I didn't have ID on me – do I look as if I have ID on me? Why was I dressed like this? Doesn't everyone dress like this on a Sunday night in March? They were all for carting us off to the nick until I persuaded them – correction, Roxy persuaded them – to phone Alex for verification of my identity. I closed my eyes and tried breathing exercises while we waited for him to arrive. They didn't work.

When we'd made our escape from the tent, Roxy had shoe-horned me into her MG Midget and roared off like a tiger. She'd asked me what was going on. I'd asked her what was going on. It seemed that neither of us had a clue. I thought she was in on the clown thing, I said. What clown thing, she asked? Darren, a friend of Joe, who was apparently the regular Sloppy Joe, was standing in today and they both did the leap on an unsuspecting member of the public' thing. She'd thought I'd be game for a laugh and had gone along with it.

Then we'd had the nightmare of being followed. Chased by two cars at high speed. She'd made Paul's driving seem positively pedestrian as she'd

169

opened the throttle and eaten up the winding country lanes, taking us further and further away from the Grange in her efforts to shake them off. We were well into Oxfordshire before we lost them and managed to head for Cheltenham and my gig. It was no good me going home for saxes because although I needed an alto as well as a tenor tonight, dear old Dexter was back at the Grange, so, with time rapidly running out, I'd asked her to drop me at the shop. I could have screamed with frustration. If Darren was right, and Tim had been in some van at the fair, just a few more minutes would have got me to the bottom of the mystery.

Alex couldn't stop laughing when he saw me. Well, not until he noticed Roxy's cleavage. She'd said she'd come and watch the gig, then run me back to the Grange. I said she didn't have to and, if Jake was there, he'd give me a lift back. She said she was coming anyway. Alex asked casually if they'd let her into the pub, dressed like that. We didn't think so. Alex lent her his overcoat. One of the police officers coughed politely and asked if they'd let *me* into the pub dressed like that. I shrieked and had to be helped out of the damned romper suit. I was frazzled before I'd even played a note.

The gig went well but Jake wasn't there and I was glad when it was all over. Alex hadn't come with us, having promised to take his wife out for a meal.

'We were nearly out the door when the police phoned,' he told me. 'A couple of minutes later, and then where would you have been?'

'In a cell at Lansdown Police Station,' I growled. 'Ha bloody ha!'

I told him we'd drop the saxophones at my place after the gig and get Raffi to take them back to the shop on Tuesday. I hoped she would be in when I got home. I'm very glad she wasn't.

I knew something was wrong before we even turned into the drive. Lights were blazing from every window and every window was thrown wide open. I must have made some sort of noise because Roxy, who'd been talking about some tightrope walker she knew, braked and asked me what was wrong.

'I'm not sure,' I told her. It didn't take long to find out. Open doors would have been a bad enough sign. Doors hanging off their hinges signalled major trouble.

'Bloody hell, Mike! I think you've been burgled!'

'No shit, Sherlock!' My mouth was dry as I approached the remains of my front door. Roxy overtook me. I put my hand on her arm to stop her going any further.

'What if they're still here?' She ignored me and moved closer. 'Roxy – do you really think this is a good idea? Maybe we should just call the police.'

We both stood still and listened. I live in a detached house with no close neighbours. My burglar alarm should have been deafening. Not a sound. Except running water. There is a stream at the bottom of my garden, but this wasn't it.

'Shit!' I plunged inside, Roxy hard on my heels and within a couple of minutes, we had a pretty good idea of the extent of the damage. Extensive.

171

The taps had been opened, transforming the house into a pretty good replica of a child's paddling pool. Which, I thought, probably meant that whoever had done this hadn't left too long ago, or we would have been swimming by now. We sloshed about, turning off taps and wondering about the possibility of ceilings collapsing through the weight of the water.

Every drawer and cupboard had been emptied and contents strewn across the floor. The TV and video looked as if they'd been hurled from one side of the room to the other, and my music centre had suffered the same fate. I felt suddenly and horribly sick.

'Bloody hell, Mike!' Roxy said for the umpteenth time. 'I hate to ask this, but...'

'I know. We ought to phone the police.'

'Well yes, but I was thinking ... well, about those other saxophones you keep here...' Her voice tailed away.

She was well ahead of me in the forward thinking stakes, and where it mattered most. I pushed past her and slid down the steps to the basement. I'd had it soundproofed and turned into a practice room where I not only keep my instruments but another music centre and copies of all my voice work. The steam coming out of my ears as I surveyed the damage should have been enough to dry out every drop of water in the house. Even Roxy looked sick and shivered, pulling Alex's coat around her. I was shaking myself, more with anger than anything else.

'Bastards! BASTARDS!' I raged.

'Are they – er – very badly damaged?'

172

I nodded yes. Truth be told, I didn't trust myself to speak. I wanted to cry, but was too stunned by the ferocity of the attack. All three saxes – alto, soprano and baritone – looked like someone had taken a lump hammer to them.

'Mike...' Roxy sloshed unhappily from one foot to the other. 'I really think you should call the police.'

I nodded and we made our way back to the kitchen. We looked silently at the mess on the wall where the phone should have been.

'Ah...' Roxy said. 'Your mobile or mine?'

Gaffer arrived just as the police were leaving. I was worried by not knowing Raffi's whereabouts, but he assured me she'd been at the Paradox all evening and, when he'd got my phone call, he'd told her to stay with a friend.

'Whoaaa!' he breathed, surveying the wreckage. 'I hope you're insured, mate!'

'I am,' I told him, inwardly cringing at the thought of what this was going to do to my premiums.

'You look like shit, Mike.'

'God! That's all anybody says to me these days!'

'Sorry!' he winced. 'What I mean is, you look like shit, so how about a nice cup of tea?'

'I'd love one, but I think the makings are all over the kitchen floor.'

'I rather thought they might be. Your phone call was pretty graphic.' He produced a giant thermos from his rucksack. Roxy had left by now, having waited with me until he'd arrived, when she'd decanted the saxes from the Midget and transferred them to the boot of his car. I asked her if she could get hold of Sloppy the Clown and give him my mobile number. This whole business was getting completely out of hand.

'You're lucky the cops came out,' Gaffer commented as he handed me a steaming plastic cup of tea. 'My end of town, they wouldn't have bothered. Just given me a case number and asked me to drop in a list of what's been nicked. What has been nicked, by the way?'

I snorted, which was a mistake with my mouth so close to the cup.

'That's the thing, isn't it?' I mopped at myself ineffectually. 'Nothing, as far as I can tell.'

'What? You mean they did all this and didn't take anything?'

'Looks that way. It's stupid. There's plenty of stuff they could have nicked but it's just been smashed up instead. Come and look at this.' I took him down to the basement, where he shook his head in disbelief, examining the instruments closely.

'It doesn't make sense, Mike.'

'I know.'

He gave me a long look, then shook his head. 'Nah! Not a nice woman like you...'

'What?' I asked.

He shrugged it off. 'If you were certain other people I know, I'd ask who you've been upsetting lately.' I stared at him, the cogs grinding slowly as he continued. 'You don't accidentally turn taps full on. You don't accidentally flatten saxophones. TVs and videos don't hurl themselves around a room. Not unless you've got a poltergeist related to Arnold Schwarzenegger.'

'I know.' I shook my head in frustration. 'But whoever did this could have done it to anyone's house, right?'

'Well, maybe.' His voice was doubtful. 'But there was a lot of stuff they could have nicked and, believe me, there's plenty of punters out there would have bought it. No, Mike. I don't like the look of this at all. Strikes me, someone doesn't like you too much.' I shivered at the thought and Gaffer mistook it for the effects of the cold and wet. 'Come on – you can't stay here like this. I'll get you back to my place. We'll sort things out in the morning. Norman's going to stay and stand guard.'

'I didn't know you'd brought Norman.' I glanced around as if the act of looking could somehow make him appear. Norman was a well-known character around town. Until a few years ago, he'd been a 'gentleman of the road', a tramp, driven there, it was said, by a speech impediment, illiteracy and long term unemployment.

'He's going to stay here until I bring in the preliminary clean-up squad once your insurance chap's been in the morning. And no, mate, it wasn't my idea, and he'll be deeply offended if you object.'

'But where will he sleep?'

'In the garage.'

'Gaffer, he'll freeze!'

'No he won't. He's come armed with a sleeping bag and a hot water bottle. Probably got his thermals on, too. Come on, Mike – he used to sleep rough, you know that. He's used to it and this, to him, is something he can do for you. As far as he's concerned, you're Raffi's Mum, and Raffi taught him to read and write.'

I knew Gaffer was right but was unwilling to concede defeat. Norman had been taken on as janitor/handyperson at the Paradox Centre, largely due to Gaffer's influence. He had a little basement bedsit on the premises, which, rumour had it, was the first roof he'd had over his head in years.

'You know I'm right, Mike,' Gaffer persisted.

'Yes. You're right. Are you sure Raffi's OK?'

'Absolutely. She's staying with Beanie's girl-friend – Beth, is it?'

I nodded. I was shivering with the cold now. There was nothing else we could do here. 'OK, Batman,' I conceded. 'Let's go.'

Chapter Eighteen

You don't realise how much there is to do after something like that. Not until you have to do it. The insurance people. The post. The telephone people. But that's jumping the gun. It would have helped if I'd had a good night's sleep. I didn't. No fault of Gaffer's. He had a nice little house, a terraced job on the edge of St Paul's, absolutely spotless unless you count the snake's nest of leads and cables writhing across the living room floor, punctuated here and there by an effects pedal or an extension cable.

I didn't mind them. It was the dog. He hadn't told me about the dog. Then again, why should he? That's the thing about things you're afraid of, isn't it? You tell the least number of people possible, so you don't look like an idiot. Fear is bad enough in itself. When it's of something that most people wouldn't think twice about, it becomes a secret and potent source of shame. You know it's irrational. Even when it's rational to you because you have good reason for the fear. You know perfectly well that just because you were savaged by a dog when you were six, it doesn't mean all dogs are going to bite you now. You know that. In your head. You know the logic. Trouble is, it's not your logical mind that's in control when you're suddenly faced with the thing you fear. It's your gut. It's the part of you that's still six years old and terrified and doesn't give a bugger about the logic or the fact that you're now pushing forty and haven't been bitten by a dog in the last thirty years. Let's face it, you've spent the last thirty years avoiding dogs at all costs, so there's no wonder you haven't been bitten. You haven't given the buggers a chance. But now you're in a room with a dog and it's bloody stupid and you hate feeling stupid. Would rather die than let someone know just how stupid you feel. Just how afraid you are.

I'd gone through the door before Gaffer. And there it was. A barking, tail-wagging monstrosity of fur and teeth and claws that had 'DOG' written all over it. I looked at it, horrified. It looked at me, interested. Probably wondering what Gaffer had brought home for a nice midnight snack. That's all it took for me to become a quivering lump of jelly. A blob. A puddle. I tried very hard to breathe. I certainly couldn't move, so it seemed like a good idea. To keep breathing, that is.

Gaffer was halfway across the room before he noticed. I was trying – unsuccessfully – to console myself with the thought that at least this thing – dog – was a damned sight bigger than Elynore's pip-squeak of a thing, and therefore more worthy of being afraid of. It only made things worse. Pip-squeak could have taken a chunk out of my ankle. Maybe reached my knees, if it jumped. This thing – dog – could bite my belly without raising its head. Tear my throat out, macerate my face, if it stretched itself slightly. With room to spare.

Imagination is a terrible thing. Good for some people, I suppose. Writers. Artists. Albert Einstein. For a terrified musician in the middle of a panic attack, it's bad. It's very bad. I had this vivid image of my belly gaping, intestines spilling out. All in glorious Technicolor. Said intestines being chewed vigorously while I was still alive. Dog's Dinner...

'Sorry about the mess. Watch where you put your feet. Trying to write some new material and you know what it's like, I... Mike?'

It was a weird feeling. Kind of tingling in my hands. Tightness in my chest. My head was sort of floating. In a tunnel. Blackness closing in around me, from the outside in. It's a good thing I was standing with my back against the door. At least it gave me something to slide down...

I came to on the sofa with my legs elevated on a pile of cushions. Gaffer must have done his First-Aid in the Workplace certificate.

'You all right, mate?' His face was a picture of anxiety.

I struggled to sit up. Gaffer helped me. I saw IT again. The dog. It was alert, ears pricked, tongue lolling out of the side of its mouth. It had big teeth. Very big teeth. My head swam. Was thrust between my knees by a concerned Gaffer.

'Didn't realise the shock had got to you that bad, mate. Bet you haven't eaten anything for hours, either. You stay put – don't try to sit up. I'll get you a glass of water.'

'No!'

'What?'

'Don't leave me. Not with ... that.'

'What?' His eyes followed my horror-stricken gaze. 'Lucy?' He sounded incredulous. I felt about six inches high.

'I'm ... scared – dogs...'

'Bloody hell, Mike – I didn't realise! Thought it was the break-in.'

I raised my eyes. Shuddered. Its – hers – looked steadily back at me. Honey coloured. Like the parts of its fur that weren't black.

'Hold on, mate – I'll put her in the kitchen. Lucy – come!'

It followed him obediently. I breathed, greedy for air. Wished I hadn't. Felt sick. Can't be sick. Not in Gaffer's house. Breathe. Gaffer returned, with the glass, without IT. The dog. Lucy. Lucy! What kind of name was that for a lump of savagery? It should be called Spike or Fang or Killer. I drank some water. Gaffer held the glass. Just as well. Don't think I could have.

'Sorry, mate. I never knew.'

179

'I know. And I know it's stupid. I'm sorry. It's me that should be sorry.' I burst into tears.

'Ah, Mike! I never thought to ask, mate. To tell you. About Lucy. Here...' He produced a box of tissues. Man-Sized. For the World's Worst Wimp.

'Honest to God, she wouldn't hurt you! Wouldn't hurt a fly! She's probably more scared of you, you know. She was rescued, see? Found her in a public lavatory in Stroud. What a state she was in! Starved. Shaking. Nearly bald through mange. She'd been abandoned there with a little Jack Russell. He was too far gone – the vet had to put him down. Wanted to put her down, too. Lucy. But I couldn't. I just – it was her eyes, you know. Pleading. Scared. The vet said he didn't hold much hope for her. She'd been beaten. Kicked. Starved. Cowered when anybody came near her. Especially men. But I was so ... so mad, you know? Outraged that anybody could do that to her. So I said I'd look after her, that I'd persevere with her. He said she had to be spayed before I could have her. Had to wait for that, too, because she wasn't strong enough for the operation. And when I finally brought her home ... she was so scared, you know. Wouldn't bark. Never barked. We reckoned – me and the vet – that she'd been beaten for barking. So I had to teach her. To bark. Took me months. She must have thought I was mad, barking at her. And the first time she did it – barked – she cowered, like I was going to thrash her. Had her tail between her legs and wet herself. And you know what? I hugged her. Rolled round on the floor with her and gave her chocolate drops. Jesus, Mike, I never knew.'

180

I was sitting upright by now, appalled by his story. Her story.

'I won't let her near you, mate. I'll lock her in the kitchen.'

'No you won't! Won't she think she's done something wrong?'

'No. I'll tell her, explain it to her. She knows what fear is.'

'No, Gaffer. I'm the one that should be locked away. This is her home. Just let me have a shower or something and stick me somewhere to sleep. I'll stay out of her way.'

We argued. I won.

I couldn't believe I'd sided with a dog. I hardly slept a wink.

The next morning was a nightmare. My house looked worse in the cold light of day although Gaffer, optimistic as ever, insisted it wasn't as bad as I thought. Norman also was cheerful, claiming to have slept perfectly in his sleeping bag on the floor of the garage. The insurance people were remarkably helpful. I was worried about dealing with them, never having had to make a claim before, but Gaffer said that was probably a point in my favour.

I had a headache by the time I'd dealt with everything, not helped by Raffi's explosive foray into her native language when she saw the damage for the first time. She'd come to check the mail, anxious about her job interview even though this was only Monday and too early to realistically expect any response.

'But how will we get the mail, Mike? And where

is Stix?'

Stix had happily spent the night curled up with Norman. Mrs Rivers, my nearest neighbour, offered to look after her until the house was habitable again. I had a strong suspicion that Stix quite often made herself at home there, anyway. Unlike dogs, with their loyalty to human beings, cats are philanderers and will spend time with anyone daft enough to stroke and feed them. But what about the mail? And the telephone? And the wreckage? I was getting into a state, already hugely overtired and stressed. Gaffer put his hands on my shoulders and shook me gently.

'Come on – I'll cook breakfast at the Paradox Centre. I'm on morning shift today, anyway – Chris is covering for me at the moment because I phoned to say I'd be in late. You're not the only one who has someone to deputise as and when necessary. Don't you worry about a thing. Just leave it to Uncle Gaffer, eh? Whatever I can't sort out myself, you can bet I know a man who can. We'll have a nice, uninterrupted talk. It'll be quiet at this time of the morning.'

It was quiet and we drew up a reasonable plan of action and got the practicalities organised. We weren't completely uninterrupted, however. Henrietta joined us, Roxy having given her the lowdown on the previous evening's events. She had Alex's coat over her arm and wasn't in the best of moods.

'God Almighty, Michal! What the hell is going on? First the yobbos at the fair and now this! Who have you been upsetting?'

Gaffer looked at her sharply. It was almost

exactly the same phrase he'd used when he'd seen the damage.

'What yobbos? What fair?' He and Raffi looked from Henrietta to me and back again.

'Has she not told you? She came to a fair with me yesterday, near Ruttersford, and there she is, off playing silly buggers with Sloppy the Clown and I'm standing by the Old Girl, selling my gear and – well, no, I wasn't actually, you ken – I was taking a break, had one of the girls I know spell me for a wee while, and I hear these three guys talking, right? They're on about how they cannae miss her because of her hair, and keep a close eye out for her and shite like that, and I think to myself, that's Michal Brodie they're talking about, so I saunters along behind them, like, and I keep my eyes and ears open and believe me, I didnae like what I was hearing. Big buggers they were, and no' making a great deal of sense, but they're looking all over for Mike. I knew she was playing the clown because a pal of Roxy's had told me, and sure enough, eventually they go into the tent and I'm holding my breath, right, but I thought she'd be OK because she had this hat on, see, and you couldnae see so much as a hair on her head.' She paused and took a bite out of the chocolate croissant she'd been toying with, brushing crumbs from her mouth. 'Anyway, next thing I know, Roxy pulls her hat off and her hair comes tumbling out and it's like a red rag to a bull. They're all excited, saying "That's her! Split up, don't lose her." And they start off through the crowd, so I signals a couple of the lads I know, tell 'em these guys are trouble, but they must have

183

known they'd been clocked, right, because *then*...'
She took another bite, dribbling chocolate down
her chin. '...before you know it, a fight breaks out,
and I'm yelling at Roxy, Roxy's yelling at Michal,
Sloppy does a disappearing act the envy of Harry
bloody Houdini, and everybody's chasing everybody else. And...' She looked at me as if it were all
my fault. '...Sloppy's no' turned up again. Not
even today. Joe – that's the regular Sloppy – is
none too pleased, to put it mildly. He needs his
stuff back. So–' She turned and looked me
straight in the eye. 'What's going on, Michal?'

Gaffer and Raffi exchanged a look before also
turning their attention on me.

'I honestly don't know.' I said.

'Up yer arse, woman!' Henrietta has all the tact
of a flying mallet when she's annoyed. 'You just
happen to be at a loose end. You just *happen* to
want to come to the fair. There just *happen* to be
some rather unpleasant people looking for you.
And now your house has been turned over. And
you don't know why...'

'This was yesterday? This fair business?' Gaffer
was trying to fit it all together.

Henrietta and I just nodded. She, because she
had her mouth full, I, because I was stalling for
time, trying to think up a plausible explanation
without bringing Tim into things.

'This is a bit of a bloody coincidence, Mike.'
Gaffer was giving me a deeply unhappy look.

'I know. And it doesn't make any sense. I'm not
sure the two things are connected, anyway. I
mean, I don't know exactly when the house was
trashed, and … look...' I flapped my hands help-

lessly. 'I can't explain it and I honestly don't know what's going on.'

'But who are these men who were after you?' Raffi was looking increasingly worried.

'I don't know!' I exploded. At least that was the truth. Not that it made me feel any better.

Gaffer took my hand. 'Look, Mike, if you're in trouble – whatever's happened – we're your friends. We care about you. Just tell us what's going down, mate. We're here to help.'

It was hard to look him in the eye, but I did it. 'I really appreciate your concern. All of you. But I really don't know. Believe me, if I find out, you'll be the first people to know.'

They looked at me for what seemed to be a very long time, saying nothing. Raffi chewed her lip. Henrietta narrowed her eyes, knowing a liar when she heard one, but unable to work out why I was lying. Gaffer was expressionless.

'All right. So what do we do now?' He threw down the question like a gauntlet.

'Go to the police,' Raffi said.

'I've been to the police. Or rather, they came to me.'

'About the house, yes,' Gaffer said. 'What about these bozos, though?'

'Right.' I shook my head. 'Excuse me, Mr Policeman, sir, these strange men chased me through three counties yesterday and I don't know why. I don't know who they are, or what they want, and I didn't get a good look at them. Oh, and they didn't actually damage me... They'll love it.'

'She's right,' Henrietta's admission was grudging.

'Well, I don't like it!' If she'd been a few years younger, Raffi would have stamped her foot.

'I don't like it either, Raffi, and I especially don't like the thought that you could have been in the house when whoever trashed it turned up for their fun and games. I want you to stay away.' Talk about stating the obvious. She couldn't have stayed there if she'd wanted to.

'All right, all right, let's think this through.' Gaffer tapped the table impatiently. 'Raffi, you do as Mike says. Is there somewhere you can stay for the next few days?'

'Yes, but Gaffer, what about the mail?'

'Mrs Rivers will intercept it,' I offered.

'OK. Leave that with me, then, Raffi,' Gaffer told her. 'I'll be there a fair bit on the clean-up operation. Now – what about you, Mike?'

'God, I don't know... I'll have to go back to the Grange, pick up my car, come back here and...'

'No.' Gaffer was brooking no argument. 'That's the one place where no shit's gone down to date.'

Little did he know, although at least, it wasn't connected to me...

'You said they want you to get to know the place, ready for doing this promo video, right?'

'Right.'

'Then what I suggest is, you go back there and do just that. Just stay there until this thing blows over or we get to the bottom of it. It's the only place we can be sure that you'll be safe.'

Right, I thought. I could buy that.

We could all buy that.

Only one problem.

We were all completely wrong...

186

Chapter Nineteen

There were further practicalities to deal with before I could go back to the Grange, particularly as far as Raffi was concerned. I, at least, had spare clothes there; she, thanks to the trashing of the house, was left more or less with only the clothes she was standing up in. I decided it was time to give my credit card an airing.

Not that we needed it much. As well as the Old Girl ambulance, Henrietta has a little basement shop in a road off the High Street and we bought a lot of stuff for Raffi from there. I'm not really into retro gear myself and decided to head off for the Arcades, but not before Henrietta had fixed me up with a couple of hats. I was dubious at her suggestion and amazed that anything fitted my unruly mop. It felt weird, but I was outvoted. Both women said they suited me. I stared at my now strange reflection as Henrietta tucked stray curls beneath the green velvet material of the second one.

'Keep your hair tucked in, now,' she admonished me. 'Remember those guys – it was your hair that was the main means of identification for them.'

'What about this?' Raffi was holding up a long, green velvet coat. 'It's a perfect match and Mike would never normally wear something like it, so that might put them off, too, if they're still after

187

her. Oh God – do they think they still are?'

I shrugged helplessly and allowed my arms to be thrust into the coat. I was surprised at how well it suited me. Henrietta saw my expression and beamed.

'There you go! We'll make a new woman of you yet! You need a fashion advisor, Michal Brodie, and we're it! Bugger the shops in the Arcade – we'll get you kitted out.' They did, too, and Henrietta even found a third hat. She chewed her lip thoughtfully and turned to Raffi.

'I'm still worried about her hair. It's a dead give-away.'

Raffi raised her eyebrows. 'You think...?'

'Aye, I do think.' Henrietta looked at me. 'We should colour it, Mike.'

'What?' My hair has never been near an artificial colourant in its life and I didn't intend to start now. 'No way! I'll wear the hats. Honestly. The only place they'll be off my head is back at the Grange.'

'We-ell...'

'No one is going to see me there,' I insisted. 'Not anyone that counts. Certainly not those blokes from the fair.' I thought of something she'd said earlier. 'Did you say that Sloppy hadn't gone home yet?'

'Aye. God knows where he's got to. And as I said, Joe – the regular Sloppy – is none too chuffed. Darren particularly wanted to do the fair yesterday and Joe said OK, he wouldn't mind a day off, but he needs his outfit and props back. Not to mention the van, of course.' She gave me her calculating, narrow-eyed look again. 'Are you sure you don't know what's going on, Michal?'

'Absolutely sure. It's clear as mud to me.'

I paid for our purchases and was given a generous discount. Henrietta couldn't be too pissed off with me, I decided.

'I still think you should colour your hair.' Her tone was threatening. I had a momentary vision of being pinned down, head over a wash-basin.

'No.' I repeated.

'Yes. You can't be too careful.'

'No!'

'Will you at least think about it?'

'Henrietta...'

Raffi took my arm and told her, as we left, that she'd work on me. I was still wearing the green velvet coat and matching hat. My head felt remarkably warm. Maybe Jake was right about most of your body heat being lost through the top of it. The coat, tailored in the bodice and waist, flared out at the hip and fell in soft folds to my ankles. I had plenty of room to stride out in. I felt good. Green for luck, I told myself.

We returned to the Paradox Centre to eat. It was busy now and I was beginning to feel more relaxed, which enabled me to think more clearly. That rather complicated things, though, as I explained to Gaffer when he took a quick break to sit with us.

'I can't stay at the Grange for more than a couple of days,' I told him. 'I've got a whole set of consecutive gigs here in Cheltenham and it would be a killer going backwards and forwards, especially once we get into race week.'

'Right. I would offer you my place to crash, but

with Lucy...'

'What kind of dog is she?' I asked. 'Apart from big?'

'She's a cross between a lurcher and an Irish Wolfhound.'

'That's big!' Raffi laughed. 'But what's the problem?'

Gaffer smiled and avoided my eye as he answered. 'Mike's allergic to dogs.'

'I never knew that! And yet you're OK with cats!'

'One of those things,' I shrugged, throwing Gaffer a grateful glance. I'd worked hard, over the years, not to transmit my fears to Raffi.

'Tell you what, mate – why don't we have a word with Aunty Joan?' Mention of her name reminded me that I needed to speak to her anyway. 'She doesn't keep pets,' Gaffer pointed out. 'When do you need to come back?'

'Thursday, I think. I've got rehearsals with the band I did the TV gig with, then a stint with the Green Glittery Jacket Mob, then straight in on the "working flat out all through race week" business.'

Raffi stifled a giggle. 'Is Lady Day ready yet?'

'I doubt it. Oh damn. It's a good thing you mentioned that. I've got the saxes I borrowed from the shop yesterday, and I can return the tenor, but with my own saxes being trashed, I'd better keep the alto and collect a soprano before I go back to the Grange. I'll need them for these gigs.'

'I'll run you up to the shop on the way to the Grange, then,' Raffi offered. 'I'm not working

until this evening, so we've got plenty of time.'
She was working in a restaurant at present.

'I'm really sorry to put you guys to all this trouble.'

'No trouble!' they said together. With friends like these, I felt bad holding back about Tim. Still, I reasoned, I didn't have anything to tell them that made any sense yet. I'd tell them when the time was right. If it ever were. I shifted uneasily in my seat, wondering if and how and when Tim would get in touch again. After yesterday's shenanigans at the fair, I was taking far more seriously his warning to 'see all, hear all and say nothing'. What had happened to Tim and Darren, though? I could only hope they'd made their getaway and were lying low somewhere. It was only as that thought crossed my mind that I realised I was connecting everything back to Tim. Which still didn't make sense.

'You look tired, Mike. Shall we make a move?'

'Sure,' I agreed, adding hesitantly, 'Actually, I was just thinking about Tim. The fire and everything.'

Gaffer looked uncomfortable. 'I don't know if you've heard, Mike...'

'About the second body? Henrietta told me yesterday. What a mess.'

'Well, yes, but...' He looked at Raffi. 'I don't know if you've heard this yet, either.'

'What?'

'Well, apparently, Tim might not have died in the fire after all.'

'But the bodies – Tim and Sherrill...' Raffi's mouth was agape. My heart was hammering.

191

'Maybe not. They haven't made a positive ID yet, but the point is, well... look, I don't know an easy way to say this, so I'm just going to have to tell you straight, OK?'

'Tell us what, Gaffer?' I watched him carefully, keeping my face blank.

'The thing is, someone reckons that someone saw Tim running away. When the house was burning. The police...'

'Running away? He's not dead? But – I don't understand!' Raffi looked at me in bewilderment.

'The police are taking it seriously,' Gaffer went on. 'They want him to come forward and help with their enquiries.'

'But they can't ... they can't think he had anything to do with it!' Her bewilderment had changed to outrage.

'I'm just telling you what I heard, OK?'

'But that's bollocks! There's no way Tim would start a fire! Or run away from one without Sherrill.'

'I know, Raffi.' I was trying to calm her down.

'Maybe it was an accident. Maybe he got scared. Who knows?' Gaffer said.

'You don't know Tim like I do, Gaffer! If he was there, he would have come forward! He wouldn't be running away! Never!'

'Come on, Raffi,' I said, taking her arm. 'It's not Gaffer's fault. Don't shoot the messenger, remember?' I stood up.

Gaffer pushed back his chair and rubbed his face. 'Hold on a sec – if you're going via the shop, Henrietta left Alex's coat here. I was going to drop it in tomorrow. You're shut today, aren't you?'

'Yes,' I confirmed, a sinking feeling assailing my stomach. I was remembering the fun and games of yesterday evening. God, was it really only last night? Would I be able to get in today without being arrested?

The answer was yes. We got in without the police paying us a visit. A couple of other people did, though. Their names were Cynthia and Dave Woodward. They were Thirty-Somethings, pale, eager and dressed in matching blue anoraks, woolly hats and jeans. They even had matching wire-rimmed spectacles. They tapped on the door as I was sorting out my instruments. Raffi shouted, 'We're closed!' and pointed to the sign on the door. They kept smiling and tapped again. Raffi rolled her eyes at me and went to speak to them.

'We know you're closed, but we wanted a word with Mrs Brodie. We're your Neighbourhood Watch representatives.' I groaned inwardly. They were probably the people who'd phoned the police last night.

'We phoned the police last night when we thought someone was breaking in. Terribly sorry, as it turned out to be you. Not that we would have known it was you, of course, ha! ha!' Dave turned to Raffi. 'Did you know she was wearing a clown outfit?'

'You were wearing what?' Raffi looked at me as if he'd said I was naked and having an orgy in the window.

'And her friend was ... well, sort of Wonder-woman or something,' his wife chipped in. She – who was stick-thin and probably flat-chested – it was difficult to tell under the voluminous anorak – looked terminally deflated.

'Roxy the Pneumatic Tattooed Amazon,' I explained for Raffi's benefit. Henrietta hadn't told anyone about that part of the proceedings.

Cynthia looked afflicted by the words. 'Yes, well...'

'Well, one can't be too careful, and we know how you've built up this business over the years, and what if it had been a gang of musical instrument thieves, eh?' Dave was very hale and hearty. Probably the most excitement he'd had in years. Seeing Roxy, that is.

'It was very kind of you – very public spirited – to be so alert on my behalf. Thank you very much.' *Now take the hint and bugger off...* Not likely.

'Not at all, not at all. That's what we're here for, and it's the least we could do. What are neighbours for, eh?'

I suddenly felt churlish and wished I'd had similar ones looking out for my house.

'You were really efficient, and I'm very grateful.' I stood awkwardly, not knowing quite what else to say, while they stared at me eagerly, earnestly, as if waiting for a pat on the back or something.

Cynthia nudged Dave, who cleared his throat. 'Er, actually, there's something we wanted to ask you, though it's not connected with that, but seeing as we found a chance to speak to you...'

'Well, it's two things, actually,' Cynthia said anxiously. 'Go on, Dave, ask her.'

I got the twin earnest looks again. Raffi, standing slightly behind them, had the kind of look on her face that forewarned an outburst at any moment if I didn't do something.

'What is it you wanted to ask?' I prompted.

'Yes. Well, first, it's to do with our daughter, Samantha.' Earnest looks again. Maybe they thought I was only disguised as a clown yesterday and believed that my real vocation was that of mindreader.

'Samantha?'

'Right. You see, she started secondary school last September and she so wants to play the saxophone, and you know how music is getting shoved out of the curriculum, and anyway, what we wondered was, you see, is do you take private pupils?'

'Would you give her lessons, that's what we're asking.'

'I'll certainly talk to her, see what her interests are.' I told them.

'Oh good!' they chorused.

'But I'm not really around much for the next couple of weeks. If you'd like to give me your address and phone number?'

Dave scrambled to do so, pulling a notebook and pen from one of his pockets. I wondered if Cynthia had a matching set in one of hers.

'And what was the other thing?' I asked as he scribbled away.

'Oh! Yes! Well, we understand that you play in several bands?' Cynthia was almost quivering.

'That's right.'

'Well, it's Dave's mother, you see. She's coming up for her eightieth birthday. Dave was the baby of the family, a bit of a shock to her, really, weren't you, Dave?'

'Rather! She thought she was having the menopause and had me instead!'

Behind them, Raffi's shoulders were shaking. I studiously avoided catching her eye.

'So...' I cleared my throat. 'It's Dave's mother's eightieth. So how can I help?'

'Well, I know it's unlikely you could do it yourself – I expect your bands are all jazz and stuff.' Dave handed me the piece of paper, making 'jazz' sound like a dirty word. 'But we thought at least you'd have the contacts, might know someone who knows someone, sort of thing? What we really want – what Mum really wants – is Thirties and Forties stuff, you know?'

Raffi had a sudden coughing fit. 'Excuse me – I must have got a frog in my throat. Isn't that great, Mike?' She looked at them, an idyllic beam on her face. 'Mike knows just the band for that job, don't you?'

She's lucky I love her. Anyone else would have had the nearest available instrument up a sensitive part of their anatomy. Not necessarily sharp end first, either...

It was a relief to finally be on our way back to the Grange. Raffi laughed so much when she got into the car, I didn't think she'd be able to drive.

'Thanks very much for volunteering the Green Glittery Jacket Mob!' I harumphed. 'Now I'll have to phone Frederick and ask if he wants the booking!'

'Then while you're on the phone, you can tell him that he'll have to get another tenor player!

196

But did you SEE them? When they left?'

I had seen them. Cynthia and Dave had walked along the road together, arms around one another's waists, hands in their partner's back jeans pocket.

'She thought she was having the menopause and she was having me instead!' Raffi mimicked. 'What a bargain!'

As she drove past the private apartments, we saw Warren, Elynore, Maggie and Jake standing together in animated conversation. Warren gave a half-wave as Jake shook his head and Maggie flapped her arms in an over-sized shrug. Elynore's face was pinched with anger.

'Looks like trouble!' Raffi muttered, slowing down and lowering the window.

'You all right?' I called.

'Michal! So glad you're back. Maggie tells us you've had a spot of bother?' Warren smiled, but anxiety showed in his eyes.

'You could say that,' I grimaced.

'Well, we've had a spot of bother ourselves. Intruder alarm. Not that we can find anyone.'

'Is anything missing?' The last thing they needed was a burglary just before they were due to open.

'No.' He shook his head. 'As Maggie says – it must have been the bloody ghost. And I don't mean my racehorse, either.'

Chapter Twenty

I learned more about the ghost, but not until the following morning. Maggie popped by briefly after Raffi had safely delivered me to Rosemary Cottage, but was obviously distracted. I felt somewhat the same myself, realising that I was more tired now than I had been before I'd arrived, over a week ago. *Some holiday this has turned out to be*, I thought. I needed to seriously catch up on some rest if I were to get through my forthcoming gigs. Maggie had been apologetic about leaving me so soon, aghast at what I told her about the trashing of my house.

'We'll catch up in the morning, Mike, I promise. I've got you down for the guided tour, if you're up to it. Also, it's Arthur's funeral in the afternoon. We're all going – the Companions are doing a guard of honour. I know you didn't know him but ... well, I wondered if you'd come? Alison's conducting the service and his nephew is coming and, as you and Alison found him...'

'OK.' I didn't relish the prospect, but what else could I say?

'Thanks, Mike. I'll see you tomorrow.'

Jake had called by later, also in apologetic mood, this time because he hadn't turned up for my gig.

'I'm real sorry, Michal. Had rather an emergency, I'm afraid.'

'The intruder alarm business?'

'No. Something else.' Whatever it was, he was obviously not going to elaborate. 'But let me have a list of where you're playing – I promise I'll come, maybe later in the week or something?'

I'd pulled out the trusty Filofax, realising with dismay that I was relying on it more and more. I was so tired and so busy, I simply couldn't seem to remember dates at present. He asked about the house trash, too, though I tried to make light of it, not wanting another interrogation about who I'd been upsetting.

'Just mindless vandalism by the look of it,' I told him. 'That's one disadvantage of living in a big house with no close neighbours.' I extolled the virtue of Neighbourhood Watch in the incident at my shop, not realising until it was too late that I was digging a hole for myself by making it necessary to explain to him what I'd been doing dressed as a clown. I wound up lying, saying that I'd forgotten the time and had to make a dash for it. I could see he wasn't convinced. He appeared to be weighing up whether or not it was worth pursuing the matter and must have decided it wasn't, because he simply asked if I'd be at the funeral tomorrow. I said yes and he left me to a little saxophone practice and an early night.

The following morning saw me at the main entrance to the Grange, being greeted by Philippa as any tourist would be in a couple of weeks' time. Maggie accompanied us and it was quite some tour. My stint with the trainee guides had not prepared me for just how extensive and sumptuous the house was. I was propelled into a different world and several other ages, so far removed from my present worries that I was lulled into a wonderland of intrigue and culture that was mine, for a while, by association. I trailed from floor to floor, staircases, corridors, alcoves, nooks and crannies providing constant surprise and pleasure. Names and dates wafted into my ears and out again, supplanted by further information. I felt like Alice in Wonderland, the tour providing a feast for the senses. Colours, fabrics, textures, paintings and furniture the like of which I'd never seen before, swamped me. History became suddenly alive, monarchs only vaguely remembered from school lessons now becoming real people. It was a glorious excursion into escapism and I was duly entranced.

I remembered the autograph room, of course, having changed my imaginary baby there, but was now being led down a corridor and up some steps. I shivered suddenly, thinking it strange that there should be such a sudden drop in temperature. Perhaps the heating wasn't working properly here.

'And this is the famous nursery,' Philippa was saying.

'Of the famous ghost!' Maggie added.

'What ghost?'

'Who didn't read the brochures properly?' Maggie pulled a face at me. 'The ghost that keeps setting off the intruder alarm! No – Philippa will tell you the proper story.'

She did. It seemed that in the 1600s, Mary de Beauvoir had been brought to the Grange as the young bride of the elderly Sir Robert de Coverley. He had been married twice before, but remained childless. Mary gave birth to a daughter, Ghislaine, but died shortly afterwards, probably of puerperal fever, so prevalent at that time. Robert was inconsolable but doted on his daughter. This room had been her nursery but one morning, the nurse entered to find only an empty bed. Ghislaine was never seen again. I had goose-bumps by the time Philippa finished telling the story.

'Is this true, or just a tourist gimmick to pull the punters in?'

'Oh, it's true!' Maggie assured me.

'They tore the place apart,' Philippa said, 'looking for the child. Searched the grounds, the village, everywhere. Even tried the nurse as a witch.'

'God! And Ghislaine was never found?'

'Never. And Robert never got over it. His dying words were "Ghislaine! Ghislaine!"' Her voice seemed to echo around the room, an eerie and unwelcome reminder of the terrible associations she had just described.

'How old was she when she disappeared?'

'Three.'

I shivered again, looking around me at what had suddenly become the scene of the crime. The room was small and quite beautiful to look at, yet still I felt uncomfortable.

'It makes me do that, too – shiver,' Philippa remarked. 'Quite illogical, of course.'

I pulled myself together. 'And this ghost – Ghislaine – sets off your intruder alarm?' I looked at Maggie sceptically. 'That's a good tale for the tourists.'

'It's not one we'll be telling the tourists! And

it's true. Let me put it this way. Since we had the system installed, the alarm has gone off several times, always indicating an intruder here. In this room. And we've never found anyone.'

'But that's ridiculous!'

'I quite agree. We've combed every inch and can find no explanation for it whatsoever. Quite frankly, it's a bloody nuisance. You can guarantee that the one time we ignore it, there really will have been a break-in, so we have to turn out regardless.'

'Could it be a fault in the system?'

'Apparently not. That's the first thing we thought of, certainly that Jake did. I don't think he's into ghosts. Rather like you, really. But no, the system is fine. Jake says so, and so do the people who installed it. Rather a mystery, all in all.'

'Could it be something like ... I don't know – say a mouse?'

'Oh, sorry to interrupt, but that's reminded me,' Philippa put in. 'The guides' staff room, Maggie – there's a most awful smell. It's only happened since the heating was put on, but I do think we need to do something about it. Mask it.'

'But what do you think it is?'

'In my previous place of employment, we used to have a similar problem, although the smell wasn't quite so bad. There, it was mice trapped behind the panelling. When they die, of course, with heating on, it causes the smell. It will go eventually, but we need to take action in the meantime.'

'Sounds horrible!' I grimaced.

'Yes,' Maggie agreed. 'We'll show Mike the

priests' hole, then I'll come and have a look at the staff room.'

The priests' hole was in a long, galleried room and ingeniously hidden.

'Heaven only knows how Arthur worked it out!' Maggie shook her head in admiration. 'That's the point, I suppose. There are no records of priests being captured here, although later testimony asserts that many were hidden. Whoever designed it knew what they were doing.' Maggie demonstrated the mechanism and invited me to go inside. I declined politely. 'It's so frustrating,' she went on. 'We know that this was very much a temporary hiding place and believe that there was a larger one which actually had an escape tunnel to the outside, so the priests could get well away. Arthur was determined to find it. I'm sure he would have, too, given time.'

'What time is the funeral?' I asked.

Maggie looked at her watch. 'Oh – we don't have long. I think we should break for lunch. Philippa can give you the rest of the tour another time.'

'OK.' They went off to sort out the smell in the staff room and I went back to the cottage. The enchantment had melted away. I was glad to get outside again, to put distance between myself and stories of disappearing children and priests hiding in fear of their lives. I not only needed lunch, I needed a good blast on the sax to chase the stories away.

The Companions of the Crooked Staff turned out in costume and in force for Arthur's funeral, six of them carrying the coffin, the rest joining in a guard of honour as it was carried out of the church at the end of the service. Arthur's nephew addressed the congregation, thanking them for the welcome Arthur had received in the village and telling them about the many letters he had received from his uncle, describing his involvement in village life and how much he had enjoyed living there.

Alison conducted the service with feeling, confiding in me afterwards that she had been almost sick with nerves, wanting so much to do it well, yet, because she had known him and had the shock of finding his body, afraid that she would break down.

'It's so much worse when you know the person,' she said.

'Can't see how it could be otherwise. Maybe that's as it should be,' I told her. 'Anyway, you did a magnificent job.'

'Thanks. Are you coming to the reception?'

'Well... I don't know...'

'Please, Mike? It's at the vicarage and William, the nephew, wanted to meet both of us. And everyone will be there. You needn't stay long.'

'All right,' I conceded. She gave me a hug.

'You look lovely, by the way – that green really suits you.'

'Thanks.' I was wearing the green coat and hat bought from Henrietta on Monday, though on this occasion, I'd allowed my curls to protrude just a little.

The reception was packed and animated. Arthur had obviously been very well liked. 'Did you organise this yourself?' I asked Alison.

'No – with help from William and Mrs Frewin

– Arthur's next door neighbour.' She indicated a plump, elderly woman sitting on a sofa talking to Edward.

'The Companions did well, didn't they?' I smiled.

'Oh yes. Edward took it very seriously.'

With so many people present I was uncomfortably warm but didn't want to take off my coat as I wasn't planning on staying long. I unbuttoned it, and stuffed the hat into my right-hand pocket. I caught Jake watching me and smiled.

'It suits you,' he said, moving in close. 'I thought you said you couldn't wear a hat?'

'I didn't think I could. Obviously hadn't tried the right sort. This was a friend's idea.'

'Here you go – oh damn!' Alison was carrying sherry for both of us and nearly spilled it as something fell from her grasp.

'I've got it!' I said, stooping to retrieve a bunch of keys.

'Stupid of me – no pockets,' she apologised. She was wearing a tailored black suit and a white blouse. 'Spare set of keys for Arthur's house,' she explained. 'I need to give them to William.'

'Well, I have a pocket to spare, so they're in there until you need them,' I offered, slipping them into the pocket that didn't have the hat in, as I eyed Arthur's nephew, who was now in conversation with a couple of very elderly men.

'Academics. Old colleagues of Arthur's.' Alison explained. 'Come on – get that sherry down your neck and let's get it over with. I know you're not looking forward to this.' Jake raised his eyebrows as Alison pulled me away.

William was a very nice man. Large in girth, with blue eyes and white hair, he had not followed the academic tradition of his family but gone into International Banking, from which he was about to retire.

'It's good to meet you, Mrs Brodie, though I wish it had been under better circumstances. Nonetheless, I must thank you, as I have Alison, for the help you gave. It must have been a shock, finding Uncle Arthur, and I'm sorry you had to go through that.'

'No, really – I'm only sorry we couldn't save him. And it was Alison who did all the work.'

'Well, I'm glad he's properly laid to rest now.' This came from Mrs Frewin, Arthur's neighbour, who was wiping her eyes with a lace-edged handkerchief. 'He was good to me, so thoughtful – a real gentleman. Always checked on me in the bad weather, offered to do my shopping and all.' She blew her nose delicately. 'It was terrible after he died. Terrible. He was unquiet, you know. Didn't rest.'

William kept a polite expression on his face as Alison gave me a warning glance.

'Really?' I murmured. Well – what else can you say to something like that?

'Really.' She nodded solemnly. 'Didn't rest for days. I heard him, you know. Heard him moving about.'

'In his house?'

'Oh yes!' She sniffed and drew herself up in her chair. '"Arthur," I said to him, "'Tis no good arguing with your Maker, the Almighty. You move on, now. You've earned your rest."' She wiped her

206

eyes again. 'It's so sad. So very sad. But I told the vicar, didn't I?' Alison nodded. 'And she came in with me. I had a spare key, you see, in case he was ever taken poorly himself. And she said prayers and all, and it must have worked, because I never heard him after that. And now he's been properly laid to rest.' She gave a watery smile.

Alison led her away, telling her that she'd feel better after a nice cup of tea. William and I looked at one another rather awkwardly.

'Strange, the way these sorts of superstitions carry on, don't you think?' he asked.

'I guess so. What will happen to his house now?' I was trying to steer the conversation to rather more mundane matters.

'Well, I'll sell it, I suppose. He left it to me. His money, he left to charities and the university, and I certainly don't need another house. I have one in Cambridgeshire and one in the Bahamas. So yes, I'll probably put it on the market.'

'Oh – Alison had spare keys she wanted to give you, and gave them to me for safe keeping.' I put my hand in my pocket only to feel a flush of panic as I was unable to find them. 'They must be here!' I assured him. I even pulled my hat out of the other pocket. Still no keys. William's polite expression was now aimed at me. 'I'm terribly sorry...' I pulled my left hand pocket inside out, only to find a hole. I shook my coat, feeling something move against my ankle. I felt a flood of relief. 'They've dropped down the lining.' Wriggling my fingers through the hole, I gathered up the material until I got to the hem. 'Here we are! That gave me a fright – I thought

I'd lost them.'

William smiled as he took the keys from me. 'You really ought to mend that, you know!'

'Yes,' I agreed, with an embarrassed shrug.

I'm awfully glad I didn't.

Chapter Twenty-one

I didn't leave the funeral reception early after all, and when I got back to Rosemary Cottage, Paul was parked outside. 'You know what they say about bad pennies!' I told him.

'That's me – I always turn up in the right place at the right time.' He got out of the car and gave me a good looking over.

'I like that green – it suits you. Even the hat. I didn't know you could wear hats.' I'd put it back on for my walk from the vicarage.

'Thanks!'

'Not at all. It rather matches the awful remains of your black eyes.'

'You're a real charmer, Paul!'

'I do try!' Smiling, he dangled a carrier bag in front of me. 'Thought you might like to look this over before your session with the lads tomorrow. I would have got it to you earlier, but there appears to have been a mishap at your house. I tried there first.'

'Honestly, Paul! Why don't you just call me on the mobile first and check where I am? You'd save yourself a lot of time and petrol.'

'And spoil my fun?' He shook his head. 'No, darling. I'd be utterly bored, sitting at home all day making phone calls. You know me – I like to be out and about and doing things.'

Paul's face showed a sudden interest in something behind me. I turned to see other members of the funeral party trailing along the path. Edward was at the head of the group of Companions. Maggie, Jake and the Myatts made up a smaller group at the rear and Alison was running to catch up with them.

'You've been to a funeral I understand?'

'How did you know that?'

'Well, oddly enough, it felt rather like a ghost town when I arrived. Couldn't find any of the usual crowd to leave the bag with.' He waved it in my face again. 'Finally, I found some young man in the garden who said there was a funeral. No one I know, I hope?'

'Not even anyone I knew.' I told him about it, briefly explaining how I had come upon Arthur's body.

'Good God, woman! That must have been hideous.'

'It was, rather. I flunked it completely, to be honest, Paul. There's no way I could have given him mouth to mouth. All I could think of was my husband's death, all those years ago. It just all came flooding back. It's a bloody good thing Alison was there. Not that it did any good.'

'You're much too hard on yourself. Anyway – take this off my hands.' He thrust the bag at me. 'I have to be off. Got a minor headache with one of my Hard Rock lot. Well – *he's* got the headache

209

– hitting the juice too much. So – look at the dots and run through, or whatever it is you musicians do. I'll see you at the rehearsal tomorrow evening. And stop beating yourself up.'

'You'll be there?'

'Of course! Having been matchmaker to your various talents, I wouldn't miss it for the world!' He looked at me, smiling. 'You want the truth, Mike? I love being with musicians because more than anything else, that's what I wanted to be. And as you well know, I can't play a bloody thing. Second-hand kicks, that's what it is. Living vicariously. If I can't be a musician, at least I can organise the buggers.'

'Well – you do it very well – most of the time!'

'I won't let you forget you said that! See you tomorrow.'

'I'll be there,' I promised.

I took the dots inside and cast a brief eye over them before going to Maggie's office to pick up more notes about the guided tour and resume proceedings. I was itching to play through the stuff, but had promised, at the vicarage, to let Maggie finish off the guided tour for me.

I hauled myself to the top of the Tower to find her with her shoes off, feet up and kettle on.

'God, I'm glad that's over!' she said. 'Still, it was a good turn out, don't you think?'

'Sure was. Who were the two old men you were flirting with?' I teased her.

'Flirting? You have to be kidding! A couple of Arthur's old colleagues. One of them was very keen to complete his research on the Grange. I said he'd have to speak to the nephew – not that it will do him much good – his papers haven't been found.'

'What do you mean?' I frowned. 'They can't just have disappeared!'

'All too likely, I'm afraid. Probably at the bottom of the pool. Honestly, Mike, he never let them out of his sight. Pound to a penny, he was clutching them when he fell in.'

'How awful! All that work for nothing.'

'Yes.' She wiggled her toes and stretched like a cat. 'Aromatherapy massage is a wonderful thing.'

'What?' She'd lost me.

'You missed your appointment yesterday, remember? So I had it on your behalf.'

'Oh God! I could have really done with that, too!'

'I'll give the Centre a ring – you could have one tomorrow, if she's free.' She picked up the phone, chatted, then looked at me and asked, 'Nine-thirty suit you?' I nodded. She confirmed the appointment and hung up. 'This time, go!' she ordered.

'I will, I will! I was rather tied up with other things.'

'Is it very bad? The house?'

'Don't ask!' I ran my hands through my hair in distraction at the thought. 'It was like Ground flaming Zero. I ought to give Gaffer a ring later, see how things are going. I feel really uprooted.'

'Oh, Mike.' She swung her feet off her desk and padded round to stand in front of me. 'Some break this turned out to be, eh? Tell you what – why don't we go away together, once the tourist season is over? Just the two of us?'

'No, Maggie – you'll be wanting to spend time with Steve and Katie!'

'That doesn't mean I don't want to spend time with you. And besides...' The kettle had clicked and she went over to make the tea. '...we'll need to talk about bridesmaid's outfits. I was thinking of shocking pink for you, seeing as how it's your favourite colour! Joke! Joke!'

I turned to her in amazement, 'You want me to be a bridesmaid? Maggie, you're crazy!' I stood for a moment with my mouth open. 'Then it's true – what Katie said! Oh my God! How can you just *spring* this on me?! I want all the details – when did Steve propose? Did he go down on one knee? And you're planning the *wedding* already? What about the engagement?' My eyes homed in on her left hand. 'Are you going to have a ring?' And then, as much to my own astonishment as hers, I burst into tears.

'Oh, Mike! You sound like Paul on speed!' Maggie shook as she hugged me. I don't think she knew whether to laugh or cry at my outburst. Crying obviously won, as her own face was wet as she held me at arms' length and proffered a tissue. 'And you, the hardened cynic!' She shook her head. 'Mike Brodie, the *un*romantic! I'll tell all later – or rather *we* will. We want you to join us – help us celebrate. Bring the saxophone to serenade us! Which reminds me – you were getting a right old earful from Mrs Frewin. What was that all about?'

'Maggie! *Now* who's changing the subject?!' She refused to be swayed and I blinked hard, struggling to change gear from the freshly-sprung eruption of her love-life to the old woman's superstitious fear, finally managing to collect my thoughts sufficiently to tell her about the old woman's belief that Arthur had been 'unquiet' after his death.

'She seriously believed that?'

'Oh yes. She was adamant. She genuinely believed that Arthur – well, his ghost – was on the loose. Reckoned he was thumping about, the night he died. Only she didn't know then that he was dead, of course. Said that's why she found it so hard to believe, when she heard the news, because she'd heard him thumping about, which apparently was unusual.' I concentrated, trying to get it straight. I'd thought I'd heard the last of the saga when Alison had taken her away for a cup of tea, but no, she'd managed to collar me again on her return, whilst William had managed to make a hasty exit.

'Yes,' I said. 'That was it. He was thumping about, only it couldn't really have been him, of course, because he was lying dead in the pool. She reckons he was at it the following night as well, and nothing could convince her otherwise. She was too scared to go round there by herself but she got Alison to go into the house with her and said most definitely he'd been there in an unquiet state because some of his things had been moved.'

Maggie looked at me sharply. 'It couldn't have been burglars, could it? Oh God – what if anything was stolen.'

I shook my head. 'That was my first thought, of

course, but both Alison and Mrs Frewin confirmed that nothing had been taken.'

'His ghost, eh? What a state!'

'Quite,' I agreed. 'Still, she seems better now,
according to Alison, anyway. He's had the proper
ceremony, so he's moved on.'

'It's the classic thing, isn't it?' Maggie mused.
'A ritual to mark something off.'

'Closure. Yes, I think you're right.'

'Paul doesn't give you any closure, though,
does he?' she laughed. 'He certainly keeps you on
your toes!'

'Oh, don't...' I groaned.

Her eyes twinkled with amusement. 'You had
the tongues wagging again – mysterious messages
the other day. Carrier bags being exchanged. And
now he's back with another one! What are you up
to?'

'Business!' I told her. 'Nothing more, nothing
less. Don't tell me – now they know he's gay, so I
can't be having a passionate fling with him, the
locals have turned him into my pimp, or think
we're drug dealing!'

'Something like that!' she agreed. 'Are you sure
you won't have a biscuit?'

'Oh go on, then – twist my arm!' I wondered if
massage was any good for getting rid of calories.
I seemed to have done nothing but eat like a
horse since I'd come here.

'Actually, it was suggested that we put Paul on
file as a useful contact for bands and such like.
He wouldn't do anything awful, would he, like
send us one of those that groan about death and
puke up all over people?'

'Even Paul's not that bad!' She flipped through her Rolodex and looked at me expectantly. I gave her his details. 'He has a mobile, too, of course, but I can't remember the number off the top of my head. My battery just died, so I can't pull it out of my own for you. It's in my Filofax, though. I'll give it to you later,' I promised.

'OK.' She looked at her watch. 'Well, Madam, I know you've had more than your fair share of ghost stories for the day, but shall we get the rest of the tour over with? Do you think you can stand it?'

'Oh, just about. But only if you fill me in on the proposal!' I heaved myself out of the chair.

She did it as we walked. Steve had gone for the works. With Katie out of the way, he'd arranged the room, filling it with candles and roses.

'Gave me the shock of my life when I walked in!' The smile as she said it lit her face from ear to ear. 'And he was shaking, poor man – could barely get the words out. He told me afterwards that he was terrified I'd say no!'

'And you're sure? Both of you?' The question was clearly superfluous but I had to ask.

'Absolutely. He loves me to bits. And I love him to bits. Katie as well. Two for the price of one! And who knows – maybe I'm not too old...' She blushed, something I'd never seen her do before. 'I'd so love to have a child with him. A sister or brother for Katie. But if I can't – well – I still have the two of them. Anyway–' she punched me lightly on the arm as we turned a corner. 'I'm serious about you being my maid of honour, though not in pink and we haven't set a date yet.

But the engagement will be announced once the opening of the Grange is out of the way. We'll get the ring then.'

'I am so happy for you, Maggie!' I hugged her, recognising even as I did so that I was suffering a pang of jealousy. Not at her happiness but at the fact that she had done for Steve what my lovers had not done for me – accepted Katie as part of the deal.

The tour was underway with a vengeance, now, and her enthusiasm was once again infectious. Coupled with my near euphoria at her engagement I got completely carried away and said, 'Wouldn't it be great if we could find the other priests' hole?'

'Think again!' she laughed. 'Dream on, even! If Arthur *had* worked it out, the secret's gone to the grave with him.'

By the end of the afternoon, I was convinced that Maggie was right. She told me of his various theories and how they'd all been tried out, without success.

'He was nothing if not persistent,' she sighed. 'Like a dog with a bone. Kept on gnawing and ferreting away. I do believe he would have cracked it in the end.'

'Well...' It was my turn to look at my watch. 'I'm going to head off, if we're finished. I want to speak to Gaffer and, God help me, I have to speak to Frederick about an eightieth birthday party gig. Wouldn't hurt to talk to Alex, either, I guess. The poor man must think I've abandoned him.'

'Fat chance!'

'I know. He's brilliant.' I waved as I walked away. 'See you tomorrow! After my massage.'

'How about before?' she suddenly asked, a gleam in her eye. 'I'll pop over in a bit. Run an idea by you.'

'OK,' I agreed.

Back at the cottage, I made my calls. Gaffer was in optimistic mood, saying that things would be sorted out sooner than I expected. He also told me he'd arranged for me to stay with Joan on my return to Cheltenham.

'Gaffer! Joan runs a hotel and there won't be a single room anywhere that hasn't been booked for race week! Punters plead to sleep on floors in people's homes, for God's sake!'

'I know that and you know that, but Joan says she's got it sorted and is looking forward to seeing you.' He didn't elaborate, so I turned to my next call.

Alex was also cheerful and pleased to have his coat back. It was, he told me, still impregnated with the scent of Roxy the Pneumatic Tattooed Amazon which might take a bit of explaining to his wife. I laughed. 'At least she's not *seen* Roxy – be thankful for small mercies! I'm sorry to have left you for so long, Alex. Things will be back to normal in a day or two.'

'Take all the time you like,' he urged. 'You need the break. Oh – and Lady Day is ready, whenever you want to pick her up.'

'Great! I might do that tomorrow, actually. I'm coming over for a rehearsal with the TV boys.'

Frederick, I left till last, having to steel myself. I practised in front of a mirror, saying 'Look,

217

Frederick, you have to get a replacement for me. I can't play with you after the end of the month,' but it didn't convince even me. To make matters worse, I was Mrs Popular when I did ring. He was delighted to hear from me, especially when he knew I had a birthday gig in a village hall lined up, for a woman of his own generation.

'Michal, I must tell you, we have a little surprise for you.' My heart leapt. Maybe he'd already found another tenor player. 'Are you free tomorrow evening?'

'Ah... I'm sorry, Frederick...' I explained about my unplanned TV appearance and its repercussions.

'But you're rehearsing with them in Cheltenham tomorrow?'

'That's right.'

'At what time?'

'Eight o'clock.'

'Well, my dear, do you think you could just pop along from seven until a quarter to eight, say? We're terribly keen for you to meet – I mean, see the surprise.'

Meet! He said meet! I felt a surge of excitement. *Maybe he really HAS found a replacement at last! Oh thank you, God!* I realised I was beginning to think in Paul-speak. This was getting worrying. So worrying, in fact, that I found myself agreeing to go along.

'We do look forward to seeing you, Michal.'

'Thanks, Frederick.' A sudden thought hit me. 'Umm... I think I might just bring someone along to meet you.' I was thinking of Lady Day, of course. Go out in style. Give them a good blast.

Soon be over, I thought.

But nothing would soon be over.

The nightmare had hardly yet begun.

Chapter Twenty-two

The day started in water and ended in blood. The transition between the two was far from straightforward, but the first is easy to explain. I went swimming. This was what Maggie had talked me into the previous evening, after my phone calls. She knows I lack confidence in the water and had wheedled me into it.

'We could go at eight in the morning, Mike. There'll be hardly anyone there, I promise, and besides, it will be good for you before the massage. You'll be so relaxed after that, you won't know what's hit you.' Prophetic words, as it turned out.

I had agreed cautiously, figuring I could emerge from the changing rooms in my towelling bathrobe and, if there were too many people around, back off and exit gracefully. I wasn't joking when I'd told Jake that I had physical scars from my run-in with a dog, and, although it was a long time ago, still carry the self-consciousness with me. We were the first to arrive, so any excuses I may have been hatching went out the window.

'You don't always open this early, surely?' I asked her.

'Oh yes we do, though not to the public!' Maggie had plunged straight in and trod water, watching as I eased myself down the steps at the shallow end. 'Staff get to swim for free at certain times of day, and this is a good time to do it. Public opening is at nine, though the influx tends to come later, when people have dropped their children at school.'

The water was beautifully warm and felt wonderful. Carefully, I dropped my knees and lowered my shoulders beneath its surface.

'Good, eh?' Maggie had swum down from the deep end, cutting through the water with a crisp, clean, front crawl. Every time I'd tried to learn that stroke, I'd rolled over in the water and panicked. I had learned to swim after a fashion, though, albeit in a rather messy-looking version of breast-stroke. It had taken Duncan a lot of time and patience to get me to that stage, but even he couldn't persuade me to put my head under the water. And so much of what he'd achieved had been undone by the circumstances of the accident that had killed him. Gingerly, I bobbed about, finally taking my feet off the bottom and going for it. Maggie swam beside me and grinned.

'You're the only person I know who can swim without getting their hair wet! Must be hell on your neck.'

'Not that I'm aware of.' I don't do it often enough to find out, is why. I was staying close to the side, periodically checking that my feet could still touch the bottom.

Two women and a man joined us. Still plenty of room. I ignored them and kept going, steadily swimming from part way down the pool towards the shallow end and back again. A head surfaced next to me. Jake. I hadn't seen him arrive.

'Morning, Michal.' He tossed a shower of droplets from his face.

'Morning.' I was concentrating too much on staying afloat to do more than acknowledge his greeting.

'Don't like the water, huh?' He had turned on his back and was floating carelessly.

'It's OK,' I told him, trying to remember to breathe.

'...just so long as you can put your feet down,' he grinned.

'That's right,' I agreed, coming back to the shallow end and doing precisely that. He stood up, too, body glistening as water ran down his almost hairless chest. I tried not to stare at the scar that curved along the left side of his rib cage. Too late. He'd caught my glance.

'You can ask.'

'I'm sorry. I didn't mean to stare.'

He smiled easily. 'Drunken brawl in my misspent youth. The guy nearly killed me. So – you up for the jam night tomorrow?'

God, was it really almost a week since we'd played together, since we'd kissed... I wanted to be with him again. Wished I had more courage. I shook my head regretfully.

'Afraid not. I have a rehearsal in Cheltenham.'

'Too bad. I'll miss you. We were good together.' His eyes lingered on my face. I slipped back into what passed for swimming mode. He turned on his back again, idling along beside me. Maggie was keeping her distance, I noticed.

'You free later on?' he asked. 'Around eleven?'

221

'I'm having a massage at half-nine. Should be free around then, yes. Why?' Hey – I'd done pretty well there, I told myself. A whole flurry of words, and I hadn't sunk.

'Oh ... I wanted to talk to you yesterday, but not at the funeral. Can I meet you at the cottage?'

'Sure.' Just the one word. I'd had to concentrate on what he was saying as well as staying afloat.

'You two all right?' Maggie had finally joined us.

'Yeah. Talking scars and music.' Jake smiled at her. 'How you doing, Maggie? How's the ghost?'

'Which one?' she asked.

'The supernatural variety. Ghost the horse is doing fine, so I hear.' He turned his head to look at me. 'Down to some friend of yours, Michal, I believe. A horse whisperer or something.'

I shook my head and laughed, floundering as I did so. Jake put out an arm and steadied me.

'Thanks. Sorry.' I was almost into mono-syllables again. I would have been, had I not realised at that point that I could no longer touch the bottom. I flailed wildly.

'Whoa! Steady! Just a couple of feet backwards. You're doing fine.' They moved rapidly in tandem, one on either side of me, moving me into shallower water.

'Thanks. Thanks. I'm OK. Really.' I stood up, sniffing and wiping water from my face. 'Ian's not a horse whisperer, but he does work wonders with them, don't ask me how.'

'Well, whatever he does, word is that the Ghost will be fit to race next week. Warren is one very happy man.'

'Great!' We'd made it to the steps by now. I turned to them as I held the rail. 'Don't let me spoil your swimming – I'm just a big baby. You two carry on.'

'No sweat. Gotta make a move soon, anyway.' Jake hauled himself out of the water and stood on the side, extending a hand to me. I took it. He pulled me up as easily as if I'd been a child.

Maggie had ordered coffee and croissants. We sat and ate them at a pool side table. Despite the near hairlessness of his chest, Jake had very hairy legs. I tried not to look at them, tried not to imagine how they would feel, naked, next to my own. I tried not to think about the kiss in the car either, the way it had made me feel. I wriggled uncomfortably.

'I believe you were asking Maggie about ghosts?' I said.

'And we still have a choice!' Maggie groaned. 'Arthur's, or the one in the nursery.'

'Arthur's?' Jake looked nonplussed.

Between us, Maggie and I recounted Mrs Frewin's tale. He sat for a moment, then looked at me.

'Do you believe in ghosts, Michal?'

'Not dead people coming back to haunt you, no.'

'There's another kind?' Maggie asked.

'Oh yes. Lots of them,' I answered cryptically, thinking about memories and phobias, amongst other things.

Jake gave me a long look before turning back to Maggie. 'I was asking about the one in the nursery.'

'Well don't!' She rolled her eyes. 'The cleaner now claims to have heard it moaning, and won't go near the place. Elynore is not amused. Speaking of whom – we'd better get ready for work.'

They stood up. 'See you later, Michal,' Jake said. 'Enjoy your massage.'

'I will,' I told him. And I did.

I felt wonderfully loose-limbed and relaxed as I strolled back to the cottage. The scent of grapefruit and rosewood was in my nostrils and I lengthened my stride, letting my arms swing free and feeling light as a feather. I had barely had time to take off my coat before Jake arrived.

'Got your car keys?' he asked

'Sure.' I picked them up. 'Where are we going?'

'Not far.' He settled into the passenger seat and gave me directions. We wound up at the point where I'd first come on to the estate the wrong way and encountered the Companions of the Crooked Staff.

'Switch her off a minute,' he instructed.

I did so, feeling a sudden niggle of unease. He got out of the car, indicating to me to do the same. We swapped places. He switched back on and set off down the track, gathering speed.

'I think it's time you had your lesson,' he told me. 'Think, now. What did you do when you first spotted trouble here?'

'I stopped. But look, I told you, I'm not interested in...'

'Right. You stopped. And that was wrong. This is what you should have done.'

He hit the brakes, slammed the car into reverse and spun her round so fast, I screamed. Then he did it again. And again. And again. We missed trees by millimetres. When he finally came to what seemed to be a regular halt, I nearly fell out of the car in my haste to get away before he had any more crazy ideas.

'What the hell do you think you're doing!' I screeched. Whether fear or anger had the upper hand, I have no idea. It made no odds. Either way, I was shaking.

'Teaching you a lesson, I hope.'

'Well, I don't need a lesson! I didn't ask you for one, and you have no right...'

'I have every right, Michal.' His voice was authoritative, tightly controlled. 'There's a lot at stake here, and I need to know just how you're involved.'

What the hell was he on about? I took a step backwards. 'Involved? In what?'

'You heard me. You're pulling a hell of a lot of trouble. Finding Arthur's body. Your house supposedly gets trashed...'

'Supposedly? It's bloody well wrecked!'

He ignored me completely, talked over me. '...and you cause trouble at a fair.'

My mouth went dry. 'How do you know about that?' I hadn't even told Maggie, so it couldn't have come from her. 'And it wasn't me causing trouble...'

'Couple of friends of mine were there.' He looked at me, eyes hard as flint.

Jesus! I thought – *the men who had caused the trouble, looking for me...* I backed away further.

'Come on, Michal – what's your connection with Arnold Niedermeyer?'

Now he had me completely lost. 'Who?' Things were making less sense by the minute.

He stared at me, head on one side. 'Nice one. Playing dumb, huh? You've been lucky, Michal. So far. How much longer do you think it's gonna hold? You're cool, I'll give you that. Got into the car with me, trusting as a babe, and drove into the middle of nowhere. You're out of your depth, and a lot worse than back there in the pool. I could hurt you, Michal. Other people are already trying, by the sound of things. I'm gonna ask you one more time. What's your connection with Arnold Niedermeyer?'

'I don't know any Arnold Niedermeyer!' I exploded. 'And I don't know what the hell you're talking about.'

'So you didn't go to meet him on Monday evening?' His expression was so sceptical it made me flinch.

I shook my head. 'What in God's name are you talking about?' I protested. 'I was here on Monday evening. You saw me, at the cottage. Checked my diary for gig dates.'

'After that.' There was just no let up.

'I was there! All night. By myself. Since when do I need an alibi and what the bloody hell for?'

'You'd better come up with something better than that. I'm not gonna be the only one asking you, and believe me, the other guys aren't gonna let you off the hook this easily. I'd hate to see you get hurt, Michal. Think about it.' He turned on his heel and walked away.

It was several minutes before I felt able to drive back to the cottage. Calming down properly took considerably longer. Any benefits I may have gained from the swim and the massage had been left behind in the woods. I was almost too frightened to think about it. To think of what could have happened. And who on earth was this Arnold Niedermeyer? All I wanted to do was find Tim and get to the bottom of this business. What on earth Jake's connection was, if any, I had no idea. To think I'd trusted him, wanted him... I felt sick at the thought that my every move at the Grange had either been under observation or reported back, in all innocence, via Maggie.

Hurriedly, I threw things into the back of the car and headed for Cheltenham. I hadn't a clue what to do, other than get as far away from Jake as I could. I felt I had to talk to Gaffer, but was still reluctant to tell him about Tim, whose warning seemed ever more pertinent. *Only when I have to*, I told myself. *And it can't be yet.*

I found Gaffer at the Paradox Centre and gave him the rundown on the morning's events, keeping it short and to the point.

'Jake threatened me, Gaffer. I can't believe it.'

'What does he look like? What's he drive?'

'Why?'

'So we can watch your back, that's why! Shit! And we thought you'd be safe at the Grange!'

'Don't remind me!' I felt sick at the thought.

'And who's this bloody Arnold Niedermeyer, when he's at home?'

'I don't know!' My nerves felt completely shredded. I ran my hands through my hair and shook my head in despair. 'Bloody hell, Gaffer! What am I going to do?'

'Well, you can't go back to the Grange, that's for sure. You'll have to give Maggie some excuse for why you've left early. I'll get on to Aunty Joan, tell her to expect you sooner rather than later.'

A couple of phone calls and everything was arranged. Gaffer would meet me after rehearsal and drive to Joan's with me. In the meantime, I had things to do.

First of all, I went to the shop and picked up Lady Day. Then I called in on Henrietta at her shop, managing to elicit, via her phone call to Roxy, the names and addresses of both versions of Sloppy the Clown.

'To say you don't know what's going on, you're awfully keen all of a sudden, or am I missing something?' she asked.

I gave her the same spiel I'd given Gaffer. 'Someone must know something. If they won't come to us, we'll just have to go to them.'

'What's with the "we"?' she asked suspiciously.

'You know what I mean. It's just a figure of speech,' I shrugged.

'Aye. And that's my point. You just be careful. And if you need any help, for Christ's sake, ask! I still think you should go to the police.'

'With what? All we've got is candy floss!'

'I don't like this, Michal.' She gave me her fiercest narrow-eyed look.

'Well, I don't exactly go a bundle on it myself,' I retorted. 'But I can't just sit around, waiting for something to happen.'

'God help us!' She gave me a thoroughly filthy look. 'Here – have another hat.' She stuffed one on my head. This was a brown fake fur jobbie.

'And I still think we should colour your hair...'

Phone calls to the two Sloppies got me nowhere, though at least Joe, the regular version, had an answerphone. I left a message asking him to call me urgently, leaving my mobile number. All I wanted to do now was sleep, but I told myself I had to keep going for just a few hours more. First of all, I had to go to Frederick's rehearsal. The drumming was what worried me most, I decided. Let's face it, if the drummer's lost it, you've had it. *Why oh why*, I thought, *if I HAVE to play with an old drummer, can't it be someone like Ronnie Varrell from the Syd Lawrence Orchestra?* Now there was a man with fire in his veins, who was still rock solid in old age and had played the best drum solo I'd ever heard. Stuff the young Turks. If I could still play that well in my seventies, I'd be one very happy sax player.

Frederick's surprise was bigger by far than I'd anticipated. Not a replacement tenor player, unfortunately, but something that made my jaw drop. He'd hired a singer. Of the six-foot-three, sleek-bodied, slick-haired, simply stunning and young variety. He was singing as I entered the room. I couldn't believe my eyes. More to the point, I couldn't believe my ears. Bugger the Green Glittery Jackets, not that he was wearing one. The man's voice was a total and utter turn-on. I nearly wet myself. God knows what he'd do to elderly ladies like Dave and Cynthia's up and coming eighty year old.

'Some encouragement for you, my dear,' Frederick beamed. 'We thought, as your contribution has had such a positive effect on us, that more young blood was in order. Nick will be the baby of the band of course – only twenty-eight. Isn't he beautiful?'

I nodded, speechless. As he turned, I did a double-take at the figure sitting behind the drum kit. 'You got a new drummer as well?'

'Ah – no!' Frederick lowered his voice conspiratorially. 'It's a toupee. Heaven only knows why, at this particular point in time. He's been bald for years, you know.'

I looked again. Oh hell. I kept my voice low, too. 'But it looks like … well...' I didn't dare say it.

'I know. Squashed guinea pig,' Frederick confirmed. 'Hopefully, it's just a phase. Perhaps best not to make any comment?' I nodded agreement. 'Now let me introduce you to Nick. Oh – and did you say you were bringing a friend? Couldn't make it after all?'

'Oh, she made it, Frederick!' It was my turn to beam. 'Let me introduce you to Lady Day...'

It was magic. She was magic. Nick was magic. Either of them alone would have been enough. Together, they were dynamite. The smouldering, long-fused-with-a-big-bang-at-the-end type. How the hell was I going to get out of the band now? More to the point, I realised, did I still want to?

I dashed off later to play with the boys from TV. That went better than I'd hoped, too, far easier because I'd had a good run-through with the dots the previous evening. The only discordant note was Paul. Or rather, his absence. We all commented on it. Even cracked a joke or two about it, but it was so out of character for him, I phoned both his home and mobile numbers, getting no response from either. We carried on without him, of course, but it concerned me enough to decide to swing by his house on the way to Joan's, to check he was all right.

And that's where the blood came into it.

Chapter Twenty-three

I have never been so sick in my life. Forget performance nerves on live TV. Forget drinking too much wine with the Myatts. This kind of sick is where the expression 'gut-wrenching' comes from. I was sick till I couldn't be sick any more, and then some.

The house looked normal enough when we arrived. There were lights on downstairs and Gaffer said, 'They're probably watching the telly.' I felt a bit stupid but, as we were here anyway, figured I may as well follow through. Gaffer accompanied me to the front door. I rang the bell. No reply. There was a faint sound that could have been the TV. Gaffer stepped back and looked round the corner of the house.

'They could be in the kitchen,' he suggested.

'Yes, but the side gate will be locked,' I told him. The words were barely out of my mouth before Gaffer had vaulted over it. I ran after him, laughing and saying, 'Gaffer! They'll think you're a burglar!' I was talking at him through the gate. It was a good six feet high and I was expecting him to open it for me. I was expecting to hear him knock on the back door, come to that, but he didn't. All I heard was, 'Jesus! Jesus Christ! Mike – Jesus! Mike – phone the police!' His voice was high-pitched, strangled.

'Gaffer – what's going on?' My skin was crawling and I found it hard to breathe.

'Phone the fucking police, Mike! Jesus! There's a dead man in here!'

I heard the sound of breaking glass as I fumbled for my mobile.

'Gaffer?'

'Maybe he's not dead. Maybe ... oh CHRIST!' The next sound I heard was that of Gaffer vomiting.

I don't know how I got myself over the gate, but I did. And I wish to God I hadn't. I ran into the kitchen through the door whose glass panel Gaffer had broken to gain access.

Blood. There was so much blood. I slipped in it, skidded, shrieked soundlessly, flailing like some BSE-afflicted cow in my efforts to get up. Maybe it was Gaffer's vomit I slipped in. All I know is, I wound up covered in blood. He was wordlessly trying to get me to leave the room. I was transfixed by the sheet whiteness of his face, the contrast it made to the bloody pulp of what had once been the back of a head. It was far worse than I could have imagined. Just monstrous, an outrage. There was no way this could be anything but murder.

The body was sprawled on the floor, face down. The back of the head, as I said, was a bloody pulp, glistening with bone and brains. That was when I was sick. Explosively so. I guess we didn't make it any easier for the forensic people...

By Thursday afternoon I felt thick-headed and groggy. It had been way into the early hours of the morning before Gaffer and I had been allowed to go home and I hadn't been able to sleep. The night's events, coupled with a strange bed, had conspired to keep me tossing and turning. Every time I'd shut my eyes, visions of that slaughter-house kitchen had swept in. I wound up afraid to sleep in case I dreamed about it.

The police, all in all, had been very good, although they weren't too thrilled with Gaffer for having broken in.

'I know you're not supposed to touch things at crime scenes,' he'd told me afterwards, 'but I wasn't completely sure until I got inside that the bloke was dead. At first, all I could see was shit loads of blood and his legs, see? It was only when I got inside that I saw his head.'

Pete, Paul's partner, had been identified, in a preliminary fashion, from stuff in his wallet, found in the back pocket of his trousers. My relief that it wasn't Paul was short-lived. The police thought Paul had done it. They were treating it as a 'domestic'. I'd protested, of course, but from their point of view, it must have looked fairly cut and dried. Paul was missing, his car gone. He hadn't come to the rehearsal. Pete was dead, battered in the home they shared. The whole thing was a nightmare scenario. We were asked a lot of questions. Gaffer hadn't much to tell, beyond the immediate circumstances, as he

233

knew neither Paul nor Pete. On the other hand, Paul and I went back a long way.

'Does he have family he might have gone to?' I was asked.

'No. I mean, yes, he has family – parents and a sister. But his parents disowned him when he came out gay. His sister lives in Canada. They write and phone, but I don't think he's seen her for a couple of years.'

'What about friends?'

I'd shrugged. 'I'm the closest, apart from Pete, of course. But yes, there are other friends and a lot of acquaintances.' I'd given them a list of names, along with my clothes, for forensic examination. They asked me to let them know if Paul contacted me. I asked them to let me know if they found him. The whole thing was surreal.

Gaffer, after going home, had now come to Joan's to visit me. Didn't look like he'd had much sleep, either.

'Do you know where he might be, Mike?'

I shook my head. 'I've no idea. I keep hoping he might phone.'

'More likely to go to the Grange, looking for you, isn't he?'

'Oh, shit! That's right! He'll think I'm still there.' What was wrong with my brain? What brain? I thought bitterly, as I punched in Maggie's number.

'Hi, Mike! Have you managed to get things sorted?' Her voice was bright, like she hadn't a care in the world.

God, I'd forgotten that, too, I thought with a flash of guilt. I'd told her that I'd had to shoot off because of an unexpected complication at the house.

'Er – no. Not yet,' I hedged. 'Look, Maggie, you haven't seen Paul, have you?'

'Paul? No. What's the problem?'

'Oh ... nothing, really – it's a bit complicated, that's all.' That much, at least, wasn't a lie. 'Gig stuff. You know how it is with him. But if you do see him, get him to give me a ring on the mobile, will you, and tell him it's urgent? Give him my number, in case he's forgotten it or mislaid it. He won't know where I am, the house being uninhabitable and all.'

'I don't know where you are, either!' she laughed.

'Oh – staying at a friend's. How's your haunted nursery saga?' I wanted to get her off the subject.

'Still haunted! I've promised to get Alison in to say prayers. It's the only way the cleaner will go back, and we don't want to lose her. Mrs Frewin's been talking, of course, saying how effective Alison was with Arthur's unquiet spirit.' She made a suitably spooky noise down the phone. 'I don't see any other way to handle it.'

'I bet you didn't expect this kind of thing when you took the job, did you?'

'Probably in the small print in my person specification! Hey – how was your get together with Jake?'

'What?'

'Your eleven o'clock meeting, arranged, if I remember correctly, whilst semi-naked, over continental breakfast by the pool! You'd disappeared before I had a chance to get the gossip!'

Enough to make your hair curl, I thought, before dismissing her question with a casual, 'There is no gossip, Maggie – it was just music stuff.'

'Mike!' She drew out my name into at least three syllables. 'It's obvious he likes you! He's been looking for you, too.'

In Maggie's romantic world-view, I should no doubt have shivered with delight. I just shivered. 'Well, you'll just have to tell him that I won't be around.'

'Mike, you're hopeless! Look, are you really all right? Is there anything I can do?'

'No. I'm fine. It'll all blow over in a couple of days.'

'So when will you be coming back?'

The six-million dollar question. God, I'd dug a hole for myself there!

'I'm not sure I can, Maggie. I really ought to get back to the shop next week, and with the gigs...'

'Please try and come back for the weekend, Mike. PLEASE?'

'I can't promise.'

'But you'll try?'

'I'll try,' I lied, inwardly thinking it would take wild horses to drag me back there. I seemed to have done nothing but lie to my friends recently, and I didn't like it.

'Sorted?' asked Gaffer, as I put the phone down.

'Yes,' I sighed. 'For now, at least.'

'You look knackered, mate. I know I am. Why don't you get your head down?'

I would have, and to hell with dreams, only we

236

had visitors. Plainclothes officers of last night's acquaintance. Joan brought them through to the kitchen.

'Paul? There's news of Paul?' I sprang to my feet.

'There is, though I have to warn you that it's not very good, I'm afraid.' The taller one, whose name was Pierce, sat at the kitchen table while Joan made herself scarce. His companion, DC Ellis, leaned against the door frame, arms crossed over his chest.

'He's not dead?' My heart was in my mouth.

'No, he's not.' I could hear the 'but' in the silence before Pierce continued. 'He is, however, in a critical condition.'

'Oh God!'

Gaffer squeezed my hand as I sank into the chair. 'What happened?' he asked quietly.

'That's what we're trying to establish. And that's why we need to ask Mrs Brodie some further questions.'

'Do you want me to leave?' Gaffer pushed back his seat.

'That won't be necessary. I'm sure she appreciates your support. I would also appreciate it, though, if anything said in this room goes no further at this stage. Do I make myself understood?'

We both nodded. Gaffer put the kettle on.

'You asked what happened. At first sight, it looked straightforward enough. Car crash.' I shuddered. 'You know the road out past Prinknash Abbey?' Gaffer and I nodded in tandem. 'He'd gone over the side. Dropped a hell of a distance – it's a wonder the petrol tank didn't explode.' He fiddled with a teaspoon. 'You know Paul well, Mrs Brodie. What do you know about his drinking habits?'

The question was completely unexpected. 'He doesn't drink,' I told him. 'He's allergic to alcohol.'

It was his turn to nod. 'The hospital said it complicated things. But still, it could have fitted. Argument with the boyfriend. Things got out of hand. He tanks himself up, full of remorse, drives over the edge.'

'No way!' I protested.

Gaffer patted my shoulder. 'I think there's a "but" coming up, mate.'

'A big "but" Mr Leonard,' Pierce agreed. He addressed the next question to both of us. 'Do you know anything about Forensic Science?'

'Only that you're not supposed to puke up all over the scene of a crime,' Gaffer muttered.

'I only know bits I've picked up from TV,' I admitted.

'Defensive wounds. Does that ring a bell?'

'Yes, it does.' I must have watched the right channel for a change. 'It's like when someone comes at you with a weapon – your instinct is to put up your arms or hands to defend yourself, ward off a blow. Something like that.'

'Exactly like that. And that's why we're almost certain Paul couldn't have driven the car himself. His arms and hands were badly slashed. Right hand so badly, a couple of fingers were almost severed.' He must have seen me flinch. 'I'm sorry.'

'Christ!' Gaffer breathed. I couldn't say

anything. 'Then..?'

'Then we at least have the possibility of a third party involved. That's the current theory, anyway. Apart from, as I said, Paul being unable to drive himself out there, no knives or other sharp implements were missing from his kitchen and there was no knife by Peter's body to indicate that he'd been the one slashing at Paul. And we know that whoever killed Peter, bludgeoned him from behind.'

'So...' I prompted.

'So, there's a couple of possibilities. Paul may have been defending himself, and possibly Peter, too, from a third person who killed Peter and, for some reason, took Paul away. You seem to know a lot about his business associations, Mrs Brodie?'

'A fair bit, yes,' I agreed. 'But – you don't think a business associate could have done this?'

'Either that, or we're looking at a love triangle. One of them was unfaithful. A jealous lover exacts revenge. Can you think of anyone who might have wanted, or had reason, to harm Paul? A shady business deal, perhaps?'

I was bewildered. 'No one even remotely comes to mind. Paul was straight-up in his business dealings as far as I'm aware. Crazy at times, yes, but cooking the books or getting into something dodgy – no. Not in a million years.'

'Another lover?'

I was feeling more and more frustrated. 'No.' I shook my head emphatically. 'He was devoted to Pete. Pete was quiet, passed for straight. Paul was much more flamboyant, but that was his personality. He'd have been extrovert even if he were heterosexual. He's been mistaken for my boy-friend on occasion.' I attempted a laugh and failed. 'I'm sorry. I'm not explaining this very well. They'd been together ... must be five or six years.'

'That can mean anything or nothing. Lots of people – gay or straight – like their bit on the side.'

'I know. I just can't imagine them... I'm sorry. I'm not really helping, am I?'

'You're doing fine. Every little helps. Think about things, will you? If anything comes to mind – anything at all – let us know, all right?'

'Of course. But Paul – you said he's in a critical condition? How bad is he? Can I see him?'

'I'm sorry.' He shook his head. 'He was taken to the specialist unit for spinal injuries.' He looked at me with genuine compassion. 'Apart from everything else, I'm afraid he's broken his back.'

Gaffer never did get round to making that tea.

Chapter Twenty-four

There was a tap on the door. I struggled upright, groggy from a heavy and dreamless nap. Raffi appeared, bearing a tray of tea and beautifully presented sandwiches.

'Compliments of Joan. How are you, Mike?'

She put the tray down on the bedside table and hugged me. I couldn't answer. She patted my back the way she used to when she was little. I used to laugh and say it made me feel like a horse.

240

'Gaffer went home to feed Lucy and take her for a walk. He should be back soon.'

I nodded. 'What time is it?'

'Evening. We wanted to let you get a good rest.'

The tea was good. Raffi caught my expression.

'Leaf tea. Joan says she can't be doing with tea bags. Says they're probably made from the sweepings.'

I smiled, and she waved the plate of sandwiches under my nose.

'Cream cheese and crudités.'

I took one, thinking I wouldn't be able to eat it. I hadn't reckoned on how hungry I was. I wolfed the lot.

Twenty minutes later, Gaffer arrived. 'Right, mates! What are we going to do? I don't know about you two, but I don't fancy staying in and being miserable all night.'

'Mike! Aren't you supposed to be playing!' Gaffer had jolted Raffi's memory.

'Yes,' I told her. 'But I phoned Patsy. I couldn't face it, after Pete and Paul.'

'Too right, mate! So what are we going to do?'

In an ideal world, find Tim, I thought. But how?

'Oh – I thought I'd got someone else for Zorba the Greek today, but she's going to France instead,' Raffi put in. 'I'll keep trying.'

Hold on. France... It was a long shot, but Tim had got to me successfully there once before...

'What night is this? Thursday?' They nodded. 'I believe there's a jazz night on at Descartes' Vineyard...'

Raffi drove, saying that Gaffer and I needed a drink. Neither of us argued with her. Gaffer

241

already knew the place but Raffi had never been before and squealed with delight at the three musical monkeys.

'Neat!'

'Wait till you see the rest...!'

Somebody was playing a pretty mean keyboard. The evening was obviously underway. I took a deep breath as we walked into the bar. Gaffer, who does Ju-Jitsu, and Raffi, who takes self-defence classes, were in deep discussion about the best way to get out of a stranglehold attack from behind. Their conversation ebbed in and out of focus as I concentrated my thoughts on a message. *Please let there be a message.*

'No, mate, I'm telling you, this can't fail.' Gaffer's voice intruded into my silent prayers and I turned to watch him. He had hold of Raffi as he spoke. 'You're using their body weight *against* them. Hands on their arms, step back and turn with your leg *outside* their forward leg and they've *got* to go down. Guaranteed.' He demonstrated the move just before we entered the bar itself, stopping an astounded Raffi just short of the floor.

'Good evening, Madame. You have friends with you tonight, I see.'

Was it my imagination, or were the bartender's eyes twinkling? I ordered the drinks. He pulled a face. 'You are driving again, no?'

'No – she's driving – Raffi that is!' I managed a laugh. 'The mineral water is for her; mine's the wine; Gaffer's is the beer.'

He nodded and extended his hand as I mentioned their names.

'Oh!' I added on impulse. 'We'll be eating, too. Well, I will be if you have a vegetarian menu.' I was trying very hard not to think of the meat map.

'But of course. Tonight I can offer you vegetable lasagne or Red Dragon pie.'

'Eating dragons is vegetarian?' Raffi looked at him as if he were mad.

'Oh yes,' he smiled. 'It is a dish of aduki beans – red – in a rich tomato and herb sauce, topped with creamed potatoes and served with a green salad.'

'So where does the dragon come into it?' I asked.

'Ah!' He tapped the side of his nose. 'The Chinese say that the aduki beans, they give you the strength of the dragon!'

'I'll give it a try,' I said. 'And it will go nicely with my red wine.'

Gaffer and Raffi chose dead pig and dead chicken respectively and we moved away from the bar to find a table. The bartender winked at me. 'I am still keeping my eyes open...' A reference to the other day, or a sign that he had another message for me?

Raffi was oohing and aahing at the decor. I was watching the band, who were playing to the right of the DWHSHTO. I was back in I-Spy mode, that being the Devil With Horns, Sticking His Tongue Out. It was a three piece combo, keyboards, guitar and alto sax, and the sax player was a gawky looking kid who managed to give the impression he hadn't seen a decent meal in weeks. He knew his stuff, though. Paul would have... I cut off the thought.

The meal was good, the band was good, the company was good. But I couldn't settle. Couldn't relax. It's not as if I was having to look out for trouble. Gaffer was well on the alert and periodically asked me if I knew people. There was no sign of Jake, no sign of the men from the fair – though, if I was quite honest with myself, I hadn't got that good a look at them. I would be glad when we could leave, when I would be given a message, if there was one.

My mobile rang. 'Mike Brodie.'

'Hi! My name's Joe Cowper – you left a message on my answerphone.'

My brain whirled, trying to place the name – the regular Sloppy the Clown. 'Yes! Thanks for coming back to me – is there any news?'

'I wouldn't be phoning otherwise.'

'News about Paul?' Gaffer mouthed. I shook my head.

'I got my stuff back,' Joe continued, 'but I don't know where Darren is. He'd just parked the van and cleared off. Owes you money, does he?'

'No. I'm just trying to catch up with a mutual friend.'

'Sorry I can't be more helpful.'

'Thanks for letting me know, anyway. And I'm glad you got your stuff back.'

'He'd be dead meat if I hadn't,' he said darkly, which is not at all the kind of thing you expect a clown to say.

Raffi and I went to the bar to get another drink. 'Oh, neat! They've got a fortune telling machine!' I smiled as she did as I had done, sticking her twenty-pence piece in the slot.

'I've got one of those, too!' I laughed as she picked up her card.

'What's it say?' she asked, peering at her own.

'Don't know – haven't read it yet!'

'You're hopeless!'

I wished I could find it, but realised it was probably still in the jacket I'd been wearing on my previous visit. Raffi's seemed uncannily accurate, stressing her connection to the earth and interest in the environment.

'Fluke!' scoffed Gaffer, getting one himself to prove his point. It didn't, nailing him to a T on his love of animals and music.

'Another fluke?' I suggested.

'Too right. You get one, Mike – if it's not a fluke, it should be the same as the one you got before, and we can check that when we get home.'

'Right.' I got another, Raffi snatching it from my hand before I could get a look at it.

Raffi's face fell. 'That can't be right. It doesn't say anything about music!'

'What?' I snatched it back. We may have lived together for years, but there was still a lot of stuff Raffi didn't know about me.

'Come on, then – read it out!' Gaffer was getting impatient.

I made a big show of rolling my eyes and shaking my head. I read it in a suitably stereotypical fortune teller's voice.

'Although you have a stubborn streak, born of a strong instinct for survival, your judgement can sometimes let you down due to a touch of naiveté. This, in turn comes from a misplaced sensitivity

245

due to emotional damage inflicted in your past, a past which you keep secret even from those closest to you. You are, however, a loyal and caring friend, willing to move heaven and earth in defence of those you love.'

'You're certainly a loyal and caring friend.'

'Thank you, Raffi.'

'Yeah – but it's your secret past I want to know about!' Gaffer rubbed his hands. 'Skeletons in the cupboard, eh, mate?'

'Oh, loads of them!' I laughed. 'Things you wouldn't even dream about!' *Not unless you wanted nightmares...*

'Speaking of dreams...' Gaffer looked at his watch. 'I don't want to be a party-pooper, but I wouldn't mind having an early night. I think everything's catching up with me a bit.'

'Me, too,' I agreed.

'Well, your chariot awaits once we've finished these drinks,' Raffi smiled.

When it came to it, I motioned to the others to go on ahead while I had a quick word with the bartender. I'd said I wouldn't be a minute, and I wasn't. There was no message.

I sat silently in the car on the way back. I didn't know what to think. More to the point, didn't know what to do next. I was beginning to feel it was the end of the road, that I'd never find Tim and never make sense of anything again.

We had a final cup of tea in the kitchen at Joan's. Tomorrow, I knew, I would have to move out of the single room she'd given me and in to what she called 'the cubby hole reserved for emergencies.' And tomorrow would see the start of what she, along with most of Cheltenham, called 'The Irish Invasion', with her regular race-goers arriving to get in a good weekend's drinking before the Festival began. I usually avoid town like the plague during Race Week. Not that I've anything against the Irish, or anyone else come to that. It's just that the population of Cheltenham explodes. You can't move. Can't walk down the street, let alone park, and parking's not good at the best of times. Also, you can't get in to your usual haunts for a coffee or a beer or a meal. It's crazy. Nice, but definitely crazy.

'What was that?' Raffi looked around nervously as a strange sound intruded our thoughts. The sound came again, a quiet but definite tapping on the kitchen door.

'Leave it to me.' Gaffer went and opened it, looking ready to fell anyone standing on the other side. 'Hiya, mate – what you doing here? Come on in.' His voice was warm as he stepped back to allow the visitor entrance. It was Norman, who looked at Raffi and I, smiling and nodding in acknowledgement before indicating that he wanted Gaffer to go outside. The door closed behind them.

'Wonder what that's about?' said Raffi. 'Hope it's not trouble at the Centre.'

We heard the muffled sound of low voices, punctuated by a loud and startled 'What?!' from Gaffer. Raffi and I looked at each other, eyebrows raised. Shortly afterwards, he came back inside.

'Do us a favour, Raffi, will you? Run Norman back to the Paradox Centre? I'm going home to get the dog.'

'Sure, but...'

He had her outside in a flash, then slipped back into the kitchen, calling something to the others about having forgotten his hat. *What hat?* I thought.

He lowered his voice. 'Mike – I'll be back for you in a minute. Stay stumm. I want Raffi out of this.'

'Out of what? What's going on, Gaffer?' I half rose at the expression on his face.

'Norman just kidnapped somebody, that's what.'

'Yeah, right!' I laughed. 'And the Pope's a Methodist and I'm playing the Hollywood Bowl next week, with Elvis!'

'Straight up, mate.' He threw me a serious glance as he moved to the door, stuck his head outside and shouted, 'Didn't bring me bleeding hat, did I? Must be going barmy!' He turned back to me. 'Like I said, Mike, Norman's kidnapped somebody. Some little shit who tried to sell him the story on who turned your place over...'

Chapter Twenty-five

I was on tenterhooks until Gaffer returned, and even worse in his car. It didn't help that he had Lucy in the back.

'I got Raffi away, all right,' he told me. 'She knows nothing. Let's keep it that way for now, shall we?'

'You're really serious?' I still couldn't take it in. 'But where is this person – the kidnapee?'

'At Norman's place. Being guarded ready for our arrival by Norman and his mate, Big Stan. You ever met Big Stan?'

'With a name like that, I wasn't sure I wanted to. 'No.'

'Old mate of Norm's. They were on the road together. Made a good pair, actually – Stan's stone-deaf – lip reads and signs. They looked out for one another, you know? Came off the road together, as well. Big Stan lives out on a farm, does labouring and stuff. Norman, you know about. Anyway...' Gaffer parked the car and let the dog out. She went straight to the back of the Centre, where Norman's bedsit was located. I followed at a distance. 'Anyway, seems Norman and Big Stan had decided to meet up for a night out. They were sitting in a pub and apparently Stan signed to Norman that some unsavoury looking character was talking about him. Taking the mickey and saying to his mate, maybe he should offer to sell him the info about Sunday night at your house. He made his move, they went out the back with him – he was on his own to do the talking – and they just picked him up between them and bundled him in the car.'

We descended the short flight of steps to Norman's home. Gaffer left Lucy sitting guard inside the back door. 'Backup,' he smiled, as I eased past her, sweating. 'You're not going to faint on me again, mate?'

'No. No. I'm all right,' I said, and we went in. The scene in Norman's living room was like a

249

Tarantino film just before the blood-letting starts. Norman and another man – I assumed Big Stan, by the size of him – sat at the kitchen table, drinking tea. Over by the radiator, a skinny young runt with a face like a weasel was tied to a wooden chair with what looked like washing line around his legs and chest, his arms pulled behind his back. Maybe he didn't really look like a weasel at all. Maybe that effect was down to the fact that he was gagged with what looked like a pair of women's tights. I wondered where Norman had got them from.

Introductions were made. The Weasel in the chair stopped struggling and started sweating when he saw Gaffer. Big Stan started signing rapidly and until Norman started speaking, the only sound was the muffled noise of music and the thumping feet of people dancing in the Centre, above us.

'Big Stan says sorry about gagging him, Gaffer. Says he knows no one would have heard him yelling, but he was fed up with him swearing.'

Correction, I thought. *Where had Big Stan got the tights from?*

Gaffer removed the gag and sure enough, a torrent of abuse streamed forth.

'I don't know what you think you're doing, but you'll fucking regret this. Do you know who I am? I got five brothers and seven uncles, and even the women in my family would eat your fucking balls for breakfast.'

'Well, well!' Gaffer turned to me. 'In case you haven't guessed, this is Skinny Sim. Youngest of the family, I believe. Guess which one, mate?'

250

I raised my eyebrows at the surname. There are less than half-a-dozen majorly serious criminally-inclined families in Cheltenham, to my knowledge. Skinny Sim's was top dog. Any one of them would whip the knickers off your arse and come back for the elastic. Usually with menaces, GBH and an assortment of other violent and singularly unpleasant habits. Gaffer pulled up a chair, turned it backwards and sat, legs splayed either side of it, looking at him.

'Do I know who you are? Yes, sonny, I do, and I don't care if your Mum's Lucretia Borgia and your father's the Pope.'

Big Stan signed. Norman said, 'He says it's wasted on him.'

'You're probably right,' Gaffer sighed. 'Actually, Sim, I know your Uncle Gerry.'

Stan signed rapidly at me. Norman solemnly translated. 'He's the biggest, ugliest one of the lot.'

'Thanks,' I said. Stan nodded and smiled.

'Your Uncle Gerry...' Gaffer mused. 'Never been the same since that accident, has he? But I'm going to let you into a little secret, Sim. That wasn't no accident. That was me.'

'Get the fuck out of here! He came off his motorbike!'

Stan signed. 'Nicked motorbike,' Norman offered.

'That was his story, was it?' Gaffer grinned unpleasantly. 'That motorbike belonged to a friend of mine. Gerry thought he'd ramp it and dump it in Pittville Lake. He'd tried that with my own the previous week. No imagination, your

251

Uncle Gerry. Tries a thing once, and if he likes it, keeps doing it until he gets caught. Like your brothers, eh? What is it? Two of 'em inside now, or is it three? Well, like I said, there he is, with my mate's motorbike. I don't like people messing with my mates or their property, see? So I was waiting for him. I got the bike back. He went in the lake. Can't think how he broke his arm and leg, though. Or his jaw. You wouldn't think water would make such an impact, would you?' He looked at me and smiled. 'Fancy a cup of tea, Mike? This could be a long night.'

A faint film of sweat was showing on the Weasel's upper lip, but he brazened it out. 'In your dreams, you lying wanker! And you – retard!' He was shouting now at Norman, who had got up to put the kettle on. 'No crap stuff, eh? I only like the bags with the little perforations.'

Gaffer was up and had him by the throat, dangling, complete with chair, before slamming him against the wall, quicker than I could blink.

'I'll give you perforations, you little toe-rag! You'd better apologise to Mr Stephenson right now, or you know what? Being the generous man I am, I might just give you a choice about who puts some little perforations in you. Me. Or my dog...'

The Weasel was looking at me now, real fear on his face. From the way my chest had constricted at mention of her, I figured the colour must have drained from mine.

'Yeah. Look at her,' Gaffer nodded. 'Have a good look. She's my mate – one of my best mates. And you trashed her house. And her saxophones. And

252

you know what?' The Weasel shook his head frantically. 'She loves dogs. Been brought up with them all her life. But my dog – no. Mine's ... different.' He turned to me, still holding the Weasel and his accessories against the wall. 'You wouldn't want me to bring that dog in here, would you, Mike?'

I shook my head and swallowed.

Gaffer shook the Weasel.

'So you're going to apologise to Mr Stephenson, aren't you, toe-rag?'

'Yeah. Yeah.'

'So do it!'

'I'm sorry. I'm sorry.'

'...Mr Stephenson. Sir.' Gaffer prompted.

'Mr Stephenson, sir.'

'That's better.' Gaffer set Weasel and his chair down again. 'And now you're going to tell us a story, aren't you? All about what you were doing at Mike's house on Sunday night. Because if you don't...' Gaffer leaned forward until his face was no more than an inch away from the Weasel's. '...well, I just might have to ask Mike to leave the room, see? Couldn't have her and my dog in the same room, could we?'

The Weasel told us a story, all right. He sang, as they say, like a bird. And it sure as hell wasn't any tune we knew.

'I didn't do nothing to her house – honest to God! On my Grandma's grave! Oh, I was going to – hands up for it. I was in there, you know, all ready for it, when I hears somebody else coming and I thinks it's the owner, but then I heard the voices, right, and it's these blokes, talking about searching the place and me, right, I'm shitting myself, see, thought it could turn nasty, me being in there and all, so I thinks, shit, I got to get out of here, only I can't because they've got this one bloke standing guard, so I had to find a place to hide till I could figure on making an exit.' He licked his lips nervously, eyeing the tea that Norman was serving. Stan was sipping his, watching the Weasel over the rim of his mug, eyes never leaving his face for a second.

Gaffer followed his gaze. 'When you've finished, Sim. Maybe. Now get on with it.'

'So where did you hide?' I asked. The thought of this little turd in my house made me feel sick.

'Upstairs. To start with. There's a cupboard in the big bedroom. Like for airing clothes, only without the slat things?' I nodded. 'Then I hears them getting nasty, and one of 'em is coming up the stairs, so I shot into the bathroom, see. What do you call bathrooms like that one?'

Clean, I thought. *Before you went in it...* 'En-suite,' I said.

'Yeah. En-suite. Right. Only you got one of them funny old baths, right? Not against the wall, and none of that funny panelling. Anyway...'

'Hang on a minute,' Gaffer interrupted. 'Before we go any further – how many men were there?'

'Three. Two inside, and the one outside.'

'Did you get a look at any of them?'

'You kidding? I was trying to hide, not get myself killed! They were real mean mother-fuckers. No, I mean, I didn't see 'em then, but I got a look later, when I was on the garage roof.' The descriptions he gave could have been anybody. Average height, average build. Nothing that meant a thing. I wondered if he was making it up, just trying to earn himself a few Brownie points so he could go home.

'They weren't very happy with you, anyway,' the Weasel continued, looking at me in a highly accusatory fashion. 'This one geezer, he says, "They've got to be here if somebody hasn't got them" – I can't remember the name, but it was some bloke's name – and this other geezer says, "Yeah, well this is a waste of time, then, because the young bloke says he has got them. If he hasn't, he knows what will happen. But you know what we've been told – cover all options. Besides, he says, why does she reckon she didn't know Arthur when she's been seen with him?"'

I bet he knows the dialogue to his favourite videos by heart.

'Hold on.' Gaffer looked at me. 'Who's Arthur?'

'The dead guy at the Grange. Well, in the village. I told you about the body in the pool?'

'That was it!' Weasel was getting excited now, eager to help. 'They talked about him getting killed...'

'Killed? But he drowned. It was an accident.' My chest was feeling tight.

'No.' He shook his head vehemently. 'That's when I knew I'd got to get out, right? I mean, I knew that anyway, but what I mean is, they were talking about killing people. He was the old man, was he?'

'Yes...'

'Right. So they're talking about him, see, how he got bumped off, but there was some other

255

bloke, too. Something to do with a horse?'

'But...'

'Right. Another so-called accident, but that guy was going to spill the beans, see, because he didn't like what had happened to the old man, only the boss guy, like, he doesn't like loose ends or something, so he shuts him up, and then they're on about this fire, and how there's nothing to lose now, and the kid had better come up with the goods and they're checking you out because you're a lying bitch and – sorry – they called her that, not me.' He flicked a worried glance in Gaffer's direction.

'Go on,' was all that Gaffer said, but he was grim-faced.

The Weasel swallowed hard. 'They said the boss said they could at least keep an eye on her, her being at the Grange and all, and they'd got a couple of blokes tailing her, seeing who she talked to.' He looked at me again. 'They didn't seem to like the fact that you had a message from somewhere. And they talked about keeping an eye on the girl, whoever that is, though they didn't seem too worried about her, but you got some poofter friend they didn't like. They thought you and him might have something going down that could cock things up.'

Big Stan signed anxiously to Norman. Gaffer held up his hand to stop the Weasel going any further while Norman translated.

'He says, is this making any sense to anybody else, because it means bugger all to him?'

'This has got to be something to do with Tim, hasn't it?' Gaffer looked at me seriously. 'They talked about a fire.'

'Yes, but they talked about Arthur, too, and the young bloke who was kicked to death by a horse. And I don't see how the hell they have any connection with Arthur.' I looked at the Weasel curiously. 'You said they called me a lying bitch?'

'Yeah.'

'What was I supposed to be lying about? Do you know?'

He nodded vigorously. 'Knowing the old bloke. Well, like they reckoned you'd said you didn't know him, only their boss reckoned you did. It was him what called you a lying bitch to them, if you see what I mean.'

'I'll second Big Stan's question, mate.' Gaffer shook his head. 'Does that make any sense to you at all?'

'No it doesn't!' I puffed out my cheeks and ran my hand through my hair. 'I never even met Arthur. I was there, with Alison, when we found the body but I didn't even look at him. Too squeamish. Bloody hell!'

'All right.' Gaffer turned his attention back to the Weasel. 'OK, Sim. Let's try this again. You hid in the bedroom cupboard...'

'Just for a couple of minutes. When I heard 'em start getting heavy, I figured they'd turn it over, see, and I'd get caught, behind the sleeping bags and shit. So then I went in the bathroom, right, and then they're coming up the stairs and I have to get out on to the garage roof, only I can't get down off it because of the bloke standing guard, so I'm lying flat, right, and they're going mad in there, total nutters, and then, like, they're in the bathroom, and they're arguing about all this, right, and I'm lying there, flat like, praying to God they don't look out and see me – I didn't have time to shut the window properly, see, which is why I could hear them. Not that they was trying to be quiet, or nothing, anyway. Pretty much on its own, your house.' He flicked me a glance. 'Nearest neighbour's down the road a way, right?'

'Right,' I acknowledged.

'So there I am, shitting myself about how I'm going to get out of this, then, I hears a mobile ring, and this one guy, he says to the other guy, "She's been playing a fucking gig and she's heading back this way. Ten minutes, tops", and they start turning the taps on and shit, and they do a runner, like, which was when I saw 'em, and they took off – I reckon they must have had cars down the road, right, 'cos I hears a couple start up, and I'm just thinking, right, I can piss off home now and get the hell out of here when she...' He nodded at me. '...turns up with this bird – fu-u-u-u-u-cking hell – sorry – this bird with big tits, and I had to wait a bit, but then I thinks, well, I won't bugger right off, see, so I went down to the culvert in the river.'

Big Stan was looking puzzled. Norman looked at him and said, 'It's just over the hedge in Mike's garden.'

'So you were hanging round there for a while?'

'Yeah. Didn't come out again till it all went quiet. But I seen him patrolling.' He nodded at Norman. 'Know who he is, like, because...'

'Watch your mouth...' Gaffer warned.

'Yeah. Right. So...'

'You thought you'd make a bob or two, eh?'

My mobile rang. I nearly jumped out of my skin. I listened, hastily turning my back on the others as I recognised the voice.

'Hang on a minute,' I said, trying to sound as normal as possible. 'Reception's not very good down here. Let me go upstairs.' I looked at Gaffer. 'Can you get me past ... er ... the dog, please?' I'd nearly said 'Lucy'.

'Sure.'

The Weasel looked suitably worried as we went to the door. I ran up the stairs and into the yard. Gaffer had gone straight back inside.

'Jesus Christ!' I exploded, free to speak at last. 'Where the hell are you, Tim?!'

Chapter Twenty-six

I ran down the stairs and hammered on the door. Norman answered it.

'Look, I've just got to shoot off for a while. Tell Gaffer it's nothing to worry about. I should be an hour or so, tops. Oh – and keep that young Skinny Weasel bloke here till I get back, OK?'

I shot off before he could ask questions, running the short distance to the hotel and stopping only long enough to collect the car and my Maglite. I'd asked Tim if he needed anything.

'Food would be good. Anything. And bring some pain killers, Mike, will you? As strong as you can get.' They would have to wait.

It took me rather more than an hour to get back to Norman's and this time, Gaffer answered the door.

'Christ, Mike! Where have you been? We were getting worried.'

I squeezed past Lucy and into the living room. All I could see was Norman.

'Gaffer – where is he?'

'Toe-rag? Calm down – we haven't fed him to the dog. He needed a pee. Big Stan's keeping him company. He did a runner from your bathroom, remember? We don't want him doing the same thing here.'

The Weasel came back into the room, sullen and tired looking, accompanied by Big Stan who was grinning from ear to ear and signing rapidly. Norman's face went scarlet. 'I'm not telling them that!'

'Right!' said Gaffer. 'I think we've got all we're going to get. I'll fill you in, Mike.' He turned to the Weasel and said, 'I think it's time you went home, sonny.'

'No!' I blurted.

Three faces looked at me in astonishment, one other – the Weasel's – in sudden fright.

'You don't understand!' I said. 'We need him!'

'For what?'

'For what he does best – breaking and entering.'

Gaffer looked at me as if I'd gone completely mad. 'This had better be good, mate!'

'Oh, it is!' I thought rapidly. 'We need two pairs of gloves. You get him in your car. Leave the dog here.' The last thing we'd need was any unnecessary noise. Gaffer gave me a long look but didn't argue, taking Weasel outside while Norman rummaged for gloves. I thanked him and took a deep breath, making sure Big Stan could see what I was saying.

'When we've gone, can you do me a favour? My car's in the yard.' I gave Stan the keys. 'There's something in the back, under a blanket. Needs rather a lot of care and attention. Will you look after it till I get back?' They nodded and I ran after Gaffer.

'Where are we going?' he asked. I gave directions and he pulled away. The Weasel was starting to gibber in the back.

'Will you shut up!' I snapped. 'I'm trying to think!'

The Weasel shut up. Gaffer looked at me in surprise. We arrived in Castle Street. It was dark and deserted. Gaffer turned off the engine and said, 'Now what?' Somewhere in the distance a fox barked.

'It's down to him.' I jerked my head in the direction of our reluctant accomplice. 'It's number twenty-four,' I told him. 'What's the best way of getting inside?'

'You can't make me do this!'

'I should have brought the dog,' Gaffer said conversationally.

'You could be right.' I turned to look at the Weasel. 'You'll do this because if you don't, you'll never see the light of day again. Do I make myself clear? It's a simple job. The people who live here are on holiday. There's no alarm system and all I want out of the place is a briefcase. It belongs to a friend of mine. Just do this, and you can go.

261

You'll never see us again.'

'Not if you've any sense,' Gaffer added.

'All right, all right! What about the back?'

'What about it?'

'What's it like? Hedges, fences, what? I don't like terraces or semis. Nosy neighbours.'

This was a mid-terrace. About as bad as you can get if you're a burglar, I supposed. 'I'm not sure,' I admitted.

'Then we'd better take a look.' Gaffer bundled the Weasel out of the car and spoke to him a low voice. I don't know if the Weasel shook because Gaffer shook him, or simply because he was scared. Anyway, he shook. We walked round the back, Gaffer with his arm slung over the Weasel's shoulder as though they were the best of mates. There was a high brick wall on either side of an equally high wooden gate. Gaffer put on his pair of gloves. I put on mine.

'What about me?' the Weasel squeaked.

'You won't be needing them. Over we go.' Gaffer virtually hauled the Weasel with him. I stood frustrated, unable to do anything until they opened the gate for me.

'Should have brought a friggin' torch!' Gaffer whispered as they let me into the yard. 'It's like the black hole of Calcutta!' I smiled in the darkness and handed him the Maglite. 'Now we're talking!'

We made the back door without incident and the Weasel set to work.

'Hope they didn't leave no washing-up in the sink,' he grumbled as he entered through the kitchen window, Gaffer once more hard on his heels. The bolts and lock on the back door sounded horribly loud as they opened up to let me in.

'OK, mate – where's this briefcase, then?'

'It should be upstairs,' I said. 'One of the bedrooms has been converted into an office. It should be under the desk.'

There were two briefcases under the desk. Weasel stood anxiously as Gaffer directed the beam of light.

'Which one? This, or the other?' He hoisted one aloft.

I saw Tim's initials and breathed a sigh of relief. 'That's the one. Yes.'

'It's got a combination lock.'

'No problem. Let's just take it and get out of here.' Skulking around in the dark was not doing my blood pressure any good.

'You're going to let me go now, right? I done what you wanted.' The Weasel looked anxiously at the pair of us.

'What do you think, mate?' Gaffer asked me. 'We let him go, or we come clean and tell him that I've run out of money for dog food?'

'Gaffer!' I indicated that I wanted a word in private but was afraid the Weasel would do a runner.

'No problem. Just make it quick.' Gaffer sat on his head while I whispered.

'Right,' he said. He let the Weasel up, gasping for air.

'You could have killed me! I could have suffocated!'

'No, Sim. I could have farted. That would have killed you.'

They let me out and locked up before climbing

263

through the window themselves. A cat jumped over the wall and onto the dustbin, frightening me half to death. Yowling with displeasure at my presence, it disappeared again. We followed the same procedure with the gate. Once back in the lane, Gaffer pinned Weasel against the wall and made a few adjustments to his clothing.

'Right, my son. Your fingerprints are all over this place, OK? But we don't particularly want the police involved, do we Mike?'

I shook my head. If I did that much more this evening, I was worried it might drop off.

'But you know what?' Gaffer dangled the brief-case in front of the Weasel's face. 'This is what those bastards on Sunday were looking for. And if you so much as breathe a word to anyone about tonight's events, it won't be the police we send after you. It won't even be me, with or without my dog. Oh no. I'll just give those fuckers your name, address and telephone number and tell 'em that you've got it. Right?'

'Right. Right. Not a word. Right.' The Weasel was so desperate to get away that even I felt slightly sorry for him by now. Entirely misplaced, of course.

'Good,' Gaffer said. 'Off you go, then.'

'What?'

'Go, my son, before I change my mind.'

We watched him scuttle off down the road like a lame crab.

'You could have given him back his shoes,' I chided.

'Yeah. And you could tell me what the bloody hell is going on...'

Chapter Twenty-seven

I let Tim do that, when we got back to Norman's place. At least he looked somewhat warmer than when I'd found him, out near the ruined Abbey on the outskirts of Winchcombe. I'd been breathless with anxiety, worrying about being followed, worrying about what kind of shape he was in, worrying if I was up to all this. My only plan at that time was to get Tim to safety and hope that between his story and the Weasel's, we could make some sense of things.

Tim was in a pretty bad way. He'd argued about coming back with me but I knew that if necessary, even I could overpower him and get him in the car. He'd given the barest of thumbnail sketches in his panic, and a garbled one at that, but it was enough to alert me to the briefcase and the potential for Weasel's role in the necessary proceedings.

'I had a key for my friend's place, Mike, but it was in the house. My house. And... – what's the use? I know exactly what's in it, and it's not what they're looking for.'

So we'd lied to the Weasel, too, to scare him into keeping his mouth shut. What we had was *not* what the bastards on Sunday were after. The briefcase was, though, at least part of the story. And now that Gaffer and I were back with it, and Tim had been fed, watered and had some minor first-aid, I hoped we'd find out the rest. He was wrapped in a blanket, lying on the sofa, and struggled to sit up as we entered, dropping a hot water bottle. Stan signed and Norman translated. 'Any longer, and he'd have had hypothermia. Dehydrated, too.'

'We should get him to a hospital!' Gaffer said.

'No!' Tim's face was stricken. 'They'd tell the police. What the ... how did you get that?' He'd spotted the briefcase.

'Carefully!' Gaffer told him. 'I'm glad to see you're not dead, mate, but I think we need to talk, right? You too, Mike.'

I explained how I'd known that Tim was still alive, and the difficulty I'd had in finding him.

'But you just phoned her tonight? Why didn't you do that in the first place?'

'I wish I could have.' He looked at me. 'I didn't know your number. All I knew was, you were staying in Ruttersford and doing some stuff at the studio complex on the Friday and might not be able to make our gig. I'd seen Raffi. She told me about it. How is she? Is she OK?'

'She's fine. Just pretty upset, thinking you were dead, and then defending your honour when the police were looking for you.'

'I daren't come into the open. There was too much at stake. But I thought if I could get at you, you could help me. It was only yesterday, when Darren finally left me, that I knew about the mobile. This woman had found us – well, him – I was hiding in the van. She was giving him hell about not taking the van back to Joe, and asking if he knew anything about the heavies at the fair.

Said she'd gone home with you and your house had been trashed.'

'Roxy.'

The name meant nothing to him. 'Like Wonder-woman?' he asked. 'With big boobaloobas? That's how Darren described her.' I smiled the confirmation. 'Anyway, she said something about your shop – I didn't know about that, either, and what she said didn't make a lot of sense, but I thought maybe I could phone there, get a message to you. I spoke to a man – pretended it was urgent musical business – and he gave me your mobile number. I've had hell's own job getting money for telephone boxes. And it ate it up when I phoned your mobile.'

'You said Darren left you – why only then?'

'He said it was one thing hiding me, another being chased by thugs. He didn't know how bad it had been until Wonderwoman – Roxy – caught up with us. She really put the wind up him. That's when he dumped me.'

Big Stan signed again. Norman nodded. 'He's been sleeping rough. Done him no good at all.'

'I can see that,' I agreed.

'Why don't you tell us what happened, Tim? Right from the start, eh?' Gaffer put in. 'Take your time, mate. You're safe here.'

'What exactly is your connection to Arthur, Tim?' I asked. 'I need to get that straight before we go any further.'

'Arthur is – was – he's dead, isn't he?' I nodded. 'He taught my father at Cambridge. They always stayed in touch. And he was pleased about me, what I was doing. When Dad told him I'd come

267

here to do my Doctorate, Arthur was delighted. Also asked if I'd do him a favour – a paid favour, actually. He was working on this history of Bewick Grange but of course, he's old school, been retired for years. Wouldn't know one end of a computer from the other. I don't think he knew how to use a video, actually. Dad joked about it once, after a visit. Anyway, the point is, Arthur wrote everything longhand. Used carbon paper, so he had more than one copy, but of course, it needed typing up. I'm just a few miles away, up to my ears in technology, so of course I said I'd do it. He sent a great wodge to begin with, then it would come a bit at a time. I kept hard copy and a copy on disk. He'd read the hard copy, make any amendments, send it back to me. This had been going on for over a year.'

'So you just used the post?'

'Basically, yes, but he'd phone me occasionally, and I'd phone him. He came here a couple of times, too. Said Cheltenham made a nice day out.'

'Did you ever go to the Grange?' I asked.

'Not the Grange itself, though I went to the village. Arthur invited me for the weekend. There was a big do on, a re-enactment of a Civil War battle. We had a great time. I met the people who own the Grange. Loads of people, actually. He seemed to be thick in with the re-enactment people – Companions of the Crooked Staff.'

'I know them well,' I commented dryly, eliciting a raised eyebrow from Gaffer. 'In fact, I'm an honorary member.'

Tim nodded. 'Well, everything was going fine,

and then I got this phone call from him. He was agitated, asking if I had the latest piece he'd sent, what he called the denouement.'

'When was this?'

'The night he died, I believe. Not that I knew about that until Sherrill and I had our visitors.'

'Go on.'

'It was Thursday evening. They seemed OK to start with – three men – well, I thought there were two at first. The other one must have stayed in the car until...' He floundered for a moment. Norman produced a handkerchief and Tim blew his nose noisily.

'What did they look like?' Gaffer asked. 'Had you seen them before? Would you know them again?'

Tim looked bewildered at the rapid fire questions and had to concentrate hard before making his reply. 'Just – ordinary. I mean, I wouldn't have let them in if I'd thought...' He swallowed hard. 'And no – I'd never seen them before. At least I don't think so...' He shook his head. 'Maybe with the Companions? Shit – I don't know!' His voice began to rise. 'At first, they just asked about the papers. As if Arthur sent them to check. Said he was worried that I didn't appear to have them. Our friends Andy and Emma were in the basement – you know I have – had – a studio down there?' I nodded. 'These men, they didn't know they were there. The soundproofing's good – was good. Anyway, they said they wanted to double-check Arthur's copy. Look at stuff. I thought it was a bit odd but I showed them the disks. They asked about the hard copy, and

Arthur's originals.'

'But I thought you sent them back to him?'

'No – he made two copies longhand, sent one to me. I walloped it in the computer and sent the print out to him, ready for amendments. I kept his handwritten stuff and a second printout. But I only had the disks at the house that night. I'd left the briefcase at Martin's. Stupid. He was going to do diagrams and graphics.' He shook his head in frustration. 'I'm not so hot on that type of thing and my machine is fairly basic. Martin's a wizard when it comes to that sort of stuff.'

Norman had made a fresh pot of tea and handed out the mugs. Big Stan signed. Norman told Tim not to drink it too quickly.

'So,' Gaffer summarised. 'These guys want to see the hard copy? They're not satisfied with the disks?'

'That's when it turned nasty. The one man said to the other, "Just like we suspected. He's going to try to cash in." Then he said, "We want the missing papers, son, and we want them now." I didn't know what they were talking about. The big one said, "Trying to up the ante, are we?" and he grabbed Sherrill.' Tim shuddered at the recollection.

'You had a fight?' Gaffer asked.

'Yes. Not much of one.' A mixture of emotions washed across Tim's face. 'I got flattened. Felt useless. Sherrill was screaming, but the other man grabbed her, hit her.' His hands were shaking as he tried to drink the tea. 'He said, to the man who was thrashing me, "I think we'd better let him know just how serious this is, don't you? Just so he realises we mean business?"' Tim's face was flushed, eyes darting. I guessed he was seeing it all in his head, reliving the horror as he told us about it. 'He laughed. The man who was holding me. Said, "Let's hot things up a bit, shall we?" Then they got the third man in.'

'How?' I asked.

'They had like a walkie-talkie thing.'

Like Jake had had, the night I arrived at the Grange? I wondered, as goose bumps rose on my flesh. Tim's voice was a whisper as he spoke his next words. 'And that's when they set fire to the house...' He was shaking now. Gaffer sat beside him.

'Steady, Tim. Nearly there, mate. We can't help unless we know.'

Tim blew his nose again and shuddered. 'The place went up like you wouldn't believe. I never thought fires could take hold so fast. And they took Sherrill, and me.' His face crumpled as realisation hit him. 'I couldn't get to the base-ment – Andy and Emma never stood a chance. Oh God...' He swallowed convulsively.

'It's not your fault, Tim. And with your help, we can hopefully nail these bastards. Now then – you said these guys took you and Sherrill, yes?'

Tim nodded. 'In a car. One of those six-seater jobs. They said I'd better deliver the goods or they'd kill her.' He looked at us helplessly. 'They threw me out of the vehicle in the middle of nowhere.'

'There was a report that you were seen running away from the house,' Gaffer told him.

Tim shook his head vigorously. 'No way. No

way! They bundled the two of us in the car and roughed us up. Said if I didn't deliver the goods... I've told you! They'll kill her!' He looked at us blankly for a second. 'You don't understand, do you? These papers they're after – I don't have them! I don't know what they want!' He broke into heart-wrenching sobs.

Gaffer rocked him like a baby. It was some time before Tim was able to continue. The room was silent apart from the ticking of Norman's clock. None of us spoke. We were all grim-faced. When Tim finally recovered himself, Gaffer asked the obvious question.

'Look, Tim – these guys take Sherrill, right? They say they're going to kill her if you don't come up with the goods. How are you supposed to deliver them? How do you stay in touch?'

'I don't stay in touch! I don't even know who they are! They said they'd killed Arthur – threw him in a pool and let him drown. They knew he couldn't swim. I checked it out the next day. Phoned his house, and a woman answered. Said she was the vicar, told me about it. She was kind, you know. Tried to break it gently and all, asking if I was a friend. There was another woman there, crying.' Probably Mrs Frewin, I thought.

'How do you deliver the goods, then, Tim? Where? When?' Gaffer was persistent.

Tim's eyes were glazed. 'I have to be at the racecourse. Next Wednesday. In a particular place. They said it would be a straight exchange – Sherrill in return for the papers.'

Gaffer glanced at me across the top of Tim's head. He looked sick.

272

'And you really don't have these papers?'

'I've told you – no! That's what I don't understand! Arthur thought he'd posted them to me. Then he's not sure. Then he says he must have. Then he's not sure again. What am I going to do?'

'We should check his house, see if they're there,' Gaffer said. He turned to me. 'Mike, do you know this vicar?'

'Yes. But it won't do any good.' I told them the Mrs Frewin saga.

'It's the first place they would have looked. And it would certainly provide a more rational explanation for Arthur's supposedly unquiet spirit.'

We were all silent. 'Let me get this right,' Gaffer said. 'What we're now saying is that, for some reason, these guys want Arthur's papers. He can't produce them, so they kill him. And when they can't find them in Arthur's house, they come after Tim, thinking he must have them.'

'Sounds about right so far,' I agreed.

'So where do you come into all this? Why keep an eye on you, turn your place over?'

I thought about it. 'Assuming that whoever is behind this is at the Grange, then the only thing I can think of is that they became aware of a connection, however tenuous, between me and Tim. I took Raffi there when we thought he was dead, remember? Talked about it in the refectory.'

'This Jake guy – was he with you at the time?'

'Yes.'

'Who's Jake?' Tim asked. I gave him a

273

rundown. He shook his head. 'Then he's got to be behind it! At least be a part of it!'

'So what do we do now?' I asked. 'I still don't think we've enough to go to the police.'

'No police!' Tim was panic-stricken, struggling to his feet. 'They'll kill Sherrill! I promised! Mike, you can't...'

'Calm down, mate!' Gaffer soothed. 'Nobody's going to the police. You're safe. And somehow, we've got to sort this out.'

'How?' I asked. *Answers on a postcard, please,* I thought. We didn't have a ghost of a chance.

Ghost of a Chance. The racecourse.

'It could be Warren,' I blurted. 'Jake could be working for Warren.' I told them about the horse. 'Didn't the Weasel talk about the guys in my house going on about next Wednesday?'

Big Stan signed. Norman asked, 'What is next Wednesday?'

'The Gold Cup, isn't it?'

'Nah!' Gaffer shook his head. 'That's Thursday. But I bet Warren's horse is running on the Wednesday.'

'But how do we find out?'

'Racing papers. Town'll be knee-deep in them.'

'Hang on,' I said. 'I still don't see how we're going to sort this out, as you so glibly put it.'

'I wasn't being glib. I was trying to bloody help.' Gaffer snapped.

'I'm sorry. I didn't mean it like that.' We were all getting very tired. 'Let's try again. How are we going to deal with this?'

We fell silent. You could almost hear the cogs grinding.

'There's only two possibilities, really, aren't there, if we're going to keep the police out of this?' Gaffer finally said. 'We either find Sherrill, or we find the papers, or both. Before next Wednesday.'

Big Stan signed, looking confused. 'He says that's three things,' Norman interpreted.

'Yes, but it strikes me there's only one way to do any of it,' I concluded. 'I'll have to go back to the Grange.'

Chapter Twenty-eight

We argued about it. Not until Tim was safely out of the way, though. We all agreed that it was too risky for him to stay in town. Quite what to do with him was a different matter, but Big Stan came to the rescue, signing rapidly. Norman signed back at him before translating for us.

'Big Stan says Tim can stay with him. It's out of town and it's safe. And Stan's handy if it does come to a punch-up.'

'Yes, but he wouldn't hear trouble coming,' I objected. 'A prowler or anything.'

'I would,' said Tim.

Norman beamed. 'So would Stan's dog.'

So it was after Tim left that we started arguing. Gaffer said I couldn't possibly go back. It was far too dangerous.

'These aren't lightweights we're dealing with, Mike! They've already killed more than once.'

'I am aware of that. I'm not exactly keen myself, but I don't see how we can get anywhere unless I do go back. The answers have to be at the Grange, and at least I have a legitimate reason for returning. Besides, if they wanted to kill me, don't you think they would have done it by now? At least had a go? No, Gaffer. I don't understand it, but thinking back to what the Weasel said was said in my house, it strikes me that they're happier with me there, where they can keep an eye on me. It might even lull them into a false sense of security.'

'You're off your trolley, Mike! There is no way you're going back there!'

We argued the toss, both of us on a very short fuse by now.

'Look, Gaffer, we're just going to have to agree to disagree for the time being. Right now, I have to get some sleep. We both do.'

He couldn't argue with that. 'All right. But we'll talk about this again in the morning. Just promise me you won't do a runner, mate – I want your word.'

'You've got it.' For all that my argument seemed logical, it didn't take much arm-twisting for me to hang fire. Logic's one thing. The bottom line, which was in my gut rather than my head, was that I was scared as hell.

Once back at Joan's, my remaining night in a decent bed was ruined by fitful sleep, punctuated by nightmares. They were more like freeze-frames, horribly vivid and aggravated by the fact that I, too, seemed paralysed and therefore unable to intervene or move away. Paul appeared. At

276

least, the upper part of his body did. He was holding up a ruined hand from which the fingers hung by the merest shreds of skin; then Jake held me in a beam of light which blinded me as well as keeping me immobile. Next came Tim, surrounded by a ring of fire which, crackling and roaring, steadily closed in on him as he screamed an endless and silent scream.

By the time morning came, I felt fragile and useless. I wasn't even up to a second round of arguing with Gaffer, let alone voluntarily mixing with murderers. Gaffer wasn't in the mood for an argument, either, though his reasons were different. He'd changed his mind.

'I've given it a lot of thought, Mike, and you're right. You have to go back. Sherrill's life is at stake. Not that I'm convinced that she is still alive, mind. Probably long killed and dumped by now. But if there's any chance – any chance at all – then we've got to do whatever we can.'

I looked at him, speechless. When I finally managed to find my voice, I said, 'Gaffer – there's just one problem. I've changed my mind. I don't want to go back. I'm scared.'

'Too right. Bloody sensible. And that's why you're not going alone. I'm coming with you.'

'You're what?'

'I'm coming with you. You don't think I'd let you go on your own, do you? No way, mate. As of now, you're stuck with me.'

'But how will I explain who you are?'

He grinned. 'I've been thinking about that, too. No one up there knows me, right?'

'Right. And they certainly haven't seen you.'

277

'So there we go. My idea is this. They all know about your stint on TV, the hoo-ha you had with Paul. So I come with you as the broken-armed sax player from that band. We'll give 'em some spiel about urgent musical collaboration or something.'

'So urgent that you're going to have to stay overnight?' I gave him my best sceptical look.

'Why not? You're not a nun. Give 'em a bit of gossip.'

'There's still a problem, Gaffer,' I pointed out. 'To be a broken-armed sax player, you'd need to have your arm in a plaster cast.'

'No sweat, mate.' He did something funny with his eyebrows. It seemed familiar, but I couldn't quite put my finger on it. 'I know a bloke who knows a girl who's doing an art course, including sculpture and stuff. Uses plaster of Paris all the time.'

'Do they still use that? For plaster casts?' I was doubtful.

'By the time it's done, no one will know the difference.'

'You can't be serious!'

'Why not? You said yourself that Maggie was dead keen for you to go back for the weekend. So that's what we do. We use today to get ourselves ready. Bone up on this stuff that Tim's been doing for Arthur. I'll get my arm sorted out and we'll go over there tomorrow, as natural as pie. What do you say, mate? Brilliant idea or what?'

I had to admit that it sounded pretty good. It certainly beat the idea of me going back on my own. 'We'll have to think of a name for you, though.'

'What's wrong with Gaffer?'

'I might have mentioned you in connection with my house being trashed.' I frowned, trying to think back through conversations. 'I can't be sure, but we'd better not risk it. Besides, I've heard of a drummer called Thrasher and a bass player called Cheesecake, but I've never heard of a sax player called anything apart from their own name.' I was lying, but he wasn't to know that. 'So – what is your name?'

He reddened. 'Bloody hell, Mike, you don't want to use that! Just make one up!'

'Come on!' I laughed. 'It can't be that bad! You're what – thirtyish?'

'Thirty-three,' he conceded.

'Well, there you are, then. It can't be Ethelred or Wilfrid or anything like that, can it? And if we just make one up, we might not remember it.' He had a very mulish look on his face. 'Come on, Gaffer – spill the beans!'

'You won't tell anyone, OK?'

'I promise.'

'Absolutely, honestly-ponestly, won't tell anyone, ever?'

'Absolutely all of that, yes. Your secret is safe with me, Inspector Morse.'

He shook his head and snorted. 'Oh bloody hell! It's Jabez. Do I look like a Jabez to you? Don't answer that..!'

I was saved from having to reply by Raffi phoning in a state of excitement to say that a letter had been safely intercepted, inviting her for a second interview.

'That's brilliant, Raffi! When?'

'Monday. Any news of Paul?'

'He's still unconscious.'

'You don't think...'

'I don't know, Raffi. I don't want to think about it. But no, at the moment, it doesn't look good.'

The police had spoken to the hospital asking if, given the circumstances, I could be treated as family. Paul's father was apparently unrelenting, saying, when told of Paul's accident, 'I have no son.' His mother, however, was distraught and wanted to see him. They were going to have a word with her.

Fortunately, I didn't have time to brood. First of all, I helped Joan to move me into 'the cubby hole'. This was, in fact, a small dressing room off her own bedroom, which led to a private bathroom.

'If you don't mind seeing me first thing in the morning, I'll close my eyes to you, love. All girls together, eh?'

'This is so good of you, Joan. Are you sure I'm not going to be in the way?'

'Of course not! First off, I sleep like the dead, and secondly, I get virtually no sleep, anyway, when the lads are here. Don't you worry about a thing.'

I told her that I'd be staying at the Grange over the weekend but would probably be back on Monday.

'You come and go as you please, Mike. You've got a key – no need to check in with me.'

I'd never slept on a camp bed before and eyed it with some misgivings. At least if I fell out, I wouldn't have far to fall. About six inches, by the look of it.

I spent most of the afternoon going through Arthur's incomplete history of the Grange. Tim had opened the briefcase for us and Gaffer had photocopied everything twice, so we could each sift through the papers.

'I know he said these aren't what those guys were after, but maybe they'll give us some clue. Especially you, Mike. You say you've been all round the place?'

'More or less.'

'Well, maybe something will ring a bell. You're more likely to pick up on stuff than me or Tim, so let's give it a go, eh? There's other stuff in the briefcase – letters and what have you – but this is where we need to start.'

I read until my eyes ached. It was fascinating work. Arthur seemed to have had a gift for making history not only accessible, but spellbinding. Some of today's pot-boilers seemed tame compared with the real-life events I was reading about. Internecine strife, political manoeuvring, betrayal – it was all there, with a vengeance. Vengeance, in fact, seemed to have been a major factor in a lot of the proceedings, anyway. It was a case of 'you murdered my brother, spurned my mother, dishonoured my sister and ill-treated my daughter's prize cow', carried on over countless generations, particularly in the early days.

Arthur also dealt with the history of the village from pre-Norman times, tracing the founding of the Grange, its expansion, decline and re-building as well as the varying fortunes of its owners. Its place in everything from the Reformation, through the Civil War to the present day tourist economy of the area was meticulously accounted for. And still I didn't have a clue why something to do with it was worth killing for.

I hadn't originally planned to play this evening, but it was Friday, and Patsy had said she couldn't cover for me after all, so I had to go. Friday nights are usually good, but Joan's Irishmen were not the only people cramming into town a couple of days ahead of the festival. The joint was jumping, the landlord was canny to it and had reduced playing space to a minimum, all the better to pack more customers in.

'Another sardine job, then,' Richard grumbled in good-natured fashion. We were used to this. Being a nine-piece band, you have to get on well, especially when you're squashed into a space where even a four-piece would have trouble playing.

'Cheer up!' I said. 'It's not as bad as that gig last month!' That really had been the limit. The venue was a tiny restaurant with a stage the size of a postage stamp. Chris had had to stand with one foot on its edge and the other on an upturned waste-paper bin, and Richard had nearly dislodged a customer's toupee with the errantly enthusiastic slide of his trombone. That aside, we wouldn't have been invited back anyway, as John had dispensed liberal amounts of good, old-fashioned sweat into the front row diners and their meals. All in an evening's work...

This evening, at least, was a great one. We played our socks off, and the crowd was the sort that were determined to have a good time, regardless. Buoyant, relaxed, and with money to burn, they drank a lot, sang a lot, and vocalised the horn lines on a couple of James Brown numbers as well as the ever-popular 'Mustang Sally'. By the time we got a break, we were hot in more ways than one. Brian, our drummer, a builder by profession, stood dripping as if he'd just come out of a shower, and was downing pints of water like there was no tomorrow.

'Bloody hell, Mike!' he gasped. 'I spends me days freezing me nuts off and now the bastards are trying to roast me alive! They've only stuck me kit by the sodding radiator!'

John was already making noises about getting ready for the second set but several of us asked if we had time to go to the toilet first.

'I'm a singer, not a schoolteacher! Make it quick!' He clapped his hands at us, shooing us away like chickens.

We played the second set, the crowd roaring themselves hoarse in their unwillingness to let us go. We encored until we ran out of material and the bouncers moved in. Then we had to pack up. Brian looked like he'd spent the last couple of hours in a sauna. He was dripping, cursing and muttering, mantra-like, that one day, by God, he'd have a roadie to do all this for him. Ian had to shoot off because his Mum wasn't well. The rest of us got stuck in.

With the doors wide open and the customers gone, the wind was whipping through the place and I slipped my coat on before humping bits of Brian's drum kit out to the van.

'There you are look!' Chris grinned. 'Mike playing the sax is just an optical illusion. She's really your roadie, Bri!'

'Yeah – she didn't break the buggering kit down for me, though!'

'What do you want – jam on it?!' I laughed.

'You look like a bleedin' leprechaun, Mike! Gone green for the Irish?'

'Well of course, begosh and begorrah!' I wrestled his cymbal bag from him. He didn't put up too much of a fight.

'Actually, you look very nice.'

'Well thank you, kind sir!' I really must let Henrietta and Raffi dress me more often. I'd had nothing but compliments on the green velvet coat.

John picked up something from the top of a speaker cab. 'Whose is this?'

'Anthony's.' Brian had glanced over.

'Do something with it, will you?' John threw it at him. Brian shrugged, grinned and tossed it over to me. 'Keep hold of it till next time, eh, Mike? If I stick it in my pocket, it'll go rusty.'

'Yeah – the incredible corrosive drummer!' Chris taunted.

'Just a bloody drip!' John corrected.

'Strewth!' I said, hefting the thing in my hand. 'Swiss Army knives never used to be this big when I was a girl!'

'Didn't think they were invented when you were a girl, Mike! Anyway – he is a tree surgeon. Needs a big one.'

'Thanks a bunch, you bastard!' I slipped it into my coat pocket.

'Here, Bri!' Chris called. 'Heard the one about the drummer who...'

'Yeah, yeah! Up yours, too!'

'Hey, Bri – how does a drummer know when his drum stool's level?'

'He dribbles out of both sides of his mouth. I've heard that one, as well.'

They were still trading drummer jokes when I left.

Chapter Twenty-nine

I heard the singing from half way down the street and decided I'd better change my tactics. I had originally been thinking of sneaking into the hotel so as not to disturb anyone. It seemed that now, trying to sneak in so that no one noticed me might be a better option. Not that it worked. I quietly let myself into the kitchen just as Joan entered it with two men in tow. They – the men, that is – took an exaggerated step backwards.

'Jesus, Mary and Joseph! I've never seen a burglar looking like that!'

'You can say that again, O'Malley! She's wearing at least one of the forty shades of green, and have you ever seen such hair! 'Tis the colour of the copper pans in old Ma Donovan's kitchen!'

'Never mind the hair, man – though sure enough, it is beautiful – will you look at that for a swag bag?'

'Swag bag, my eye! You're an ould fool, that's

what you are! Unless me eyes are deceiving me – which I have to admit, is a distinct possibility to be taken into account, given the amount of liquor I've imbibed so far this evening – I'd lay a fair bet that it's none other than a musical instrument case!' They looked at Joan, feigning shock, and clapped their arms around her shoulders.

'Joan! Lord save us, you laid on entertainment and never told us!'

'Hello, Joe! Hello, Charley!' I grinned as I put down the sax case to hug them.

'Michal, darlin' – how are you...?'

That was the start of the second part of my evening. Or should I say the first part of my morning? Either way, by the time I got to bed – around 4 a.m. – I neither knew nor cared. The lounge bar, into which I was led like a prize exhibit, was thick with bodies and thicker still with Irish brogues. Joan and I had the only English accents to be heard and were the only women. After an exuberant welcome, it took all the tact I could muster to convince them that it wouldn't be a good idea for me to play right now, thank you, because, you know, it was late, or early, depending on your point of view, and the neighbours might not appreciate it. I did tell them, however, that I would be playing, free of charge, from Sunday night onwards with not one, but two of my bands. They promised to come, and I knew John would bless the day he made the deal with that landlord. How Frederick would take to such an audience, I wasn't sure, but we'd soon find out.

Joan had evidently told them about the reason

for my stay with her, because they muttered darkly about what they'd do to the hooligans responsible for driving me out of my house and home, if ever they laid their hands on them. They were a disparate bunch, some of whom I knew, some whose faces I could vaguely remember but at the expense of their names, and some, I was convinced I'd never seen before. The big thing was, they all had a common interest in gambling, drinking and horses, not necessarily in that order, and never more so than when the three came together in Cheltenham during Gold Cup Week.

Charley and Joe, who'd greeted me in the kitchen, I'd first met several years ago. They'd attended the same school and married two of the sisters of another school friend, Dermot, who'd emigrated to America. In their early fifties, perhaps – I've never been very good at guesstimating people's ages – Joe was a farmer and Charley, unbelievably, a member of the Irish Parliament. I got the same warning from the others every year.

'You'll have to watch him, Michal! You know what they say, and no doubt 'tis true in England, just the same – never trust a politician.'

'Unless he's giving you a racing tip! Any horse that comes off his tongue is placed. Lord knows how he does it.' This piece of advice came from Thomas, the oldest member of the group.

'Talking of horses...' I said.

'Which we weren't!'

'For a change! But go ahead anyway!'

'What do you think of Ghost of a Chance – running on Wednesday?'

Charley was the in-house spokesperson, having a pact with the devil and all.

'Good horse. Sound. A real beauty. Same colour as your hair, Michal, come to think of it. I would have put my money on him, but there's been a rumour that he's not on form.'

'Somebody tried to nobble him, so I heard,' Joe put in.

'Oh, he's fit!' I assured them. I told them what had happened.

'And this friend of yours – the one that's treating him – he's really that good?'

'Yes.'

'Then put your money where your mouth is, woman. What's the odds, Thomas?'

As if Charley didn't know! It was just a kind of ritual. Thomas was always the one to tell you the odds.

'Sixty to one this morning.'

Charley thought for a moment, and looked at me solemnly. 'He's really that good, this friend of yours?'

'Really.' I nodded slowly and emphatically to further the point.

'Then, if you've a hundred pounds or so to spare, I'd put it on him. On the nose.' He took in my blank expression. 'That means, to win. As opposed to each way, which is for a place. Do it in the morning. There's a bookie's just down the road.'

I looked at him dubiously. 'I've never been to a bookie's. I wouldn't know what to do.'

'You don't know how to place a bet? Lord love us, you're an innocent!'

288

'She's sensible!' muttered Joan.

'Well, we'll take you in the morning and give you a lesson in unsensibility.'

'Sure, and there's no such word, you ould fool!'

'She knows what I mean!'

They looked set to start singing again. I made my excuses, saying I had to go to bed.

'And just where is she going to lay her pretty head, Joan? Are we not taking up all your rooms?' Joe asked.

Joan explained my sleeping arrangements. There was a chorus of protest.

'She can't be doing that! What kind of men would we be, allowing Michal to sleep on a camp bed...' Joe made it sound like 'bed of nails' or 'the rack'. '...when we have Dunlopillo and all?'

'Well, she can't sleep with you lot!' Joan laughed.

'No, but she could have my room. 'Tis a single.' Thomas offered.

I held up my hands. 'No, really – it's fine. I'm going away for the weekend anyway,' I told him.

'All the more reason you'll be needing your beauty sleep! I'll be hearing no argument, now.'

'Hold on a minute!' said Joan. 'You think I want you sleeping in my dressing room, Thomas Cullen? I'm not so green as I'm cabbage looking, I'll have you know!' Raucous laughter greeted her announcement.

'You think this old goat would be bothering you, Joan, darlin'?' Charley was bent double at the thought. 'God love you, he lost the lead in his pencil years ago! He'd need an instruction manual, I'm telling you!'

''Tis the truth, I have to admit. Not that you're not a fine woman and all, Joan...' Thomas agreed mournfully. But he winked as I was ushered up to his room.

The next morning was a real eye-opener. Once I could get my eyes open, that is. I overslept horribly and had to ring Gaffer to stop him thinking that I'd been kidnapped. I met Charley on the half-way landing of the stairs. His face was cut and his right arm was in a sling. He was blocking my descent by standing at the payphone and behind him, where the window should have been, emptiness gaped. I looked from him to it as he finished his conversation with his wife.

'Yes, everything's fine, darlin', just fine. You take care now, and kiss the little one for me.' He gave me a sheepish shrug as he replaced the receiver.

'What on earth happened to you?' I asked.

'Ahh ... 'twas nothing much. They tell me I lurched a little on my way to bed, and fell through the window.'

'You what?!' I looked down at the flagstones. Joe was scrubbing at them with a yard brush and a bucket of soapy water, aided by a younger man I remembered from the night before.

'You landed there?!' The bloodstains spoke for themselves, but I still had to ask. Charley shrugged again and winced slightly.

'Must have rubber bones. Never broke a thing. Never felt a thing, come to that. Not at the time, anyway...' He headed up the stairs as I went down to eat.

The dining room was full but strangely silent, inhabited by bleary-eyed, unshaven men suffering various degrees of hangover. One was perfectly dressed from the waist up but still wearing his pyjama bottoms. I hoped someone would remind him before he decided to go out.

Joan came in with a tray of coffee. She had an expression of disbelief on her face, the corners of her mouth tucked into a funny little smile. How odd, I thought. She must have seen all this before. Then I caught sight of Thomas. He was sitting in the corner, clean-shaven, dapper, and with enough of a glow to his cheeks to put paid once and for all to his vampire reputation. He looked at me, nodded, smiled, and gave a long, slow wink...

Chapter Thirty

I picked Gaffer up from Norman's place. He had sneaked in to avoid anyone seeing him with his arm in plaster, fearing it might lead to awkward questions. He'd also dropped off Lucy to be looked after while we were away. I was relieved he wasn't taking her with us, figuring I had enough to be scared of without worrying about being on a dog's menu as well.

'Well – how do I look?' Gaffer asked as we were about to leave.

'Impressive!' I wasn't only talking about the plaster cast. He was wearing a blue suit, jacket slung round his shoulders, a grey silk turtle neck sweater, shades, and a highly embroidered, multicoloured smoking cap.

'Think it's suitably jazz-ish, then?'

'Cool School. Definitely. And the plaster cast is very realistic.'

'Tell me about it! It weighs a ton. I told Julie not to make too good a job of it, but she said if she made it too thin, it would crack.' He pulled back the cut off sleeve of his sweater to give me a better look. 'Just mustn't get it wet. Real work of art, eh?'

It certainly was. Suitably aged to suggest a couple of weeks' wear, it was covered in cartoons, rude messages and autographs.

'I ought to add mine to that,' I told him.

'Yeah. We can mucky it up a bit with damp fag ash.' Neither of us smokes, so we had to wait while Norman rolled up for our benefit. Finally, everything was done.

'Right then! Suppose we'd better get going, mate.'

'Yes.' How come I felt so reluctant? Cowardice, I supposed, though, to be fair, with rather more reason for it than usual.

'Did you bring the music and stuff?'

'It's in the car.' If we were supposed to be working on some musical collaboration, we'd thought it better to play the game properly and take the necessary accoutrements for cover.

'Did you have to take time off work to do this?' I asked as we drove out of Cheltenham. We had a pretty free run, but traffic going into town was chock-a-block.

'Nah. I was off this weekend anyway because I'm working straight days all through next week. You know what it's like – racing breakfasts. Packed lunches for the racecourse. We're doing special offer eat-in lunches as well as the usual evening stuff!'

'You'll be knackered!'

'Yeah, but rich. They don't half tip well.' The generosity of race-goers, especially the Irish, during Gold Cup week, was legendary. Raffi had waitressed at the racecourse several times and had always come home with a small fortune.

'Thanks for ringing this morning, Mike. Take it you got nobbled by the Irish Contingent?'

'You can say that again!'

'Great bunch, aren't they?'

I gave him a potted version of events, neatly editing out my suspicions about Joan and Thomas.

'So what's the plan when we get to the Grange, mate? Strikes me we could do with Baldrick right now.'

'Baldrick has a cunning plan, milord!' we chorused, laughing. Anything to ease the tension.

'I'm not sure,' I admitted. 'But let me bounce some ideas round with you, OK?'

'Fire ahead.'

'On one level, I'm thinking that going back to the Grange should look perfectly natural. It's well known that I have unfinished business, so going back to wrap it up before Race Week shouldn't look suspicious. On the other hand ... do you fancy a coffee?' I'd spotted a roadside cafe which would make a welcome break before the final leg of our destination. More prevarication, I knew, but I couldn't help it.

'Yeah, why not?' Gaffer agreed. 'Let's get things straight and psyche ourselves up.'

We continued out conversation inside. 'On the other hand,' I repeated, 'whoever is behind all this may think we're getting too close for comfort, and I don't like the idea of that, Gaffer.'

'JB remember?'

We'd settled on that abbreviation to lessen his embarrassment. 'Oh, shit, yes! JB. JB.' I ran it through my head like a mantra whilst he stirred his coffee thoughtfully.

'I can see where you're coming from, Mike, but maybe that's not such a bad thing – as long as they don't go too OTT. What I mean is, if our being there turns the heat up a bit, maybe they'll get nervous, make a mistake.'

'Or kill Sherrill.'

He looked at me over the rim of his cup. 'You really think she's still alive? Seems to me they've wiped out everybody else that got in their way.'

'Don't!' I said. 'Don't say that! It's only the chance that Sherrill is still alive that's making me go back at all. Besides...' I added. 'Thinking about it logically, why kill her before Wednesday? They're banking on Tim delivering the goods, right? He's not going to hand anything over without seeing her first. So there's no point in killing her before then.'

'Maybe. But he's got nothing to hand over, mate. And if they clock that – which they may already have done – then why keep her alive? She'd be a liability. And they've got to be worried in case he's gone to the police.'

'With the police suspecting him of arson and murder?' I shook my head. 'I don't think so.'

'Let's hope you're right.'

We sat in silence for a moment. Finally, Gaffer put down his cup and sighed, looking me straight in the eye. 'Well – sitting here isn't going to get us anywhere, is it?'

'No, it's not,' I agreed, and stood up. 'Let's go. JB.'

Our arrival at the Grange was uneventful and unremarked. No one seemed to be around.

'Bit quiet, isn't it?' Gaffer commented as we unloaded the car and took things into the cottage. I'd phoned Maggie to let her know I'd be coming back and given her the spiel on JB's presence. There was a note under the door. It said, *Don't know what time you'll be arriving, Mike, but we'll be riding and brunching as usual. Big do with the Companions this afternoon. Would you and JB like to come for a meal with me, Steve and Katie? Lots of love, Maggie.*

I showed the note to Gaffer and looked at my watch. 'Well,' I said, 'I think they should be brunching by now. What do you think?'

'Let's do it!'

The refectory was heaving. I hadn't expected to see so many people and hesitated just inside the door. Maggie soon put paid to that, shooting over and enveloping me in one of her hugs. I introduced her to JB, who took it all in his stride.

'I wasn't expecting a fancy-dress party at this time of day!' he grinned.

'The Companions of the Crooked Staff,' she

told him. 'Mike will fill you in.'

'I didn't know there were so many of them,' I confessed.

'That's because you've only met the hard core local lot. There are more of them who don't live locally, often miles away. They train closer to home and Edward – their leader, and our Head Gardener,' she put in for JB's benefit '–co-ordinates them for the big events.'

'Where is Edward?' I asked, noticing his absence. There was no sign of Jake, either, or Warren, come to that.

'Off collecting his "elite unit". From Birmingham, would you believe?'

'I'll believe anything here!' Gaffer – JB – laughed.

We sat down and made ourselves at home. Katie, who had been playing under a nearby table, squealed with delight when she saw me. 'Mike! Did you bring Dexter again?'

'Indeed I did!' I confirmed. 'And I brought my friend, JB.'

She admired his plaster cast and smoking cap in equal measure, staring round-eyed at his head when he took off the cap for her to play with.

'Are you really, really old?' she asked.

'Katie...!' Steve bit his lip to suppress a laugh.

'Positively ancient!' Gaffer grinned. 'Why?'

'I thought only really old people were bald but you don't look old. Your skin's not all wrinkly like old people.'

'Ah! That's because I shave my head. Like your dad shaves his whiskers. Oh – maybe not!' He had just realised that the bearded Steve was the father in question. He wiggled his eyebrows at her and she rocked with laughter. That eyebrow business still reminded me of something and still, I couldn't put my finger on it. Gaffer then got into a conversation with Steve and Katie, leaving me free to catch up on news with Maggie.

'We are definitely going away, Mike, once all this is over!' she announced. 'Just you and I, and I won't hear any argument! It's been worse than not having you here at all, having you popping in and out like a yo-yo. Especially with me up to my ears over the opening.'

'Bad timing,' I conceded. I glanced round the room. Elynore was talking to a gaunt-looking man dressed in Companions' garb. Maggie followed my gaze. 'Dave Turley – he's in charge while Edward's away.'

I nodded. 'Where's Jake?' I asked.

'Away with Warren. Something to do with Ghost of a Chance. They're inseparable at the moment. Warren and Jake, I mean.'

'Ghost's not unfit to run?' I asked, thinking of the hundred pounds I'd put on him this morning.

'Oh no. Fit as a fiddle!'

'And when will they be back?' I was wondering what they might really be up to.

'Tomorrow. Keen to see Jake, are you?'

'Not at all, actually.'

She opened her mouth, caught my expression and thought better of it.

'So when's all this Companions stuff happening?' I asked.

'It'll be starting in about an hour's time. Should

297

be fun. Are you and JB coming for tea later?'

'Sure. We'd love to.'

She looked at him curiously. 'Not your type, I would have thought.'

'Strictly business. Besides, you should know me by now, Maggie – I don't have a type.'

'I know...' she muttered. 'But I can still live in hope!'

Elynore was happy for me to give Gaffer my own version of a guided tour, particularly when I told her that we were thinking of writing a piece fusing classical music through the ages with a jazz interpretation of the history of the Grange. I'd made this up off the top of my head but Gaffer really came up trumps, nodding as if he'd known about it all along, enthusing about history, culture and the "third space between public and private, being and becoming" and how music "transcended dualistic modalities and the constraints of written language".

'I didn't know you had a degree in bullshit!' I told him as we started our tour.

'I don't. It's in Cultural Studies, Masters level. Some people say it amounts to the same thing, actually!'

'You're kidding!'

'Just because I spend my time playing the guitar and slaving over a hot stove, it doesn't mean I can't think, mate! Right – get me oriented.'

Having Arthur's manuscript had shed new light on things and gave us greater urgency.

'So why is everyone so sure that a second priests' hole exists?' Gaffer asked. 'I must have been nodding off by the time I got to that bit.'

'Early records. Contemporary accounts of its use.'

'You reckon Sherrill could be being held there?'

The idea startled me. 'I don't see how, when it's never been found. Even the previous owner didn't know where it was, and Arthur couldn't find it.'

'Hmm. What about the haunted nursery, then? What do you make of that?'

I took him to it, to make his own judgement.

'Jesus, they got a draught in here or what?'

'Not that I can find. Weird, isn't it? And it looks so homely, so pretty. I can't account for its coldness.' I shivered uncomfortably.

'Your psychic investigators would say the drop in temperature is indicative of paranormal activity. And the kid's ghost is supposed to haunt the place, eh? How do you pronounce her name?'

'Zhilane.'

. 'I never did French.' He shook his head ruefully. 'Embarrassed myself something terrible when I was a new Undergrad. at University. Only went and asked for a book on "Dezcarteez". I don't know how the librarian kept a straight face.'

We knocked and tapped our way around the room, almost carrying out a fingertip search, to no avail.

Gaffer was thoroughly exasperated. 'So where's all this crying and moaning coming from?'

'The cleaner probably just has an overactive imagination. You know what it's like – one whiff of anything out of the ordinary and it tends to get embellished. Attention by association.'

'Yeah. Well. Whatever. But there's something not right in here, mate. I can feel it in my bones.'

We left the house and watched some of the Companions in a skirmish on the South Lawn before heading over to Steve's for tea. Gaffer was pressing me to let Maggie in on things in the hope that she may be able to shed light on what was going on.

'No, Gaffer. We'd be putting her at risk. This is her employer we're talking about, for God's sake!'

'But she's your mate, Mike!'

'Exactly. Which is precisely why I don't want her involved.'

'OK. But I still think we need to get someone on our side. And what was it we were talking about the other night – we need to get into Arthur's house. I know, I know...!' He staved off my interruption with a wave of his hand. 'The bad guys must already have turned it over. But what else have we got to go on?'

'You're right,' I acknowledged. 'And if we want to get into Arthur's house, I think we should go and see Alison.'

We walked round to the vicarage after our tea with Maggie, Steve and Katie. Gaffer had scored an even bigger hit than he'd made with his brunchtime performance, using his one free hand to join in 'Chopsticks' and 'The Monkey's Wedding' on the piano, and schmoozing scat to one of my own compositions on saxophone. We promised to go back for an encore the following day.

The route I chose to take to Alison's was not the most direct, and took us past the ornamental pool where she and I had found Arthur's body. Gaffer and I stood in silence. It had been bad enough when I'd believed – when we'd all believed – his death to be an accident. Knowing now that he'd been deliberately thrown in there, that the people responsible had known he couldn't swim, horrified me beyond expression. It brought my own near-drowning experience into uncomfortably sharp focus. At least that had been an accident. But these men... Had they watched him thrashing around, I wondered? Did they hang about, waiting to make sure he was dead? Had they – God forbid – held him under?

'Come on, Mike.' Gaffer put his unplastered arm around me. 'There's nothing we can do for him now. But maybe, just maybe, we can do something for Sherrill, eh?'

We left the pool and made our way over the short distance to the back of the vicarage. Alison let us in, wearing teddy bear slippers and with her hair in rollers. We told our story only after swearing her to secrecy and priestly confidentiality. I wasn't sure if the C of E worked in the same way as the Catholic church in that respect, but she understood what we meant and promised to tell no one, especially the police, until after Wednesday. We figured we only needed her word that far because if we hadn't unravelled the mystery or found the missing papers by then, it would be too late anyway. Gaffer had his own ideas on that, however, arguing that, if necessary, we could stage a last-ditch rescue attempt at the racecourse with the help of Joan's Irish contingent. Alison sat silently as we argued about this, finally saying, 'That's enough! You'd better start at the beginning!' So we did.

We were lucky that Arthur's house hadn't been cleared yet. William, the nephew, had asked Alison to do it in return for a generous contribution to church funds, but she hadn't got round to starting yet.

'I'd pencilled it in – making a start, that is – for next week. Are you quite sure about all this? About Arthur being ... killed. On purpose?'

'Murdered? Yes.' Gaffer seemed to be the only one with the stomach to say the word. I recounted what the Weasel had told us.

'Dear God! We have a duty to get to the bottom of this. For Arthur, as well as Sherrill.'

Gaffer shook his head. 'I don't understand how they let Arthur be buried,' he said.

'Why not? The postmortem showed that he'd drowned. There was no evidence of foul play. The body was released for burial and the inquest set for a later date.' Alison paced the floor, making the ears of her teddy bear slippers flap dementedly. 'What you're looking for – it could help bring Arthur's killers to justice?'

'Absolutely.' I sounded more confident than I was really feeling. 'And if we can find evidence, we can go to the police. That's our biggest problem at present – having to keep them out of it. I also hope it will clear Tim and enable us to get Sherrill back safely.'

'Right. Give me a minute, and I'll be with you.' She went off and came back a few minutes later with her hair brushed and free of rollers and with sensible shoes on her feet. She took a coat from a hook behind the door and said, 'Come on – I'll take you to the house.'

It was dark and quiet and the streets were almost deserted as we made our way, on foot, through the village. It reminded me somewhat of the similar trek Gaffer and I had made on our trip with the Weasel. At least we had keys this time, though.

'What about Mrs Frewin?' I asked. 'She's bound to hear us and wonder what's going on.'

'I don't think so – Saturday night is the Beetle Drive at the old village hall. She's been regular as clockwork for years.'

A few minutes more and we stood outside an end-of-terrace house. Alison inserted the key in the lock and stepped inside. It was the kind of house where you stepped straight off the street into the living room. Alison turned on the lights and closed the curtains. We stood for a moment, unsure as to quite what to do next. Despite the purpose of our visit, there was a lingering feeling of invading the dead man's space. We meant him no harm – quite the contrary – but somehow, it still felt like a violation.

The front room had obviously been used as an office and seemed a logical place to start our search. We showed Alison the type of papers we were looking for and all set to work. Nothing. Piles of papers, yes, but not what we were looking for.

'We'll have to try the other rooms, I suppose,' I said. 'We...'

There was a loud knocking on the door. We froze, looking at each other in horror, like cornered rats. 'In the back!' Alison hissed. Gaffer and I scrambled for the door, then we were through it and behind it, standing in the dark with the door ajar so we could hear what was happening.

'Hello, Jake! What brings you here?'

Alison's voice sounded absolutely normal. My heart was pounding. I don't think I could have done so well. 'He's supposed to be away with Warren until tomorrow,' I whispered to Gaffer.

'Hi, Alison – lights!' came the Texas drawl. 'I was concerned, you know. Thought someone might have broken in.'

'Oh, right! No – just me, I'm afraid. I'm supposed to be packing everything up for Arthur's nephew. Just thought I'd bring a few boxes over in readiness for the task.'

'Sure. Hope I didn't scare you.'

'No, no. You were right to check up.'

'You need a hand at all?'

I closed my eyes and held my breath. *Pleease* make him go away.

'No, I'm fine, thanks. But thanks for the offer.'

'I'll be on my way then. Oh – have you seen Michal at all? Mike Brodie?'

My heart may have been pounding before. It was in my mouth now.

'I heard she was back,' he continued, 'and I – uh – I need to speak to her.'

'Mike? Yes, she is back, I believe. Have you tried the cottage?'

'No reply. I guess she could be gigging. I'll have

a word with Maggie. Thanks, Alison. Goodnight.'

''Night, Jake.'

Gaffer and I remained motionless, even after we heard her close the door. I was holding my breath, worried he'd come back. Alison stepped into the back room with us, turning on the light as she did so.

'Jesus Christ! Sorry, vicar.' Gaffer let out a huge sigh of relief. 'Hey, Mike – are you all right?'

I was staring at the photographs on the wall. At one of them in particular.

'Oh my God...' I breathed. My mouth was dry and I was suddenly smitten with goose bumps. 'Alison – that man – in the photo – was that Arthur?'

'Why yes. It was. Mike – you look as if you've seen a ghost.'

'Oh God. I have. Let's get out of here. Gaffer...' I said, clutching his sleeve. 'We've got to get hold of Raffi.'

Chapter Thirty-one

Gaffer didn't catch up with me until I was half-way down the street, shouting at my mobile in frustration, with Alison struggling along behind.

'Raffi?' He grabbed my arm. 'Why have we got to find Raffi?'

'She's got the key to this whole thing! At least I think she has. I had it all along, and didn't even know! Oh God, if she's thrown it away...' I was almost incoherent with panic.

'Mike...!'

'We've got to get away without Jake seeing us! Shit!' I'd caught sight of the church clock. 'I've got this bloody gig and I can't get out of it and...'

'Slow down, Mike, and come out of scramble! I haven't understood a word you've said!' Gaffer shook me, and I struggled to gather my thoughts.

'I'll explain on the way.' I turned to Alison, who had caught us up by now. 'Just pray I'm right about this. Pray that Raffi hasn't thrown it away. I'll fill you in later. We have to go.'

'What about Jake?' she asked.

'If you see him again, do what you did back there – just stall. Don't risk your own neck, for heaven's sake.' She nodded. We ran.

'Are we likely to meet Jake on the way to the cottage?' Gaffer asked.

'I hope not. He said he'd already been there, and if he was serious about asking Maggie where I am, he'll probably go to Steve's. Damn! She knows about the gig and she'd see no harm in telling him!'

'Don't you worry about that! I'll be there, remember, keeping an eye on you.'

'No you won't – you'll be finding Raffi! She's not answering her mobile.'

'You think she's in danger?'

'No – would I be doing a bloody gig if that was the case?! It's classic Saturday night – she's probably in a club with a load of mates and can't hear it. But we *have* to find her!'

We reached the cottage, and, leaving Gaffer to keep an eye on things outside, I changed and hurriedly threw Lady Day into the car, mind whirling.

'Oh God!' I said as we turned onto the main road. 'She's got that job interview on Monday – what if she's spending the weekend in London?' The car should know the route to Cheltenham by heart now. I wished it had autopilot.

'You've lost me again, mate! What the hell has Raffi got to do with this?'

Swiftly, I told him.

We arrived at the pub with little time to spare. Gaffer had become paranoid about leaving me there to go and find Raffi, but we both grinned as soon as we walked in. Joan's Irishmen were out in force, although there was no sign of Tom, or Joan herself.

'I'll have a little word...' Gaffer set off towards them as I hastily unpacked the sax, apologising to Frederick for having cut my arrival so fine. Nick looked scrumptious. He, I noticed, had not been afflicted with a Green Glittery Jacket but was wearing a tuxedo and a green bow tie without the spots. Gaffer whizzed over as I settled myself behind my music stand. 'I'll be back...' he intoned, like Arnold Schwarzenegger.

'Yes please!' I grinned. And please, God, let him find Raffi, or at least find out where she is. I knew Gaffer would soon have everyone we knew and their cousins looking for her and my best bet was to stay put, right here.

'And Mike–' Gaffer gave me a lecturely look before finally disappearing. '–you don't leave here without me. Not even outside to pack up, OK?

307

I've briefed the boys. If they get this signal from you...' he demonstrated, '...or if they spot Jake themselves, they'll handle it, OK?'

'OK.' I had given Gaffer a good description of Jake to pass on.

'Ahem!' Frederick was looking disgruntled. I felt suitably guilty. 'If you're quite ready, Michal? It would be nice to start on time, especially as Nick is making his debut...'

'Of course. I'm sorry.'

'Very well, then...' He took up his position and tapped his piano lid as if he didn't already have our attention. Nick looked set to provide additional percussion until it was time for him to sing. He was discreetly positioned by George, the drummer, who was looking resplendent with the squashed guinea pig on his head. I closed my eyes, determined not to laugh.

Quickly, I scanned the audience. Mainly older people, the Irish contingent aside, which was to be expected for this kind of music. No sign of Jake, thank God, Joe and Charley waved to me and raised their glasses. They had set themselves, like sentinels, at either end of the row of Irishmen which had, by now, become an informal barrier between the band and the rest of the audience.

We started to play. Not perfectly, but unless my ears were deceiving me, better than we had in a long time. The audience clapped. We played another instrumental, and as we finished, Nick smoothed on down to the vocal mike in time for us to go straight into his first number, Frederick's special arrangement of 'Moon Love'. The change in atmosphere was electric from the moment he opened his mouth. You could have heard a pin drop. He had the punters in the palm of his hand. His voice was smooth as silk and warm as velvet. Listening to him became a tactile experience, his voice caressing every nerve ending you possessed. It was Lady Day's debut, too, and with him leading, she swung out from behind and covered him with kisses in a solo so sensual, it was the closest I've come to an out-of-body experience. When the number ended, there was silence. It hung, palpable and quivering, before exploding into a roar of approval from the crowd. Those who had been sitting were standing now, clapping and whistling. Those already standing were stamping their feet as well as clapping and whistling. Those of us in the band were stunned by the response.

Things got better still. As Nick played the audience like fish on a line, the evening simply took off. *God knows how we're going to keep him*, I thought. With a voice like that, he just had to go on to better things.

Close to the end of the night, I was on such a high from playing that it's a wonder I noticed Jake at all. He was standing at the back, near the door. Our eyes met and locked, mine swinging away as the chill of fear gatecrashed my happiness. What they focused on next caused the fear to bite deeper still. On the opposite side of the room were three men. Three men among many in the audience, but I knew, just knew in my bones, that they were the men who'd broken into my house. They looked at me steadily, making no attempt to disguise their interest. One of them bore a striking resemblance to a gorilla. I darted a glance back at Jake. He looked from me to the three men and simultaneously, they started to move forward. My mouth felt like sandpaper. Joe's eyes narrowed as I made the pre-arranged signal, indicating that trouble was approaching on two fronts. Frederick, oblivious to the brewing storm, was announcing that Nick was going to sing 'Careless'. Gaffer walked through the door just as my Irish friends launched into their own special version of 'The Camptown Races'.

'I know something you don't know, Doo-Da! Doo-Da!' they sang, turning to face the rest of the audience. Frederick turned back to the band, baffled and affronted, as Nick, rather more alert to trouble, raised his eyebrows at me, moving within earshot.

'Bandits, ten o'clock and two o'clock,' I told him.

'Are you in trouble?'

'We all could be...' I answered as the fight broke out.

Jake disappeared, knocked to the ground, and Gaffer ran forward, treading on people in his haste to get to me. Nick picked up a mike stand as Gaffer tried to grab my arm.

'No!' I yelled. 'He's on our side! Don't hit him – hit HIM!' He caught the expression on my face just in time, ducking and swivelling in one flowing movement, to jab one of the Gang of Three straight in the balls. The Irish contingent, still singing, dragged his victim away as Gaffer yanked me forward into the fray, heading, as a lot of the more sensible people present were doing, for the door. My one glance back was incredulous. George, squashed guinea pig over one eye, was brandishing his high hat stand at an interloper. And Nick, I noticed, had a very neat left jab.

Lady Day was still slung around my neck and I clutched her to my body with one hand, the other firmly in the grip of Gaffer's unplastered arm. We ran down the street as fast as we could, people scattering in all directions. I'd had to park the car some distance away and knew we couldn't stop until we reached it, and safety.

We reached the car, all right, but it didn't equate to safety. They'd got us well sussed, I thought. One of the Gang of Three rose up from the other side of it. It was the Gorilla, and he looked pretty pissed off.

'Back off, mate,' he growled at Gaffer. 'No need for trouble. It's just her I want.'

'Then you've got trouble,' Gaffer replied, 'because if you want Mike, you're going to have to come through me.'

I glanced around, senses straining for any sign of the others.

Gaffer dropped the jacket from his shoulders as the Gorilla ambled round to face us. We had parked under the only street lamp in the car park, which was basically wasteland. Gaffer and the Gorilla stood facing one another to my right. I turned to watch them, afraid to stay and afraid to run.

The Gorilla looked Gaffer up and down, then spat on the ground.

'You're a big bugger, I'll give you that. But

311

you've already got one broken arm. I don't think you really want to make it a matching pair.'

'Oh, I don't know...' Gaffer's voice was eerily quiet and matter-of-fact.

'By the time I've finished with you, you'll never play the saxophone again.'

'That's all right,' Gaffer told him. 'I never have.'

He did the funny wiggling thing with his eyebrows and moved to put himself squarely between me and the Gorilla. Of all the stupid times for the penny to drop...

'Tom Selleck did that in a film, once,' I said idiotically.

'Did he now? Well, I bet Tom Selleck never did this...'

With one sweeping movement, Gaffer swooped forward like a wrecking ball and hit the Gorilla full in the face with his plaster cast.

Funny, isn't it? In the movies, the hero walks away unscathed from a run-in like that. Real life is rather different. From the amount and volume of swearing, and the strange sort of war dance he was doing, I figured that Gaffer really had broken his arm. I wanted to take him to Casualty.

'Yeah, right! And how do I explain the plaster cast, eh?'

'Fancy dress?' I suggested. He didn't look impressed. He did look distinctly unhappy and was shedding shards of plaster all over the floor of the car.

'Besides,' he added, 'Casualty would not be a good place right now. Jake and his mates could be there. We need to put as much distance as possible between us and them.'

That, I wasn't going to argue with. Gaffer, however, argued down my suggestion of taking him to Casualty elsewhere. Gloucester or Worcester, for instance.

'Just drive, Mike, all right?'

We hadn't hung about to question The Gorilla. Although he had gone down under Gaffer's blow, he hadn't stayed down for long, and in between his cursing and war-dancing, Gaffer had made some comment about the hardness of the man's skull that was quite the most obscene thing I'd ever heard. We'd got into the car in double-time, Lady Day having to be slung, uncased, on to the back seat. So I drove while Gaffer muttered to himself.

'Look,' I interrupted. 'Where exactly are we going? I don't know about you, but I don't fancy staying in the cottage tonight. If our friends show up again … well, we'd be sitting ducks.'

'Right, but we need to be back at the Grange. They're getting rattled, Mike. What about the vicar? Would she put us up overnight?'

'We can try. Gaffer...' In the mêlée, I'd completely forgotten about his mission. '...did you find Raffi?'

'No.' He shook his head and nursed his arm. 'It's like you said – Saturday night, and she'd be out and about along with just about everybody else in town. But I've left messages all over the place, saying it's absolutely vital she rings you asap, and there's plenty of other people looking for her, too.'

'I'm still worried she's gone to London.'

'Look, Mike, there's nothing we can do. If she

has gone up the Smoke, one of her mates will let us know. We'll hear something from someone soon, OK?'

I drove on, avoiding my usual route to the village through fear of being followed. I've never used my rear view mirror so much, I parked as close to the vicarage as I could but was acutely anxious that the car would give us away.

It took a while for Alison to answer the door. It was, of course, very late by now and judging by the all-in-one sleep suit that matched her teddy bear slippers, we'd woken her up. I pushed Gaffer forward.

'Alison – is there anywhere we can hide the car?'

'Put it in the double garage at the back.' She gave me directions on how to find it and I left Gaffer to her ministrations. When I returned, she was drinking coffee and Gaffer had his arm in the kitchen sink, trying to soak off the remains of his plaster cast.

'I hear you've had quite an evening!' she said,

'That's something of an understatement. I don't suppose you can persuade him to get his arm looked at?'

'No, she can't!' Gaffer threatened. 'Anyway, it's all right. I can wiggle my fingers – look.'

I went over to the sink and did as I was told. Sure enough, his fingers moved. 'But does it feel any better?' I asked.

'Yeah. Mind you, that's probably because I've taken a couple of painkillers.'

It was some time before we had the whole thing off and got him properly cleaned up, but at least nothing gruesome was visible. My mobile beeped, signalling that the battery was on its way out.

'Christ, that's all we need!' I could have thrown it against the wall.

'Don't you have a spare battery?' Alison asked.

'Oh yes.' I rolled my eyes at the thought. 'In my sax case. Back in Cheltenham. Probably wrapped around someone's head, by now.'

Gaffer waved the towel he was drying his arm with. 'But your charger's at the cottage, right?'

'Right.'

He put the towel down. 'I'll go and get it.'

'No you bloody won't! Those goons are probably looking for us, and that's the first place they'd go!'

'Those goons are probably in hospital!'

We stared at one another. I turned to Alison. 'Can I use your phone?'

'Sure. But it's rather late. Whoever you're after – will they still be up?'

'Oh, they'll be up!' I told her.

I wasn't wrong. The hubbub at Joan's was hardly a candidate for 'least intrusive background noise'.

'Oh, Mike – thank God you're all right!' she shouted. 'When they told me what happened ... we've been so worried. Will you SHUT UP!!'

I barely managed to get the phone away from my ear before permanent damage was inflicted.

'Not you, Mike – them!' Joan continued in her normal voice. 'Couldn't hear a bloody thing!' Her voice was muffled as she called out to the room, 'It's Mike – she's all right.'

'But are they all right?' I asked.

'Oh yes. No serious damage done.'

'Can I speak to Charley or Joe?'

'Hang on. Joe! Mike wants you!'

There was a scrabbling sound as the phone changed hands, then Joe's voice, thanking Jesus, Mary, Joseph and all the saints, for my safe escape from harm.

'Joe – the men who caused the trouble – what happened to them?'

'Well, two of them are in the slammer, I'm pleased to say.' He chuckled to himself. 'I'm not sure the police would have taken our word for it, being Irish and all, but that singer of yours – Lord save us, what a voice! Well, he's telling the police that it was them that caused the trouble, and your band leader was all outraged and backing him up and there was this other chap – looked like he had a dead cat on his head, or something...'

'George, the drummer. It's a squashed guinea pig, masquerading as a toupee.'

He laughed. 'Well, anyway, with the band backing us up, the police carted them off and are holding them for affray or some such... Your singer – Nick, is it? He's come back here with us to have a drink. Lovely left hook on him. Just beautiful. Would you like a word?'

I didn't have a choice, as it happened, but not to worry. From the descriptions Nick gave, I felt fairly confident that only Jake and the Gorilla were still on the loose. Only...!

The background noise was rising again, confusion, surprise and protestation coming to the forefront. I thought it was time I rang off.

'Thanks, Nick. You saved my life. I owe you one.'

'I'll remember that! Wait – Mike – someone else wants to speak to you...'

Bloody hell, now what? I was thinking. Then an unmistakable voice came down the line and my body sagged with relief.

'Raffi!'

Gaffer and Alison, hearing her name, would have been standing point, ears and tails rigid, had they been dogs instead of people.

'Raffi!' I repeated. 'Thank God you're there! My mobile's just gone down and...'

'That's why I'm here! I got Gaffer's message and tried to call you and when I couldn't get you, I came here as fast as I could. I thought you'd have come here after the gig...'

'It's a long story,' I told her. 'Listen, cast your mind back to when I brought you to the Grange after we heard about the fire at Tim's. Paul gave you a lift back, remember? Called you Ravioli? And I gave you a couple of carrier bags...'

'Yes, the presents were lovely, but...'

'Raffi, where are the carrier bags? PLEASE tell me you've still got them?'

'Well, no, but...'

'Raffi!' Alison and Gaffer jumped at my wail.

'Calm down, Mike! What I mean is, the one bag had presents in, didn't it? That's at Corinne's. The other one...'

'You threw it away...' I closed my eyes as my voice tailed away, fearing the worst.

'No. It's in the boot of my car. It had magazines in or something. I'd forgotten about it, to be honest, but I was cleaning the car out yesterday and found it. Thought I'd take it to London. Pass the time on the train. I'm going tomorrow, remember?'

'But tomorrow's Sunday!'

'No, it's Sunday now, Mike. Only the early hours, but...'

'OK, Raffi, I've got you. Now listen to me. This is vitally important. I need that bag. Or at least, something I think might be in it.'

'Might be? Mike...'

I told her what to look for. Basically, anything that wasn't a newspaper or magazine. Could be loose papers. Could be in an envelope. Could be anything. *Just please let the papers be there*, I prayed.

'But just what are these papers, Mike? Are you sure it can't wait until I come back?'

'Raffi, this could literally be a matter of life and death.'

'I'll bring them over, then. Are you at the Grange?'

'Sort of. Look, I really don't want you coming over here...'

'At this time of night? Too right! Anyway, I've had a couple of drinks, so I couldn't drive over. How about the morning?'

Gaffer was shaking his head and asking me to fill him in. 'Hold on, Raffi.' I covered the mouthpiece and told him what she was suggesting.

'No way. We can't let her come over here. I'll go and pick them up, if I can use your car.'

'Hold on a minute!' Alison put in. 'If it's just papers, why can't she just fax them? I've got a fax machine in the study.'

'Listen, Raffi – I want you to fax the papers if they're there, OK?'

318

'From where?'

'From where?' I relayed the question. 'It's Sunday now, right? Nowhere will be open.'

'She can fax from the Paradox Centre,' Gaffer said. 'Tell her to go to Norman's. He's got keys. I'll phone him, tell him to let her in.'

'OK.' I directed my voice back to Raffi again. 'Raffi, go to Norman. He'll let you into the Paradox Centre. There's a fax machine there.' I glanced at the note Gaffer was scribbling. The noise at Joan's was reaching a new crescendo and I had to shout to make sure Raffi heard me.

'Have you got a pen? I'll tell you the number to fax it to.'

'Hold on a sec! Joan – have you got a pen?' There was a pause from Raffi, while she waited, then a roar, and, quite distinctly above the clamour, a voice shouting, 'Raffi – watch yourself! Oh no! The drunken ould fool...'

The line went dead and stayed that way.

Alison looked at me in dismay. 'Not more trouble?'

'Not that kind. At least I hope not. I think someone just fell down the stairs...'

Gaffer grinned. 'They do it all the time. Drunk,' he explained, for Alison's benefit. 'Let me phone Norman.'

'Get him to give her the fax number when she goes to the Centre.'

'OK.'

That done, there was nothing more we could do until the pages came through – if Raffi had them.

Except catch up on some sleep.

Chapter Thirty-two

Sleep. So tired. Must wake up now.

Eyes so heavy. Must open my eyes.

Open... Blackness. Black. Dark. Black... Dream. It's just a dream. Breathe. Breathe. Count, Michal. 1-2-3... Now, open my eyes...

It wasn't a dream. Nothing happened. I opened my eyes and I couldn't see. I cried out, panic washing over me like a tidal wave. The sound bounced back, mocking the suffocating terror which swamped my senses. I think I must have passed out. When I came to, when I realised that this horror was truly for real, I had to fight hard not to just scream and scream.

Think, Michal, think! You can't see anything? OK, what about your other senses? Listen, listen... Nothing but my own ragged breathing.

Feel, then – what can you feel? Cold. So cold. And hard. Like a cellar. OK. Think. Make sense of your surroundings. Come on, think! It's dark, it's cold, why the hell do my arms ache so much? Why can't I MOVE my arms? Because my hands are tied behind my back, stupid...

Oh shit. My ankles were tied, too. I yelled again, got the same mocking echo, forced myself to lie still and breathe, breathe... Anything to calm myself down. There seemed to be something the size of a football hammering inside the middle of my chest, threatening to break my ribs and burst through my breast-bone at any second. Oh God – please don't let me have a heart attack! Please don't let me die!

Die... I fought the fuzz at the periphery of memory. *Who had said that? Something about dying... What was it? 'I couldn't let you die without seeing it.' Seeing what?*

'O-o-o-mmmm...' I released a big, deep sound, forcing myself to breathe from right down in my belly. My head felt full of sawdust.

'O-o-o-mmmm...' *Where the hell am I? How did I get here?* 'O-o-o-mmmm...' *What's the last thing I can remember? Really remember?*

'O-o-o-mmmm...' *I went to bed at Alison's. At the vicarage. I slept upstairs in a spare bedroom. Gaffer slept downstairs on the sofa because he wanted to be on hand to clobber anyone who might try to get in.* 'O-o-o-mmmm...' *Right. I must have got up in the morning. We were waiting for a fax from Raffi...* Sawdust again. Why did I think there were two faxes? Why would Raffi send two faxes to the same place? *No, no, it wasn't the same place, it was...*

'O-o-o-mmmm... O-o-o-mmmm...'

Slowly, I began to piece things together...

Alison was out for the first Sunday service of the day when I got up. Gaffer was already down-stairs. Made breakfast for both of us. There was no fax from Raffi.

'It's early yet, Mike. She'll come through, you'll see.'

Alison had left a note for us, telling us not to answer the door to anyone and saying if anyone asked, she would say she hadn't seen us. We waited. Still no fax.

The phone rang. Alison's answering machine kicked in and we heard Maggie's voice, asking if she knew where we were. 'I was hoping they could join us for the Companions' Lunch at one o'clock.' I felt guilty for not letting her in on things.

'Maybe we should go,' Gaffer had said.

'What? To the lunch?'

'Why not? Keep our ears to the ground. Safety in numbers, too.'

I thought about it. 'Hmmm. How would we explain your miraculous healing powers?'

'Oh!' His face fell. 'I hadn't thought about that...'

Alison had returned just after midday. She'd been conducting services in other villages. She listened to the answer phone messages – there were two others by now, calling on her pastoral services – and agreed that joining the Companions' Lunch would be a good idea, and pondered the problem of Gaffer's arm.

'You still haven't had the fax?' she asked us.

'No. Gaffer's phoned Norman twice, and Raffi still hasn't arrived. Joan's phone is still out of order.'

'Well, Mike, why don't you come to the lunch with me? That way, you're not alone and Gaffer can stay here, ready for the fax.' She turned towards him, pre-empting his objections. 'I won't let her out of my sight. And I'll bring her back here with me when you get the fax – we'll phone periodically to check whether it's arrived.'

'OK. That's cool.'

We decided it would be best if I took my car, saying Alison had spotted me heading for the Grange and flagged me down to pass on Maggie's message. I would then, of course, have given her a lift to the pub the Lunch was being held at. If anyone asked about Gaffer in his guise as JB, the Broken Armed Sax Player, I would say he'd had a problem with his plaster cast and had stayed in Cheltenham, having had to go back to the hospital.

'I don't know what I'm going to do about Jake, if he's there,' I said.

'Blag it, mate.' Gaffer looked at Alison. 'Any big guys with white hats going to be there if he gets out of hand?'

'Oh, I think so!' she'd laughed.

Alison got in the car with me and I drove to the cottage before going on to Lunch. I was in urgent need of getting changed, still being stuck in my Green Glittery Jacket. Also, I wanted to pick up the battery charger for my mobile. The sooner I was back in contactable mode, the happier I would feel.

The pub was packed when we arrived. As we squeezed through the bodies and entered the courtyard en route to the Function Room, I was thinking of Joan's crazy Irishmen and started to whistle, 'Oh, Susanna'.

'What's that got to do with anything?' Alison laughed.

'Oh, hello, Jake.' The tune fell from my lips. He stood with Elynore and Warren.

'Hi,' he said. 'That was quite some fight at your

gig last night.'

'It must have been, if your face is anything to go by.' My heart was hammering. His cheekbone was bruised and he had a black eye. I forced myself to smile at the Myatts. 'I got out while the going was good.'

'Sounds awful!' Elynore said. 'Where's your friend? JB?'

I fed them the line we'd agreed on. Alison plucked at my sleeve. 'Look – there's Maggie!' We smiled and moved past them, into the safety of the Function Room. Alison muttered, 'Are you all right?'

'Yes. Just caught me on the hop a bit...'

I couldn't hop now, I thought, back in the dark. I had cramp in my right calf muscle and was shivering with cold. Lying on my side on a stone floor was doing me no good at all. I forced my legs straight and turned my feet outwards in an effort to create slack in the rope – I assumed it was rope – that was binding my ankles. *Which will do no good at all if I can't get my hands free*, I told myself, countering my own argument with, *Well, at least I could walk...* I rolled over to my left, tangling myself in my coat through my efforts to turn without crushing my hands in the process.

'Ow!' Something dug into my leg, just above the ankle. Probably a stone, I thought, trying to move myself away. The stone surface beneath my cheek was damp and smelt of ... what? I lay still and sniffed. It wasn't just the floor, I decided. It was in the air, too. Unfamiliar and unpleasant, had I been an animal, my hackles would have risen.

Hackles had risen at the Companions' Lunch, I remembered. I hadn't really followed the argument, distracted by explaining to Maggie why she had been unable to raise me on the mobile. I'd blathered about having stayed in Cheltenham overnight, the charger being back at Rosemary Cottage. But hackles had been raised, and it seemed to be something to do with an extremist wing of battle re-enactment groups.

'You tell him, Edward!' one of the men had called.

'Realism, yes, to a degree, and historical accuracy, absolutely. But we are not in the business of blood and guts and leaving body parts scattered all over the battlefield. Besides our own interest and enjoyment, we're here for education and entertainment – and that's *family* entertainment, not giving children nightmares.'

'Oh, right – so education shouldn't include bringing home the horrors of war?' someone else had shouted.

'Not when you've got a mixed age range and limited understanding...'

The disagreement had rumbled on for a while, someone sitting close to me grumbling about it. 'There's always somebody who gives groups like ours a bad name.'

Edward caught the comment. 'That happens whatever you're into. There's always a lunatic fringe.' He raised his voice. 'To the Companions of the Crooked Staff! We do it well, and we do it right!' Tankards had been hammered on the table.

My head was hammering now, as I made ever more futile attempts to free myself. God! That stone again! I pulled at my coat, barely able to move my arms from the middle of my back to my hip. Velvet might be warm when you can walk around in it. It wasn't doing me much good right now. I lay still. Wiggled my feet. Thought suddenly of Alison's keys. Thought about my last gig with the Howlin' Blue Horns. Goose-bumps rose, and not because of the cold, this time. *Please let me be right*, I breathed. Tortuously, I began to turn over...

'Coming to the Ladies?' Alison had asked.

'I thought you'd just been!'

'No – I had to make a phone call.' Her look was loaded with meaning.

'Ah. Right.' I'd followed her into the corridor.

'I was checking in with Gaffer.' She dropped her voice. 'He's got the fax.' She'd paused to get the information straight. 'Let me get this right – Raffi told Norman she was sorry she was so late. Apparently she stayed at some hotel last night and said that she got – and I quote – "shit-faced with a load of Irishmen and an Anglo-Italian who turned her knees to jelly". Does this make any sense?'

'Oh yes,' I'd laughed.

'Well, Gaffer's looking at it now. The fax. Said there's reams of the stuff. I told him we're going to the Grange to see the final Companions' run-through, then we can amble back and see if he's made any sense of it...'

The pain in my arms now made sense, I supposed. They felt like they were being wrenched from their shoulder sockets. I had managed to pull enough coat material around to reach the pocket. Trying to pull the lining material through the hole in the pocket was a different matter. With painstaking effort, my muscles quivered and burned in protest...

After my conversation with Alison, I'd accompanied Maggie to the bar and we'd been split up in the crush. My nerves had protested at that, but I'd reasoned that there were far too many people around for anything serious to happen. Elynore had touched my elbow. She was smiling, but there was ice in her voice as she brought her face close to my ear.

'He thinks I don't know. But I do know. I knew, right from the start. I was well aware, Michal, of what I was getting myself into. So if you're thinking of blackmail, it won't work. I've had to deal with people like you before and believe me, it's far too late now.' She glided away, still smiling, as Maggie fought her way towards me, elbowing enough space to pass a tray of drinks to me.

'You take those – I'll bring the rest.' I nodded dumbly as I made my way back to the Function Room. She knew! Elynore knew, and she'd done nothing to stop him! I fought down a wave of nausea.

'Let me take that for you!' Warren intercepted me in the courtyard and had the tray out of my hands before I could blink. He stood squarely in front of me. 'So you found out, huh? Think you're pretty damned clever. Well, I've worked too long and too hard to let you spoil things at this stage of the game. If you're sensible, you'll clear out while you can. And keep your mouth shut.'

'Are you threatening me?' I was incredulous. Husband and wife, one after the other.

'No. I'm making you a promise.'

Maggie emerged from the bar, laughing with one of the young Companions. She looked at me and rolled her eyes, happily oblivious to what was really going on.

'Trust you to get the Lord of the Manor to help! Come on – we're losing drinking time! We have to be back at the Grange soon...!'

Back in the darkness, I had finally retrieved the Swiss Army Knife from my coat lining. I lay exhausted, clutching it for dear life, terrified I would drop it and be stuck down here for ever. And where the hell was Gaffer? He should have missed me by now, raised the alarm. *This is not a film,* I reminded myself. *There is no all-action hero to come rushing in and save me. It's down to me. I have to do this myself.* I closed my eyes. Why, given the all-pervading blackness, I don't know. I took a long, deep breath. *Get on with it, woman,* I told myself. Slowly and with infinite care, I opened one of the blades...

Blades had been much in evidence as the Companions had resumed their battling on Sunday afternoon. The place seemed to be swarming with steaming, sweating men intent on belting the hell out of each other. One skirmish had taken place on the South Lawn and this was where Alison and I had stood to watch. A lone Companion approached us, a Royalist, by the look of him. He announced himself with an elegant bow and a Birmingham accent.

'Mistress Brodie? Mistress Mallory doth require me to inform thee that she hath a facsimile message for thy attention. Bugger this!' He shook his head and laughed. 'You've got a fax, love. Maggie found it when she let one of our lads use the phone in her office.'

'Oh thanks. She didn't give it to you, then?'

'Said it were personal. Summat about Raffles or Ruffles thinking you'd given her a wrong number, so she sent it again? Make any sense?'

'Yes. Thanks.' I glanced at Alison as she fell into step beside me, my stomach contracting as I took on board the possible implications. 'What the hell was Raffi thinking of, sending it here when Norman clearly gave her your number? I hope to God no one else has seen it.'

'Well, let's play it safe,' Alison said. 'We'll go up, get it and get out of here. Back to the vicarage.'

If only it had been that simple...

If only I'd have got a decent blade when I opened the Swiss Army Knife. *Oh no*, I thought. *Sod's Law.* The Law of Sod stated that I had to get, first time out, something that made no sense to my fingers at all. Probably one of those things for getting stones out of horses' hooves. Bloody useless, in other words, for a bipedal Homo Sapiens with Doc Martens on her size five feet.

I tried again. Second out of the Swiss Army

Knife was something that felt like a corkscrew. All I succeeded in doing was stabbing myself with it. I exaggerate. I pricked my finger. *Please, God*, I prayed, *let it be third time lucky*. I knew I was on the verge of hysteria and knew equally well that I could not afford to go over the edge...

Maggie's Tower steps had loomed before us. 'I hate these...' I had sighed as Alison and I had begun our ascent.

'I suppose you've heard the story of people being thrown off the top?' Alison had asked.

'Yes. Jake told me when I first arrived.' We had only got part way up, then. I was in the lead, and turned as a voice called, ''Scuse me, vicar? Can I have a word?' One of the Companions had poked his head inside the door.

'Don't tell me someone needs the last rites!' she'd laughed. She glanced up at me. 'You go on. I'll wait for you down here.'

Down in the darkness, God, luck or sheer mathematical odds had at last given me a usable blade. More than usable, actually. It felt like a miniature saw and it was very, very sharp. I exhaled slowly, convincing myself that my fingers were warm and I was not going to drop the knife at this late stage. Gingerly, I set to work. It was just the rope I wanted to cut, not my wrists...

My wrists were fine but my legs were aching as I'd approached Maggie's half-open office door. 'Bloody hell, Maggie!' I'd called. 'Couldn't you just have stuffed it in an envelope and saved me the hike?' I'd pushed the door open, entered the room and barely had time to register the fact that Maggie wasn't there before someone hit me from behind and the lights went out.

I don't know how long it took me to free my hands. Longer than it took to free my feet, that's for sure. I exhaled in a mewling series of small explosions as the circulation returned to my extremities. Then I wept with relief.

Then, I carefully retrieved the other object from the lining of my coat.

The Maglite.

Chapter Thirty-three

Now I knew why my voice had echoed back at me. I fought down a fresh tide of panic as I cast the torch beam around. I appeared to be in a stone cavern and at first sight, there seemed to be no way out. Illogical, I told myself, trying to remember when I'd last put new batteries in the Maglite. Cautiously, I ran my hand along the wall. *Someone got you in here, Michal*, I told myself. *There has to be a way out.*

There was, but I didn't find it until after I found the source of the smell I had been unable to place. It was a body. The body of a man. I did some tricky breathing, trying not to be sick. When I got myself sufficiently under control, I turned the beam back on his face. It was distorted by decomposition, but I didn't think I knew him. There was no outward sign of violence, but I made the assumption, based on the unnatural angle at which his head was lying, that he had suffered a broken neck. There was still no sound other than my own breathing. Cautiously, I knelt and directed the beam to his jacket. Over-riding the distaste I felt, I lifted the edge between the merest tips of finger and thumb, and felt in the inside pocket. It was empty apart from a business card which told me that he was – or rather had been – an American Private Investigator called Arnold Niedermeyer. The man Jake had been so convinced that I knew.

I stood up slowly, slipping the card into my pocket. It was high time I got out of here. I felt my way along the wall again, using the beam to high-light any possible outlet from the cavern. There had to be a way out... There was. A passageway. I let out a couple of swift, sharp breaths and started walking. I'm not sure how much time had passed before I saw the light ahead. Oddly enough, it hadn't occurred to me to look at my watch. Time was irrelevant down here. All that mattered was that I keep breathing and keep moving.

I thought I was imagining the light to begin with. It was hazy and indistinct, and to the left of my present bearings but as I got closer, I realised that it was emanating from another passageway which made a ninety-degree angle to the one I had been proceeding along. I stood in the entrance, turning off the Maglite and looked at the now visible expanse in front of me. Cables and lights ran along this tunnel. I hesitated.

Someone had obviously installed the lighting for some reason. Who might I bump into down here? I fingered the Swiss Army Knife, now closed and nestling firmly in the right-hand pocket of my coat. The one without the hole. I had to go on. My heart was hammering as I moved as swiftly as I dared, ears straining for any sound not of my own making. Despite my boots, I was light on my feet. I had learned from experience to cough when approaching people from behind, especially in the dark, having frightened several by my soundless approach. Now, I least, I could use this to my advantage. I hoped.

The passageway opened eventually into another chamber. This was no pitch black cavern, however – lights and cables had been run in here as well. I stood breathless with shock. At the back, was a rudely fashioned altar. In the centre, a roughly hewn block of stone, surrounded by a double row of elaborate metal railings. On top of the stone sat a small sarcophagus.

I approached slowly, circling the block of stone before moving in to examine it more closely. The sarcophagus was surrounded by an odd assort-ment of items. Jewellery. Crucifixes. Rosary beads. Candlesticks. A sword.

'Beautiful, isn't she?'

The hairs on my neck prickled. The sound came from above me. Above and behind. I didn't dare move.

'Ghislaine. The beautiful, missing child. Kept here all the time. Murdered by her uncle. In remorse, he created a shrine here. Made penance. But inherited the Grange anyway. I don't suppose you can read the inscription?'

'No,' I answered, strangely calm. 'I really ought to get my eyes checked. But I bet you know it by heart, Edward.'

I turned now. Turned to look at him.

'You are an enterprising one! Took lessons from Houdini, did you? Or was it David Blaine? I was just coming back to give you the ex-officio guided tour.'

'Before you killed me?' Now I remembered.

'Oh yes. I should have done that much earlier. I seriously underestimated you.'

'No,' I told him, backing away to place the sarcophagus between us. 'You seriously *over*estimated me.'

I could now see the stone steps by which he'd descended. 'People do it all the time,' I told him. 'It's like being called "Mistress Scrappy". Maggie told you my band nickname, right? Came about because I got involved in a fight at a gig. Supposedly saved our trumpet player from being bottled by an irate punter. Irate because we wouldn't play "Rawhide".'

'Sounds like a rerun of The Blues Brothers.'

'Something like that. They thought I'd decked him. Completely wrong. I got between them, he took a swing, I dodged. He was so drunk, he fell over.'

'Does this tale have a point?' He was making no attempt to come closer.

'Oh, I think so. You see, whatever you may think, Edward, I don't know shit. You obviously want to protect this underground complex from becoming public knowledge, but I don't know why. I certainly didn't know you were involved, either. I'd sussed out Warren and Jake, and Elynore's threat surprised me, but...'

He laughed, like a bark, shaking his head. 'Dear oh dear! You are in a mess, aren't you? That's disappointing, really.' He moved forward. Relaxed. At ease. As if he owned the place. 'It's all very simple. I'm just protecting my own interests.'

'Which are what?'

'This!' The sudden ferocity in his voice shook me. 'The Grange. It's mine. Should have been mine. I was deprived of my inheritance, just like Ghislaine.' He laughed again, came closer. 'You still don't understand, do you? Oh it's not as final as murder, but it might as well have been. Sir Ranulph was my father. Not that I knew that, until after my mother died. She'd always refused to name him. You're younger than me, don't know the stigma attached to illegitimacy then. Not like now, when no one gives a damn, where girls flaunt themselves, spawn multiple bastards by any number of so-called fathers!' He was spitting the words. 'No. Back then, being a bastard... And my mother covered for him. Never got a penny. Slaved herself into an early grave. Took in washing. Took in lodgers.' The implications he put into the final word were quite clear.

My eyes never left his face, contorted now as he spewed out his memories. We seemed to have unconsciously engaged ourselves in a mesmeric dance around the long-dead Ghislaine, his every step forward matched by my own retreat.

'Once I knew, I came back here. As his gardener.'

'Did you kill him?' I asked.

'No.' He looked surprised by the question. 'I found this. The underground complex, as you call it. Much sweeter revenge, and all by accident. He had a dog. Stupid little thing. A terrier. I was out one day, walking it, and it disappeared down a hole. I dug it out. The rest is history. What better way to get revenge. Not just on him. On the lot of them. The Aristocracy.' He rolled the word round his mouth as if it were distasteful to have it there. 'They think they're safe. Above the law. Hanging on to their treasures. Well, not any more. Not since I've had my little operation going. How much did you earn last year, Michal?'

The question threw me. I stopped moving.

'Come on – don't be shy! The taxman need never know. £50,000? £70,000? Or am I over-estimating you again? Want to know what I made? Just last year? £2.5 million.'

I stared at, him stupidly. The gap was closing. I took a flurry of steps backwards, almost tripping over. He smiled at me, highly amused.

'And where do you think you're going to go? Don't fight the inevitable. I'm just keeping my word, telling you so you won't die, not knowing. I don't suppose you remember me saying that, though. You were only half-conscious when I brought you down here.'

I said nothing, locked once more into the obscene circling.

'I use my elite group Michal. For robberies. Stately Homes. Country houses. And all the spoils stored and shipped out from here. When Arthur got too close, action was called for. We

336

were going to move the last of the stuff out next Wednesday, when everyone would be off to Cheltenham for the Races. But he and you...' His look was calculating. '...you've caused me an inordinate amount of trouble. Where did she send the other fax, by the way? Not that it matters now, but I had to move swiftly when it arrived. Originally, I'd have had my lads hiding out down here, ready for Wednesday. As it is, once we'd sent the locals off, I had to bring things forward. Which is why there's a robbery taking place right now. Even as we speak. At the Grange. There'll be nothing to connect me. As for you – we'll give you a good send off. The Companions, that is. If your body is ever found.'

'What did you do with Sherrill?' I asked him.

He laughed. 'The black girl? She's still here. Insurance. We would have done the swap, you know. You really shouldn't have interfered. Now? Well, we'll keep her until we've got the stuff away. Then...' He shrugged. 'She'll have served her purpose.'

We had both come to a halt now. The steps by which he'd entered the chamber were ahead of me and to my left. Edward was on the opposite side of the sarcophagus and to my right. He could cut me off. He knew it and I knew it. We both also knew that, at some point, I had to try. He stood, hands on hips, and laughed. He gave me a Cavalier's bow.

'Go for it, Michal! I'll give you a head start!'

Our eyes were locked now, the corners of his mouth twitching. He was going to kill me and do it smiling.

'Go on!' He stamped his foot, feigning his move over and over, teasing me, taunting me.

In the end, as we both knew I had to, I went for it, throwing myself forward with all the force I could muster. I hit the stairs at a gallop, only to be yanked backwards by my coat, landing in a tumbled heap on top of him. He was still laughing, arms around me like it was some playful lovers' game. I lifted my head and smacked it backwards, into his face, rolling free as he let go of me, blinded by my own pain and wondering if I'd fractured my skull. I grabbed the rails of the sarcophagus stone, using them for support to pull myself up, hands scrabbling, sending the artefacts flying. Edward's nose was pouring blood, his eyes streaming, and he swore profusely as he got up, shaking his head.

'Bitch!'

I ran again, not even reaching the stairs this time. Edward had his arms around my neck, pulling me backwards, cursing about how he hadn't expected this much resistance from me, but then he hadn't expected much from my poofter friend either, and look what had happened there...

More than anything now, I didn't want to die. And running far deeper than the fear was anger, so cold, so terrible, I didn't know what to do with it. He was responsible for Pete, for Paul, for Tim's two innocent friends, trapped in that burning basement hell... His hands were throttling me, my mind recoiling from the awful knowledge that I was next.

With one almighty effort, I grabbed his arms, swung my right leg back and out and forced my

338

body to follow it.

It was Gaffer's Ju-Jitsu move, and it worked.

He went down, all right.

Straight onto the upturned blade of the sword, wedged and protruding where it had fallen, between the elaborate iron railings of Ghislaine's secret shrine.

Chapter Thirty-four

I tore up the steps, stomach heaving, mind desperately trying to block out the sight I was leaving behind. I was expecting to come up into the nursery, but had got it badly wrong. I gulped in huge lungs full of air to stop myself being sick and stood bewildered as my eyes became accustomed to the gloom of the Chapel. It wasn't completely dark. The door was ajar and a shaft of moonlight cut a diagonal across the main aisle. I had emerged where Sir John's sarcophagus should have been. It was askew now, giving access to the steps and chamber below from where I had made my desperate escape.

I moved swiftly to the door, peering cautiously around the edge before risking emergence into the silvery light outside. It was as well I did. A large van was parked by an open door at the back of the Grange, two men carrying a heavy object to its rear. They lifted it onto the tailgate before going back inside again.

I crouched low and ran for the nearest cover,

which was to my left – ironic, as Edward himself had nurtured the hedges which afforded me shelter now. I had to get help. I don't think I realised where I was heading. The only thing that mattered at that moment was getting and keeping the Grange behind me, so when the blackness of the conference centre rose in front of me, I stopped short, cursing my lack of forethought. I skirted the main building, noting only one light on the ground floor. Jake's room. Moving slowly now, I kept going until the courtyard annexe accommodation block came into view. It was also in darkness, and its layout meant I did not have the benefit of moonlight here. Surely the guest rooms would have telephones? I switched on the Maglite, shielding the beam with one hand, allowing myself only enough illumination to be sure of my footing. Could I break a window without being heard? Would a mullioned window break sufficiently to let me in?

I never had chance to find out. I'd taken off my coat, wrapping it around my arm to take a swing, when a muttered, 'What the hell...' swung me round instead. I snapped the light off, lurching to the left as Jake leaped forward. I was too slow. He cannoned into my right shoulder, the force of his body carrying me backwards and slamming me into the door. I don't remember yelling or screaming, but he knew it was me.

'Michal! What the hell do you think you're doing?'

I brought my right knee up, pushing him backwards at the same time. He staggered, fell, and grabbed my leg as I tried to run past him. I wobbled, frantically trying to stop myself pitching forward, and, completely off balance, sat down heavily on top of him. A leg whipped round, knocking me over, and I wound up face down, with him on top of me. He moved quickly, pulling me to my feet, swinging me round and shaking me like a doll. I tried to kick, tried to punch, but it was useless. I'd used the only move I knew on Edward.

'Go on then – kill me! You bastard! Bastard!'

'What? Stop it! Why in God's name would I want to kill you?'

'Isn't that what you were trying to do at the gig?' He held only one of my arms now.

'Michal, I was trying to stop those goons moving in on you. I've been riding shotgun on you as much as I can since things started going haywire, especially after I checked out the Niedermeyer business more thoroughly and...'

'Oh yes! Arnold Niedermeyer! And I suppose he broke his neck accidentally, did he?'

'What the hell are you talking about?'

'Arnold flaming Niedermeyer! He's dead, down in the passageways. Are you really telling me you don't know?'

'Michal ... I have no idea what you're involved in, but you have to believe me – my main concern has been watching Warren's back.'

'Warren?'

'How did you know? I thought he was heading for a heart attack when he heard you whistling.'

'Whistling? What on earth are you talking about?'

'"Oh Susanna." His Alabama background.'

341

I wanted to scream. 'You're mad!' I said. 'This whole bloody place is mad!' I felt like I was in the middle of some nightmare Munch or Dali canvas, an incomprehensible Samuel Beckett play. I clutched at him, desperate for reassurance. 'You're not part of Edward's gang? The burglaries?'

'What burglaries?' He pulled me closer. 'Michal, read my lips. I'm a good guy. Now – what the hell are you talking about?'

I blurted it out, lost for words, unable to make sense. All he got was that the Grange was being burgled and there was at least one hostage being held, I didn't know where. 'You really didn't know?' I asked again.

'I've been here all evening with the Myatts! Business meeting. Jesus!' He caught his breath. 'Elynore just sent Warren back to the Grange!'

I ran after him to his apartment. He burst in, picked up the phone and looked at me. 'It's dead!'

'What on earth...' Elynore, sitting in a high-backed leather armchair, had risen to her feet. She caught sight of me. 'You! What are you doing here?'

'The Grange is being burgled! We have to...'

'Hold it, Michal.' Jake's voice was low as he moved towards her. 'Why shouldn't she be here, Elynore?'

'Why... I – it was just a figure of speech. She startled me. I mean – look at her.' She flapped her hands as if trying to shoo away my doubtless ragged appearance.

'I am looking. And the first thing I'd have asked

342

her is, what's wrong?' He turned to me. 'You said Edward is behind it?'

'Yes. He...'

'Warren got it wrong, then. He thought Elynore was having an affair with Howard, not Edward.'

'What is this?' Elynore was on her feet now. 'That's outrageous! I would never...'

'No, probably not. Howard's wealthy, but not rich enough for your blood, huh? Not as rich as Warren. So why Edward? He's not your usual style, Elynore. He's not rich.'

Oh yes he is, I thought. *Or rather, he was.* I watched as the colour drained from her face, leaving bright red spots of anger in the middle of her cheeks.

'If you think I would have an affair with my gardener ... this is not *Lady Chatterley's Lover!* Ask Edward. The whole idea is preposterous.'

'Where is Edward?' Jake asked me. I felt suddenly faint, my stomach knotting at the scene I'd left below the Chapel.

'I... He's... He's dead. I...'

'Dead? Dead!' Elynore hurled the table over, knocking me down as she hurtled towards the door. Jake was after her in a flash. I scrambled after them, winded and suddenly more afraid than ever.

The scene outside was chaotic. Elynore's vehicle was pulling away, engine roaring, and Jake was hauling himself to his feet, face as white as a sheet and his left arm hanging uselessly. 'Reversed into me. Got me against the wall.' He was fumbling for keys, urging me towards his Land Rover. 'Drive, Michal! Drive!'

'Oh shit!' I swore as I stalled the engine. I hadn't driven a manual in fourteen years.

'Use the clutch, dammit!' I used the clutch and kangarooed painfully down the road before getting the hang of it. The back of the Grange came into view. Elynore was now out of her vehicle, gesticulating towards us.

'Take a right – head for the village!' I swung the wheel, gave it more gas and was halfway down the track before I saw the car ahead, facing us and blocking our escape.

'Reverse! Reverse!'

'Where is it?' I yelled, cursing the vagaries of gearboxes. I eased off the accelerator and slammed the clutch down as Jake changed gear for me, shouting, 'Go! Go! Go!' He kept his eyes on the car ahead as I looked behind me and gave it more gas, screaming backwards down the track. Off to the left, I could see running figures. They distracted me enough to be aware only of a sickening crunch as we came to an abrupt halt. We leapt from the vehicle just in time for me to see what the running figures had been doing. They had loosed the dogs.

It was like a magnified version of my arrival at the Grange, only this time it was for real. Behind us, barking and baying rang out over the sound of voices. Ahead of us was blackness as the Tower loomed, blocking out the moon. *Oh God!* I thought, as my flying feet ate up the South Lawn, praying that its door would be open. It wasn't.

Sounds of confusion carried on the wind, across the expanse of grass we'd left behind us. We skirted the Tower, edging along, then ran across a flower bed and slammed ourselves against the nearest wall.

'They've got this place sewn up tighter than a duck's ass,' Jake whispered.

And then we saw her. Elynore. She was dragging and pushing something – someone – through the window of the library. As she moved more clearly into the moonlight, realisation struck. 'Sherrill!' I breathed.

Elynore's car was parked, engine running, several yards away.

'Get her car,' Jake said. 'I'll head her off.'

I nodded silently, darting to the hedge on the other side of the gravelled path as Jake called out to her.

'Let her go, Elynore! It's over.'

She whirled around, moonlight glinting on the knife she held at Sherrill's throat.

'Elynore – come on! Why be the fall guy? You can blame it all on Edward. Say you knew nothing about murder. You don't want to commit cold-blooded murder, now, do you?'

'Why not? I've done it before.' Her voice was cool and clear. I eased myself along, opposite her now.

'Husband number one. I know.' Jake's voice was level. 'Only no one could prove it. Still can't. Especially now you got Niedermeyer out of the way, right? Which is why you don't want to kill her, Elynore.' He gestured towards Sherrill. 'No one has a thing. Why give 'em *prima facie* evidence? A witness?'

'What witness? You won't get out of here.' She laughed at Jake then, Sherrill's feet dragging along the gravel as Elynore backed away from him.

'No?'

I was beyond her now, just feet away from the car.

'No. And with Warren dead...'

'You sent him over here on purpose, didn't you? What was the plan? He'd walk in, surprise the bad guys and get killed in the ensuing fight? And I would have been your alibi, right? There you were, all innocent, oblivious to the crime that was taking place, talking business with me. I'm surprised you kept him this long, Elynore. Max didn't last half the time.'

'Warren lasted this long simply because I chose that he should.'

'Money and danger. They're your aphrodisiacs.'

I was directly opposite the car now. Knew I'd have to dart across, make my move. She was completely unaware of my presence, focused entirely on Jake. And then I froze. A bloodied figure, pursued by Warren, rushed for the van, got in, gunned the engine. Elynore swung round, startled, dropping the knife. Sherrill stumbled forward as Jake made a dive for her, knocking her over and rolling the pair of them clear of the path of the oncoming vehicle.

Frozen in the glare of the headlights, Elynore Myatt's last facial expression was one of total disbelief.

Chapter Thirty-five

It was an unusually quiet gathering at Joan's on the following Friday evening. Not that we intended it to stay that way. It was the last night before the Irishmen were going home, and this was to be the get-together to celebrate the fact that those of us involved with the Grange had survived, and to piece-up the picture for those whose involvement had been peripheral.

'You've never heard so many Jesus, Mary and Josephs in your life!' Joan had told me. 'Once the news started breaking on the radio and TV, the lads were demented – said they would have stormed the place if they'd known what was going on!' We'd dissolved into fits of the giggles as we'd pictured such an event in our minds. I'd hugged the lot of them, happy in the knowledge that Edward hadn't been the only one with an elite unit at his disposal.

We were in Joan's lounge bar, squeezed together like Band Sardines because of our extended numbers. Big Stan was positioned opposite me, between Norman and Gaffer, so he could lipread. Henrietta and Roxy the latter demurely dressed in trousers and a baggy sweater, sat alongside them. Sherrill sat on Tim's lap and I, unbelievably, was sitting on Jake's. Nick had come not only in a personal capacity but as representative of the Green Glittery Jacket Mob, who were

347

anxious to hear all the news. He had also returned Lady Day's case.

'I thought they would all have turned up!' I told Nick.

'They all wanted to, but Frederick put his foot down. Said it wouldn't be seemly to invade your privacy and having one person to report the story back would suffice very nicely, thank you.'

I gestured expansively, taking in the entire room. 'Privacy? What privacy?!' and everyone laughed.

Raffi had returned from London on Wednesday, oblivious to the drama which had been going on around her. She'd got the job, which I still knew next to nothing about, having been tied up myself – metaphorically speaking – with the police. She was now squashed between Nick and Liam O'Donnell, the youngest member of the Irish Contingent, who looked more than happy with the arrangement.

Alison, Maggie and Warren were unfortunately not present, still having their hands full at the Grange, the official opening of which had been put back to accommodate the police and the sense of shock in the village. Apart from that, we were all there. Except Paul.

Tim told his story first, which set the scene on how everything had started.

'God help us all!' Joe declared solemnly. 'Just to set fire to the place like that. 'Tis wicked.'

'They genuinely appear not to have known about the couple in the basement,' I said, aiming a sympathetic look towards Tim and Sherrill. 'Not that it's any excuse, of course, and quite frankly, I think they'd still have done it anyway. They certainly pulled no punches later,' I said.

'And you, dear girl – you must have been terrified for your life.' Thomas, sitting a discreet distance from Joan, addressed Sherrill.

'I was,' she confirmed. 'All the time. They didn't hit me again after they threw Tim out of the car, but I was always cold and mostly in the dark. I really thought I was going to go mad, that they'd just leave me down there to die. They moved me after a while. That man – Edward – said I'd been heard, that people thought I was a ghost. Said I soon would be if I didn't keep quiet.'

Sherrill's original hiding place – the elusive second priests' hole – had been discovered during the police search of the Grange, and sure enough, it was in the nursery. Between Arthur's material and a detailed map found at Edward's house, a lot of things had come to light.

Next, I gave my account of how I'd received Tim's note and made my initial visit to Descartes' Vineyard, and this was followed by Henrietta and Roxy giving their accounts of the uproar at the fair.

'And you do fire-eating and juggling and such, do you?' Joe's face was a picture. 'We have a fair coming up back home, if you're interested. You'd go down a storm, so you would!'

'Cause a riot, more like!' Charley laughed.

No one laughed when I told them about the break-in at my house and what Gaffer and I had learned from the Weasel, thanks to Norman and Big Stan.

'But what were they after, Mike? Did they really think you had these papers?' Charley asked.

'That's where things start getting really complicated,' I told them. 'Edward wasn't aware of any connection between me and Tim until I took Raffi to the Grange when we thought he was dead. He was already suspicious of me, though, because he'd seen me talking to Arthur the day after I arrived, and I was there when Arthur's body was found. Also, of course, the first time he'd officially met me, I was standing right by the tomb in the chapel which led to the secret entrance to the underground passages. So when I said I didn't know Arthur, he started to worry, and all the more so once the connection to Tim came to light. He thought I must be on to something and started having me followed. It was bad enough for him that he couldn't work me out, but Paul was a real wild card. He was backwards and forwards to the Grange like a yo-yo, and Edward put two and two together and came up with five, assuming, because of another musical connection, that Paul knew Tim as well. At any rate, he had to check him out, because we must have seemed like a massive threat to his operation. But that – when his hard guys paid Paul a visit – went massively wrong.' I stopped, had to clear my throat, remembering the carnage we'd found. Jake squeezed my shoulder as Gaffer took up the story for me.

'They were getting desperate. They knew that once Arthur made his findings public, they'd have to move their storage operation elsewhere, remove all traces of what they'd been up to. The awful thing is, if Arthur hadn't got so close so soon, it would all have worked out. They knew he was pretty close to cracking things and had arranged to get everything out of the Grange this Wednesday, when everyone would be at the races to see Ghost of a Chance. How they would have stripped the passages of evidence of the lighting Mike told us about, I'm not sure. Anyway, what was vital, was to keep the lid on things until then. Arthur was a serious academic and his research was immaculate. He was kind of like a time detective, I suppose you could say. He made a connection between the tunnels built to hide illegal tobacco growing from excise officers in – when was it Mike? Seventeenth Century?' I nodded. '...between them and stories he'd dug up of a so-called mythological Monk's Walk from much earlier times. And he talked about it, of course, especially at the Companions' meetings.'

'Edward egged him on,' I added, 'superficially encouraging his work and its ramifications for the Companions, but really, to keep a check on how close he was getting. So when Arthur turned up in a state of excitement, saying he believed he'd found an entrance to these secret passageways, Edward nearly had a fit. Of course, he said it was far too dangerous for Arthur to explore on his own and volunteered himself and a couple of his men to accompany him. Arthur was thrilled, and mentioned, during his little foray, that he'd written up his theory to Tim and would confirm it and add more after their expedition. That's why it became so vital to sit on

351

those papers until everything had been moved. They couldn't find the papers when they broke into Arthur's house, of course, but Tim was easily traced because of the correspondence there between him and Arthur.'

'And you had them all the time and didn't realise!' Tim said.

I explained how Arthur and I had literally bumped in to each other outside the post office. 'It was such a scramble, picking things up. The envelope with the latest papers, ready for posting to Tim, was caught up inside a magazine I never got round to reading. And I unwittingly passed it on to Raffi.'

'But what about Paul? What exactly happened there?' Joan asked. She had comforted me after my visit to the hospital, where I'd had a painful conversation with Paul's mother.

'They meant, so they say, to put the frighteners on him. Pete was upstairs when they arrived. He came down and leapt to Paul's defence and was struck down from behind – one of the goons was behind the kitchen door. Paul made a dash for it but was caught and bundled into his own car. They used his and one of their own, driving him out to an isolated barn where they forced alcohol down his throat in an effort to loosen his tongue. He's allergic to alcohol, of course, and was also desperate to get help for Pete, not realising he was already dead. God knows how he did it – he'd be the first to say he's not the most physical kind of guy going – but he put up a hell of a fight...' I had to stop again, and asked Gaffer to continue.

'That's when he got the injuries to his arms and hands. They weren't expecting trouble from him, not to that extent, and one of the guys pulled a knife. How he drove the car like that, God only knows...' He told of Paul's almost severed fingers. 'Sheer desperation, I guess. He knew he had to get help for Pete and himself, but between the alcohol and loss of blood, he lost control of the car and went off the road.'

'And what's his condition now, Michal?' Joe asked.

I bit my lip. 'He'll live. But the doctors say he won't walk again.' There was silence.

Charley cleared his throat. 'But these men never actually grabbed you – why?'

'They were basically supposed to keep an eye on me, suss out my connections and generally intimidate me. They were, however, supposed to grab me after the gig where you lot saved my bacon. Edward had had enough, by then. Just wanted to haul me in.'

'Ah, what an evening that was...!' Joe breathed. 'You've heard about your Irish tour, have you?'

'What? You are joking, of course?'

Nick grinned. 'Afraid not. You know I came back here after the fracas at the pub? Well, your friends here said they can organise a load of bookings. I said I'd have a word with Frederick, see if he was interested...'

'And?'

'He is. They all are. Really up for it.'

'Oh my God...' I buried my head in my hands.

'You'll love it, Michal! Right up your street!' Charley assured me. It sounded so like Paul's usual spiel, I had to blow my nose. 'Come on now, anyway – back to that evening – is this where Jake comes into things?'

Jake leaned forward to reply. 'Well, I came into it earlier, really, but from Mike's point of view... well, it really does get complicated. She thought I was in on it, one of the bad guys, and it didn't help matters that I'd given her the third degree, thinking she was connected to something quite different.'

'Arnold Niedermeyer...' I offered.

'Right. Maggie was out one day a while back when I got a call from a guy asking to speak to Elynore. Said to tell her he was a friend of Max's – Max was her first husband. She accepted the call and a few minutes later, he's back on the phone to me, saying why don't we meet up? He's coming to see Elynore and will be staying nearby, and says how it sounds to him like he and I are from the same neck of the woods. We chatted and sure enough, it turned out that he lived about twenty miles away from my old home in the States. Anyway, I thought it was kind of odd that Elynore didn't say anything and didn't book him into one of the holiday cottages or guest suites, but you know how it is – you have other things to get on with. Thing is, of course, I go off to meet the guy at his hotel and he doesn't turn up. I ask at the desk, and they tell me he checked out after meeting a friend. A friend called Mike Brodie. I ask if he left a message for me and I'm told no, the only thing he left behind was a business card. As soon as I see he's a PI, my chain starts rattling, you know? I ask Elynore if she kept her meeting with Niedermeyer and it's obvious to me that she thinks no one knows she had a meeting. Meanwhile, she appears to be thick in with Michal, getting her to do a promotional video and stuff.' He squeezed me gently. 'That's the point when I started going about things completely the wrong way. I made a couple of calls to the States, starting asking questions about Niedermeyer and find he's a shady character, suspected of blackmailing certain of his clients. I also find out about Max's death, that, while nothing could ever be proved, Elynore had been a strong suspect in some cops' books for killing him – or having him killed – and setting it up to look like an accident. Michal, of course, denied knowing Niedermeyer, which had me wondering how the hell she was involved and what she was up to.'

'Hold on, hold on – you've lost me, young feller!' Tom was looking confused. 'If Michal didn't know this character, how come her name was mentioned in connection with him?'

'Wouldn't we like to know!' I said. 'I don't like my name being taken in vain.'

'Best as we can figure it, Elynore had a strong suspicion of what he was up to. Maybe he was straight up front about it. We figure she probably said she would negotiate through an intermediary – Michal. Probably just used her name for convenience and to make sure her own wasn't mentioned at the guy's hotel. When I went back there and asked more questions, I was told that Niedermeyer had left with *Mr* Brodie, and got a description, so it obviously wasn't our Mike. By then, I was becoming increasingly concerned about the scrapes she was getting into and wanted to apologise and find out what was going on from her point of view. Too late, of course. Because of the way I'd questioned her in connection with the Niedermeyer business, she was avoiding me like the plague, thinking I'm a bad guy. And I'm getting increasingly worried that Elynore is planning to get rid of Warren, so I'm trying to stick to him like glue. Going back to the night we're talking about, when I got to the gig and saw those boneheads moving in, I moved in to try and head them off, and all hell broke loose.'

'We broke loose, you mean!' Charley chuckled. An impromptu version of 'I know something you don't know' followed, for the benefit of those who hadn't been there.

'So what happened next?' Raffi asked when the singing ended. 'Before you phoned here?'

I told them about Gaffer's Tom Selleck impression in the car park and our flight to Alison's. Joan held her hands over her ears in horror.

'I was really worried the next day,' Jake continued. 'There was no sign of Gaffer, and Michal is back at the Grange, whistling "Oh Susanna" bold as brass. It hit Warren like a bombshell. He was convinced she was going to try and blackmail him.'

'About what, if he wasn't involved in any of these shenanigans?' Joe asked.

'You need to know Warren's background – it's a long story.'

'Sure, and don't we have all night ahead of us, young feller! Get on with it, man!' called Thomas.

Jake settled himself more comfortably and I adjusted my position on his lap.

'Warren, basically, was born dirt poor Alabama white trash. Got in trouble with the law at an early age and struggled for years to overcome it, forged a new identity for himself and sure as hell didn't want any reminders of what he'd come from. Most importantly, he didn't want Elynore getting any whiff of it She was an English lady, as far as he was concerned, and he thought if she knew, it would completely blow his chances of marrying her.' He turned to me. 'She told you she knew?'

'Yes,' I confirmed. '"From the start", she said.'

Jake shook his head. 'Then that's where another death may come in. Warren had a close friend, Homer Marshall, who apparently committed suicide just before Warren and Elynore got married. My friends in the States haven't finished digging yet, but it looks like Homer was on the periphery of the investigation into Max's death. The theory at present seems to be that he wasn't too happy when he realised Warren was going to become husband number two.'

'Did he go to Warren with his suspicions?' Nick asked.

'Without evidence, and with Warren besotted, that would not have been a good idea. My guess is, he tried to turn the screws on Elynore in an effort to get her to leave Warren alone. Maybe played poker with her, if you like, pretending he knew more about Max's death than he did.'

'And then he conveniently kills himself? You really think this wretched woman was responsible?' Joan shook her head.

'It would fit with her threat to me,' I said. 'She told me she'd dealt with people like me before, and when she said that, she thought I was going to try to blackmail her.'

'She must have been paranoid by then, Michal. With Edward's suspicions of you on the Arthur front, coming out with "Oh Susanna" was simply too much.' Jake shook his head.

'So you got kidnapped at the Grange, Mike, when they decided to cut their losses and move the plan forward – but what about you, Gaffer?' Raffi asked.

'Don't remind me!' he groaned. 'I'd stayed at the vicarage, waiting for your fax, Raffi. Alison had been lifted the same time as Mike, but taken into the house. Once the ordinary Companions had been dismissed and were having a booze up, word went out that Jake had put a security exercise into operation, so that the Grange and estate were effectively sealed off. Edward's elite squad, then suitably balaclava'd and the rest of it, go into action and round up the few people left on site, like Maggie and the cook. They also start ransacking the place as well as moving the stuff left in storage. I didn't know this at the time, of course – I was busy reading the stuff you'd faxed.'

'It's all my fault!' Raffi said. 'I thought Norman had given me the wrong fax number. When I went to his place, with the carrier bag, there was a Grange brochure in it and the number on that was different to the one he'd given me, so I thought I'd better send it to both, just to be on the safe side.'

'It wasn't your fault, Raffi – it was his!' said Joe,

pointing at Charley. 'If he hadn't fallen down the stairs, tearing the phone off the wall in the process, you wouldn't have been cut off from speaking to Michal.'

'It's nobody's fault but Edward's and Elynore's,' I said firmly. 'You did what you thought was best, Raffi. It's just unfortunate that Edward was in Maggie's office with one of his elite squad when it arrived. He really had to move fast, then.'

'And this Elynore was having an affair with the feller, was she?' asked Thomas.

'The couple from hell!' I snorted.

'And probably burning in it right now, the pair of them. If I wasn't sitting in your lovely hotel, Joan, I'd spit on them, so I would,' Joe admitted.

'God knows how it started, if they were,' said Jake, 'but after what Michal's been telling me, I'd say that for Edward, it was obviously some sort of revenge thing, a power kick, from his point of view of being the rightful heir to the Grange. Maybe she found out what he was doing, or found the underground complex and him in it. She was certainly genuinely interested in Arthur's work. She'd be thinking in terms of what it could do for the Grange, in other words, her income. Money was the only thing that mattered to that woman, and I can't figure that out, when she was born to it the way she was. Warren, now, as I said, was dirt poor when he started out – worked for every nickel and dime he ever made, yet he's a generous man. Never showed the obsessional greed she had.'

'There's nothin' so queer as folk,' Thomas observed.

'So what happened to Gaffer?' Raffi persisted.

He shook his head ruefully. 'Like I said, I was sitting reading your fax. Seems like Edward had been suspicious, Mike turning up with Alison, plus he wasn't convinced I was out of the way, after hearing what happened to the Gorilla. Anyway, just to be on the safe side, he sent a delegation to the vicarage. I got clobbered good and proper. Wound up trussed up like a chicken and carted back to the Grange to be left with the others during the robbery.'

'Well, thank God you're all alright!' Joan said. 'What an almighty bloody mess.'

Nick was on the edge of his seat. 'So to top it all off, Mike, you and Jake raised the alarm?'

'After Elynore was killed by the van, we used her car to get to the village,' I told him. 'The elite unit had recalled the dogs and were clearing out faster than expected because one of the gang had found Edward dead, under the Chapel, so they were already on the edge of disarray when Warren arrived on the scene. He put up quite some fight, totally ruining Elynore's plan to have him killed, and, of course got outside just in time to see her run over.'

'It was Warren who released me, too, so I was able to pitch in, indoors.' Gaffer added. 'I do not want an evening like that again. Ever.'

'But...' Thomas raised his hand. 'Will the others be brought to justice? With Edward and Elynore dead? That's the bottom line now, surely?'

Gaffer nodded. 'Oh yes. The van and most members of the gang were rounded up. They soon started spilling the beans and blaming each other. Trying to distance themselves from murder charges, I suppose.'

'They're still accessories, though, the lot of them!' Joe said.

'Well, let's drink to your safe deliverance!' Charley stood up, glass in hand.

'And to Raffi's job!' Joan beamed.

'Well done, girl! When do you start?' Thomas asked.

'September,' she replied.

'That's a long wait!'

'Oh God – talking of long waits...' I said, 'we never got anyone else to work for Mr Clerides – Zorba the Greek.'

'Yes, we did,' said Raffi. 'All done and dusted! And you might like to know, Mike, that a lot of time in my new job will be spent on an EU project just outside Athens, so my summer work with Mr C. will be a perfect opportunity to start to learn the language.'

'We'll certainly drink to that, then!' Charley beamed from ear to ear. 'Finished with this Grange business for now, have we?'

Those of us involved looked at each other and nodded.

'Then have you got that DVD, Michal?' Chancy asked.

'Sure.' Raffi and Joan had particularly asked me to bring along the DVD I'd made with the Howlin' Blue Horns at the studio complex.

'We've a little bet on with Raffi and Tim,' Joe told me, tapping the side of his nose.

'What?' I looked at her suspiciously. 'What bet is this?'

'It's not Raffi's fault,' Tim laughed. 'It's just that, when she told me you were going to do it, I said "Oh good", because we could finally settle a little dispute she and I have had over your playing.'

I squirmed on Jake's lap. 'What's wrong with my playing?'

'Nothing – the dispute is over whether you stand on one leg or two when you take a solo.'

I stared at him with my mouth open. 'Well, two, of course! What reason would I have for standing on only one leg?'

'Care to put your money where your mouth is, now?' Joe interjected.

I looked at him suspiciously. 'Have you had a sneak preview?' I asked. I'd given the thing to Joan on my arrival.

'Absolutely not!' said Charley. 'But my tip for Ghost of a Chance came up trumps, did it not?'

It certainly had. My hundred pounds had come back to me with a whole lot of interest. 'This is different,' I said. 'You're asking me to bet on myself. And you're not telling me which way to bet, either.'

'Well, now – you should know whether you stand on one leg or two! Should be a sure-fire certainty!'

'I stand on two,' I insisted.

'Ha! We'll see!' said Raffi. 'Who's got the remote for the video...?'

I lost.

I really am Mike, 'The Stork' Brodie.

I stand on one leg when I play solos. At least, I had done that day. And I never knew...

The evening from then on degenerated into a lot of singing, drinking and generally having a good time. I wasn't drinking, however, because I'd promised to take Jake back to the Grange. Elynore had dislocated his shoulder when she'd backed into him and he still wasn't entirely pain free. I went to fetch my jacket. Feeling in the pocket for my car keys, I found a card. The original card I'd had from the fortune telling machine at Descartes' vineyard. The Irishmen had said we must all go out for an evening there next year, it sounded so good. I told them it was, and decided I'd take at least one of my bands up there to play for free. I owed them one, and owed Descartes' Vineyard one, too. I looked at the card, read it and smiled to myself. It was all about sticking one's courage to the mast, not being afraid of being out of one's depth. Trusting the desires of one's heart...

'Maybe it's a psychological thing,' Jake suggested as we drove into Ruttersford village.

'What is?'

'Standing on one leg when you play a solo. Maybe, subconsciously, you feel you're going out on a limb.'

'Is that right?' I said. 'Nice pun. Very funny.'

I pulled up at the conference centre and switched off the engine. He stroked my hair, my cheek, my neck.

'Do you remember that we took a rain check a while back?' he asked.

'We did?'

'Uh-huh. I asked you – seems like a lifetime ago

– if you'd like to come inside, sit by the fire, share a bottle of wine and swap life stories.'

'That's right,' I acknowledged.

'I'm asking you again now, Michal.' He kissed me, softly.

I wanted more...

'But if I sit by the fire with a bottle of wine,' I reasoned, 'I won't be able to drive home.'

'That's the whole idea.'

'Really?'

'Really.'

This time, I said yes.

Acknowledgements

Descartes' Vineyard, as it was, no longer exists, although it looked exactly as described in this book. At the time of writing, its name has changed to The Swan at Coombe Hill, and gigs of various kinds are still held there.

There are many people to thank for their assistance and inspiration in the writing of this book: Robert Swindells, who, many years ago, talked to me about his job at Sudeley Castle, Gloucestershire; Freddie, who provided inspiration for the character of Henrietta Satterthwaite; Dik Cadbury, Dave Bell and Mick Dolan, with whom I've had great fun on the voice front over the years; and Ian and the late Kay Brown, of Secondwind, who looked after my saxophone so well. If only I were as great a player as Mike!

Last but not least, to the guys who made up Blue and the Rude Tubes – Mike 'It's in C!' Pullen, Joe Nourse, Dave 'Cheesecake' Gray, Rich Grainger, Richard 'Shaggy' Rees, Chris Slatter, Karoline 'with a K' Wadsworth, Warren Dunn, Anthony Bethall, Brian Chu, and not forgetting Chris Kear, in whom the spirit of Stevie Ray Vaughan is definitely alive and well and doing apparently impossible things.

Thank you all for a fantastic four-and-a-half years!

The publishers hope that this book has given you enjoyable reading. Large Print Books are especially designed to be as easy to see and hold as possible. If you wish a complete list of our books please ask at your local library or write directly to:

Magna Large Print Books
Magna House, Long Preston,
Skipton, North Yorkshire.
BD23 4ND